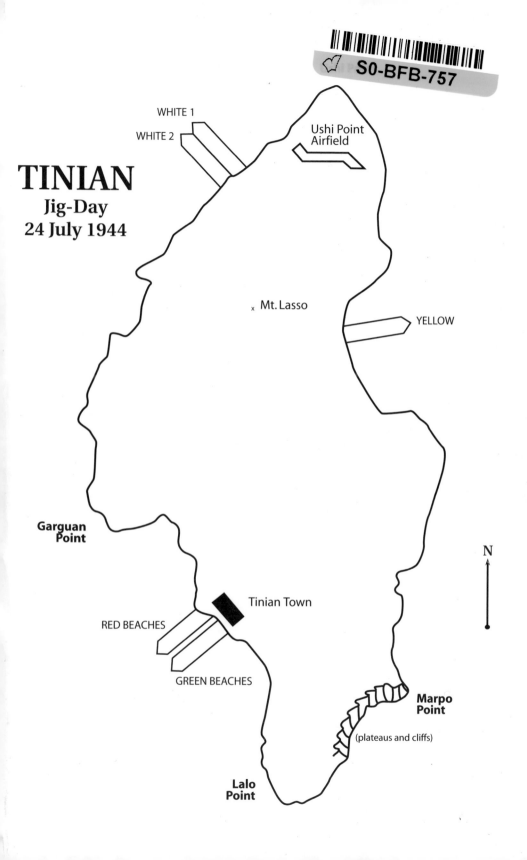

WHITE 1

WHITE 2

Ushi Point
Airfield

TINIAN
Jig-Day
24 July 1944

x Mt. Lasso

YELLOW

Garguan
Point

N

Tinian Town

RED BEACHES

GREEN BEACHES

Marpo
Point

(plateaus and cliffs)

Lalo
Point

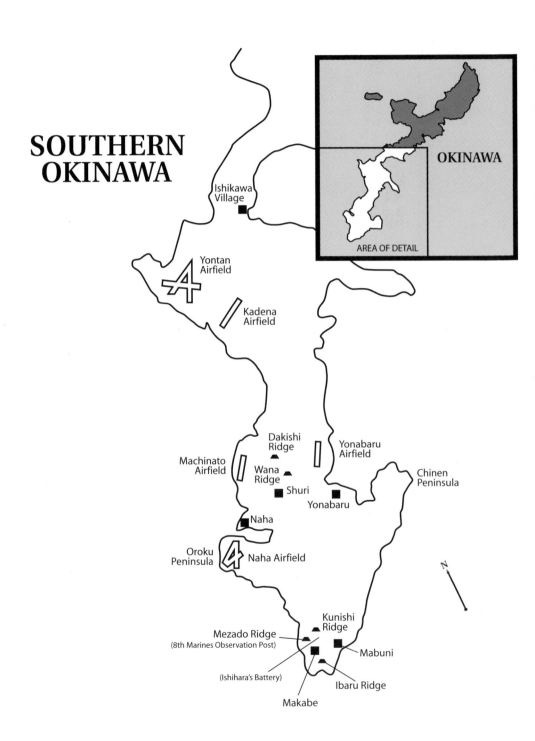

SOUTHERN OKINAWA

OKINAWA

AREA OF DETAIL

Ishikawa Village

Yontan Airfield

Kadena Airfield

Dakishi Ridge

Machinato Airfield

Wana Ridge

Shuri

Yonabaru Airfield

Chinen Peninsula

Yonabaru

Naha

Oroku Peninsula

Naha Airfield

Kunishi Ridge

Mezado Ridge
(8th Marines Observation Post)

Mabuni

(Ishihara's Battery)

Ibaru Ridge

Makabe

N

The Spirit of

Semper Fidelis

"Reflections From the Bottom of an Old Canteen Cup"

Major Rick Spooner, USMC Ret.

Second Edition
July 2005
3000 Leathernecks

Library of Congress Number
ISBN 0-932572-44-8
© Copyright 2004
by

ℙhillips
Publications

P.O. Box 168
Williamstown, NJ 08094
Phone: 609-567-0695
Fax: 609-561-4967
Printed in the United States of America

Acknowledgments and Dedication

This book would not have been possible without the encouragement, able assistance and great patience of Mr. Jim Phillips, of Phillips Publications and of persons too numerous to list here including the distinguished members of "The Privates' Mess." My supporters know who they are and I hope they will accept my sincerest thanks.

The author wishes to acknowledge the dedication, courage and sacrifices of all those who have borne the title of United States Marine. This book is respectfully dedicated to them and to the perpetuation of those fine old customs and traditions which have added strength, character and color to our Corps of Marines for well over two centuries.

To the Marines of today and to those of yesteryear who march gallantly through the pages of American history from our war for independence to the global war on terrorism. Doing more, and at times sacrificing more, in every clime and place, than their countrymen may ever know. They upheld the honor of our Corps.

Shanghai Pooley once said, "No one is really dead until he is forgotten." This book is an attempt to keep those gallant raggedy assed Marines of yesteryear from being forgotten.

Richard T. Spooner
Major of Marines, Retired
Quantico, Virginia
15 June 2004

SEMPER FIDELIS

Major Rick Spooner, USMC Retired

Prologue

The adventures depicted herein are based on events of sixty years ago and thus cannot be related with absolute accuracy. The names of commanders and senior officers, Japanese and American are real as are the places, ships and campaigns. The dialog is generally fictitious. The dates are as accurate as the author's memory permits.

Most military units in this book are real except that the author has borrowed the 2nd Battalion, 8th Marines as the parent organization for his characters. This was done because he served in that battalion and it seemed a logical choice. The Marines are composites of men the author knew and served with and are not intended to be accurate representations of any individual, living or dead. Nicknames are frequently used since many "old Corps" Marines were referred to by their nicknames.

If the author has given any of his characters the names of actual people, living or dead, other than as stated above, it was unintentional and none of the actions attributed to them should be construed as factual.

Jim "Chic" Yancey was a teenager who had grown up in a big city on the west coast. He was from an average American home with strong family values. Exposed to the Marines of the 1920's and 30's, he couldn't wait to grow up and find a way into the Marines. When the Japanese bombed Pearl Harbor, they helped him to realize his dream.

Daniel Reed Lane, "Lucky," was a junior at Ohio State. He was an above average student who lettered in football and wrestling. Lane was fearful that if he stayed in school the war would end before he could get into it. Passing up the opportunity to become a commissioned officer following graduation, he quit school and enlisted in the Marine Corps as a private.

Francis Xavier Quinlan was an orphan. Raised by foster families in and around Boston, Massachusetts, he had an obsession with girls and thought that the best way to impress them would be to join the Marines. He was particularly fond of the dress blue uniform, which he never had the privilege of wearing. Quinlan was nicknamed "Fearless Frank" by his drill instructor during the first week of boot camp and for a variety of reasons the name stuck.

David Donahoe, "Deadly Dave," was the son of a WW I veteran who had lost his arm in France. His mother died when he was very young and he and his father were avid hunters and fishermen. Dave Donohoe grew up in Montana and Wyoming. He played varsity football, basketball and baseball in high school and excelled in all of them. His nickname, Deadly Dave, was acquired not on the field of battle but while on liberty with his buddies in Los Angeles, California.

Paul Pooley, "Shanghai," joined the Marine Corps in 1930, during the Great Depression. While serving in Nicaragua, he showed an aptitude for languages and proved himself to be an excellent field Marine. During much of his early career he was assigned to the Office of Naval Intelligence (ONI). He was trained as a specialist and received rapid promotions up to the rank of gunnery sergeant. Stationed in Shanghai, China, Pooley made frequent trips to Japan and was educated in the language and customs of the Japanese. Administratively assigned to the 4th Marines in Shanghai he was carried on their muster rolls. Pooley was tried by General Court Martial, convicted and reduced to the rank of private in 1939. He subsequently reenlisted as a private and during WWII, served as a sergeant/squad leader.

John Black, "Blackjack," enlisted in the Marine Corps with his brother Milton. Jack liked the Marine Corps and stayed in. Milt got out at the expiration of his enlistment and joined the Marine Corps Reserve in their home town of Galveston, Texas, where he attended college and got married. Jack reenlisted and served tours in China and at sea. He was a platoon sergeant during the war.

Carl Johannsen, "Gunny," enlisted in the Marine Corps in 1916 and was sent to the Mexican Border. He later served in France with the 4th Marine Brigade. He remained in the Marine Corps for more than 20 years and retired. During World War II, he volunteered to return to active duty. Johannsen spent the last year of the war as Fox Company's gunnery sergeant.

Kevin Mulcahy, "Choirboy," was one of the many under-age Marines who had managed to fraudulently enlist in the Marine Corps during the height of World War II. He had a remarkable voice which endeared him to the men of his company. Mulcahy wanted desperately to be accepted by the older Marines. All were fond of him and many thought of him as a surrogate kid brother.

W. Maxwell Netherland, "The Music," had prior service in the Corps and in 1939 had been assigned to the World's Fair Detachment in New York. Following his discharge he became a sidewalk reporter for Mandel Brothers Department Store in Chicago. A con-man, he enlisted in the Marine Corps Reserve in 1942 in hopes of remaining in Chicago, working with the recruiters and evading overseas duty.

"Chief" left the reservation at a young age and quickly adopted the ways of the white man. The Great Depression found him destitute in St. Louis where he was accepted into the Marine Corps because he could speak Spanish. Sent to Nicaragua following boot camp, he met and served with Private Paul Pooley. Chief was a competent Marine who learned quickly; he was promoted to corporal after only two years in the Corps. He became an alcoholic and was subsequently reduced to private and re-promoted a number of times. He was a professional private who had found a home in the Marine Corps.

The above ten were only a few of the many characters who moved in and out of Fox Company while it was in the Pacific during World War II. When the company was at full strength it was comprised of 244 men. Most of them, wartime warriors, were young reservists who had enlisted out of patriotism and intended to serve for the duration of the war and then get out of the Corps and return to civilian life. Many of the survivors did get out of the Corps but the Corps would never get out of them. Once they became Marines, they were Marines for life. This book tells a little of what that life was like for a few of them during the war years.

Authors Note

Jim Yancey had always wanted to be a Marine. When he was a small boy he used to watch the Marines and Sailors coming ashore from the huge gray battleships and sleek cruisers of the old U.S. Pacific Fleet.

To a youngster in those long ago days Marines in their dress blues walking tall looked as though they owned the world. They were impressive role models for a boy.

Some wore the French *Fourragére* around their left shoulder indicating their wartime service in France with the Marine Brigade. They spoke of the fighting at Belleau Wood, Soissons, St. Mihiel or Blanc Mont Ridge. Battles Marines had fought and won during what, at that time, was called the World War.

They knew service on the high seas and in the tropics and had chased Agosto Sandino through the mountains and jungles of Nicaragua and some had served in Santo Domingo or with the Gendarmerie in Haiti.

Some spoke fondly of duty on the old Asiatic station and they told fascinating tales of adventure with the 4th Marines in the enchanting city of Shanghai and of going up through the gorges on gunboats with the Yangtze River Patrol. Some had served with the Legation Guard at Peking and a few spoke of the Horse Marines.

Jim Yancey could hardly wait to grow up so he could be a Marine.

*   *   *   *   *

When he finally became a Marine, the "Old Corps" was rapidly disappearing. It was being transformed into a dynamic modern corps of six fighting Marine divisions and four air wings that were to fight their way across the Pacific in some of the bloodiest battles in history.

After boot camp and training in the States, he was sent overseas as a teenaged Pfc and had the great good fortune to be assigned to the Fleet Marine Force.

His battalion had a reputation for being in the first wave. When you are in the first wave of a contested amphibious landing, you need a lot of luck. You also need highly motivated, well-trained Marines and superb leadership. The battalion was blessed with all of these.

"The Marines I knew and served with in the Second World War were the finest, toughest, most profane and yet the most compassionate men I have ever known and there wasn't an atheist among them. There are no true atheists in combat.

"Don't misunderstand me, the Marines I served with in the Korean and Vietnam wars were great guys and fine Marines. I respected them and I liked them and many have remained close friends over the years. The old timers of WWII just had a uniqueness about them that made them different. They were a very special breed.

"Most of those who survived the war were destined to get out of the Marine Corps once the war had ended but the Marine Corps would never get out of them. They considered themselves 'Wartime Warriors' but deep in their hearts, they knew they would be Marines for the rest of their lives. Like all Marines who came before and after them, the Spirit of Semper Fidelis lives on in their hearts.

"I've been asked just what it is that makes the Marine Corps so special. The Corps means different things to different people and it would be impossible for me to define in just a few words what it is that makes it so special. Let me share some memories with you:

"Many Marines have experienced this. You are a young Marine home on leave for the first time and are wearing your uniform. You see envy and respect in the eyes of civilians who hardly seemed to notice you before.

"In my day, stateside duty meant living in a barracks with a centerline squadbay. The windows were half-masted or quarter-masted and the aroma of Bay Rum, Hoppe's Gun Oil and Kiwi Shoe Polish prevailed. There was a special code of ethics and integrity among Marines. If someone inadvertently left his wallet on his bunk and went off to chow, when he returned the wallet, and its contents, would still be there.

"In garrison it was the crisp clear notes of 'Reveille' shattering the stillness of a quiet morning or a bugle sounding

'Attention' and then 'Morning Colors' as the beautiful flag of our country was briskly hoisted to the peak of the flagpole.

"It was a snappy salute properly given and promptly returned with that special friendly greeting that distinguishes us as Marines.

"It's the comforting feel of your trigger finger taking up the slack when you've lined 'em up at six o'clock and have a perfect sight picture and are ready to squeeze a round off.

"Its a frontal assault on a heavily defended position. All the protection you've got is your rifle and helmet but the enemy to your front is well protected in his bunker. There's a flight of planes overhead. They come in low and slow and blast hell out of the enemy directly to your front. One of the planes circles back over the beach. The pilot dips his wings. He's saying "It's okay men, we got 'em!" He's also telling you that he's a Marine.

"You're on a combat-ravaged island and you're exhausted. Your throat is parched, your shoulders are raw, your pack's too heavy and you've walked and crawled and fought too long in the blazing tropical sun. You feel that you simply can't go on. A salty old sergeant utters fiery words of encouragement and Marine, you know you can go on - and you do.

"It's the hot sand on your sweaty face as you flatten yourself out on the bloodstained slopes of Saipan's Mount Tapotchau and pray as you crawl forward that the next round won't have your name on it.

"It's a Navy corpsman stumbling across a pockmarked battlefield under fire to apply a tourniquet, give you a swig of water and clean and dress your wound.

"It's a flag-draped coffin and the three volleys fired over the grave of your best friend. God, he was a good Marine!

"A Marine Band is playing 'Semper Fidelis' and then they play 'The Marines' Hymn.' There's a tingling sensation up and down your spine and warm tears course down your cheeks. You suddenly realize that sometimes Marines are not so tough after all.

"Nearly all Marines have experienced something like this; a stranger walks up to you on the street and says 'I was in the Corps one time, I sure wish I'd stayed in,' and you know he means it.

"You're a commissioned officer on a sleek gray cruiser with white teakwood decks and shiny polished brass. Your Marine Detachment is in full blues standing honors on the quarter-deck. You grasp the hilt of your Mameluke Sword and as you draw it from the scabbard, you can feel more than two-hundred years of history and tradition in your very hands. You are a Marine and the Spirit of Semper Fidelis is upon you and will remain with you forever.

"It's the tremendous feeling of pride and accomplishment that surges through you as you pin the gold bars of a second lieutenant on your son and administer the oath to him.

"All of these things and more are what the Marine Corps means to me. Being a Marine is a state of mind, it's a deep feeling of dedication, it's a vocation. It's so many things - some of them make you glad, some make you sad, some make you smile, and all of them make you feel that special spirit of the Corps.

"It's difficult to describe but its good and it's right and when deep down in your heart you truly feel that Spirit of Semper Fidelis, you become someone special. You know it, God knows it and your country knows it."

To any young Marine who may read this: In the words of the late Marine Gunner Gene B. Robinson and of this old warrior, "Take good care of our Marine Corps."

Semper Fidelis

The Spirit of Semper Fidelis

Reflections from the Bottom
of an Old Canteen Cup

Chapter I

The Marines

The Fury of Hell

Hawaii - 15 May 1944

The convoy of 2-1/2 ton trucks moved over the seemingly endless road. They passed through the lava flows between the great volcanoes Moana Kea and Moana Loa as they left the Parker Ranch and Camp Tarawa behind them forever. The road was exceedingly dusty and the bumpy ride would have seemed even more uncomfortable if it hadn't been for the anticipation of high adventure and the possibility of a good liberty port.

Knowing looks were exchanged between Platoon Sergeant Jack Black, and Sergeant Paul Pooley. They knew they hadn't spent the last six months of training just so the troops could go on liberty. The two of them remembered the first time they had traversed this road in late November of 1943. It was colder than a well digger's ass in January and they had no warm clothing. Returning to civilization from the bloody battle of Tarawa they had expected something different from what they actually experienced. A return to New Zealand would have met with the approval of all hands. Hawaii had been unexpected and especially this godforsaken part where it was as cold a place as any of them could remember.

When they had first arrived on "the big island" they disembarked at Hilo Harbor and immediately boarded open trucks. It was a cold, bleak trip from the docks at Hilo up to the Parker Ranch and Kamuela through the snow flurries. Many of the men were surprised to learn that it snows in Hawaii. They had eventually gotten their pyramidal tents set up, replacements started arriving and the division was soon back on an intensive training schedule. The six months had passed by very swiftly and now once again the division was combat ready and on the move.

Leaving the dusty road bound for Hilo they found themselves on an asphalt highway. They glimpsed parts of the city of Hilo as they passed through on their way to the docks where they went aboard ship. Someone had arranged for some local musicians and a troupe of hula dancers to be on the dock to see them off. Aloha Oe.

Once aboard ship little more was heard about Hilo. Rumors were rampant that after a big landing exercise on Maui with the 4th Marine Division, they would be heading for another campaign. Following the landing the division steamed into Pearl Harbor and Hilo was forgotten.

The word was passed; there would be no liberty in Honolulu for the embarked troops. The ship was only to take on stores and ammunition and form up in convoy in preparation for combat operations. All of this suddenly changed when the quiet of a Sunday morning was shattered by a series of tragic explosions. The sailors and Marines who were at Pearl Harbor on 21 May 1944 would long remember the incident at West Loch which many described as "The Fury of Hell." Until that moment few of the embarked Marines had even heard of West Loch – after this moment, none would forget it. West Loch was a channel in Pearl Harbor to the west of Hickam Field and south of the Waipahu Peninsula. A number of LST's and other small ships had been berthed there for loading and minor repairs.

Some work had been needed on LST 353, which was berthed along with several other LST's loaded with 2nd and 4th Marine Division troops and equipment. Mortar shells and other ammunition were being removed from 353 so the welders could accomplish the necessary repairs. Details of the cause of the tragedy remain uncertain but after 60 years unfounded rumors still persist about Japanese saboteurs or careless welders.

LST 353 exploded and sank as billowing clouds of brown and black smoke enshrouded it and all the ships nearby. A series of detonations rocked the island of Oahu reminding some of that fateful day in December 1941 when the Japanese attacked Pearl Harbor. Those who had been present at both events proclaimed 21 May 1944 at least as loud as the "Day of Infamy" and just as surprising. LST 179 had been berthed alongside 353 and it too was blown apart and sank in a matter of minutes.

The explosions continued and damage was so extensive that a total of six LSTs were eventually destroyed. In spite of the tremendous efforts mounted to rescue victims, 163 men were killed and 396 were seriously wounded. Over the next several days, human body parts were found floating among the debris littering the surface at Pearl Harbor. It was another grim reminder of the fragility of human life, in or out of combat.

Survivors from the lost LST's were quickly transferred to available shipping and replacements were requisitioned from the Marine Transient Center at Pearl Harbor. Ranks depleted by the loss of the dead and wounded were quickly filled by the replacements. The destruction of six ships would not cancel Operation Forager.

The departure of the force was delayed by the release of "The Fury of Hell" at West Loch. As a result many of the men were granted a limited amount of liberty. The division made a sincere effort to let the Marines get ashore in Honolulu for up to six hours at a time. With liberty granted for such a brief period, there was much grousing among the embarked troops. Honolulu was a good liberty port.

The younger troops were lonely. It was a loneliness that was hard to describe and even more difficult for others to comprehend. To someone who has never lived on a troopship, it's difficult to understand how men can be lonely while in the midst of three thousand other men. It's not easy to explain, but the loneliness is there and it's real. Perhaps it was that the men were tired of being aboard troopships or maybe some were just plain homesick.

The Convoy

Pearl Harbor, Hawaii - 30 May 1944

Ships had been gliding to and fro all day long and as time went on, the movement became more intense and Pearl Harbor more congested. The great gray ships of the US Navy were everywhere.

On the afternoon of 30 May the men were advised that if anyone wanted to write letters home they should do so soon. The ship's mail was being sent ashore in an hour.

After dark, the shadowy forms of ships could be seen drifting across the inky waters. For the past couple of days ships had been quietly pulling out of Pearl. Silently, one after another, the great gray ships had slipped their moorings and were steaming out into the vast Pacific Ocean. Never before in history had so many ships of the US Navy been in Pearl Harbor at the same time. Now, the time had come for the vast fleet to depart. And depart they did, moving out of the harbor one, two or three at a time. The huge gray hulks gliding silently, gracefully out to sea were heavily laden with troops and the implements of war.

There were massive battleships and cruisers and great gray aircraft carriers towering high above the sleek destroyers and destroyer escorts slipping silently out to sea throughout the night.

The men of Fox Company had been wondering when their ship would be shoving off. They knew it would be soon and wondered how far they would have to go across the sea to engage the enemy. What was their destination? There had been talk that they were going to Wake Island. The Japs had taken Wake from the United States in December of 1941 and it would be a great victory if the Marines could recapture it.

Or perhaps it would be Guam; the Japs had taken it as well. They all wanted to go to China but they knew there would be many islands to take before they got to the coast of China. The code name for their operation was "Forager" but no one would reveal to them anything further about it.

It was late at night and Jim Yancey was sleeping. He

thought he heard something about setting the special sea and anchor detail, but he wasn't certain. Perhaps he was just dreaming. After a few minutes, he sensed movement and felt the faint but steady throbbing of the ship's engines and knew they were underway. He immediately awakened two of his buddies who were sleeping over him on bunks that had been stacked six high.

Chic Yancey, "Fearless Frank" Quinlan and Wetzel the "Weasel" were soon up on the deck leaning over the rail and straining to get a last glimpse of the blacked-out island of Oahu as it slipped slowly from their sight and into a fading memory on that nearly moonless night.

On the first morning at sea, the loudspeaker system, referred to aboard ship as a 1-MC, was busily blaring out instructions and the shrill whistle of the boatswain's pipe was frequently heard preceding orders and announcements.

All hands were required to lay up to their debarkation stations for abandon ship drill. This was done leisurely the first time, but then it was done again with a greater sense of urgency but not quite rapidly enough to satisfy the ship's captain. The third time was better. The bugle call and the loud bleating of the klaxon sounded "General Quarters" next and again the drill was repeated until the men's response was satisfactory. Shipboard drills at all hours of the day became a part of everyday routine for the embarked Marines.

Later on the first afternoon at sea, following another drill, the bugle had just sounded "Secure from General Quarters." Chic Yancey nudged Fearless Frank Quinlan and said, "Let's move up forward to the fo'c's'l where there aren't so many people around and have a smoke."

They were soon joined by "Little Ski" and "Deadly Dave" Donahoe. It was a clear morning and the sea was a bright, glistening, almost royal, blue. The young Marines were awestricken as they looked out over the Pacific. Ships! There were hundreds of ships! They noticed that everyone on deck was looking at the vast armada. The great number of ships in their convoy was simply unbelievable. Several onlookers started to count but it was a hopeless and impossible task. There were far too many and there were even large numbers of them beyond the horizon where they could not be seen.

Years later Chic was to learn that there had been 535 ships in that impressive convoy.

On this day the beautiful blue Pacific Ocean was as calm and majestic as its name implied. The day was sunny with puffy white clouds scattered throughout the azure sky. It was a perfect day, calm and serene. Little Ski exclaimed:

"Listen! What the hell is that? It sounds like an air hose or something has sprung a leak."

It was the soft hiss of the ship's prow cutting through the blue sea.

"Damn Ski! I thought you were a Marine. You're nothin' but a landlubber! That is the sound of the ship slicing through the water. Up here on the fo'c'sl is the best place on the ship for you to really hear it. That is, you can hear it if the sea is calm and everything else is quiet. I've always liked it; it's a good sound. It means that we're really underway now and we're headed for new adventures." Yancey proclaimed.

As they looked out across the ocean in all directions, a full 360 degrees, as far as the eye could see and beyond there were hundreds of warships. They knew it was a convoy of extraordinary proportions. They knew that Operation Forager was going to be a very important campaign indeed.

Down in the troop compartments, the bunks were white canvas stretched tightly and lashed onto metal tubes. The men slept six high on bunks that were only two feet above one another. Air in the men's berthing compartments was hot and muggy. After lights out had been sounded, the overhead white lights were extinguished but there remained the sub-dued blue, green and red standing and emergency lighting. The continuous humming and throbbing of the engines made everyone aware that the ship was alive and moving. At first, sleep did not come easily to the embarked troops.

In time, the men became so accustomed to life on a transport that they climbed into their bunks and felt safe and se-cure, rarely thinking about the dangers from enemy aircraft or submarines. They adjusted to the lights and sounds and felt comfortable with the rolling and pitching of the ship and the passing of time made many of them complacent.

No one liked the cold saltwater showers and saltwater soap that often failed to lather but fresh water was a precious commodity. The ship's evaporators could not produce enough to take care of the needs of the embarked troops. It did not take long for the men to adjust to Navy transport chow. Marines casually filled their canteens from scuttlebutts dispensing fresh chilled water. They would, before long, passionately remember those scuttlebutts with great yearning and desire. Drinking water was to become their second most longed-for commodity. The first, of course, would be ammunition.

During the first few days sleep was difficult in the hot, foul-smelling, cramped berthing compartments and the men spent as much time as possible up on the weather decks. Many found suitable spaces to sleep on deck. Some would often lean on the rail talking and wishing they could smoke but during darken ship it was not possible. Showing a light, even briefly and no matter how small, was a deadly serious offense. The men savored the fresh sea air and were mesmerized by the sounds of the ship and the sea and by the phosphorescent glow in the ship's churning wake on a dark night.

Seagulls had been following the convoy and they landed on the water and rode the crests as they gorged themselves. They screeched and dove hungrily at floating scraps. The seagulls playfully shrieked back and forth as they circled high overhead. Some were soaring and diving as they scolded wildly at nothing in particular and sometimes at one another. After a few days the seagulls were gone.

Schools of porpoise and flying fish were welcome distractions from the monotony of the usual calm seas and bright sunshine. Once in a while, the bugle would sound general quarters and as the claxon's loud barking pierced the silence, a voice announced over the ship's 1-MC "This is a drill! This is a drill! General Quarters, General Quarters! All hands man your battle stations, that is, all hands man your battle stations!" And the loud, piercing claxon barked on endlessly, shocking the men into instant action.

The massive convoy continued steaming westward. Days and nights started to run together and time became blurred. One lone consistency that was a welcome sight was the ensign overhead flapping in the breeze. There was always something very special about the American flag. The brightness of that red, white and blue banner radiated a special strength and confidence that transferred itself to the men. They felt good about being Americans and were fiercely proud of being Marines.

The monotonous routine of steaming over the sea on a lazy day made the men lazy too and, at times this life seemed almost pleasant. The illusion never lasted for long. Reality frequently descended like a thunder clap with the piercing whistle of the boatswain's pipe or the blaring noise of the claxon as "General Quarters" blasted away or another of the many bugle calls sounded as various ship's drills were called away. The Navy wanted to be sure the Marines didn't mistake their transport for a luxury liner and none of them did.

*　*　*　*　*　*　*　*　*　*

Life at Sea

June 1944

Days upon days of steaming in a zigzag course across the vast Pacific became tremendously monotonous. Waiting in line for chow twice a day for what seemed like hours, then being served the same dull fare was part of the routine.

On most nights the Navy would show movies on the mess decks. It was stuffy and hot but it was a distraction from the monotony of life on a transport. In peacetime, movies would have been shown up on the weather decks where there was fresh air to breathe but this was wartime and "darken ship" meant precisely that. All portholes and hatches were covered to keep any light from escaping. This practice also resulted in keeping the heat in and kept the fresh air out. The men would force themselves to go down and sweat profusely as they watched the old movies then they'd try to remember how many times they'd seen the same picture before.

As Fearless Frank and Big Ski sat on a hatch cover smoking and talking about nothing in particular Big Ski drifted into deep thought.

"Hey Ski, are you still with me, this is me, Fearless. Is something wrong? You look like the weight of the world is on your shoulders. What's with you?"

"I've been doing a lot of thinking lately Fearless and y'know, I'm gonna get married. I'm gonna marry that little Women's' War Service Auxiliary gal, Stella. You know, the one who had a job workin' for the Navy down at the Aotea Quay in Wellington? I've already asked her and I know she must be close to acceptin'."

"What! How can you know that Ski?"

"Well *Cobber*, I've asked her in each of my last four letters. I think I must be close to wearing her down by now. Stella's really a great person Fearless. Do you know what that gal did for me? Why, one time when we were sittin' in a little pub, you remember that little place down by the Quay near where she worked? We were just shootin' the breeze about things in general when we each realized that the other wanted to go to the flicks at the cinema and then go out and have a nice dinner. I wuz nearly broke and I had to admit it to her. So she just says to me 'Come along Yank, it's my treat tonight'. Now what do you think of that?"

"Well, this is only about the tenth time you've told me that story Ski, but I guess you got yourself a really good girl at that. She sounds like a keeper to me."

"I know you've got lots of girl friends Fearless, but I think I'm strictly gonna be a one-woman man. I sure hope they send us back to Paekakariki after this campaign."

"You're not alone Ski, I think that is what every Marine in the division is hoping for." A few of the embarked troops were sometimes allowed to slip into the crew's working spaces by a friendly or sympathetic sailor where they could listen to a radio. The English language programs usually came from Japan and featured "Tokyo Rose" with good "Stateside" music and a melodramatic newscast of pure propaganda.

Smoking on deck was permitted during the day but was forbidden at night during blackout. Drills were conducted at odd times of the day and night and with a frequency that increased as the convoy moved farther into enemy territory. Nearly three thousand men crammed onto the one transport made the ship seem like a lonely world all unto itself until one looked out across the sea at the hundreds of other ships all with the same destination and purpose. We were not alone.

Chic was with Deadly Dave and Chief, standing on the fantail and leaning over the lifelines and talking while waiting to haul in the lines that had been tied securely around their laundry and thrown over the stern. The churning seas in the ship's wake did wonders for a sweaty old pair of dirty dungarees. Every transport in the convoy had numerous lines bouncing along in the ship's wake tied to Marines' laundry.

The chow lines were long and boring. They seemed to go on forever winding around the ship. Two meals a day wasn't up to the expectations the Marines had when they enlisted but, it was wartime. Waiting in the slowly moving lines gave the men an opportunity to read the pocket books that had been distributed by the Red Cross back at Pearl. As each book was read, it was passed along to another man who usually had one to swap for it. When shuffling through the line and not reading, the men would tell "sea stories" and basically grouse about shipboard life. There was much speculation about the coming campaign, Operation Forager.

Besides reading, much time was spent playing acey-deucey or cards. Poker was the most popular of the card games and what would generally start with small wagers of nickels and dimes soon became staggering as large amounts of money were won or lost on the troop transports. Remarkably, some poker games lasted for days on end, shifting below decks during darken ship, with friends and confederates relieving one another occasionally for sleep. There were some old salts in the Navy and Marine Corps who took their gambling very seriously.

From time to time, the 1MC would announce that the ship's store would be open for a limited time to serve the embarked troops. The men would queue up in long lines to buy stationery and writing supplies, candy and tobacco products. There was little variety but the men didn't care, they would buy whatever was available. Most of the things in the ship's store, candy bars, toothpaste and other personal items reminded them of home.

The Marines paid special attention to cleaning their rifles, bayonets, K-Bars and other personal implements of war. After all, this was not a pleasure cruise; they knew they were headed for combat.

Lying back on the gray canvas stretched over the wooden hatch cover Chic could feel the steady, hypnotic throbbing of the mighty ship's engines far below him. His buddies Ross and Muldoon were lying in the sun beside him, as was poor Eddie Malone, one of the replacements picked up at Camp Tarawa. Malone had been having second thoughts about his enlistment in the Marine Corps. He had done well in boot camp and was one of the best men in the squad while in training but since boarding ship, a depressing change had come over Private Malone. He was scared. Not scared like everybody else in the outfit, his case was different. He had developed a case of deep fear of going into combat that seemed to grow worse each day. The other men felt sorry for him and tried to encourage him.

Shanghai Pooley, the squad leader, had tried to gently encourage Private Malone when he first became aware of his problem with fear but now Shanghai was fed up. He could put up with almost anything, but cowardice was the one thing he would not tolerate. Shanghai was beginning to have reason to believe that one of his own men was a coward. One night when Malone was up on deck talking to Epstein and "Stash" Stahoviak, Shanghai happened to be walking by in the dark and heard Malone talking about how he didn't want to die. In one swift movement Shanghai Pooley reached out and grabbed Malone by the front of his dungaree jacket, bent him back over the rail and held him there as he said, "Listen to me you sonofabitch! I'm not going to tolerate a coward in my squad. I don't want to hear another word out of you about how scared you are. The other men are afraid too. But, they don't keep telling everybody about it. Do you have any idea how the other men feel about you going into combat with them? Do you think they would dare depend on you when things get rough? Remember, it's not courage that makes ordinary Marines perform, it's the fear of letting down the Marines who are counting on them. I will not have you let down those other Marines."

Shanghai's eyes flashed as he continued, "Now listen to what I'm saying to you Malone and understand me. Fear is one of those things that will reduce your effectiveness to mediocrity. Your civilian upbringing has taught you to fear -

its developed fear in you from birth, very slowly and methodically. But just like (snap!) that, you can let it go - and let go of mediocrity. You can come back to us and be a Marine again just by the force of your own will! I'm going to give you the benefit of the doubt and let you have one last chance. I'll assume you are going to be as good a Marine as anyone else in this squad but if I hear one more word out of you about how scared you are, I'll solve your problem my way.

"You won't have to worry anymore about the Japs killing you because I'm going to throw your worthless ass over the side and let the sharks fight over you. You are very bad for the morale of my squad Malone."

Eddie Malone was bent so far back over the side of the ship that he thought sure Shanghai was going to drop him into the sea whether he said anything else or not. Shanghai pulled Malone back to the standing position said "Goodnight men" to Stash and Epstein and walked on down the deck into the darkness.

A trembling Private Malone looked into the night after Shanghai and quietly asked,

"Just where is that sonofabitch from anyhow?"

Stash answered, "I'm not sure exactly where he's from".

Epstein spoke up knowingly, "I don't know exactly where he's from either, but I know one thing, its gotta be somewhere in hell!".

* * * * * * * * * *

During daylight hours noncommissioned officers went to great lengths to locate, and then stake out, suitable areas up on deck. They needed space to talk to their men and conduct training but more likely than not, once their classes were underway, the deck force would be out with their big hoses washing down the decks and hatches again. Classes on military subjects had to compete for deck space with marathon poker games where many of the passengers and members of the ship's company had become mesmerized. In many cases, the stakes were not only high they had become astronomical.

Topside, Marines were scattered everywhere. Many, like Chic and his buddies on the hatch cover, were more asleep than awake. The tropical sun was overhead and its warmth was totally relaxing. Chic's thoughts were a million miles from Operation Forager and all that it implied. The men who were engaged in serious poker games were undaunted by the tropical sun, they were awake and intense and remained so for hours on end.

"Avast you damned Jarheads, move it! Off that hatch and get your butts over on the starboard side! Its time for a clean sweep down. Move NOW or you're all gonna take a cold salt-water bath you won't like!"

The demanding voice was that of a grizzled old chief petty officer from the ships deck force. He was one of the salty chief boatswain's mates who pretty much ran the ship from the deck up or at least thought they did. The Marines thought they did too and grudgingly but expeditiously moved from their chosen places of relaxation to the starboard side while the deck force manning large fire hoses sprayed salt water over all the areas of the deck where troops might gather.

The bright tropical sun dried the water in a short time and the troops soon returned to their old positions. If Fearless Frank was nearby, some undoubtedly listened out of curiosity as he described his exploits ashore with some of the world's most beautiful women. Fearless Frank was considered very successful with the fair sex. Some men played cards and groused about the chow until the next hose down. Hose downs usually occurred twice a day.

It was late one afternoon when the first sergeant sent for Shanghai to come down to the compartment shared by the sergeant major with all of the first sergeants and company clerks. Shanghai exclaimed, "Wow Top, this place is a regular beehive of activity; I've never seen so many office pinkies and assorted administrators and first pay graders crammed into such a small space before. Why there's hardly room for the typewriters."

The first sergeant looked at Shanghai and stated: "Okay Shanghai, knock it off. We didn't expect to sail on a luxury liner. This space is suitable for our needs but it is overcrowded as hell. Let me get my cover and we'll go up on deck. I need to talk to you."

The first sergeant was relaxed and composed as he leaned

on the rail chewing on his stub of a cigar. He seemed lost in thought for a moment then exhaling a stream of smoke, he turned to look at Shanghai with a pair of determined eyes that riveted him right where he stood.

"What's this about you gonna kill one of your men?"

"Aw hell, it's nothin' Top. I just wanted to get his attention so I told him I was gonna throw him over the side if he didn't shape up and stop acting like a damned coward. He's a good kid but he could do a hell of a lot of damage to the squad and even to the platoon by always talkin' about how scared he is and how he doesn't want to die. It just reminds all of the other men of what they don't want to hear. Could be infectious if he doesn't stop it."

The Top maintained eye contact with Shanghai as he stated, "Dammit Pooley, that kid could put you on report for threatening him and you could wind up a private again. Everyone who knew you in the old days, from Jim Crowe and the Skipper to the sergeant major, have all been going to bat for you and hoping they could find a way to get you promoted back up to gunny. So what do you do? You threaten one of your privates."

"If you want him to stop being scared, threatening to throw him overboard is piss poor psychology. From now on, think before you open your mouth. You know things are different now. It just isn't like it was back in the old Corps."

Then the first sergeant added, "These new wartime warriors are a different breed than the professionals we knew in the old days."

Shanghai Pooley wasn't sure just what he was going to do to get Private Malone over his intense fear of combat. This was a leadership challenge he had not previously encountered.

* * * * * * * * * *

Unforgettable Characters

At sea in the Pacific - Late May 1944

"Hand Grenade" Harrington shouted, "Hey Epstein, Catch!"

"Hell no, dammit!" Epstein retorted, "I don't want to play catch with you. You're dangerous! Those grenades aren't baseballs, the way you throw them, they hurt!"

Harrington had a reputation for throwing practice grenades at anyone who just might try to catch them and throw them back. He loved to play catch. In the company area back in Hawaii he would have another Marine toss a practice grenade towards him then he would whip his helmet off and toss it over the grenade, covering it, then he'd dive for cover. Some of the men watching simply decided he was nuts but a few were impressed at the skill and speed with which he could move to cover the grenade and then dive for cover. No one knew whether it would work in combat with a real grenade but Harrington contended that the helmet being blown apart would absorb some of the grenade fragments and slow the others down thus perhaps saving lives.

Hand Grenade Harrington was totally captivated by America's favorite pastime, baseball. He had played sandlot ball as a kid and in high school he was pitcher on the varsity team. In most respects Harrington was a very normal Marine. He did his job efficiently and stayed squared away. Harrington was quiet most of the time and was always friendly and was well liked by his shipmates.

Harrington had just one idiosyncrasy that could not be overlooked, in fact, it just about drove all his buddies nuts! He was a baseball freak. One might think that all young Americans would be interested in baseball; after all, it was America's national sport. With Hand Grenade it was an obsession. He would quote baseball statistics for as far back as records had been kept. He knew the names of players, long dead that few others had even heard of. Using the light blue practice grenades, he constantly played catch with anyone he could find who would throw the grenade back.

Shortly after joining the company, Harrington had picked

up the nickname of "Babe Ruth" but it didn't last. To be in Harrington's squad or even in his platoon could be a very trying and harrowing experience. No matter what subject was being taught or discussed, Babe Ruth Harrington always managed somehow to equate it with baseball.

Babe Ruth Harrington finally came into his own during grenade practice at Camp Tarawa and that was when he lost his nickname of Babe Ruth and picked up his permanent name of "Hand Grenade" Harrington. He also managed to endear himself to his platoon sergeant. Grenade practice was an essential part of training but it was usually pretty dull. First Lieutenant David Stacey had suggested to Platoon Sergeant Black that they should try and come up with a means of making grenade training more interesting for the troops.

"Blackjack" got together with his squad leaders and decided to generate a little interest by making the training competitive. The squad leaders decided that the winning squad would be relieved of all police duties for a week and the squad that came in second would perform those police details. The squad that came in third of the three would provide men for the camp guard detail for a week in place of men on the winning squad.

Hand grenade training was pretty simple. Targets were made from poles about the size of long 2X4's. They were set up with a square opening at the top. They looked something like window frames on stilts. The idea was for the men to be in the prone position and on a given command get up and prepare to throw, and finally to throw their grenades on command and if successful, their hand grenade would go through the opening in the boards. This was done at increasing ranges after each practice grenade was thrown. Practice grenades were nothing more than regular Mark II fragmentation hand grenades with the fuse and powder removed. For identification purposes, they were painted a light blue.

The men got ready by assuming the prone position. One man from each squad participated at a time. The lieutenant, platoon sergeant and platoon guide were the scorekeepers, judges and referees. When the lieutenant gave the commands, the men did just as they had been instructed and assumed the ready position, simulated pulling the pins and finally, on command, threw their grenades through the targets. At close range, all did fairly well. Then they moved back, five yards, then another five, and so on.

After observing the special skill displayed by Private Harrington, Blackjack was beside himself. The results of his platoon's grenade tossing competition were an inspiration to Platoon Sergeant Black. He simply could not resist challenging the other platoon sergeants in the company. Just to make it interesting, Black decided that there would be only one Marine representing each platoon. Harrington of course was his man. The stakes were dangerously high; two kegs of Hawaiian brewed Primo Beer to the winning platoon. The dangerous part didn't occur until after the men of the winning platoon had drunk the two kegs of beer.

*   *   *   *   *   *   *   *   *   *

During one particularly uneventful day at sea a Marine newly joined to Fox Company was standing just in front of Chic Yancey in the chowline. He casually commented to Chic, "I wonder how that little guy Quinlan who hates corpsmen so much ever got the name of Fearless Frank. He doesn't look to me like he has any more guts than anybody else in this outfit."

Chic replied, "Well, maybe he has and maybe he hasn't, but if you really want to know how he got his name, I can tell you 'cause it just so happens that I was present at his baptism."

The replacement answered, "Yeah, I've always thought he was kind of a character, why don't you tell me about him."

Chic replied, "Well, as you know, Marines and Navy corpsmen have a lot of respect for one another and they always seem to get along well. The only exception I know of is old Fearless and his case is pretty unique. It all started during the first couple of days in boot camp back in October of '42."

"It was an excited Private Quinlan who asked anyone who might have the answers, 'Shots. Shots! Someone said we are going to get shots! When? What for? How many? Do we all have to get them?'

"His answers came from the DI who snapped, 'Fall in! Right

face! F'ward march! Awn hup treep, treep fow ya left.'

"The building didn't really look much like the Sick Bay, it was a small white wooden building, not much more than a shed. It had none of the normal trappings of a dispensary or hospital. It did smell like a dispensary however and suspended over it on a pole was the Red Cross flag.

'Column of files from the right, March! All right people, guide into that hatch and keep moving until a corpsman tells you where to stop,' the DI shouted.

"What happened next would be unnerving to almost anyone but to brand new Marine "Boots" lined up and waiting to get their shots, it was catastrophic. Four Navy corpsmen emerged from the building carrying a stretcher upon which a young Marine was reclining. He appeared to be unconscious. His face was very pale. After they placed him into a waiting ambulance and closed the door, three of them returned to the building. Presumably to continue giving inoculations.

"As they passed by the file of Boots waiting to enter, one of them commented half to himself.

'It was that square needle in the left nut that got to him, that's the shot that really separates the men from the boys.'

"The corpsmen passed into the building and were out of sight when Private Francis X. Quinlan turned to me. The color had drained from his face and his voice was quivering. 'Chic, did you hear that? They really are going to jab us in the left nut with a square needle! Those guys in Platoon 1006 weren't kidding when they told us that.'

"Quinlan looked very weak and shaky but before I could answer or reassure him in any way, the voice of the DI broke the silence.

'Okay you guys wanted to be Marines, now act like it! Close up that line, keep moving, we don't want to be here all day. You don't have to worry about these shots, every Marine in the Corps has had to take them. They won't hurt you a damn bit,' the DI was in charge.

"Francis X. Quinlan was not reassured. The rest of us could see him faltering almost as though he wanted to find a means to escape what was about to befall him. We kept shuffling forward and stayed in line. Most tried to look brave and unconcerned, but for some, it was their first real test of courage and a few just didn't appear to be up to it.

"We were inside now and very close to the corpsmen who were giving the shots. As the recruits filed through, one corpsman on each side would give their respective shot, withdraw the hypodermic needle, swipe an alcohol impregnated cotton ball over the puncture and then say 'Step forward.'

"This went on until all seven shots had been administered. When it was Quinlan's turn to step forward, he stepped but went downward instead of forward. He was out cold on the deck! One of the corpsmen called for assistance and Quinlan's limp body was dragged out of the way. Looking out of the corner of my eye, I could see that Quinlan, now revived, sat up almost immediately, but he was not to avoid the dreaded shots. A young pharmacist mate's striker held an enameled pan of hypodermics while a seasoned chief petty officer administered a full series of shots to Quinlan while he sat there as if in shock.

"Quinlan would not be punished for holding up the shot line, but there were lessons to be learned and so there would be ample "extra military instruction" for the platoon this night. Private Quinlan was honored by the drill instructors in being given the privilege of being the first in line whenever subsequent shots were to be given to the platoon.

"The Drill Instructors let it be known that hereafter, Private Quinlan's nickname would be "Fearless." None of us guessed then that the nickname would stick and that he would indeed be fearless. He turned out to be one of the fiercest barroom brawlers in the naval service and is probably one of the only U.S. Marines who has gone through life, to this day, harboring a passionate dislike for all Navy corpsmen. So now you know how Fearless got his name and I guess I should add just one more thing, don't be fooled by his small size and don't mess with him. He's really a good guy but he's had lot's of experience fighting swabbies in barroom brawls and its made him pretty tough."

Another of the company's most colorful characters was "The Knife Fighter," Pfc Samuel K. Barkdahl, III.

It was a known fact among the men in the 2nd platoon that the Knife Fighter had never actually killed anyone with a knife but at least he had studied books on the subject and had done a lot of practicing. He had honed his skills to a "razor's edge."

* * * * * * * * * *

It was the disturbed voice of Fearless and it cut to the quick. "Knife Fighter, you sonofabitch, you've sold us out haven't you?"

"What are you talkin' about Fearless?" responded the surprised Knife Fighter.

"I saw you talkin' to a couple of those swabbies yesterday and the same ones were up on deck with you again this morning lookin' around on the foc'sl as though you were partners in some kind of a shady deal. This afternoon, the same swabbies were up on the fantail with you rigging up a rack with some planks of dunnage. What the hell's going on?"

The Knife Fighter smiled and with a shrug replied, "Geez Fearless, they are just swabbies, they ain't corpsmen and they aren't going to stick anyone with needles. You remember my set of throwing knives don't you?"

An irritated Fearless answered, "Yeah sure we all remember your phony carnival act. So what?"

"Dammit Fearless, when you're a knife thrower like me, you know, a real professional, you need constant practice. I had to find a way to get those planks put up and the only way I could do it was to get the swabbies involved. I wanted it up on the foc'sl but the ship's First Lieutenant wouldn't hear of it so we compromised and I got the fantail. I promised that if they helped me I'd teach them knife fighting techniques."

Fearless was incensed as he said, "Damn! You really have sold out! You don't think those sailors want to learn to fight with knives so they can kill Japs do you? Those bastards will probably use what you're teaching them in barroom brawls. They'll be out there fighting Marines and slashing and stabbing your own brothers."

The Knife Fighter responded, "Fearless, in this life, you do what you hafta' do and I had to promise those sailors a few lessons that's all."

"Knife Fighter, I think you're nuts!" Fearless stated. Then he asked, "You've got six knives in that throwing set, right?"

"Yeah, right there's six of 'em and I'm telling you, they are a perfectly balanced set. They were made just for throwing and they're really great. You've seen what I can do with those knives."

Fearless responded with, "Well, I've got an M-1 rifle and it fires a clip of eight rounds. When it goes "pinng!!", and the empty clip flies out of the receiver, I reach into my cartridge belt and take out another clip of eight rounds and load it. That's security. Now tell me Knife Fighter what are you gonna do after you've thrown away your six knives and some Nip is still comin' at you with a bayonet on the end of his rifle?"

The Knife Fighter chose to ignore his young friend's question. He too was armed with an M-1 and Fearless knew it. He established himself on the ship's fantail and for a day he conducted demonstrations in knife fighting and throwing which was impressive to a large number of Marines and sailors but the novelty quickly wore off. Marines dragging their laundry over the fantail on a line got an adrenalin rush and were somewhat perturbed each time they heard the "kerchunk" made by a sharp knife imbedding itself in a wooden plank a foot or two beside or behind them. The following day, the Knife Fighter was restricted to conducting his classes and demonstrations during just one hour daily commencing at 1500 and all hands were restricted from being beside or behind his target.

It was to the Knife Fighter's everlasting credit that in throwing his six knives at the plank scores of times daily, he never injured anyone and he never lost one of his precious throwing knives over the side. Samuel K. Barkdahl, III, turned out to be more of a professional than many of his buddies had realized.

* * * * * * * * * *

Chic, Fearless and Deadly Dave were on deck with Corporal Al Jerden when a small bit of excitement occurred. The ship's surgeon was being sent over to a destroyer to take care of a medical emergency. The troops lined the rail to watch the doctor being high-lined. There was all too little excitement aboard a crowded troop transport on a long slow voyage across the Pacific. The men thought about "Lucky" Lane and his medical emergency at Tarawa. His untimely appendectomy on a troop transport on 18 November, D minus 2, was something Lucky would never live down, although the appendectomy probably saved his life in more ways than one.

Jerden asked if "Riverboat" Brown had found out about Lucky's scar yet. Deadly Dave didn't think so but he commented that the facts were bound to come out sooner or later. They chuckled as they remembered the first time Riverboat had seen Lucky's new scar. Lucky had just left the tent to take a shower. Jerden, Sam Barkdahl, (the Knife Fighter), Hand Grenade Harrington and a new replacement, a corporal by the name of Brown, walked with him. While they were showering Brown noticed the healing scar on the right side of Lucky's groin and asked, "What happened to you Lucky, where'd you get that?"

Lucky quietly mumbled, "Tarawa."

Riverboat's interest was aroused as he stated, "Damn, it sure musta' been rough on that island. Was it from a bayonet? I'm glad I wasn't with y'all on that one. Was it from a Jap bayonet, Lucky?"

Corporal Jerden and the Knife Fighter looked at one another wondering what Lucky's response was going to be.

"Nah, it wasn't anything like that, but if you don't mind Corporal, I'd just as soon not talk about it."

"Sure Lucky, I understand."

Corporal Brown may have thought he understood, but he did not understand. The Knife Fighter and Hand Grenade Harrington just grinned at one another; they knew and Al Jerden knew that sooner or later Lucky would have to confess about his appendectomy aboard the transport at Tarawa while the rest of the battalion was fighting their way ashore.

Thinking about Lucky's fortuitous scar reminded them of another of his brilliant strokes of luck. The time he almost got promoted to Pfc but was saved, just in the nick of time, by being sent on meritorious liberty.

It was only a squad of men but they were to be representatives of the company. They had been carefully selected by their platoon leaders as men who were most deserving of a special liberty. All had worked hard and trained hard and they were excited about this reward. Liberty in Hilo, Hawaii, was very rare for junior enlisted Marines in the 2nd Marine Division. They put on their best summer khaki uniforms and climbed aboard the 2½ ton truck that was to transport them the 60 miles down to Hilo.

The singing Marines had some difficulty climbing back aboard the 2½ ton truck for their return trip to Camp Tarawa. With the help of the driver and his assistant, they finally all climbed and stumbled aboard. The assistant driver, who had a small ukulele slung around his neck in addition to the two flower leis he was wearing, slammed the tailgate shut and was attempting to secure it when he heard the driver call out that he was departing. The assistant driver ran through the mud along the right side of the truck and jumped in beside the driver as he jerked the vehicle into motion.

They had gone but a few yards when the tailgate dropped and Private Lucky Lane dropped with it. He was sprawled in the middle of the muddy road painfully grasping his right arm which he thought was broken. The truck ground to a shaky stop and two of the liberty party jumped from the truck bed and went back to retrieve Lucky. This time, before the truck moved out, the tailgate was properly secured.

The men continued their long ride back to camp amid much singing and frivolity. Lucky Lane had the last seat on the starboard side. He was filled with disgust and was experiencing quite a bit of pain in his right arm. He hadn't seen a group of men act this way since his freshman year at Ohio State. One inebriated Marine stood up in the truck bed and started to stagger toward the tailgate. Lucky was certain the man was going to fall off the back of the moving truck unless someone did something to stop him. The others were all singing and were oblivious to the danger at hand. It was up to Lucky.

He reached out and grabbed the unsteady lad who promptly sprayed him with vomit. It was in his hair, on his face and all over the front of his rain-soaked shirt. As the long ride progressed, the singing became almost unbearable to Lucky who had long since realized that he was the only sober member of the group of unruly celebrants. In typical Hawaiian fashion, the rains had started almost without warning. The men were drenched. Passing through the lava flows, they traveled past Moana Loa and Moana Kea and the rains stopped. The drenched Marines were cold and shivering as they pulled into their area at Camp Tarawa.

As the unsteady passengers alighted from the truck, Gunny Littleton met them and called to Private Lane. He acted as though the cargo of drunks didn't even exist. He had to speak to Lucky Lane. Lucky stood before the gunnery sergeant in his muddy khakis, soaked to the skin and reeking of vomit with his right arm in a makeshift sling. "Lane, the Top wants to see you right now."

"I can't see anyone right now, I've got to get cleaned up, that damned Private Green puked all over me and I'm soaked to the skin from the damned rain and I've got to get to Sick Bay and find out if my arm is broken. Tell the first sergeant that I'll be there as soon as I can get cleaned up."

"You must not have heard me Lane, I said the Top wants to see you now! You can get cleaned up later." The gunnery sergeant reached out and, somewhat reluctantly, firmly took Lane by the arm and marched him to the company office. The first sergeant had been waiting for the special liberty detail to return. He had finally managed to get the captain to sign the warrant promoting Private Lane to Private First Class. The first sergeant believed that Lane had been a victim of circumstances. He was one of the sharpest and brightest Marines in the company and yet he was only a private. Some unfortunate thing always seemed to happen to Lane when he was up for promotion but this time, the first sergeant had convinced the company commander and the warrant was signed and in his hand.

Private Lucky Lane was escorted into the office by the company gunnery sergeant who was doing his best to hold his breath. The smell of ripening vomit was exceedingly unpleasant. Lane stood before the first sergeant in his soaked, muddy uniform. The Top couldn't believe his eyes, Lane had been his sharpest man. Captain "Marty" Barrett couldn't believe his eyes either as he asked: "What the hell is that Top?"

The first sergeant replied, "Private First Class Lane, Sir. I can't believe it either, but it really is Lane."

The captain snorted, "Private First Class my shirt! Give me that warrant!"

The Top handed Lane's Pfc warrant to the captain who

promptly tore it in half and directed, "Dismiss this man and see that he takes a shower immediately! I mean immediately. BEFORE removing his clothes! And by the way first sergeant, I don't want to see his name on a liberty list again ever, not as long as I am in command of this company. Is that clear?"

Lucky Lane's arm was not broken but he had a bad sprain that kept him out of the field for some time. There were those in the company chain of command who felt that if he couldn't perform his duties in the field, he sure as hell shouldn't be promoted. Lane's streak of bad luck was holding, in fact it was so tenacious, it had all the appearances of becoming a permanent curse.

* * * * * * * * * *

A Cup of Joe

Steaming in the Pacific May/June 1944

On duty with the ship's guard, Chic found himself in the loneliest spot on the ship. He was aloft in what seemed like a small gun tub without the gun. It was apparently a platform used for signaling. He liked being so high up as it gave him a chance to see the ship's decks from a different perspective. He was able to see farther out on the horizon than he normally could from the deck far below. It was a hot day with the bright tropical sun beating down on the steel ship. The heat of the sun seemed to drain the strength from him, as his dungarees became sweat-soaked. Just putting his hand on the steel plates could result in a burn.

The gentle dipping and swaying of the ship was much more pronounced from way up where Chic was than it had been down on the main deck. It was practically rocking him to sleep. He hadn't realized how sleepy he was until he'd been on watch an hour or so. His eyelids became very heavy from the strain of searching the bright sky and the sea. He was really sleepy. He knew he would never allow himself to fall asleep on post, but he did want to find something to lean back against and just close his eyes for a moment or so.

It was about that time that he heard sounds on the ladder. Someone was climbing up to his post. A Navy steward scurried up with one hand on the ladder and the other hand carrying what appeared to be a large bucket-like container.

Navy stewards periodically went to each of the remote posts where the men were required to look out over the vast sea for four hours at a time in hopes of spotting something unusual or of importance. The stewards had large coffee pails and classic heavy Navy porcelain china cups into which they poured steaming hot coffee for the watch standers. Chic declined the offer of coffee. A gruff voice beckoned the steward not to leave without giving him a cup of "joe." It was a swarthy Navy Chief Quartermaster who had come up the ladder after the steward and stepped into the tub.

The Chief was obviously not about to trust the security of his ship to amateurs. As he stood sipping his black java, he scanned the sea with a pair of binoculars that were suspended from his neck. Spotting nothing, he turned his attention to Chic. "Been in the Corps long, son?" He asked, knowing full well what the answer would be.

"No Sir, Chief, not very long."

"Well then, let me ask you a question. Have they ever given you any instructions on the Articles for the Government of the Navy? The Rocks and Shoals?"

"Oh sure Chief, that's required in the Marine Corps. We're given a class on the Rocks and Shoals once a month."

"Well then, son, I guess you must know the penalty for sleepin' on watch. Sleepin' on watch in time of war. Its pretty serious you know."

"Yes Sir, I know it's serious."

The Chief spent a few minutes remarking to Chic about his time in the Navy and especially how he hated the Japs for starting the war and screwing up his erstwhile good duty on the Old Asiatic Station. He said that Shanghai would never be the same after the war. That was where the Chief had obviously spent much of his foreign shore duty.

Finally, he looked at Chic with a stare that seemed to bore right through him and remarked:

"Kid, the next time the stewards come around and offer you a cup of joe, I strongly recommend that you accept it.

Remember, you are up here to watch for enemy aircraft or periscopes and you've got to be alert at all times. It's a boring assignment. Just looking out over the sea can be pretty tiresome and the roll of the ship can lull you to sleep. Four hours is a long watch. It would be easy for a young fella like you to doze off from time to time. Let me give you an important piece of advice, don't fall asleep on post. When they offer you coffee, drink it and drink it black and if you can get them to pour you another cup, take it. Coffee may help you to stay awake.

"I asked if you knew the penalty for sleeping on post in time of war and you said you did. Just in case you have forgotten what it is, let me remind you. You can be awarded the death penalty, son. They can shoot you for sleeping on post in time of war.

"Now son, you could be shot by the enemy after you get ashore on Saipan but that is different. If you are shot for jeopardizing your shipmates' lives by sleeping on post, you will be tried, convicted, shot and you'll be forgotten. If you die fighting over on that beach, you may die a hero, and in the Marines, heroes are not soon forgotten. That's it son, take your choice. We're all gonna die sooner or later. You've got a chance to be a dead hero or just dead, it's up to you," advised the Chief.

The old chief descended the ladder and disappeared but the memory of him lasted. Chic wondered to himself just what Saipan was and where it might be. He became a serious coffee drinker on that day in early June of 1944. Frequently over the decades when he poured himself a cup of joe he thought about the old chief quartermaster high aloft on that Navy transport so many years ago.

* * * * * * * * *

Operation Forager

June 1944

The word had been passed for the platoon to assemble up on deck around hatch number two. Platoon Sergeant Black had staked it out and the three squad leaders were all there protecting the space. Two of the sergeants had brought up a large relief map and with the platoon guide were displaying it on the hatch cover. Blackjack got the men's attention and Lieutenant David Stacey stepped up onto the hatch cover. This seasoned veteran of the fighting on Guadalcanal and Tarawa clutched his swagger stick in his right hand gently slapping his left palm as he glanced at the faces of his men mentally appraising each of them as was his way.

The men looked back at their lieutenant - each making direct eye contact with him. It was their silent acknowledgement that he had their full and complete attention. The diagonal scar across his left cheek hinted that this warrior-leader was not new to armed conflict. A look into his steady, knowing eyes proved it.

"All right leathernecks, gather 'round. Those of you in front get down so the men behind you can all see this map. You've been wondering just what Operation Forager is all about and now you are going to find out. Men, we are going to seize, occupy and defend the Mariana Islands."

The swagger stick now pointed to a chain of islands on the map before them.

"The Mariana Islands are the key to our wresting control of the Central Pacific from the Japanese. These islands dominate the Jap lines of communication.

"The capture of the Marianas will provide bases for the Pacific Fleet to attack the enemy in a variety of strategically important locations. We'll be able to strike at the Palau's, the Philippines, Formosa or China from the Marianas."

The lieutenant paused as he looked at the men of his platoon and then he continued: "Just in case you haven't figured it out yet, an attack on such a sensitive area may be what it takes to finally bring out the Japanese Fleet. We've waited a long time to engage the Jap Navy in a major fleet action and this may be our best opportunity.

"Another thing that makes this operation really important is that the Army Air Force wants to base their big bombers like the B-17's and B-24's in the Marianas, for the bombardment of Japan (The giant B-29 Superfortresses had not yet been heard of by the Marines.). We are going to start by seizing the northern Marianas commencing on 15 June.

"For the purposes of today's briefing, I'm going to concentrate on the island of Saipan, because men, that is where we are going to land," explained Lieutenant Stacey.

The swagger stick in the lieutenant's steady hand now moved down a small chain of approximately fifteen islands and came to a stop on an island midway in the chain. It was the second largest of the Mariana Islands. This was Saipan.

Chic Yancey now understood what the old chief had been talking about. The Navy chief had learned that Saipan would be their destination even before the Marines were briefed.

"This campaign will be different than what we've done in the past and its going to be challenging in many ways. In the first place, this will be the first island where Americans have landed that has a Japanese civilian population. We'll have to handle the civilians differently than we do their soldiers. You'll find that this piece of real estate has white sandy beaches, jungles, cultivated fields, a city and mountains with steep cliffs, caves and all manner of natural obstacles. If that is not enough of a challenge for you, the intelligence people estimate that there may be as many as 10,000 Jap soldiers on the island along with a number of sailors and Marines. All of this is on an island that is approximately twelve miles long and six miles wide."

Blackjack, the platoon sergeant, couldn't wait to voice his opinion: "We've finally mastered the technique of attacking the flat coral atolls like Tarawa and the Marshals so where do they send us? To a place with mountains, cliffs, caves, jungles and civilians to deal with. This is going to be a helluva lot different than anything we've dealt with in the past."

The men who had been in the platoon longest wondered if anyplace could be tougher than their previous operations on Guadalcanal and Tarawa. They were soon to find out.

The lieutenant added that a nearly unbroken ring of coral reefs surrounded most of the Marianas and Saipan was no exception. The troops showed considerable interest as they remembered the reef at Tarawa. Some had to wade through the lagoon from the reef all the way to the beach under intense enemy fire. The lieutenant spoke again.

"Men, these islands are a thousand miles from the nearest American base. They constitute the most remote and formidable targets encountered by American forces so far in this war and we have been given the privilege of taking them. We're going to assault along with the 4th Marine Division and there's an Army division, the 27th, that will be our floating reserve. Now before we dismiss you I've asked Gunnery Sergeant Paul from the Machine-gun Platoon to brief you on a couple of items that are very important and may save your lives."

Gunny Paul stepped up onto the hatch cover holding a gas mask in one hand and a life belt in the other. Epstein nudged Stash and asked, "What the hell is he gonna tell us about those stupid things that we don't already know?"

Stash reminded Epstein that there were some replacements that were new to the platoon and had not been in combat before. They needed to be reminded of the value of these two "encumbrances". Stash did concede that they were the first two things he was going to get rid of when they hit the beach.

The gunny held up the life belt and unscrewed the two retaining covers and inserted two small steel CO_2 bottles and then screwed the covers back on. After fastening the belt around his waist he inflated it, and showed the men how it was done.

"Once you men put this belt around your waist it simply becomes an additional item of interference. It's cumbersome, it's clumsy, it's in your way and it serves no useful purpose," declared the gunny.

There was a confused grin on Epstein's face. Surely the gunny couldn't be agreeing with his evaluation of the lifebelt. Then the gunny continued: "That is, it serves no useful purpose unless you want to stay alive. If you should need it, it's the best friend you'll ever have. But if you don't need it, get rid of it just as soon as you get ashore. Now the gas mask is another matter. You won't know if you're gonna need it until after you are ashore. You'll see a lot of wise guys who think they know everything who will drop their gas masks just as soon as we hit the beach. Well, if the Japs decide to use gas on us, the only thing that's going to keep you alive is your gas mask. The guys who drop them on the beach are gonna feel pretty stupid just before they die."

Before stepping down off of the hatch cover the gunny remarked that he was tired of hearing the men constantly griping and complaining about the cramped quarters, poor chow and a multitude of other inconveniences aboard ship.

"Just remember, after you've been over on that beach for a few days, you'll wish you could swim back out to this old rust bucket. It is gonna seem like a luxury liner to you and you'll wish to hell you were back aboard. Now I recommend that all of you stop your bitching and start learning just as much as you can about Saipan. Frankly, I never heard of it before, but I guarantee you that none of us will ever forget it once we've assaulted that beach."

Up on deck in the evening, Chic moved from group to group and listened with keen interest. Self-styled "experts" expounded on Saipan Island. He heard many versions of what the next landing would be like; none appeared to be based on fact or on optimism. He heard a great deal about the flora and fauna of the island, the Chamorro people, the terrain and the weather during the rainy season. All of this from sources who until the previous day had never even heard of Saipan.

Sergeant Black, the platoon sergeant, had just finished giving the lieutenant his morning report when he added: "Lieutenant, I think we may have a problem with Private Malone. The kid's a good Marine in most respects but he seems to be on the verge of a case of combat fatigue and he hasn't even been shot at yet."

"Yes Blackjack, Doc mentioned something about Malone the other day. He's really concerned about him too. I don't know what we can do for him. The other men are scared too and they have a right to be. Hell, I'm scared myself but it's just something we've got to live with." the lieutenant continued, "Perhaps I should have a talk with him."

Blackjack responded, "Well Lieutenant, that might be a

good idea but you know you can't talk a man out of being scared. That's something he's just going to have to deal with himself."

"Nevertheless Blackjack, I want to see him. Make it as inconspicuous as possible so the others won't know what's going on. Give him a message to deliver to me or something and let me know when you're going to do it so I can be alone up on deck where he and I can talk privately."

"Aye aye, Sir."

* * * * * * * * * *

Another Day at Sea

13/14 June 1944

"Now hear this, now hear this, Reveille! That is, Reveille! All hands heave out and trice up! There'll be a clean sweep down fore and aft! The smoking lamp is lighted on all weather decks. All hands, that is all hands, carry out the ship's plan of the day."

Another signal from the boatswain's pipe and a bugler sounded first call followed by chow call five minutes later.

The troops stumbled up the ladder to the deck to start shuffling through the chow line and noticed that the dawn was having a hard time breaking. It was still nearly dark and they wondered if reveille hadn't been accidentally sounded a couple of hours earlier than it should have been. That turned out not to be the case. The sky was a solid mass of dark clouds, it was an unusually overcast morning and the sea was flat and lifeless.

The dark clouds in the sky were various shades of gray. The sea had taken on a washed out dark gray drabness that appeared dull and hostile. The gray of the ship was depressing. Only the spirited rippling and snapping of the Stars and Stripes and its bright red, white and blue contrasted with the depressing gloom of the ships and the sea. As long as the Marines could look at that flag they could feel the spirit of America, it was the emblem of home and so many of the things they loved and missed.

Troops lined the rail and watched with interest as an officer was brought aboard via high line. The officer, wearing Navy khakis and a life vest, made the harrowing trip from another ship steaming alongside. He proved to be a chaplain that had been brought aboard to conduct services and minister to the troops. As soon as he arrived on board he was escorted up to officers' country presumably to freshen up and have a cup of coffee.

It was not long before the shrill whistle of a boatswain's pipe pierced the air followed by a bugle sounding the mellow notes of church call. As the bugle was sounding church call, a quartermaster snapped the white and blue church pennant to a halyard and quickly hoisted it. Then the announcement: "Now hear this, now hear this, church call, that is, church call. Protestant divine services are now being conducted on the fantail. The smoking lamp is out; knock off all card games; maintain silence throughout the ship."

Services were well attended and when they were finished, the chaplain took a brief break then he held services again for the men who couldn't get close enough to participate in the first service.

The sun, the blue sky and the puffy cotton-like clouds were back and the drab gray sea had changed to a vivid blue again. The Marines who were bored with shipboard life and were preoccupied with thoughts of Operation Forager and the island of Saipan generally overlooked the natural beauty of the sky and the sea.

Private Eddie Malone climbed the ladder up to the next deck. He was now in officers' country and felt somewhat uneasy about it. Malone was to deliver a packet to Lieutenant Stacey. He moved over to the port side and glanced fore and aft. There was his lieutenant up forward he was all alone just leaning on the rail and smoking his pipe.

Malone saluted smartly and stated: "Sir, Platoon Sergeant Black sends his respects and asked me to give this envelope to the lieutenant."

"Thanks Malone, I've been waiting for this. Stand easy." Looking up from the report the lieutenant glanced at Malone and asked.

"How's everything going with you?"

"Okay Sir."

The lieutenant queried, "When they brought mail aboard the other day did you hear from your folks back in Cincinnati?"

Malone responded, "Yes Sir, I got a few letters."

"Have you been writing to them?" asked the lieutenant.

Now beginning to see where this was going Malone responded, "You know I have Sir, you must read my letters when you censor them."

"Malone, you may be surprised to learn that I censor many letters but I don't really read any of them, I can't. We are required to screen the mail for classified information and that's what we look for. We don't have the time or inclination to actually read the letters or even to look at who wrote them," explained Stacey.

Taking a long drag on his pipe, the lieutenant turned to look squarely at Malone and asked, "Eddie, have any of the old timers in the platoon been telling you about what its going to be like when we go ashore in this next operation? I know it's your first time in combat and I want to be sure you learn as much as you can from the men who have been through it before."

The private responded, "Yes Sir, we talk about it a lot. I guess I'm a little nervous about going into combat but then I suppose everyone is." He anxiously added, "I really don't want to die Lieutenant."

In a fatherly way the lieutenant replied, "None of us do Eddie, but some of us will. That's just the way it has to be. I'm not going to tell you that no one is going to get hurt in this campaign. We're going in there to kill Japs and their job is to kill us if they can. You understand that don't you?"

"Yes Sir, I understand." Said Malone.

"Well, if it helps any, I will say this, there are over 20,000 Marines in this division and over 20,000 Marines in the 4th Marine Division. If they have to call in the reserves, the Army's 27th Division, that's probably going to be another 20,000. You remember when I briefed you I told you the intelligence estimates were that the Japs had 10,000 defenders on Saipan. Eddie, there'll only be 10,000 of them against 60,000 of us and you'll have to admit that's pretty good odds in our favor." explained the officer.

"Yes Sir" acknowledged Malone, "I guess we've got a pretty sizeable advantage over them."

Trying to inspire confidence, the lieutenant added, "That's not the half of it. Wait until you see what Marine and Navy air will have done to that island before we even get there. And another thing that will really impress you is what the Navy's big guns will do to it. We'll have battleships firing their 16-inch main batteries at that island for days before we arrive. By the time they're through with it, the damned rock will be just about ready to sink. I may be wrong but I really can't see how the surviving Japs will be able to put up much of a fight after the punishment they will have received before we go ashore."

Not completely convinced but feeling somewhat better, young Malone said "Yes Sir, thanks for talking to me about it Lieutenant. I really feel better about it now that I've talked with you, Sir. I guess I'm not so scared now."

At sea approaching the Mariana archipelago
14 June 1944

The great convoy continued steaming on to westward and the boredom of the troops increased with each passing day. NCO's held classes on the weather decks and the men were told everything known about the island of Saipan which turned out to be remarkably little. Lookouts would occasionally spot bits of floating debris causing much speculation as to its origin. Rifles and BARs were repeatedly cleaned and machine-gun belts were loaded by hand. "General quarters," "fire in the paint locker," "abandon ship" and an assortment of other drills continued to be held at unexpected times.

Schools of porpoises swam past the bow, as flying fish leapt out of the sea in large arcs that really did make it seem that they were flying. Sunsets were an amazing array of color and were so magnificent that it seemed they were a special gift from God to all that beheld them. A humming ventilator on deck gave off the delightful smells of freshly baked bread. As the troops filed by in the slow chow line they hungrily inhaled the pleasant aroma.

The platoon was on deck listening intently to a final briefing by their platoon leader. When the lieutenant was finished
Platoon Sergeant Black told the men to stand fast. He'd asked
Gunny Littleton, the company gunnery sergeant to spend a
few moments talking about his experiences on Guadalcanal
and Tarawa and telling the men what he could about how the
Japanese fight. The Gunny held the men spellbound for about
ten minutes and was just about to leave when he hesitated
long enough to remind the men: "Don't you forget what I am
about to say to you now. You have heard it before but it's
important so I'm going to say it again. When you get over on
that beach, you will be fighting for your lives and for your
buddy's lives. It's down and dirty men and there are no rules.
Always cheat and always win! Remember, the only unfair fight
is the one you lose.

"One more thing, you must always have a backup. Everyone knows that you've got to have a plan but the best damned
plan in the world won't do you a bit of good unless you've got
an effective backup plan. Why do you think the backup plan
is so important? 'Cause your first plan is not going to work
that's why. And that's just the way it is in combat," advised
Gunnery Sergeant Littleton.

Blackjack dismissed the platoon and as the men moved
away some of the NCO's lingered on to chat with the Gunny
and one another. Shanghai walked over to the rail with the
platoon sergeant. He cupped his hands against the wind and
lighted a cigarette then said, "Damn, Blackjack, I don't know
what the lieutenant said to Malone but I sure wish he'd say it
to me. That sonofagun has really turned around lately. He
can't wait to get ashore and start killing Japs. I've never seen
such a change come over a man before. He's like a one man
cheering section. The squad has picked up on it and morale
is soaring. I guess enthusiasm really can be contagious."

The platoon sergeant studied Shanghai's face carefully then
answered simply, "Yeah, so is panic. There's a fine line between infectious enthusiasm and infectious panic Sergeant
and you are not a qualified psychologist so keep your eyes
and ears open and watch out. Don't let those men of yours
get too enthusiastic about killing Japs 'cause when the shoot-

ing gets too heavy there could be a hell of a psychological reversal. This is where good old effective Marine Corps leadership really counts."

It was 14 June. Back home it would be Flag Day but aboard the troopships, it was D minus 1. They had finally arrived off the island in the darkness of night. All had been curious about Saipan but they were unable to see much of it; only the barest outline of the island was visible along with multiple fires.

The results of the naval gunfire that had been, and was still, pounding the island were quite visible. To Private Eddie Malone, it looked like hell had risen up out of the dark sea and was just floating there burning. He watched huge white-hot explosions occasionally followed by spires of orange flames licking up into the blackness of the sky. There were detonations all along the beachfront and he could see many fires burning. Lieutenant Stacey had been right. Navy and Marine air and naval gunfire had just about destroyed the whole damned island. There were even several fires burning up on the slopes of Mount Tapotchau.

A feeling of exhilaration and enthusiasm swept over Malone as he witnessed the devastation of Saipan. It was good to be on the winning side. His previous fears were virtually forgotten.

"Holy cow! That island is really taking a beating. I don't see how anyone could live through a bombardment like that, do you Stash?" asked Malone.

Stash thought about it before answering. He remembered how the lieutenant hadn't believed any Japanese could live through the bombardment at Tarawa. He also remembered how none of the survivors could ever forget the bloody reception they had received from the Japanese defenders.

Stash knew that Eddie had been having serious problems with his obvious fear of combat and he could easily become a liability to the platoon. The U.S. Navy was doing a tremendous job of destroying just about everything on the island and Stash was starting to feel fairly confident that they may have an easy landing after all. He fervently hoped so. He finally made up his mind that the best way to help keep Malone from cracking up would be to agree with him and try to put his own fears aside and show some enthusiasm.

"Yeah, Eddie, I've never seen anything like this before. The Japs may even raise a white flag and surrender tomorrow when it gets to be daylight. That is if there are enough of them left to surrender. I've got to admit to you that up to now I've been pretty scared about this operation myself, but I'm starting to feel good about it now. I think those Japs are whipped."

An enthusiastic Malone replied, "Yeah, Stash, I can see that. Look how many fires are burning over on the island? And the good old Navy is still lobbing those big rounds at them. It almost makes you want to feel sorry for the poor bastards don't it?"

"No! I've lost too many buddies to feel sorry for the sonsabitches. But I'll tell you one thing Eddie, thank God that we aren't over on that beach now. I just don't see how anyone could live through that kind of fire. If anyone is still alive over there, they will be deaf from the detonations and surely they will have been driven mad from the concussion and being shot at so much with that big stuff."

Private Eddie Malone was no longer possessed with an overwhelming fear of death. He could hardly wait to redeem his tarnished reputation by storming the beach in a heroic manner the next day.

Chic was standing on deck with Deadly Dave and Fearless Frank watching the fires burning on the island they were to invade in the morning and thinking about this rust bucket they were finally leaving.

They thought about the many inconveniences of shipboard life that they would no longer have to put up with: the uncomfortable tight quarters; only two lousy meals a day; the excessively long chow lines; the deck crew always hosing down the decks where Marines were assembled; the frequent drills; saltwater showers; barely two feet between bunks and a multitude of other inconveniences including the threat from submarines and general quarters being sounded at ungodly times of the day and night.

They also silently thought about the sailors who would be staying on board. They would be able to turn on a scuttlebutt and get cool fresh water anytime they wanted it. If there were squalls or heavy weather, they could go below decks and be dry. The food was not the best but at least it was hot and the aroma of fresh baking bread coming through the ventilator up on deck would be missed, as would the clean, fresh sea air and electric lights to read by. Most importantly, the steel armor plating of the ship was much better protection from enemy fire than the thin cotton of Marine dungarees. Yes, in spite of the many inconveniences they were Marines and Marines were at home aboard ship, they would miss it.

* * * * * * * * * *

Land the Landing Force!

Saipan Island – 14/15 June 1944

They all knew that Shanghai carried an American flag but not all had seen it before last night. He had gently removed it from his haversack and had Chief help him shake and carefully refold it.

Sergeant Childs asked, "What're ya doin' with the colors Shanghai?"

"Do you know what the date is, Childs?" Shanghai inquired?

"Sure, it's the 14th," Childs stated with an air of confidence.

"That's right, it's the 14th of June. Back home in the States its Flag Day. Don't you think it's appropriate for me to take my flag out and refold it on Flag Day? Do you want to know something else about this flag, Childs? It's the flag that's going to fly over Emperor Hirohito's Palace in Tokyo after the war. And I just happen to be the guy that's going to put it there. Who knows, I may even let you help me put it up. In the meantime, if we need to raise a flag on Saipan this one will be available right here in my pack," Shanghai stated.

The men's packs were carefully assembled and rolled, rifles and equipment meticulously checked and rechecked. Another shrill command from the boatswain's pipe, then a bugle call and the troops were absorbed into a seemingly endless line that wound its way up a ladder, down a passageway and out onto the weather decks where it slowly snaked toward the troops' messing compartment. Once on the mess decks the troops picked up their steel trays as they started through the line and held them out for the Navy mess cooks to load them up with what was to be their last meal aboard ship. For some it would be their last meal - ever.

The U.S. Navy, always benevolent to Marines on the morning of a combat landing, had been able to produce a breakfast of steak and eggs. The steaks were small, tough and rather well done and the eggs were powdered but they seemed delicious to the perpetually hungry Marines. Steak and eggs had become a D-day tradition.

Young Marines tried to mask their uneasiness at going into battle and yet there was considerable uncertainty and deep concern within them. The troops wondered how they would perform when put to the ultimate test. The replacements like Eddie Malone and many others were untried and were about to get their first taste of real combat. All were well trained. They knew their jobs but still there was an uncertainty they hoped would never show. They must not let their buddies sense their fear. They were Marines, they had to act and fight like Marines.

The old hands knew what the boots were thinking and feeling. They had lived through that same inner terror themselves. The old timers looked confident and professional but deep down inside every one of them was experiencing the same gnawing feeling in the pit of his stomach. Would this be it? Was their luck about to run out or would they survive another campaign? They must never let the new men sense their fears; it could destroy the combat effectiveness of the unit. No matter how they really felt they had to act like Marines.

The shrill whistle of the boatswain's pipe sounded strangely different this time and it had an electrifying effect on all hands. It was followed by the announcement they had all been waiting for and some hoped would never come.

"Now hear this! Now hear this. Prepare to Land the Landing Force! That is, Prepare to Land the Landing Force! Men assigned to Boat Groups one, three, five and seven who are in the first and second waves lay up to your debarkation stations."

For the embarked Marines, their time had come. It was

almost like a bad dream, a nightmare. No, a nightmare could never be as frightening as the real thing. The horrors of D-day - going over the side in the morning darkness - being jostled and weighted down by packs, rifles and helmets that seemed to weigh twice what they did in training. Climbing down a cargo net as it heaved and slapped against the side of the massive ship, three men abreast and God only knows how many men below and how many above. Hands on the verticals and feet on the horizontals, down they went, one precarious step at a time. Without hesitation, without delay, to stop could lead to tragic consequences.

They descended toward the "Mike" boat as it rose and fell with the sea, hoping to drop just at the right moment and land on the heaving deck without breaking a leg, or worse. Finally, the boat is loaded. It moves away from the security of the "mother" ship and rolls and bobs in the sea for what seemed an eternity.

Dawn is breaking. The darkness has put up a fight but it is gradually losing and slowly fades into oblivion. The tropical sun asserts its presence and reigns supreme, illuminating the ships, the sea, the aircraft overhead and the mysterious island crowned by Mount Tapotchau looming high above with the now visible strip of white sandy beach below it. The beach that must be taken by force of arms.

The Marines hardly noticed the transformation from darkness into daylight. They were preoccupied by more pressing matters; the weight of their packs, clumsy helmets and precious rifles. Some carried extra cans of machine-gun ammunition. Others carried mortar rounds or batteries for radios. They were further burdened with some of the most pressing thoughts and fears of their lives. Once again, it was "D-day," a day that's memory would be permanently etched into the minds of those destined to be in the assault waves. That vivid memory would remain with the survivors for the rest of their lives.

Finally, they were climbing out of the heaving Mike boats and into the amphibian tractors, "Alligators," the landing craft that would take them to the beach. The "amtracs" were bobbing in the turbulent sea like corks. Every man who could possibly fit was stuffed aboard.

With no room to spare, the men of the squad crouched over so as not to present a target to the enemy. They were jammed against one another, smelling the foul diesel fuel and being jostled by shipmates. They were still in full combat gear with packs, rifles and a full unit of fire that now seemed to weigh much more than it had hours earlier. There was the additional burden of the gas masks, which most Marines planned to drop as soon as they hit the beach.

The uncomfortable hours spent circling in the Mike boats and then, after having transferred to the smaller amtracs that were to take them on in to the beach, proved to be just too much for many of the men under such extreme stress. Sea-sickness descended on them like a plague. Few were immune to this added misery, even many of the "Old Salts" succumbed.

The terrible noise of war had started with the occasional bombing and strafing of Saipan by carrier-based planes. By 11 June, naval gunfire from the battleships and cruisers had been added. Now, on 15 June, the morning of D-day, all hell had surely broken loose. A continuing chorus of 16-inch naval rifles was fired by the bombarding force of battleships and sounded like scores of massive freight trains rumbling overhead. There were deadly eight-inch rifles from the heavy cruisers, every type of small arms fire imaginable, and of course, there was a proliferation of deadly enemy return fire.

The Japanese anti-boat guns, artillery, mortars and machine-gun fire was continuous and devastating. To the Marines churning ashore under that canopy of shrieking steel overhead, death was riding the skies and it lay in ambush on the bloody beaches ahead or for those that survived the beach, death may be lying in wait in the jungles beyond.

The Navy laid down a smoke screen along the length of the beach to cover the approach. It was eerie - was it really smoke? Was it ours? Or was the enemy using gas? Would the little bastards actually dare to use gas? Perhaps not everyone would discard their gas masks when they hit the beach.

While crossing over the reef the amtracs had to pass through a heavy curtain of plumes and geysers of water and flying fragments of coral and steel caused by the Japanese mortar and anti-boat gun fire. It did not seem possible to get through it without being hit. Several amtracs full of Marines were blown out of the water. What a relief it was for those who got safely over the reef to be churning toward the beach - still alive!

Row after row of amtracs moved through the lagoon toward the shore. They were no longer bobbing up and down like corks in a turbulent sea while circling and waiting. They were forging ahead now, all in the same direction. As they continued moving they were met by intense fire. More of the amtracs were hit and were either sunk or disabled. A total of twenty amtracs were destroyed in the water before getting to the beach. Scores of men, with their rifles held overhead, attempted to wade ashore past the floating broken bodies of other Marines.

The sky was full of aircraft, some were strafing the beaches, and some were bombing inland. Not all of the planes were friendly. Some had a big red "meatball" painted on their wings and fuselages.

The naval gunfire was like huge, multiple, unseen thunderbolts directly overhead and all heading for the beach. It was an ungodly roar, breathtaking and frightening. It must have been sheer hell-on-earth for the enemy troops on the receiving end. The fast-moving freight trains each suddenly came to an abrupt halt as they detonated on target with horrendously loud explosions. The naval gunfire and aerial bombardment of the beach was impressive enough to give some Marines false hopes that the defenders would be wiped-out before we landed. Those who had been with the battalion at Tarawa knew better.

The amtrac's two machine guns were firing now. Requests for information went unheeded by the Marines who were manning the machine guns and were in a position to see and fire at the enemy. They were much too busy for small talk.

Private Jerome (Just call me Jerry) Bronson could take it no longer! He was seasick like most everyone else. He had been pushed, squeezed and shoved in a craft designed for half as many men as there were on board. He was frightened by the incessant, terrible noises of firing everywhere. He was sickened by the persistent smell of diesel fuel coupled with the plunging and rolling of the amtrac. He had been vomited on and crushed by the pressing bodies of the other Marines and he was scared out of his wits. He just had to see what was going on.

Bronson stuck his head up to get a look around and vowed to the others that he would tell them what was really happening. It happened only seconds after Bronson raised his head above the gunwale, he was exclaiming, "My God, you guys ought to see....!" And then it was over for Private Jerry Bronson, his head and neck seemed to vaporize in a streak of red that flashed across from the starboard gunwale to the port bulkhead. Bronson's head and helmet wounded two Marines. The top of his body was open from shoulder to shoulder. Blood spurting from the convulsing body sprayed nearly everyone, in varying degrees, with the warm sticky fluid. Bronson had indeed told them what was happening. They were back in combat.

Bronson's broken dog-tag chain with one of his dog tags and a little Star of David that he had worn had struck McLaughlin's helmet and fallen to the deck. Shanghai told Mac to pick up the bloody dog tag and before he disembarked to give it to one of the amtrac crew. He didn't want one of his Marines to be buried as an "unknown."

Mac, badly shaken, trembling and scared to death would carry out the orders of his squad leader before he left the amtrac. Shanghai's men always obeyed his orders without question. He was an 'Old Corps' Marine who commanded the respect of all who served with him.

* * * * * * * * * *

The White Sands of Hell

Saipan - 15, June 1944

Amphibian tractors were designed to deliver their human cargo safely onto the beach and in our case they were to carry us all the way over the beach and up to the 0-1 line. It did not happen that way. We left our amtrac at the water's edge under enemy fire. The amtrac had sustained hits and the crew seemed determined to move it off the beach expeditiously. Shanghai's booming voice could be heard above the din of battle, "Liberty call! C'mon you Devildogs, let's go ashore!"

Splash! Jim Yancey was flat on his face. Before he could get ashore he had to get back on his feet and get out of the water. He crawled on all fours toward the waters edge only yards away. The water was up to his neck. He did not bother to inflate his life belt as it was not needed. He released it and considered the gas mask. He remembered the smoke screen then wondered at the possibility of the enemy using gas. He decided the gas mask may be worth keeping for a while.

Once on the beach it was obvious that the tremendous amount of softening up done by the Navy, with its big guns and Navy and Marine aircraft, prior to the invasion had been inadequate. Within seconds, dead and dying Marines joined the dead Japanese littering the beach where they were soon scattered everywhere up and down the white sands of hell. Scores of Marines' bodies were floating in the lagoon. Chic was on the beach, soaking wet, he felt like he'd gained fifty pounds.

They had to continue advancing in the face of what for some was almost certain death. They saw shipmates and buddies blown apart as they moved forward - they had to keep moving. To hesitate could be fatal. A moving target is always more difficult for the enemy to hit. The sound of firing and detonating grenades and mortars was unnerving. The mixed smells of cordite, coupled with the odors of the island, diesel fuel, burning amtracs and burning flesh, human flesh, was everywhere.

Soft-needled ironwood trees were growing just beyond the beach and an occasional bright flame tree could be seen interspersed among them. Behind the trees was a Japanese tank trap 8 to 10 feet deep and about 10 yards across. Two hundred yards to the southeast, a short distance inland from the beach and just beyond the trees and tank trap was the Charan Kanoa fighter strip.

Chic Yancey, soaked to the skin and weighed down by his helmet, pack, M-1 rifle and a full unit of fire (80 rounds) in his cartridge belt, could hardly carry his own weight. He kept running in a zigzag pattern, bent over with his rifle at the ready. The deep white sand slowed him down. He had to move fast; had to get beyond the beach where there would be a little cover. If he could just move up to the tree line he felt that he would find cover and some concealment. The enemy fire was devastating. The Japanese were dug in and intended to stay there until they annihilated the invading Marines or pushed them back into the sea. A fusillade of rifle fire from very close range convinced Chic that the Japanese occupied the tree line!

More men were ashore now, hitting the beach and crawling forward. They tried to get up and run in the deep white sand with bullets kicking up all around them. Some men were yelling and every now and then, a scream was heard amidst the firing that even the uninitiated knew was a shriek of death. Marines were trying to find somewhere to hit the deck on a beach strewn with the debris of battle and the dead of two cultures.

The battalion had been ordered to land on Green Beach Two. In the tremendous confusion of combat and after penetrating the Navy's smoke screen, and a hail of deadly enemy fire, the battalion, minus several amtracs that had been destroyed, learned that they had actually landed far to the left of their objective on Green Beach One. The battalion found itself in a hornet's nest of activity. Resistance on the beach was heavy.

"All right you people! Move to the right and keep firing!"

It was the demanding voice of the company gunnery sergeant hell-bent on reminding the Marines of what they had been trained to do and in the process, probably saving some of their lives.

"Watch that tree line up ahead, that's where the Nips are. Let's have some covering fire over here! Fire a few rounds and get up and move dammit! You can't stay here - these mortars will blow you all to hell. Move out!"

Chic Yancey took a few deep breaths, fired a couple of rounds and cursed himself for being in such a hopeless situation. A quick glance to his right told him that his buddy Eddie Malone had made it okay so far. He turned his head to the left and recognized Corporal Jerden, the old salt from Guadalcanal and Tarawa who was just a few feet away.

Malone was scared and said so. Chic, also scared out of his wits lied, "Don't worry about it Malone, unless one of those bullets has got your name on it, you are not gonna buy the farm and that's all there is to it."

"I'm not worried about the one that's got my name on it. Dammit, the Japs don't even know my name. It's all these other bullets flying around here that have me worried."

Corporal Jerden fired a few rounds in the direction of the tree line, turned his head toward Yancey and Malone and snarled, "Okay, you guys knock it off and listen up! This ain't like Tarawa. You haven't got a damn coconut log seawall to cower behind. There's no protection on this beach. We either get up and move now or you're gonna die where you are! Follow me!!

Chic got to his feet. He was soaked with the salt water from the lagoon and felt like he was lifting a ton. Why were his pack and rifle suddenly so heavy? He tried to run as fast as he could, but the sand slowed him down. He could sense several rounds really close to him. He imagined that he could feel the heat from the bullets, as they whined past him too close for comfort. He was running now as fast as his legs would carry him. Zigzag! He had to remember to zigzag!

With all hell bursting around them in the midst of the devastating artillery, mortar, rifle and machine-gun fire, Chic felt as though his world was coming to an end. For many Marines and Japanese, it did. While running down the beach with a handful of other Marines, he was horrified to see Japanese infantrymen running toward them with rifles and fixed bayonets. Now he knew the world was coming to an end! Knowing that he couldn't fire accurately while running, he nevertheless persisted in shooting at the rapidly approaching enemy troops. Thank God for the M-1 rifles. They were semi-automatic and those eight rounds before reloading were a blessing.

Some of the Japs fell as others continued closing; one wild-eyed Jap coming right for them had no rifle but was clutching something in one of his hands. He was unarmed except for a hand grenade! Chic continued firing and moving. Pfc Sam Barkdahl, who was running beside Chic shrieked "Owww!" as his rifle flew out of his hands, the stock shattered. The unarmed Jap was now only feet away!

Barkdahl, the Knife Fighter, swiftly reached his right hand down and in one unbelievably quick movement drew his K-

Bar knife. The screaming Japanese soldier closing fast threw his arms around Barkdahl's neck and flailing both his arms violently, he started beating the Knife Fighter on the back with the grenade and his fist. Barkdahl's right hand firmly grasping his trusty K-Bar shot forward toward the enemy's mid-section. The soldier was screaming an unintelligible battle cry as he continued to beat on the Marine's back. The Knife Fighter was also screaming.

Japanese hand grenades operated differently than U.S. hand grenades. To arm a Japanese grenade it was necessary after pulling the ring to strike the detonator against a hard object thereby igniting the fuse and fully arming the grenade.

"Help! For Crissake you guys, help me! I can't get the goddam thing in! My knife won't penetrate! Get this crazy sonofabitch offa' me!"

Chief was coming up on Barkdahl's right. Without missing a step the powerful Indian delivered a crushing blow to the Jap's head with his rifle and continued moving down the beach. The soldier was dead before his body hit the sand.

During the short time Barkdahl remained with the platoon, he seldom mentioned anything about edged weapons. Still referred to by the troops as the Knife Fighter, Sam no longer seemed to glory in the title. In fact, he was rather uncomfortable with it.

Chic heard the ungodly shriek! — It was another incoming mortar or artillery round and it was terrifyingly close. Chic and the shell hit the deck simultaneously and he hugged the earth with such an intimacy that he practically became a part of it. Hot shrapnel, sand and shards of coral fragments flew wildly in every direction. Men were blown apart just a few yards away. Little that was recognizable was left of Private Eddie Malone. The left side of Chic's face, pressed hard against the sand, felt strange. He didn't dare move or try to ascertain what it was. He was paralyzed with fear.

Jerden and the gunny had been right. Chic knew he had to make himself get up and move. Stumbling out of the rubble and smoke he was covered with white sand that adhered to his wet dungarees and made him look like a ghost. He would have been a ghost too, had that shell been any closer.

He could not stop trembling and cursed himself for it. Fear

was more of an enemy than the Japs. Everyone is afraid in combat but a Marine has to be able to live with it and still function effectively. This can be one of life's greatest challenges.

Oh God, he wished he could make himself stop trembling! The left side of his face was caked with sand and felt odd. He reached his hand up to brush the sand off his face. His fingers came away coated with sticky blood and sand. He knew it wasn't his own blood. Some other poor bastard had been hit in the very same spot where he had just been and he had slammed his face down into it as he instinctively threw himself to the ground.

He was on his feet and running down the beach again. He recognized many of the other Marines who were running with him desperately attempting to get to Green Beach Two where they were supposed to have landed. He was thankful to hear the voice of Deadly Dave yelling at Fearless and the Weasel to keep moving. Some, scattered along the beach dead were harder to recognize. Maybe it was because he made a conscious effort not to look too closely at them. He was more concerned about the enemy fire. In the midst of running and firing, hitting the deck and rolling, getting back on his feet and thinking each second was going to be his last, he couldn't help but wonder if the blood on his face was that of another Marine or a Jap. He thanked God it wasn't his.

Poncho Gutierrez fired his rifle from the hip while running and killed a Jap less than a dozen feet in front of him. As he passed the body, he kicked it brutally. Epstein stopped briefly to insert a clip in his rifle and as Poncho passed him, he forcefully pushed Epstein to the ground. This did not endear Poncho to Epstein but it may have saved his life.

The battalion continued moving down the beach to the right. Slowly, painfully they were able to seize and occupy Green Beach Two. The Marines shared the beach with considerable debris of battle and scores of enemy dead.

Just beyond the beach was the Japanese airstrip. Elements of the 4th Marine Division would take the southern half of the airstrip. The northern half was assigned to the 8th Marines. Small-arms fire came from across the strip. Orders were to cross the deadly strip as rapidly as possible, eliminate the enemy and take cover on the far side.

The Marines moved through the line of trees down into, then up past the long trench-like tank trap and then crossed the tracks of a narrow-gauge railroad. They moved swiftly across the airstrip braving enemy rifle and machine-gun fire as they did. There was no cover, no concealment, and no hope that all would make it. Many did and some did not — the airstrip was in U.S. Marine hands by noon.

* * * * * * * * * *

The Sandcrabs

15/16 June 1944

The battalion started moving again and the price continued to be high. Beyond the airstrip was what they had been told would be Lake Susupe. It would take some imagination to qualify Susupe as a real lake. What they found was a swamp. Heavy Japanese action to halt the drive to Susupe was slowly and painfully overcome. The Marines continued to pay a price in blood. The marshy area around the Susupe swamp was reached by 1300.

The word quickly spread from man to man that "Jim" Crowe, their beloved battalion commander, and a living legend in the Marine Corps, had been shot at Lake Susupe. He was evacuated to the aid station on the beach where he was again seriously wounded, this time by mortar fragments.

When the colonel was transferred to a hospital ship Major Bill "The Professor" Chamberlain, the battalion's executive officer, though wounded himself, assumed command of the battalion. The men would later learn that all of the original battalion commanders in the 8th Marines had been casualties on that first day of fighting.

Word was passed for Lieutenant Stacey to report to battalion operations (Bn-3) for a briefing and some special instructions. The platoon sergeant asked the lieutenant whom he wanted to take along with him as a bodyguard.

"Who's up next to be the runner?" asked the lieutenant.

"Pfc Baker is supposed to take the next run Lieutenant. Do you want him to go with you, Sir?" responded Blackjack.

"Yes, that way I can leave him at the battalion message center and he will know the way back if anyone has any message traffic for us later. I'll be coming back alone Sergeant, it's a very short distance and I really don't need anyone with me." Blackjack answered with an "Aye, aye, Sir!"

The lieutenant checked his map to be certain he could pinpoint his location in relation to the command post (CP) back in the defilade of the tank trap they had crossed earlier.

Stacey snapped, "C'mon Baker, let's move it."

The lieutenant had instructed Blackjack to take charge of the platoon and keep putting pressure on the Japanese. He and Baker moved out. Stacey was glad to have Baker with him. Baker had been in the platoon on Guadalcanal and Tarawa and was a combat-wise Marine.

Chief was lying in a firing position beside Barkdahl. The big Indian looked over to his right and said, "Hey, Knife Fighter!"

"Yeah Chief, what is it?" replied Barkdahl.

"You owe me a front hand guard. How about taking one off the next M-1 rifle you see that ain't needed anymore?"

Barkdahl snapped, "What the hell do you mean I owe you a front hand guard?"

The Chief replied, "Mine broke when I killed that poor little Jap that was tryin' to embrace you back on the beach."

"Oh, yeah, Chief, thanks, I guess you really saved my butt when you clobbered that guy. I'll pick up a front hand guard for you as soon as I can. There are plenty of rifles lying around. Damn, we sure took a lot of casualties, didn't we?" said Barkdahl.

The lieutenant had long since returned from the CP when Pfc Baker was given a message to run back to Fox Company. He had gotten to within 100 yards of his destination when a bullet tore into the left side of his chest. He screamed with pain and cried for help but the sounds of war were everywhere. A faint human voice could not compete with the roaring artillery and machine-gun fire. Crumpling onto the trail and bleeding profusely, he wished he had not been alone. As he lay on the trail bleeding and crying for help, his strength was rapidly diminishing and his eyes glazed over. He opened them once or twice then they closed forever as his life slowly faded. He prayed that another Marine would come along the trail soon but instead it was the Angel of Death, always lurking nearby, that he would next encounter.

Before dark on that first evening, the 8th Marines who had been attacking eastward were ordered back from Lake Susupe to strengthen the division's lines. Marines always hate giving up real estate they have taken by force of arms, especially when there have been casualties. In spite of the troops griping, whoever gave this order knew what he was doing.

The regiment fell back and straightened its lines. They were strung out from Afetna Point inland almost to the Lake Susupe swamp and from just north of Charon Kanoa to the Japanese radio station between Red Beach 3 and Green Beach 1, where they were tied in with the 6th Marines. An item of great concern was that darkness was rapidly descending and contact with the 4th Marine Division to the south had not yet been firmly established.

They were behind schedule because of the time lost after landing on the wrong beaches and taking such heavy casualties during the day. The first day's fighting had resulted in the Marines getting barely half way to the 0-1 line, their first day's intended objective.

Rumors had been circulating among the troops that they were facing an enemy force three times as large as their previous intelligence briefings had estimated. According to the company commander's radioman, Field Music First Class W. Max Netherland, the rumors were true.

In George Company's area Afetna Point was being bitterly contested. Heavy fighting persisted throughout the day but by nightfall the company had knocked out or captured seven enemy anti-boat guns and had taken the northern half of Afetna Point.

An unusual but effective aspect of the fighting on Afetna Point was that every other man in George Company was armed with a shotgun. The wide dispersal pattern and short range of the shotguns was ideally suited for killing the nearby enemy on Afetna Point without endangering the Marines from the 4th Division who were fighting farther to the south. The shotguns proved highly effective in combat at close range.

Blackjack gathered the platoon together and said, "Okay men, here's the hot scoop from the old man. As most of you know, the battalion had a special assignment for the lieutenant so, for the time being, I'm in charge.

"We're gonna move back to Afetna Point and support George Company with a blocking position. They've been catchin' hell all day. We'll dig in just inside the tree line where the little bastards can't see us, then George Company will fall back and pass through our lines to a better position. When the Gooks see George Company falling back, the arrogant little bastards will think they've whipped the Marines but we'll be right there inside that tree line waitin' for them.

"We've got two of Gunny Paul's machine guns attached. I want one of them on our right flank and Steinmetz, you put yours over by Chief on the left. You men remember now, the Japs have orders to fight to the death. Marines don't need any such orders. We will gladly accommodate the sonsabitches by seeing that they do fight to the death.

"When the Japs realize that George Company is gone they'll probably move forward. They like to operate at night. The only logical avenue of approach for them to pursue George Company is to come right across this field. They can't go to the right and if they try goin' around their left flank they'll have to swim. They've gotta cross the field right toward us and there ain't no place for them to hide while they're comin' across.

"With a little luck, we'll be able to catch them with illumination flares while they're in the field just before they get to us. Don't anybody move or make a sound until I give the word to open fire. When we cut loose on 'em, we're gonna make those slant-eyed sonsabitches think they've just entered the main gates of hell!" Proclaimed the confident platoon sergeant.

Blackjack's tactics seemed sound enough to the troops but the Japanese failed to cooperate the way he had planned. They had a tactical plan of their own. They fired across the field with a light machine gun, spraying the tree line where they must have thought George Company had stopped. Then the Japs walked a knee mortar barrage past George Company's old positions into the tree line. It was only after that when the enemy commander decided to commit his troops.

The early moonlight disclosed two of them crawling across the field directly toward the center of our position. The platoon sergeant had expected the whole outfit to get up and just walk across the field like they were strolling down the Ginza. That's not what was happening.

"Remember men, hold your fire and wait for my command. If we open up too soon, we'll lose most of them and Marines will die. You've gotta be patient and let those first two crawl right into the tree line and into our position. Wait till they're out of sight of the other Japs then kill 'em with a bayonet or entrenching tool, but don't open fire!

"We need to entice the rest of them into following the first two. I want to see them out in the open in that field to our front. When they're just about 20 yards from us, I'll call for illumination then I'll open fire. That will be your signal to open up as well. Remember dammit, I want carefully aimed rifle fire! At this range, every shot should be a kill." The sergeant stated it emphatically and the men knew he meant it. They waited patiently for the enemy to advance and for the signal to open fire.

Blackjack took up the slack on his trigger and continued to squeeze gently but firmly as he aimed carefully at the first of the advancing enemy soldiers. Illumination flares started popping overhead and the enemy troops were caught in the bright light of the flares. They were in the open field to the front with no cover or concealment available to them. "Blaam!" Blackjack's first deadly round was fired and it was followed by a fusillade of rifle fire. The two machine guns were firing from the flanks. The Japanese appeared to have been mowed down by the fire but the Marines were taking no chances. They called for support from the company's 60mm mortars and their fire was effective.

Lieutenant General Yoshio Saito of the Imperial Japanese Army had prepared his defenses well. His troops, many of them seasoned veterans of the fighting in China and Manchuria, were well trained and determined to hold their positions. As the first day's fighting wore on and the weary sun slowly descended into the west, visibility was gradually diminished and darkness and fear became the enemy's ally.

Marines spent the first sleepless night on Saipan withstanding heavy artillery shelling and periodic enemy counter-attacks. Uneasiness swept through the ranks as heavy clouds covered the moon from time to time intensifying the darkness. Danger lurked in every sound and shadow. The counterattacks and shelling kept nerves on edge and successfully deprived the Marines of much-needed sleep. Nervous fingers gently caressed triggers and safeties of M-1 rifles and BARs. Eyes strained to discern an unseen but expected enemy. There were sounds, lots of sounds as on most battlefields - but there was one sound here that was different.

Someone or something was approaching our positions. They were close, very close. The damned Japs must be crawling right up and into our foxholes! We could hear them, we could all hear them, we even thought we could hear them breathing but no one could see the little bastards! Where were they? How could they be so close and yet remain invisible? And then, in the darkness of the night, heavy with fear and confusion, someone who had a firmer grip on reality than most discovered the source of those unnerving sounds crawling through the white sands of hell, SANDCRABS!

* * * * * * * * * *

Bugles in the Night

Saipan - 16 June 1944

The thundering artillery was deafening as its impacting shells lit up the night skies. Pleas of the wounded and dying were a continuing reminder of the fragility of human life. All who heard the screams and moaning hoped never to hear such agony again but they knew in their hearts that the sounds and the memories of this nightmare would live with them forever. The incessant fire of a determined enemy was intended to push the Marines back into the sea and every Marine ashore knew it.

The night of 15 June was only one of many that would prove to be sleepless. The crashing and booming of powerful artillery continued as it roared its defiance throughout the night. With each passing hour the sounds of the impacting murderous artillery crept closer. To men whose only protection was a shallow hole in the ground, where they crouched low, intermittently cursing and praying, the roaring thunder of the artillery seemed designed for the purpose of driving them mad before killing them. Would it ever cease?

To the survivors of this night of horrors, it was long and frightening — there were many on both sides who did not survive. Friendly counter battery artillery fire streaking loudly overhead was as nerve wracking as the enemy's fire. The only grim relief from the Japanese artillery was when it was lifted just prior to each of their several attempted counterattacks.

As the night wore on rifle and sporadic machine-gun fire seemed to be increasing in volume and moving closer. The enemy was obviously intent on closing with us on the ground. Their pale pinkish-yellow illumination flares were a further indication that they desired visibility for some planned activity. Every Marine in the line knew instinctively just what that activity would be.

Two green star shells signaled the first counterattack, which came shortly after darkness and was near the left flank. This attack was driven back but not before several invisible infiltrators had taken advantage of the darkness and confusion to slip through our lines. They would be a problem in the days to come. There were other counterattacks during the night but the worst of all was right in the center of the line shortly before dawn on the morning of the 16th. The advancing Japanese were stopped. Many died within feet of our foxholes.

As the Japs were being beaten back some bold Marines moved forward in the darkness to rescue their wounded buddies. One Marine dashed out to bring his wounded friend back. He immediately sustained multiple hits from a Nambu machine gun, giving up his life in a futile but heroic attempt to save a friend. The Japs had moved their light machine gun up from somewhere. It was out in the darkness just forward of our lines. The machine gun was apparently there to cover the Japs withdrawal and it was playing havoc with the rescue attempts.

Superior Private *(Jotohei)* Akiro Hayakawa was carefully

inserting a curved 45-round magazine into the Nambu Light machine-gun. Corporal *(Gocho)* Hiro Yamaguchi, the squad leader, was lying behind the Nambu firing short bursts. There were lots of targets in this area. He could hear them through the darkness. Yamaguchi wanted to remain where he was and kill the Yankee Devils but his Lieutenant *(Chuii)* would be waiting, he must move on. Swiftly, and as silently as possible, Yamaguchi and Hayakawa disengaged and withdrew to where they hoped to meet with the remainder of their company and their *Chuii*.

Lucky Lane had been slightly wounded twice but his injuries were not serious and he had returned to duty. There were some dried bloodstains on his bandages and dungarees, giving the big Marine the appearance of a battle-scarred combat Marine just as Hollywood may want to depict one. Far from a Hollywood actor, Lucky Lane was the real McCoy.

In the uncertain light of a flare he watched as his friend Buddy Blair went down while attempting to move back from an untenable position. Lucky started forward to go after the fallen Blair but he was physically restrained by Donahoe and Chief. "Let me go! Buddy's out there and he's hit! Let me go dammit! I've got to help him!"

"Knock it off Lane! The Japs have got a machine gun out there and you're stayin' right where you are."

We all knew that Buddy Blair was dead. The dead would have to wait until after the living were recovered and treated, preferably in the morning, when there was light and when we had beaten the Japs back for good. Lucky Lane sobbed, "I've got to go get Buddy!" Donahoe and Chief relaxed their vice-like grips on Lucky Lane only after they were certain he had been subdued and was again calm. We had already lost far too many Marines on this damned island.

The Japanese had allies on that first night ashore. There were hordes of persistent mosquitoes and an onslaught of noisy little sand crabs. The sand crabs crawled in and around our foxholes as they made their fiddling, grinding sounds. The annoying sounds could be heard when they were very close to us and in our holes or whenever there was a quiet moment between the bursts of small-arms fire and the crashing of artillery. What a distraction! We swatted mosquitoes, wiped the sweat from our eyes and silently prayed as we waited for the enemy to close on our positions.

Japanese prisoners and captured enemy documents revealed that the enemy forces ashore were nearly three times as large as previously estimated. Marine casualties had been considerably higher than expected. The invasion of Guam, scheduled for 18 June, had to be cancelled and would not occur until 21 July.

George Company had only taken the northern half of Afetna Point on the first day. The attack was resumed at 0700 on the morning of the 16th and contact was finally made with the 23rd Marines of the 4th Marine Division. The Charan Kanoa pier was taken and the entire Afetna Point zone and Green Beach 3 were secured by noon. After securing Afetna Point the Marines concentrated on locating and exterminating infiltrators that had come in through the left flank and the center of the line during the previous nights' counterattacks.

Word had been received from division that the Japanese were massing tanks and troops in the Lake Susupe area. The regiment must again move to the northeast toward their previous day's positions west of Lake Susupe and clear the area. Marine artillery and tanks would be in support. The Marines were relieved to note that some of the tanks rolling up to support them were equipped with flamethrowers. They were truly awesome and effective weapons.

By the time the regiment had started closing on the marshy area they were again sustaining substantial casualties. Thank God for the supporting tanks and artillery. Heat from the blistering sun was oppressive and seemed to add weight to the men's already heavy packs and ammunition belts. Flies were out in droves that far surpassed those of the previous day. There were more cadavers now to attract and sustain them. Chic noted that the putrid smell of dead horses and water buffalo, swelling under the tropical sun, was nearly as bad as the odor of dead humans.

Enemy rifle and machine-gun fire was sporadic but effective and came from all around the swamp. Japanese artillery was delivered from well-camouflaged positions somewhere up on the slopes of Mount Tapotchau and at times it was devastating. Our supporting artillery sought them out and delivered what we hoped would be effective, counterbattery fire.

Calls for corpsmen were heard and they became more and more frequent. Stretcher parties strained under the heat of the sun and the weight of the wounded Marines they were carrying to the rear. Sam Barkdahl, "The Knife Fighter", was grumbling and cursing as he stumbled his way towards the beach. He stated for anyone willing to listen that he only had "a little scratch" on the back of his left thigh and that he would be back on the line as soon as a corpsman applied a tourniquet to stop the bleeding and put a proper dressing on it. Barkdahl continued to the rear and sickbay but he never returned to Fox Company. The colorful antics of the Knife Fighter would be missed.

The chaplain probably should have been in a safer area somewhere to the rear. Instead, he was up on the line visiting the troops. He was hit but not seriously. He'd been knocked out briefly by the concussion and there were some tiny bits of shrapnel in the side of his face, hardly enough to bleed. A piece of grenade fragment had scratched his left arm and caused him to bleed a little through the sleeve of his dungaree shirt. The concerned company commander had him escorted back to the battalion aid station for treatment. The Padre looked a lot worse off than he was.

The battalion aid station, still located near the beach, was an exciting place. Enemy mortar rounds were sporadically crashing nearby as friendly naval gunfire zoomed loudly overhead. There was a constant stream of casualties being brought back from the Lake Susupe area, which was hardly more than 600 yards ahead. Every now and then a Japanese plane would start a strafing run down the length of the beach until it was shot down or driven off. Many of the casualties being brought in were serious and a few were already dead.

It was not unusual for the stretcher bearers, after gently placing their patients down at the aid station, to practically collapse on the sand in near total exhaustion. The more frequently mortar rounds dropped nearby, and the closer they got, the quicker the stretcher bearers would recover and become eager to move back up to the lines.

A brief barrage of mortar rounds finally found its target. Several of the rounds exploded among the wounded Marines lined up on stretchers on the beach awaiting evacuation. Some were killed and several were again wounded. There was a flurry of activity among the doctors and corpsmen as they attempted to continue their life-saving efforts with a renewed sense of urgency under extremely hazardous conditions.

It was only natural that the chaplain would want to be useful. In spite of his own wounds, he moved from man to man giving encouragement and in some cases administering the last rites. He approached one stretcher bearing an age-less, mustachioed, Marine and was startled as he realized that it was Lieutenant Colonel H.P. "Jim" Crowe.

Jim Crowe, a living legend, was known throughout the Marine Corps as a colorful character and an officer who was loved and greatly respected by his men. Crowe's Marines would eagerly follow him into the jaws of hell then proudly brag that they had been there with him. The young priest was cha-grined at seeing this vibrant, dynamic leader in his present pale, drawn condition. Crowe had a large red "M" painted on his forehead with iodine, indicating that he had been injected with morphine to ease his pain and suffering. Jim Crowe was down but not out, he was still a fighter.

The chaplain spoke softly to Colonel Crowe, asking if he could do anything for him. He was not expecting the answer he got. Crowe answered with less than his usual volume, but still maintained his unique brand of command presence and colorful language.

"You bet you can Padre. Get me a radio so I can communi-cate with Chamberlain and my battalion. If these medical marvels insist on evacuating me out to a hospital ship, I'll have to have some way to maintain command of the battal-ion. Don't waste any time dammit, get me an SCR-300 and do it now! If you can't handle the assignment yourself, find some-one from the 2nd Battalion and let them know where I am and what I want. Do it quickly before I fall asleep from this damned morphine!" The colonel added, "If you don't come through for me on this Padre, I'll put you on report. And you can forget all about the military chain of command 'cause I'll run your ass all the way up to the Pope!"

Easy and George companies were on line and Fox Com-pany had moved back a few yards into a defiladed area with overhead concealment from the trees. The men, thankful for the respite, were reclining in defilade in the wooded area where the concealment gave them a chance to relax, take a swig from their canteens and have a smoke before moving back up on line. All this while the war went on around them.

Muldoon was expounding to the squad on Private Ross' recklessness in sprinting across the Jap airstrip without periodically hitting the deck or zigzagging.

"He really took a chance trying to be a big hero by running across the airstrip the way he did yesterday morning just to be the first one across. He could have been killed by any one of the damned Japs that were firing at us from over there."

Muldoon had either not noticed or had not cared that the company gunnery sergeant was sitting nearby leaning against a tree. Gunny Littleton turned around and glared at Muldoon:

"Listen Private Muldoon, there's somethin' you'd better understand. I know you've heard this before but now you're gonna hear it from me. A moving target is a helluva lot harder to hit than some poor scared SOB that is tryin' to take up permanent residence in a damned hole in the ground. Watch for an opportunity to move and when it comes, take it! Run like the devil himself was after you 'cause Lad, that's just who the hell it's gonna be."

Muldoon was not convinced. Lying on the ground in defilade seemed a lot safer to him than running across an open area under fire. Discretion being the better part of valor, the private was not inclined to further voice his opinions on this matter within earshot of Gunnery Sergeant Littleton.

Taking his cue from the company commander, the First Sergeant looked around at those reclining nearby and took one last drag on his cigarette before carefully field stripping it. A habit not easily forgotten, even in combat. He strode to where the 1st platoon was sitting, got their attention and stated: "All right men, the smoking lamp is out. Fieldstrip your butts, get on your feet and man your loads. Pass the word back to the rest of the company, we're movin' out."

While he was adjusting his pack, the "Top" muttered almost as an afterthought: "You know, there's an expression I once heard that goes, 'Fortune favors the brave'. We need all the good fortune we can get, so you sonsabitches had better be brave. Now, man your loads and stand by to move out!"

As the platoon filed past Gunny Littleton, he reached his hand out and grasped Private Muldoon's arm then walked along beside him for a few steps. In a voice that could be clearly heard and understood by all in the immediate vicinity the gunny said: "Lad, in combat, the greatest risk of all is in NOT taking one! And don't you ever forget it. If you're gonna play in the big leagues, you gotta play to win! Remember what the Top said, fortune favors the brave." The incident concerning Private Ross had not been forgotten.

The company moved up on line and relieved Easy Company as Easy fell back into the reserve position. As the battalion approached the swampy area that surrounded Lake Susupe there were two companies up and one back.

Pointing, Shanghai barked and said "There's a dead Marine on that knoll over there. Two of you men get his cartridge belt and weapon and check to see if he has any grenades on him. Better get his canteen too if it's full, we'll need all the drinking water we can scrounge before this day is over."

The sergeant reached for his little green notebook and entered the name, serial number and location of the deceased. A party would be sent back later to retrieve the body. It was the Marine Corps' way not to leave their dead.

The men were thankful that the area designated for them to defend on the perimeter of Susupe Swamp seemed to be on reasonably dry ground for at least part of the battalion. Digging their foxholes was a cruel surprise and disappointment and an exercise in futility to some. As they dug down, the bottoms of their holes promptly filled up with water. This additional inconvenience was acceptable. After all, for the time being, they were still alive.

The God of Darkness had been lurking in the east but now came forward and moving westward soon spread his dark shroud over the island of the dead. From Green Beach to the Susupe swamp Marines strained their eyes and ears in the darkness as they scanned the area for any possible movement in the likely avenues of approach.

Frightening sounds were heard as on the night before. The nerve-wracking artillery fire thundered from both friend and foe, but mostly it was from the foe, and the sounds of small-arms fire was not too distant. Thus it was during the darkness of the first several hours of 16 June 1944, the second night ashore on Saipan - as we watched and waited.

By midnight the small-arms fire had grown closer and increased in its intensity. It seemed to be coming from the direction of Garapan. The 6th Marines had responsibility for that area. The 1st Battalion, commanded by Lieutenant Colonel Bill "Willie K." Jones, a superb Marine officer, was blocking the enemy's advance.

In the late hours of this night of horror there were new sounds to accompany the thundering blasts of the artillery, mortar and small-arms fire. The distant blowing of bugles in the night was heard and a din caused by hundreds of human voices approaching as they chanted their threats and battle cries causing heartbeats to accelerate rapidly and adrenaline to surge. Private Wetzel turned to his foxhole buddy Pfc Frank Quinlan and in a less than confident voice uttered: "Damn Fearless, it sounds like the whole Nip army is comin' right down the beach after us."

"Yeah Weasel, but before they get to us they're gonna have to get through a hell of a lot of other Marines."

An ominous sound was the eerie creaking and squealing of a large number of Japanese tanks as they loomed out of the unknown darkness and into the world of reality--the death and destruction along the narrow battle zone from Red Beach inland to the narrow gauge railroad tracks.

The U.S. Navy fired illumination shells by the score and they cast eerie shadows as they descended. Phantom troop movements were detected where only bushes and small trees actually existed. Terrain features seemed to keep changing and every moving shadow became an imagined enemy moving forward on an avenue of approach, which in reality may not even exist.

The blowing of bugles in the night announced, like the fanfare for a cheap Hollywood movie, that the enemy was upon us. It was frightening and seemed unreal as the attack rapidly grew in intensity. The darkness came alive with unintelligible shouting in Japanese but often the word *"banzai!"* could be distinguished. It soon became everyone's' fight as there were plenty of Japs left over for the 2nd and 8th Marines after the battered and bloodied 6th had absorbed the point and the main body. The shouting was accompanied by the detonation of grenades, a fusillade of small arms fire and screams of the wounded and dying.

As the melee increased, the night exploded with the firing of every weapon on the beach and strong-willed men did their utmost to kill one another. Fear and uncertainty were never strangers to the battlefield but Marine Corps training and discipline proved their worth. Teamwork, dedication and the spirit of Semper Fidelis prevailed. By the grace of God and a few very brave Marines, the attack was repulsed.

The dawn's early light on the morning of the third day revealed hundreds of enemy bodies. They had made a valiant, but futile, attempt to rid their island of the invading U.S. Marines. The battlefield also contained the hulks of twenty-four of Colonel Gota's destroyed Japanese tanks from the 9th Tank Regiment.

Two battalions of artillery from the 10th Marines had fired in support during the night but they had received so much counter battery fire that by daylight, one of the battalions had only three pieces left that could fire.

The beauty of the bright tropical morning was wasted on the weary Marines as they moved forward walking through the enemy dead. Many of the dead were soldiers of the Imperial Army's 135th Infantry Regiment. They wore Japanese army uniforms and helmets with their red star, but among them was a large number who were wearing *ryakubo* (the soft peaked visor cap was called *ryakubo*) that bore an insignia familiar to the men of the 8th Marines. They had first encountered it on the bloody beaches of Betio, it was a cherry blossom superimposed over an anchor.

Someone exclaimed, "Marines! We were fighting the Jap Marines! No wonder they fought so well." They died like warriors as they had charged forward to meet their fate. What a strange feeling — it was as though a bond of some type existed — they were the hated enemy, but there was something special about them, they were Marines. In peacetime, under other circumstances, we may have swapped a few sea stories and maybe had a smoke together. Poor little bastards, lying there so grotesque and disfigured in death.

A sniper's bullet struck some debris close to Big Ski and the *Rikusentai* were immediately forgotten. The Marines became intensely alert again as they continued moving northeast through the carnage.

Chapter II

Supporting Arms

Saipan - 17 June 1944

As the company moved forward the Weasel asked Fearless Frank:

"Where do you think we're headed for now Fearless?"

"How the hell should I know Weasel? I'm just an enlisted man. You gotta be somebody important like a field music bugler or a corporal or somethin' to get the word around here."

Weasel persisted, "I wish they'd take us back out to a ship where we could get a shower and some hot food Fearless."

"Boy, you really are a dreamer! You ain't goin' aboard ship again Weasel until we secure this damned island."

"How much longer do you think it's gonna take us to secure it Fearless?"

"Weasel, we haven't even gotten to the 0-1 line yet and this is already our third day on this stinkin' island. We're so far behind schedule now it'll probably take us another month to secure it."

"C'mon Fearless, you heard the briefings we got on the ship. They said we'd probably secure the island in a week."

"Yeah Weasel, I remember the briefings but they lied."

Little Ski spoke up, "Hey Weasel, if you are so curious where we're goin' why don't you ask the field music. The captain's comin' back this way and Netherland's right behind him."

"Hey Music, what's the scoop? Where are we headed?"

Field Music First Class W. Max Netherland had little time for the Weasel.

"Stow it Weasel, I can't talk to you now. The captain and I have an important briefing to attend at battalion. If the opportunity presents itself, I'll let you guys know what's going on when we get back."

The captain returned to his company and assembled the platoon leaders for a briefing. The field music, eager to show his importance to the troops, couldn't wait to give his slightly embellished version.

He cleared his throat in a somewhat pompous manner (which was quite natural for the radio announcer turned bugler when he was attempting to get his listeners' undivided attention).

"If it were up to me, I'd maintain contact with the 6th Marines on our left and the 23rd Marines from the 4th Division, on our right. D'ya see the high ground up there to the northeast? Those foothills to our right front? Well, I'd have the battalion take that high ground as soon as they can and then with plenty of softening up from artillery and air support, I'd move up and take Mount Tapotchau. That's where the Jap artillery is that has been punishing us. It also commands a great view of the entire island. That gentlemen, would be my objective.

"And, oh yes, I did hear a rumor somewhere that our air observers have spotted large concentrations of Nips to our northeast and very heavy concentrations of 'em just to the south of Tapotchau. Thought you boys ought to know about that."

Deadly Dave Donahoe shook his head.

"I sure hope that information is purely the music's opinion and not based on anything he really overheard at the briefing. Do you guys see what it would be like trying to take that high ground leading up to Tapotchau? We'd lose half of the battalion, or half of what's left of it, and it would probably take us a couple of weeks at the rate we've been moving so far."

When the new lieutenant got back from the Skipper's briefing he was amazed at how the men seemed to already know what he was about to tell them. These Marines certainly showed a lot of professionalism. They had evaluated the situation and had arrived at the same plan of action as the commanding general and his staff. The only problem with the plan was that the men didn't have the confidence in it that the general apparently had. They pointed out to the lieutenant just how much jungle and steep rocky terrain and even sheer cliffs they would have to traverse before they could get up on Tapotchau.

The naïve young lieutenant was saved by a mature and savvy platoon sergeant who advised him that the troops had been privvy to what the battalion commander had said during his briefing. It had been from an outside source, not always totally reliable, but with just enough information to be dangerous. The platoon sergeant assured the lieutenant that the 'outside source' would be taken care of later. Right now, the word was being passed to move out. As they moved forward the 2nd Platoon's 536 (walkie-talkie radio) started crackling:

"Fox 2, that is Fox 2, this is Fox 6, over."

"Fox 6, this is Fox 2, over."

"Fox 2, Skipper advises 3rd Battalion, 2nd Marines is now on the 0-1 line. Left flank of the 6th Marines is also on 0-1. Right flank of 6th still tied in with us but contact with 23rd Marines on our right has been broken. Next time we hold up, dispatch a squad patrol over to the right flank and make contact with the 1st Battalion of the 23rd Marines. Over."

"Fox 6, this is Fox 2, received your last concerning patrol. Wilco, out."

The patrol was dispatched but contact with the 23rd Marines would not be reestablished anytime soon. The left flank of the 8th Marines finally made it to the 0-1 line by 1210 but the right flank was held up with 200 yards left to go. As the gap between the 8th and 23rd Marines widened, an enemy counterattack was developing. The 23rd Marines, already having a difficult time because of the brutal terrain, were meeting with an increasing volume of enemy fire.

Spotter planes overhead warned of Japanese troop movements advancing toward the area between the 8th Marines and the beleaguered 23rd. The 8th quickly attempted to move to the right as the 23rd made a valiant effort to continue moving to the left in an attempt to close the line. The squad patrol caught in-between took up firing positions facing the enemy's direction of approach and prayed as they waited.

Artillery and close air support were called in to stop the Japanese attack. The artillery forward observer was a gunnery sergeant named Mike Malloy who had served aboard the battleship *Wyoming* with Blackjack back in the days when they were both privates.

"Let's get a bracket on those little devils Mike. As soon as you get one over and one under, adjust and fire for effect. They'll never know what hit 'em."

"Okay Blackjack, that first round was over by about 50 yards. Let's play it safe. We'll drop it a couple of clicks and call another one in."

Blackjack smiled, "Look at that baby Mike we've got 'em bracketed. Raise it just a click, suck it up, say a prayer and call it in."

Mike keyed his radio and exclaimed: "Right on guys! Up two and fire for effect! Okay Blackjack, you'll feel those babies coming over in just a minute, we're right on the gun-target line."

"We're on the gun-target line? Holy cow! What about a short round?"

"Short rounds? Hell, don't worry about short rounds, if one hits you, you'll never know it."

One of the rounds dropped perilously close to the front of the Marines' position.

"What the hell is going on Mike? Was that a short round or just a bad call?"

"Was it a bad call? Hell no it wasn't a bad call and don't blame the cannoneers either! Blame the politicians for that World War I surplus ammo we're still getting."

Friendly artillery fire fell in the 8th Marines area inflicting several casualties before the screaming Malloy could make the necessary adjustments. The gap between the two Marine regiments continued to close as the Marines were actively engaged in repulsing the fanatical Japanese. Lieutenant Swift was an acquaintance of Lieutenant Yoakum's. He had been with the battalion since D-day and had gotten to know some of the officers pretty well but the troops on the line had seen little of him. He was a pilot from the 2nd ANGLICO and was assigned to the battalion as a forward air controller. He may have called in close air support for the other companies before but this was the first time the men of Fox Company had seen what he could really do. Lieutenant Swift had an ANGR-9, radio for talking to the Corsair pilots and some of our Marines were assigned to crank the generator to give him power when directing the planes. Lieutenant Swift and his Angry-9 became an instant hit with the troops when he violated the rules and got his buddies in the Corsairs to fire less than a hundred yards in front of our lines.

With Marine pilots, close air support was an art form. They were good at it and frequently proved it by saving many Marines lives when they came in low and slow over our positions and fired at the enemy directly to our front. Thank God for supporting arms. Close air support worked and so did artillery.

Stash remarked, "Boy, that Angry-9 is some radio isn't it? I wish we had one of them with us all the time. The damned thing actually worked and that's more than I can say for our 536's."

Corporal Jerden answered, "Yeah, with the 536's the batteries are either dead or dying and at least with the Angry-9 you don't need batteries, just Marine power and we've got plenty of that."

Stash responded angrily with, "That's easy for you to say Jerden, you're a corporal. If you were a private or a Pfc you wouldn't be so ready to employ Marine-power. There's a lot of work cranking that handle to generate power for the Angry-9."

Jerden said, "Look Stash, I don't care how much work it is or how many men it takes to crank the handle or what their rank is. Dammit, it works. Did you see the way those Marine Corsairs came in right over our heads and shot the hell out of the Japs to our front?"

It was Fearless Frank who spoke up next, "Yeah, and I saw the way that last plane banked then dipped his wings and waved at us when he dropped those two green star shells.

Those Corsair pilots are just great! Boy, I'd sure like to fly one of those planes."

In addition to the air strikes and artillery fired at the advancing Japanese, a tremendous volume of rifle and machine-gun fire was directed at them. The enemy advance finally sputtered to a stop. The friendly artillery was lifted and the planes dropped two green cluster flares, signaling that the mission was completed, and flew off. Suddenly the battlefield was unusually quiet. Air observers reported seeing large numbers of dead bodies scattered in front of the Marines' lines.

*   *   *   *   *   *   *   *   *

Body Count

17 June 1944

The company commander and Lieutenant Yoakum were talking with Blackjack who motioned to Shanghai to join them. When he arrived the Skipper greeted him and directed: "Shanghai, take one of your men, one of your best men, and get the hell out there and let me know what's going on! And Sergeant, be careful, I want you back."

"Aye, aye, Sir!"

Shanghai considered all of his men to be good men and good Marines but he knew there wasn't another Marine in the regiment with the experience and skill of Private First Class Chief. The two-man reconnaissance was completed in less than an hour and the sergeant and Chief returned to make their report to the company commander.

"What did you find out there Old Man? What did you two see?"

"Sir, if you don't mind me saying so, its my opinion that there are a couple of companies of ghostly Japanese infantry marching across a heavenly plain toward the Shrine of the Righteous Souls at Yasakuni in Tokyo. And Skipper, you'll be pleased to know that we couldn't see any live Japs out in front of our position. I've picked up some unit identification and personal papers and one map that I'll turn over to battalion."

"Good work, Old Man. Now, about how many Japanese bodies would you say are out there?"

"Hell Cap'n, I didn't know you wanted us to count the damned bodies. I don't know how many of 'em are out there. But I can tell you one thing, there's a hell of a lot of 'em - maybe 200 or more."

"Dammit Shanghai, I've got to make a report to the Old Man and he's going to want to know how many there are. Chief, what do you think? About how many dead Japs were out there?"

"Gee Skipper, I don't know how many there were but I can tell you one thing for sure, there was a whole shitpot full of 'em!"

"Well, based on a report like that I guess I've got all the answer I need. That kind of language will really impress the Old Man. Thanks men, you both did a fine job and I'm glad you made it back safely. When you get back to battalion be sure to fill your canteens and see if you can scrounge some extra cans of C-rations for your boys."

When Shanghai and Chief returned to the company the word was passed for all hands to dig in. We were to stay in position for the night and would be moving out with the battalion on line in the morning. There was to be plenty of support from artillery and Marine air. All hands could sense that something was up. The next day's advance was going to be important. It was not long before the booming voice of the company first sergeant was heard: "All right people, the word's been changed! Man your loads Marines! We're movin' out!"

The only certainty about combat in the Corps is that nothing is for certain. The men moved through the enemy corpses and swarms of Saipan flies swarming over the bloodied, putrefying dead and constantly attempting to land on their hands and faces. They were reluctantly adjusting to the millions of flies but none of them could ever fully adjust to the sight and stench of battlefield dead.

The line was temporarily held up and the troops squatted among the scattered enemy hoping the word would soon come for them to move out. They were repulsed by the thought that they may be told to dig in where they were. All dreaded having to spend the night amongst the scores of corpses. The sickening smell of putrefying flesh would increase as each hour passed under the broiling tropical sun. Some of the dead had already commenced to bloat.

As the troops sat waiting and eager for the word to move forward Stash, in keeping with the humor of the time, took a healthy swallow from his canteen, removed a C-ration can from his pack and looking at it asked, "I wonder if we'll have time for a light lunch while we're enjoying ourselves here in the outdoor morgue."

Taking a drink from a canteen was not a simple task in this gruesome environment. When a Marine attempted to place the canteen up to his lips to drink, the irritating flies would immediately land in the corners of his mouth. No one could evade the nasty hordes of giant blue-green flies that were everywhere on the island of Saipan.

Private Denny Brennan was one of the most recent of the teenaged replacements that had joined the company. Brennan, sensing his good fortune in being assigned as assistant to such a capable Marine as Deadly Dave was doing his best to fit in with the experienced men but his actions gave him away. He couldn't help staring at the cadavers and finally commented that he was surprised to see how well fed the Japs appeared to be. Most of their uniforms were too tight and the Japs actually looked stuffed. Deadly Dave calmly explained, "Denny, these Japs are not well-fed; you won't find a fat soldier in the whole Japanese army unless they've started recruiting sumo wrestlers. What you see is the sun baking them and as they cook, the gasses created by the heat are causing them to bloat and swell. Some of them will eventually blow up like balloons and if you are close enough when one of them pops, you'll get that body fluid on you and nobody will want to dig in with you for days. The smell of death doesn't wear off soon and there's no way for you to wash it off of your clothing when we barely have enough water to drink."

Donahoe screeched, "Hit the deck!" and everyone did, except Donahoe. He stood holding his BAR firmly against his hip and moving it slowly from right to left and back again firing short bursts of 3 or 4 rounds until the magazine was empty. Deadly Dave Donahoe had detected some movement among the Japanese "dead." A grenade detonated and Brennan went down, Deadly Dave Donohoe doubled up in pain momentarily but soon straightened up, removed the magazine from his BAR and inserted a fresh magazine of 20 rounds. He was prepared to resume firing but had no target left. This time the Japanese really were all dead.

Corporal Jerden shouted, "Brennan's been killed! Take his weapon and get that BAR belt off of him and see if he had any grenades. We're gonna need all the firepower we can get when we start movin' toward that damned mountain."

Chic was still in the prone position and he was trembling. He had not been wounded but had felt a tremendous jolt to his helmet when Brennan was hit and when he saw Deadly Dave double up in pain, he was sure his buddy had been killed. Dave had stood straight back up a moment after the grenade explosion and he was apparently all right. Chic's eyes scanned the area around them and marveled that they were completely surrounded by so many Japanese soldiers all lying there motionless in death.

Doc Butcher casually strolled over to where Deadly Dave was sitting and knelt down beside him.

"Let me take a look at you old man, I saw you double up when you got hit. Where does it hurt?"

Donahoe had a badly bruised stomach. A piece from the grenade had struck his BAR belt and dented a magazine severely enough to ruin it and jam the bullets in it. Donahoe breathed a sigh of relief as he realized the 20 rounds of ammunition in that magazine could easily have detonated and blown him apart.

Chic's head ached; it had been ringing since the grenade exploded. He removed his helmet and was surprised to find a crease in it and to see that his camouflaged cover was ripped. Had it not been for his helmet, the grenade fragments would have gone right into his skull. He finally stood up and hoped that none of the others could tell that he was still trembling. He had been afraid ever since they had landed but there were degrees of fear. At times it didn't seem so bad and at other times it was nearly too much to bear.

Chic Yancey had just become a true believer in the value of the steel helmet. There had been some discussion among the troops concerning the helmet's usefulness. It was questionable to some as they had seen bullet holes shot clear through helmets and some had even been blown to pieces. As far as some of the old time professionals were concerned, the helmet's value was purely psychological, providing a 'security blanket' of sorts to the troops new to combat. It was another required encumbrance serving only to lessen one's combat efficiency. There were, of course, many serious exceptions to this opinion concerning the helmets uselessness and Chic had just become one of those exceptions.

As his men were wrapping Private Brennan's body in a poncho, Shanghai Pooley removed the little green notebook he carried in his dungaree shirt pocket. He noted the time and location of Private Dennis R. Brennan's death. They would be back before dark to recover their brother's body.

Without further command, the men automatically went into a tactical formation as they cautiously moved forward. No one was told to take the point or guard the flanks, they were professionals, it was just done automatically.

Lucky Lane suddenly snapped, "Look out Buddy! Stop! There's a tripwire right in front of you. Get off the trail and do it carefully. We've got to defuse that damned thing before it kills somebody. Damned Japs! Why can't they just get up and fight instead of being such sneaky little bastards?"

The Chief answered, "Be careful what you wish for - it may just happen. You know the Japs are merciless, aggressive SOB's when it comes to fighting."

The squad leader cautioned, "Okay, pass the word back to hold it up and take cover. We've got to defuse a booby trap. When we move out again you men keep your eyes open and be damned careful where you step."

When the column moved forward all hands exercised a higher degree of caution than before. A second trip wire was soon discovered and defused. The men moved on. The company front shifted and moved until finally in the diminished light of impending nightfall the men were told to halt and dig in. Artillery fire crashed and boomed throughout the night. As the time for daylight crept closer, the artillery gradually lessened until in the pre-dawn darkness, it was finally stilled and a strange quiet fell over the battlefield. The pre-dawn silence was eerie and ominous. The men, fatigued but battle wise, sensed that this was a silent prelude to some great or important event.

* * * * * * * * * *

The Jaws of Hell

Saipan - mid-June 1944

The dawn was just starting to push back the darkness of the tropical night when the silence was shattered. It was the beginning of a barrage of serious proportions. A thunderous roar that shattered the nerves of strong men and shook the island like an earthquake. The sky above was filled with fierce, unearthly sounds, the shrieks and rumbling of shells light and heavy. The battlewagons and cruisers, backed up by our own close-laid Marine artillery batteries, were taking more than a casual interest in the terrain to our front. It was a blistering barrage, laid down close at hand and the men knew they would soon be moving forward.

The shelling ceased but the smoke still clung to the treacherous marshy ground to the front. It was through this smoky haze smelling strongly of cordite that the battalion must move. Visibility was restricted - theirs and ours. We had to move out rapidly but cautiously before the smoke cleared and the enemy regained their wits after the heavy shelling, it would only be a matter of precious minutes before we came into their view.

A quick backward glance to the right revealed the towering smokestack that rose high above the remains of the Nanyo Kohatsu Kaishai sugar mill at Charan-Kanoa. Chic Yancey briefly marveled that the smokestack could withstand the tremendous amount of fire that had been directed at it and still remain standing. He hoped that he too would still be standing when this fearful day was over.

As the morning sun overpowered the gray dawn and advanced toward its appointed place overhead, its glittering rays were reflected on the bayonets that glistened through the morning haze. A battalion of Marines cautiously advanced with rifles slanted at the high port, the sparkling sunbeams danced on the cold steel of the bayonets.

The determined expressions on the men's faces and their methodical, professional movements masked the fear that was in their hearts. The word had been passed. There was an objective to be taken. The Marines grimly moved forward.

Jim Yancey's attention was quickly diverted to the right front as the blistering rattle of a Japanese light machine gun started chattering. The rapid rat-tat-tat of the light was soon joined by the ominous chug-chug-chugging of a heavier machine gun somewhere way over on the right flank.

The fear could not be disregarded, but one must learn to function in spite of fear. To be a Marine was a great source of pride and satisfaction to a young American. To be a Marine, one had to pay his dues. It was not cheap and no one ever said it would be easy. On this day, as on the terrible days before it, some would pay the ultimate price for the privilege of being Marines.

A clump of tropical scrub rising slightly above the Susupe marshlands like a small island harbored a handful of trapped enemy soldiers less than a hundred yards out to the left front. A grenade was thrown and detonated harmlessly in the mud. It was well out of range. Then there was another and then two more. The barrage of grenades wasn't close enough to the advancing men to be effective although each detonating grenade blew up a considerable fountain of mud. An ambitious attempt but the Japanese had overestimated their ability to throw hand grenades. The grenades were a dead giveaway to the enemy's position. A healthy amount of random rifle fire was directed to whence the grenades had come. It was fired offhand and almost casually, as determined men kept moving forward over the marshy terrain. No more grenades were lobbed at them from that particular position.

A handful of freshly dead Japanese soldiers was seen on a small rise within a clump of heavy tropical vegetation. The Marines continued moving cautiously forward past the place of death from where the grenades had been thrown.

The rapid chattering of rifles sounded as though a string of Chinese firecrackers had been set off out to the front. The line halted as all dropped as one. Shouts of "Corpsman!" could be heard amidst the crackling rounds. When forward movement resumed, the men would be creeping and crawling through the saturated marshland. The effects of the naval gunfire and artillery had worn off and the enemy was now fully alert. There was no need to present a larger target to the Nips than necessary. Forward movement now would be strictly by fire and maneuver.

There was a time when every American schoolboy had to learn Tennyson's, "The Charge of the Light Brigade." Jim Yancey had not learned it well but he remembered parts of it and he was certain it was appropriate to the situation he now found himself in. Surprisingly, amidst the confusion of the battlefield and the fear that had become his constant companion, a portion of "The Charge of the Light Brigade" kept coming to mind. And so it was that when he heard Jock Ross, who was crawling forward on his immediate right, ask no one in particular, "How much farther do we hafta go before we are completely surrounded by the damned Japs?"

Tennyson's words came to Yancey, "Half a league, half a league, half a league onward, all in the valley of death rode the six hundred."

Jim Yancey had no idea how far half a league was and he didn't much care, but he surely knew what the valley of death was, he was in it. And he was learning what the jaws of hell were, he could feel them closing around him!

As they advanced forward, there were scores of places providing cover and concealment from where the Japanese could fire at them. There were clumps of trees and there were sugarcane fields large enough to conceal a regiment, there were rocks and boulders, cliffs and caves and always - out on the periphery - the jungle. The advances were for shorter and shorter distances and each one took more time than the one before it. Casualties were mounting on both sides and in time men became impervious to the grotesque bodies, only recently human beings, that littered their way.

An occasional group of civilians would be found, Japanese and Chamorro. They were terrified, many were in shock, all were hungry, disoriented and dirty, and several had wounds that had not been treated. General Sherman was right "War is hell"!

Someone had found a position from where he could observe the enemy fire and determined the location of their positions. Mortar fire started falling to the front. First the company commander's weapon of opportunity, the 60 millimeter mortars followed soon after by the heavier 81's from the battalion. Supporting mortar fire was music to the ears of advancing infantry but terrifying to the poor natives and Japanese civilians who were caught up in the confusion of the battlefield.

To the front! A line of civilians stumbled toward us, dazed and confused, they had walked right through the mortar fire. They didn't know any better. They could not know if the fire was friendly or enemy though it really did not matter, all fire was deadly. You did not have to be a soldier to die on the field of battle - you merely had to be present.

Whenever the advance was delayed and enemy civilians were encountered, the plight of the people was heart rending. Old men, women and children many wounded and all frightened and obviously hungry and thirsty were so helpless and pitiful no civilized human could disregard them. The Marines, cynical, battle hardened and calloused - and filled with hatred for the Japanese - did something peculiar to Americans. In spite of their strong feelings they reached into their packs for whatever rations they had, opened their canteens and shared their precious little food and water with those who were obviously more in need than themselves. Later that fateful day or later in the campaign, many of those same Marines would be killed by Japanese fire. A good deed may not be long remembered but no good deed goes long unpunished. No one ever said war was fair.

The Japanese seemed to have but two objectives, to kill Americans and to give their lives for the Emperor. Some of the caves were well stocked with weapons, ammunition and dedicated Japanese soldiers. No matter the odds, Japanese soldiers did not surrender. If a Marine was foolish enough to approach a cave, the Japs would often hold their fire until he was in the entrance, that way they were sure of a kill before giving up their own lives. Thank God for the flamethrowers. In many cases, they were the only really effective means of neutralizing caves.

When the day was nearing an end and it was time to stop moving and go into a defensive posture for the night, the bone-weary men dug their fighting holes in ground that it seemed only a jackhammer could penetrate. They were beyond the Susupe Swamp now and the spongy marshland had given way to hard coral. Through a seemingly super-human effort they somehow managed to do it by hand, using the entrenching tools attached to their packs. It is surprising what a man can accomplish when properly motivated and fear is the greatest motivator in the world. Men nearing the point of exhaustion were again tested. Some had to be sent back through the marsh to supply points on the beach to hand-carry five-gallon expeditionary cans of precious water and boxes of ammunition, grenades and rations.

Those who went to the rear were shocked when they realized what a short distance the long day's advance had actually covered. The grueling day's fighting had resulted in a gain of but a few hundred yards.

As the day slowly vanished into the west, darkness came forth and beckoned the creatures of the night, real and imagined, to come out and test the mettle of tired men who would sooner be elsewhere doing other things. Decisions were made as to who would take the first watch and who the next. Always, one man must be awake and alert in every two-man fighting hole. Lives depended upon it.

Throughout the night Marines strained their eyes and ears while scanning the area for any possible movement in the likely avenues of approach. The sounds of the wind and the moving shadows cast over the battlefield by descending parachute flares have been known to conjure up strange visions in the creative minds of young Marines. This can be further exacerbated by the sound of small-arms fire not too distant. And thus it was in the first several hours of another night ashore as we watched and waited.

*　*　*　*　*　*　*　*　*　*

The No-Hitter

Saipan cane fields · June 1944

Dawn was breaking as Chic silently recited the 23rd Psalm to himself. He was thankful that he was still alive to see another day. He carried a small prayer book that his Mom had given to him just before he had left for boot camp. She had written asking him to open the book and read the 23rd Psalm whenever he felt the need. He no longer had to read it, he had memorized it.

> *The Lord is my shepherd; I shall not want. He maketh me to lie down in green pastures; He leadeth me beside the still waters; He restoreth my soul; He leadeth me in the paths of righteousness for His names sake. Yea though I walk through the valley of the shadow of death, I will fear no evil; For thou art with me; Thy rod and Thy staff they comfort me. Thou preparest a table before me in the presence of mine enemies; Thou anointest my head with oil, my cup runneth over. Surely goodness and mercy shall follow me all the days of my life; and I shall dwell in the House of the Lord forever.*

He watched as the pale blue-gray streaks slowly brightened the night sky. In a matter of minutes, it was daylight. Throughout the night everything had been quiet out to their immediate front. He was relieved that this time there had been no discernable enemy activity. He looked at his friend and buddy, McLaughlin, the Marine asleep beside him in the small hole in the ground. Mac slept in the sitting position, forehead on his knees with his helmet precariously on the back of his head. His rifle was close beside him. Chic thanked God that he had lived to see another day. It was full daylight now and they would soon learn what fate had in store for them on this another day on the island of the dead.

His reflections were soon interrupted by the deep, commanding voice of Blackjack the platoon sergeant as it shattered the morning silence and seemed to descend on them from the heavens above. All could hear and understand his intended humor with equal clarity.

"Another day in the history of our glorious and illustrious Corps! Gird yourselves and be well armed my lads for today we sally forth once again to slay another of the deadly dragons of the East!"

C-rations were opened and hastily devoured as heat tabs warmed water in canteen cups into which soluble coffee had been stirred. Morning ablutions were taken care of as teeth were brushed without benefit of water. When the coffee had been consumed the canteen cups were used for shaving and the stubble of beards was scraped away with a safety razor dipped in as little precious water as possible. Combat or no combat, the Skipper insisted that his men look like Marines. Shaving was not optional, it was required.

The platoon guide checked to be certain that all-hands had a full unit of fire for their rifles and as many grenades as could be spared. Each squad sent two men to the company CP carrying the empty canteens of their squad mates to be filled from five-gallon expeditionary cans. Oil and thong cases were removed from wells in the stocks of M-1 rifles and brushes and patches were drawn through rifle bores. Rifles were wiped clean with a special care that only those who have lived in harm's way can truly appreciate. They heard the platoon sergeant's booming voice once again as it created a sense of urgency among the men.

"Alright you reluctant dragon-slayers, man your loads! We're movin' out!"

They had their gear on now and were starting to move. Chic was petrified. It was as though his feet were glued to the ground. He didn't want to go. He didn't want to move out. Not another day of being shot at time after time and scared nearly out of his mind. Not another hour of sheer terror while crawling forward to help pull the body of one of his dead buddies back to friendly lines while some crazy Jap with a machine gun was firing just inches above them.

Sergeant Childs rose up from his hole and in a crouching position started moving cautiously forward. Corporal Jerden over on the left moved out and Chief stepped from his hole on the right. Fearless and the Weasel soon followed. They moved bent over and at high port with fixed bayonets. No one knew what this day would bring but all hoped it would be better than the nightmare days that had just passed. The rest of the men moved forward. They were in a skirmish line now, slowly, cautiously, moving at the high port ready to drop to the ground and take up firing positions at the first hint of the enemy.

As Shanghai, the squad leader, moved cautiously past Chic, he snarled out of the corner of his mouth, "C'mon you sonofabitch! What're you waitin' for, an engraved invitation?"

The sergeant's voice cut to the quick. Shanghai was an Old Corps Marine, a professional. The men up ahead forming the skirmish line were moving more confidently now. They were Marines, his brothers, he needed to be with them. He was scared, really scared, but then he'd been that way off and on ever since they'd landed on the damned island. He thought of something one of the sergeants used to say back at Camp Elliott while lecturing them on his experiences on Guadalcanal and telling them what combat would be like.

"They write of valor but never the cost of it - because they just don't understand it and there's another thing they don't understand, fear. I am highly educated in fear. I know every kind of fear there is."

And then the sergeant would add, "Don't ever confuse fear with cowardice, there's a big difference between the two."

Chic was filled with fear but he was not a coward. He swung the M-1 rifle off his shoulder, fixed his bayonet to its lug and moved forward with the squad. That's what being a Marine is all about. No one ever said it wouldn't be challenging.

The company was to move into and through a cane field in a column of files and cross rapidly over to the edge of the jungle. The cane stalks were eight feet high. A whole regiment could have moved through a field that size without being seen. The 2nd platoon was to lead off; the 2nd squad took the point. It was easy to follow the straight furrow between the rows of cane. The cane leaves crackled and crunched noisily as the men trudged along.

Visibility was severely restricted and a man could only see the backs of one or two of the men ahead of him. The leading squad had gone about 50 yards into the maze when there was a Thud! Thud! Thud! A sickening Whoosh! Whoosh! Whoosh! was followed by an equal number of detonations.

They were Japanese "knee mortars" and by the grace of God they were overshooting the column.

The men instantly dropped to the ground and struggled to burrow themselves deeper into the furrows between the rows of cane as all hell broke loose in a heavy volume of rifle and machine-gun fire exploding just inches above the ground. Combat-hardened Marines trembled in fear and cursed in anger, as they lay helplessly between the rows of sugarcane with bullets passing so close over them that they imagined they could feel the heat from them. The thick rows of cane stalks provided the enemy with perfect concealment.

As the volume of fire lessened the squad leader, moving to the next furrow over, crawled recklessly from man to man, daring the enemy fire to hit him as he coolly advised his men that the safest way out was with hand grenades. The Japs were close, very close, but they too were blinded by the proliferation of cane stalks. Their fire had been aimed at the sounds the men made as they walked through the cane field, not at anything they could see. Now, the Marines were not making any more sounds but the sporadic Jap fire was. We knew the direction of their fire. All that remained was to guess the range and then get close enough to start lobbing grenades and pray for accuracy. Shanghai Pooley, the squad leader whispered: "Harrington!! I know you'd like to pitch in the World Series someday. How'd you like to pitch a no-hitter? And I mean right now, today?"

"What do you mean Sergeant?"

"Kid, this is gonna be the Marine Corps' version of a no-hitter. Here's your chance to pitch in the really "Big Leagues" and I ain't talkin' about baseball. This is no game Harrington, it may well be the greatest test of your life. You either put those grenades right where the Japs are or we die, that's what I mean. You've gotta do it right the first time 'cause we may not get a second chance."

Throwing hand grenades from a furrow in a cane field was no simple task when the stalks were more than eight feet high. It took skill and courage to stand up and carefully aim and throw the grenades in a high trajectory under sporadic enemy fire. Only a few men were up to the task. Hand Grenade Harrington finally came into his own. He was at his best on this day. The men would never again make jokes or kid him about practicing grenade throwing. Once the second round of grenades was thrown, the men must get up and move quickly through the rows of cane toward the enemy, firing rapidly (though blindly) from the hip as they advanced.

They struggled through the thick cane - firing as they moved - but they didn't have to move far. The Japanese had been a mere 40 feet from the 2nd squad when they had opened fire. As the squad entered a small clearing near the center of the cane field Shanghai pushed forward and standing in the midst of eight freshly killed Japanese soldiers confronted his men.

"Alright you birds, take a close look here! This is the enemy! These poor little dead Japanese soldiers are what held you up. They couldn't see you when they opened fire; they just heard you moving through the cane like a heard of cattle. When they fired those "knee mortars" which are nothing more than a poor man's grenade launcher, and pretty damned inaccurate at that, they made a gross error in judgment. In the first place, their range was way off and in the second place they would have killed a few of us, maybe all of us, if they had opened up with their rifles and that Nambu first. The mortars overshot their target and gave us a chance to hit the deck and on top of that, the Japs couldn't see what they were shooting at. Without realizing it they must have been aiming high. If we had returned their fire instead of throwing those grenades, their aim would have improved and some of you would most likely be as dead now as these guys are."

Deadly Dave Donahoe tried to salvage the light Nambu machine-gun but quickly gave it up when he saw how badly damaged it had been by the grenades. Poncho Gutierrez, dazzled by a sparkling gold tooth in the front of a tall dead Japanese soldier's mouth moved with the speed of a true professional in his salvage operation, which never failed to disgust the entire squad. Fearless Frank Quinlan had a smile on his face as he proclaimed to Wetzel the Weasel that the luck of the Irish was still with them.

"But Fearless, I ain't Irish."

"Shut up and do what you're told and someday, if you're lucky, I may declare you an honorary Irishman, you dumb

Kraut. Eight dead Japs and not a Marine hit. What a break! Okay Weasel, check out the Samurai sword on that one over there. Is it in pretty good shape or did the grenades get it too?"

Wetzel was now squatting down beside the dead Japanese officer. He had no way of knowing that the Katana was much older even than the United States Marine Corps or that it was of considerable value.

"The sword's kinda' worn and it's scratched up a little Fearless but its good enough for trading material. Would ya look at the shirt this Nip's wearin'! Maybe he was thinkin' of comin' over to our side."

All eyes glanced at the dead Japanese officer. He was wearing a U.S. Marine dungaree shirt.

"Check the pocket Fearless; he's blocked out the Marine emblem with black ink or somethin'. I wonder how he got the shirt?"

"The little sonofabitch probably killed a Marine and took it Weasel."

Wetzel handed the sword to Quinlan for his inspection as Riverboat Brown shook his head and proclaimed,

"You know what the scriptures say; He who lives by the sword shall die by the sword."

Looking at Riverboat Fearless quipped; "I don't know much about what the scriptures say Riverboat but in my book, them that lives by the sword gets shot by them that don't!"

Hand Grenade Harrington's nickname was no longer used in jest; it had suddenly become a title of respect. Even the company gunnery sergeant and the Skipper started referring to Harrington as Hand Grenade. He had really earned his nickname and it had acquired a certain dignity, which pleased him immensely.

Once clear of the cane field the company went into an assembly area where they waited and enjoyed a brief break as a group of replacements came trudging through the cane field after them. The replacements had brought rations, water and mail.

Two important lessons had been learned about moving through cane fields. The first of which was simply not to do so (unless absolutely necessary). The second, if it was absolutely necessary, it had to be done silently (and with as few men as possible).

Among the new replacements was a corporal named Nesbitt. He was a nice guy, but why in the world had they sent him out here as a corporal? He had come from Hawthorne, Nevada. Yancey had never heard of Hawthorne, Nevada and neither had anyone else in the 2nd squad.

Nesbitt was a squared away Marine, but he was not experienced in the field. Like so many of the replacements the only infantry training he'd had was when he was in Boot Camp. When this batch of replacements first arrived, Nesbitt, like most of the others seemed to be in a daze. To these squared-away Stateside Marines, it must have come as quite a shock to first encounter the seasoned combat veterans they would be serving with.

The old hands were a motley crew. Their pallor was a sickening yellow from the Atabrine tablets they all took daily. They had seen much of life and far too much of death to have the appearance of normal, civilized Marines. They were lean and mean and obviously looked it. Dungarees were tattered and worn and faded with perspiration stains. They seemed held together by little more than bloodstains, dirt and dried mud. The men's tempers had grown short and their language was colorful and somewhat bizarre.

At first, the replacements must have been awed by the appearance and language of the men with whom they would be serving. Having spent so much time under primitive and oppressive conditions, the troops had reverted to using profanity to a marked degree and were practically unaware of it. It was not only second nature but had nearly progressed to the point where it was an art form. Along with the profanity, they had picked up and frequently used expressions from Samoa, New Zealand and of course a few phrases from the old China hands. Within days the replacements, without an apparent awareness of it, were speaking the same jargon as the veterans.

All the men were eager for news from home. They wanted to hear what the new replacements had to say, without becoming overly friendly towards them. They had all lost too many buddies. The men couldn't let themselves develop new close friendships again only to lose them.

Most of the old hands were still in their teens and early twenties but to them the replacements, regardless of age, were rookies. Replacements were seldom fully accepted until after their first firefight. After you had served in combat with a man, age made no difference. Deeds are what counted. If you could depend on a man while under fire, it didn't matter how young or how old he was.

Nesbitt had only been in the Corps a couple of years so he must have been a pretty good Marine at Hawthorne to make corporal. On his first night with the company, he dug-in with Corporal Al Jerden who was a pre-war Marine who had been in the outfit since before the 'Canal' and had been overseas somewhat longer than Nesbitt had been in the Marine Corps.

"Jerden, I keep hearing the word *Cobber*. What does *Cobber* mean?"

"Why hell, Nesbitt, even you should know that! It's New Zealand. It means the same thing as *Pongyo*."

Corporal Nesbitt scratched his head and quietly resolved to himself that it may take him some time to learn the language. He also recognized that he would have to be a very good listener and be very patient if he wanted to survive in this outfit. He wondered just what in the world a *pongyo* was.

Like most of the other replacements, Nesbitt learned fast and soon acted like he was at home climbing the cliffs or on a jungle trail. He already knew how to curse like a mule skinner.

Hey, Childs did you know that Nesbitt guy was a "Horse Marine"? asked Jerden.

"Hell no," replied the sergeant, "There ain't no more "Horse Marines." They disbanded them over in Peking before we got into the war."

Nesbitt had some photographs of himself and some of his buddies back at the Naval Ammunition Depot at Hawthorne. The troops were surprised to see that they wore regulation Marine Corps green uniforms with green riding breeches and leather puttees. Chick thought the last of the "Horse Marines" had gone when the Marines left North China, but Nesbitt assured them that there were still Horse Marines and he had been one of them. Corporal Nesbitt of the Horse Marines immediately acquired the nickname of "Barnsmell." He advised any would-be Horse Marines that in addition to Hawthorne, there were mounted Marine Detachments at Hingham, Massachusetts and Lualualei, in the Territory of Hawaii.

All of the "cowboys" in the company immediately decided that as soon as they got back to the states, if they got back, they would put in for assignment to the Horse Marines. The troops thought the uniform looked really sharp with riding breeches and leather puttees. Barnsmell Nesbitt gained rapid acceptance among the old hands in the platoon simply because he had the unique distinction of being a Horse Marine. Others among the new replacements were not accepted so quickly. The old hands resented the fact that so many of the new men were corporals and sergeants and the long service privates in the outfit didn't hide their feelings.

Having cleared the cane field and absorbed their new replacements the company entered the jungle. As they moved forward, it was necessary to follow the trails. The jungle growth was so dense it was all but impossible to move unless they stayed on the trails. As they moved forward, the elevation increased and so did Chic's apprehension.

Trudging along with his rifle cradled in his arms, Corporal Alvin Jerden was livid!

"Damn!"

"What's that supposed to mean Jerden?"

"It means we're up a creek without a paddle, that's what it means. The Navy has bugged out on us again. Just like they did when they left us on the "Canal.""

"How did you come up with that gem of wisdom?"

"I got it from a very reliable source and I know damn well it's true. I'm tellin' you guys, they've done it again! Damn those Navy sonsabitches!"

The platoon sergeant and Shanghai, the squad leader, remembered the incident on Guadalcanal with misgivings. They took Jerden aside where they wouldn't be heard by the other men and told him to stop it.

"Belay it Al, that kind of talk is bad for morale. You are gonna scare hell out of the new men with that kind of BS. You know its only scuttlebutt and it's not true."

Black and Pooley were both veterans of Guadalcanal and

they knew the U.S. Navy would never do such a thing again.

The rumor persisted that the Navy had pulled out and left the Marines on Saipan to fend for themselves. Corporal Alvin Jerden had seen it happen before and so he believed the rumor. He was reliving Guadalcanal where the Navy did indeed leave the Marines ashore with inadequate supplies of food and ammunition.

Jerden looked at his two superiors and fervently wished that he could believe them but he knew the rumor was true. His confidential source had been none other than W. Max Netherland, the field music. The music had stated that Admiral Spruance's fleet had left Saipan. Somehow, the music always knew what was going on and Jerden was sure that this time was no exception.

When the company was told to halt and take up defensive positions on line and prepare to dig in for the night the rumor spread like wildfire. The Navy had bugged out again! Word was soon passed down the line that the Skipper wanted all platoon leaders and platoon sergeants to lay back to the company CP for a briefing. The company commander was more than a little disturbed.

"Gentlemen, some dumb sonofabitch is spreading bum scoop that is totally erroneous and furthermore could be detrimental to the efficiency of this goddam company and I want it stopped immediately! If I find out who is responsible for this damned scuttlebutt, I'll be sorely tempted to shoot the sonofabitch myself. Whoever has done this is guilty of conduct prejudicial to good order and discipline and furthermore it might even be construed as giving aid and comfort to the enemy in time of war. Now that Gentlemen, is serious!"

The captain went on to tell his subordinate unit leaders just what was really happening, or at least as much as he knew about it: Part of the fleet had indeed left. They were on their way to seek out and engage the Japanese fleet. This was to be the U.S. Navy's first significant opportunity to engage the Imperial Japanese Navy on a grand scale. The captain hoped this would have the immediate effect of giving his men a respite from the Japanese air raids and perhaps preclude the possibility of a Japanese assault and counter-landing to engage the U.S. forces on Saipan.

The fleet commander, Admiral Raymond Spruance, had higher aspirations. He wanted to destroy the Japanese fleet. Spruance was hopeful that in attacking Saipan, one of Japan's most important possessions, he would force the Japanese fleet to come out and fight. He was certain they would take the bait but his problem now would be to find them in time to strike the first decisive blow.

The usual working parties had been sent back to battalion to carry ammunition, water and rations up to the company. Fighting holes were being dug and prepared for another sleepless night of God knows what. The chaplain arrived from the CP with the carrying party and the word was passed for men wishing to receive communion to fall back to a defiladed area behind the company CP in small groups. At least one man would standby in each hole until his buddy returned, then the others could go a few at a time.

Corporal Jerden knew that chaplains were much easier to talk to than most other officers were and they usually had access to plenty of scuttlebutt. They were generally a ready source of information. After receiving communion, which in his mind had become almost like receiving the last rites, Jerden approached the chaplain.

"Padre, you're around a lot of the senior officers, what have you heard about the Navy shoving off on us again?"

"Shoving off? You mean like they did on Guadalcanal?"

"Yes Sir, that's exactly what I mean. We've been hearing rumors about it all day."

"Well Corporal, if it makes you feel any better, I can tell you that the Navy did not 'shove off' as you say. Many of the ships are right over the horizon out of sight but nearby if we should need them. Admiral Spruance has sent a part of the fleet, including Admiral Mark Mitscher's Task Force 58, out to challenge the Japanese Navy in the Philippine Sea. If they're successful, we may not have to put up with 'Washing-Machine Charley' dropping his bombs on us in the middle of the night anymore."

"Yessir, that's all well and good, but what are we gonna do when the ammunition and rations run out? Everything we need is aboard them ships Padre."

"Corporal, if you could see what I've seen back at the beach you'd really be amazed. The Navy has off-loaded several ships already and we have the biggest ammunition, fuel and supply dump down on that old Japanese landing strip by Charon Kanoa that I have ever seen. You just can't imagine it until you see it for yourself. And for your information, the admiral didn't take all of the ships. The transports and AKA's have just moved over the horizon a few miles out to the east. They'll still be nearby when we need them. You may not see many of them because they have dispersed so they won't present too attractive a target to enemy aircraft and submarines, but they are just over the horizon. This is not going to be anything like what you experienced on the Canal."

"Thanks Padre, I know I can trust you. I'll let the men know what you have said."

Corporal Al Jerden returned to his buddies in the 2nd platoon and told them of the important intelligence he'd gleaned from his personal conversation with his good friend Father Grace. He reminded the men that Catholic priests don't lie and he further advised them that they wouldn't have to worry about Washing Machine Charley anymore. Task Force 58 had gone out after the Japanese fleet and the chaplain had assured him that they would soon eliminate Japanese airpower over the Marianas.

Later that night in the midst of an artillery barrage with mortar and small arms fire thrown in for effect, the men were straining their eyes and ears to locate and fire at approaching enemy troops. Sickening whines announced the arrival of a series of aerial bombs that detonated and caused the earth to tremble with even greater ferocity than the Jap artillery. Japanese aircraft were dropping the bombs. Searchlight beams pierced the sky and locked onto and followed the bombers overhead. Orange tracers from the ships nearby and the anti-aircraft positions on the beach filled the sky as the bombs continued to drop. So much for reliable scuttlebutt from the chaplain. Sometimes the men just didn't know who they could trust.

* * * * * * * * * *

The Book

Saipan - 19 June 1944

A gentle breeze brought the smell of impending rain and a skyward glance confirmed that the rain clouds were positioning themselves overhead and the sky was darkening. The Marines continued down the trail, rifles cradled at the ready and alert eyes darting from one possible danger or target of opportunity to the next. Soon the putrid smell of death was detected and the beauty of this once lovely island was lost to them.

The 81mm mortars had given considerable attention to this position the day before. The patrol was to go in and eliminate holdouts and snipers and ensure the safety and security of the area. As they moved in they could see there was not much left but ruins. None of the original buildings were standing intact. From the looks of the debris this must have been an area where some Japanese officers had been quartered.

Dead humans and the carcasses of several chickens and two small pigs littered the clearing. Over by the ruins of one of the houses were scattered clothing, a photograph album, toilet articles, writing paper, and some weapons.

Harrington started for a body lying in the middle of the clearing. There, right where it couldn't be missed, was a Samurai sword lying across a dead soldier's body. Shanghai's command stopped Harrington in his tracks. "Belay there, you half-baked idiot! Stop!! Look on that Jap's collar. He is wearing the tabs of an *itohei*. If you touch that sword it's liable to blow you to kingdom come! Harrington what makes you think a dead Jap private would have an officer's Samurai *katana* unless it was booby trapped?"

"I don't know Sergeant, but it sure would be a good souvenir for tradin' with the Army. We could probably get a half-case of C-rations or a couple belts of ammo for it."

"You could get yourself killed too. Wait till we're ready to leave and I'll have Donahoe fire a burst into the body with his BAR. If that doesn't blow it all to hell, you can go ahead and take the sword. Carefully though, remember souvenirs can be deadly."

Chic was looking with wonder at a book lying on the ground across the compound. A shaft of sunlight had found an opening in the heavy cloud cover and the white pillar penetrated the overhead canopy of green and shone diagonally down, spotlighting the book. A gust of wind had started the pages flapping. The light breeze following the gust was just enough to keep the book's pages turning slowly one after another. He did not know what kind of a book it was but he fantasized that it was someone's life story. The pages turning faster and faster in the gentle breeze eventually stopped. It was over; there were no more pages for the breeze to turn. The book was finished, the pages lay flat and still, like the enemy dead lying about the compound.

All of the things scattered on the ground throughout the clearing had belonged to people who had used them and cared about them. The items now scattered in disarray caused a slight glimmer of understanding to come over Chic. The dead had recently been real people, human beings. They had feelings just like he had. Prior to this moment it had been difficult for him to think of the Japs as being human. All of the live ones he had encountered, thus far, had been brutal and merciless. Somehow the simple possessions, strewn about this clearing humanized the Japanese.

A suitcase of woven wicker with brown leather fittings was lying open on the ground. It contained clothing and personal articles but something on the top caught Chic's eye. There was a straight razor and shaving brush a packet of letters and beside them a medal, a military medal. He reached down and picked it up from the open suitcase. He had never touched a real medal before although he knew a couple of Marines who had been recommended for medals. Holding it in his hand he was fascinated by it and wondered what it represented. He inspected the medal carefully.

It was distinctly Japanese; on one side it had a large bird with wings spread, sitting on two flags. Above the bird's head and between the spread wings was a classic Japanese chrysanthemum symbol. The ribbon was tan with shades of blue on the ends and a pink center with a red stripe down the middle. The other side had three mountain peaks jutting up above the clouds with the sea below and four Japanese characters across the clouds. Chic wondered what great act of bravery had been performed to earn such a medal. He wondered if Hirohito, the Emperor himself or maybe Premier Tojo had pinned this medal on the proud recipient. As he glanced around the clearing, he wondered which of the broken bodies had been that once proud and great warrior.

Shanghai reached out and took the medal from Chic's hand, briefly looking at it he said, "It's the China Incident War Medal." Casually tossing the medal onto the ground he stated: "That thing's no good as a souvenir, they're not worth a damn. All the Nips who served in China or Manchukuo since 1937 are entitled to one of them. They're a dime a dozen."

Pfc Jim Yancey wanted to bend down and pick it up off the muddy ground but his pride wouldn't allow it. He was beginning to realize that looks can be deceiving and that some things just may not be what they seem. How was he to know that over a million Japanese were entitled to wear that medal? It had looked pretty special to him. The squad moved out and the medal was soon forgotten but not the broken bodies and what was left of their possessions scattered in the mud throughout the clearing.

The slowly turning pages of that book lying in the mud with the shaft of sunlight shining on them had made a lasting impression on Chic. He fantasized that the turning pages each represented a day and once turned they were gone forever and could not be relived or rewritten. He thought of it as the book of life. Chic had become painfully aware that life was fleeting and fragile and ended much too swiftly.

As the men moved the short distance back toward the company, Harrington was grinning to himself. He had proudly slung the Samurai *katana* diagonally across his back. It had been crudely booby-trapped but was defused by Shanghai himself. The sword would be excellent trading material. Chic's thoughts were of the many men that had been lost on Saipan thus far. They had only been ashore for five days and nearly one third of the platoon had been killed. He could easily recall the faces and names of his dead comrades but hadn't learned the names of the new replacements. He surprised himself with the realization that he didn't want to get to know the new men. He missed his dead buddies.

Once back with the company, the platoon was in reserve. They followed the other two platoons through blackened sugarcane fields. The burned cane gave off a pungent odor and the sticky black residue and ash adhered to everything that touched it. The company was forced to hit the deck when they came under fire from Japanese artillery. After creeping and crawling through the burned cane field the men, their dungarees and their packs were a sticky, dirty black. Their only chance to bathe would be when it rained.

Passing through the cane field they entered a grove of coconut palms. The wind, gusting intermittently, caused the tops of the trees to sway and bend ever so slightly. The rustling of the fronds sounded like whispering. They seemed to be sharing a special secret mere mortals were only meant to hear, not understand. The company was soon clear of the whispering palms and the gentle breeze was joined by a light but steady rainfall. The terrain ahead was rough and the men wondered what they would next encounter. So far, the artillery pounding they had received while passing through the burned out cane field was the only enemy fire they'd sustained. It was their first half-day not to be under small arms fire.

The company was on line with George Company on the left. They had halted and would be in position until joined by Easy Company who would be tying in on the right. It was time to relax, open a can of C-rations and brew a canteen cup of soluble coffee.

Mac hollered over to Stash, "Hey Stash, lend me your oil and thong case will ya? These government issue thongs are no good, mine's broken again. I don't know how they expect us to keep our rifles clean without ramrods."

Stash snapped open his rifle's butt plate and withdrew the metal cylinder that was his oil and thong case and tossed it to McLaughlin. He then took two cans from his haversack and looked at the heavier one then carefully glanced around at his buddies to see if any looked as though they might be willing to trade for another "heavy."

"Hey you guys, does anyone want to trade with me? How about you Barnsmell? I've got one of those tasty cans of meat and vegetable hash."

"Who are you kiddin' Stash? I had one of those last night and another one this morning and you wouldn't trade with me. I've got meat and vegetable stew this time and I'm not tradin' with anybody. And, I don't even like meat and vegetable stew. I don't like meat and beans either but I have to break the monotony once in a while."

Stash persisted, "Aw c'mon Buddy, just this one time?"

Barnsmell Nesbitt shook his head in a negative manner as he uttered, "Semper Fi Mac, Semper Fi!"

Stash shot a quick glance at Barnsmell and in a half-whisper warned, "Damn, watch what you say Barnsmell! You don't ever want to let old Shanghai or Blackjack hear you saying Semper Fi in that way. To them, and a lot of the other Old Corps guys, Semper Fi is almost like a religious term. It doesn't have the same meaning to them that it does to us. They really take it seriously, so knock it off."

The new replacements still had much to learn.

*　*　*　*　*　*　*　*　*　*

The Snipers

19 June 1944

He crawled up to the rocky ledge then slid over to his left making room for the lieutenant. The new lieutenant crawled up beside the platoon sergeant and stopped.

"Lieutenant, would you mind letting me use your binoculars for a moment?"

"No I guess not, what do you see out there?"

"Shhh, keep your voice down, Sir. I'll show you in just a minute."

The sergeant fixed as if in a trance, stared through the binoculars without moving a muscle. Slowly taking the binoculars down and handing them back to the lieutenant, he pointed with his right index finger and quietly whispered: "Look right over there across the draw under that overhanging rock ledge, and tell me what you see?"

"Hell, Sergeant Black, I can see them without my binoculars. Japs, at least two of them and they've got some kind of a crew-served weapon."

"Right Lieutenant, that's what a Jap heavy machine gun looks like. If Shanghai was up here with us he could tell you the model and everything you'd want to know about it. He's a real expert on Nip weapons. They've got it trained on that area down to our right. That's where Easy Company is supposed to tie in when they catch up."

"Sergeant the skipper said Easy Company would be in position in about a half hour." The lieutenant glanced at his watch then continued, "We haven't got much time Blackjack."

"Sir, the lieutenant may not want to say anything about time to the men, I want to use a couple of them as snipers to take those Jap machine-gunners out. If they know how little time we've got, it will just add to the stress and pressure they are going to be under.

The sergeant motioned for the lieutenant to crawl back down to where the troops were waiting then he silently followed. As Blackjack approached the 2nd squad he said, "Shanghai, gimme your two best marksmen, we're gonna kill us some gooks."

Shanghai looked around at his squad and instinctively pointed to Dutch Shute and motioned him over. Shute cringed inwardly and silently wished that he had not been a gun enthusiast or ever fired expert. This was not an assignment he relished.

"Private Shute is a good shot. He fired in matches back home when he was a civilian and in boot camp, he fired high expert. He may even become a team shooter someday if he stays in the Corps."

Private Muldoon quickly moved up beside the sergeant.

"I heard you say we're gonna kill some gooks. I'm your man Sergeant."

"Like hell you are! The platoon sergeant needs men who are high experts. We may only get one crack at these birds and I can't take a chance on you missing."

"Dammit Sergeant I've lost some of my best friends to those Nips and you know it. Remember poor old Jerry Bronson who never even made it to the beach and Eddie Malone who never got off the beach? And old Baker and Buddy Blair and just this morning they even killed that new kid, Brennan and you know all the others. You know how many good friends I've lost on this damned island. There ain't a man in this outfit that want's to kill Japs any more than I do."

"We've all lost good friends Muldoon and we'll most likely lose a lot more before this fiasco is over. You'll have your chance to kill plenty of other Japs, but not these. I want expert riflemen and you are only a marksman. I can't take a chance on you. Mc Laughlin what about you? You fired high expert didn't you?"

"That's right Sergeant, I guess I'm your man."

The squad leader pretended not to notice the others who held back or quietly turned around not wanting to be noticed. They were reluctant to volunteer to kill unless they had to.

The lieutenant, with his runner in tow, told the platoon sergeant that he was going back to the CP to advise the skipper of the location of the machine gun and see if he could delay E Company from moving up until the gun was neutralized.

Blackjack looked at his two marksmen and stated, "Dutch and Mac, leave your packs where they are and take off your cartridge belts and helmets and leave them too. You are traveling light and believe me, you two experts are going to earn your shooting pay. We're going to crawl up to that ledge where the lieutenant and I saw them. I don't want either one of you to make a sound, you got that?"

Dutch and Mac each managed a quiet, "Yes Sir."

Blackjack instructed, "When you see me stop on that rise up ahead, start crawling toward me. Once you are up there come alongside me and maintain complete silence. You're going to see a rock formation across the draw from us. Look in the shadow just under the overhang. I'll point out the targets to you and you acknowledge silently. Your targets are going to be the two Japs manning a heavy machine gun. Dutch, you take the one on the left and Mac, the one on the right is yours. You will each fire one round and one round only. If either one of you misses, Marines are gonna die. Do you understand clearly how important this is?" Dutch and Mac understood.

"Just lie there and don't make a move unless you do it in

very slow motion and that includes breathing. Clear your thoughts and minds of everything except killing those Japs. Check your sights and adjust your slings as though you were on the firing line back at Camp Matthews.

"Now here's how I want you to do this: Sight in on your targets, line 'em up carefully and take a deep breathe then let it part way out. Stay completely relaxed except for your mind, the grip on your rifle and your trigger finger. Do this two or three times without squeezing off a round just so you will have confidence that you can do it. When you are ready to go for the kill, each of you try and fire as close to the same moment as you can without sacrificing accuracy.

"Once you've taken them out, don't move for a few moments then slither back down here quietly and slowly. If there are any more of them, I don't want the little bastards to know where you fired from. When you two have successfully made your kills we'll wait a while and then I'll go back and stick my head up there and see if there are any others. If there are, we'll kill them too and eventually, we are gonna get that machine gun. They're heavy as hell to carry but one of those babies will sure give the platoon a boost in firepower."

CRACK-crack! The two rounds were fired almost as one. Private Shute didn't even know when his rifle was going off. His trigger squeeze had been excellent, as had his sight picture. He saw the enemy soldier drop instantly as the round struck his head. McLaughlin's quarry plunged forward and fell down the hill sprawling awkwardly with arms outstretched. He appeared to be dead.

Back with the squad, Dutch and Mac put on their helmets and cartridge belts. Someone had brought up water and ammo so they drained their canteens and refilled them. Dutch sat down beside Lucky and Chic and lamented,

"I feel like hell. I've never had to kill anyone like that before. I just sighted in, squeezed a round off and killed him. Damn! Whenever I shot at anyone before it was 'cause they were tryin' to kill me. This poor guy wasn't even lookin' in my direction. Blackjack shoulda' let Muldoon take him. He'd probably feel good about killin' the guy".

Lucky put his hand on Dutch Shute's shoulder and looked him in the eyes. "Don't be a jerk! You were given a job to do and you did it. Be glad you guys got the little sonsabitches. They didn't have that big Nambu up there to shoot clay pigeons dammit; they were waiting to kill Marines."

Chic sensed that Dutch was deeply disturbed and no amount of talking would change his mind.

Blackjack motioned for Shanghai to follow him. They crawled back up to the firing point and looked at the enemy machine gun and the dead Japanese soldiers.

Blackjack said, "I've gotta be sure there's no more live Nips up there Shanghai. Easy Company will be on our flank in less than 10 minutes according to what the lieutenant says. If the Japs man that machine gun again they can really clobber us. What kind of a gun is it anyhow; you're supposed to be the expert on Nip stuff?"

Shanghai answered, "Hell Sergeant, I can't tell from here, it's a heavy machine gun, that's all. Probably a T-92, I've seen plenty of them the past few days." Then looking at Blackjack he asked, "Look! Do you see that?"

"You bet your ass I see them. I wonder how many more of 'em there are and if they have any idea where the rounds came from that killed their two gunners? Quickly, move back down to where the lieutenant is!

"Dammit Shanghai, I can't send your snipers back up there; we'd be pushing our luck tryin' the same trick twice in succession. They'd probably spot your men this time; the element of surprise is gone. Then they'd call mortars or artillery down on the whole damned battalion. What are we gonna do to take them out?"

"Well Blackjack, the 60mm mortars are no good because of that overhanging ledge. Rifle or machine-gun fire may kill the ones we can see but we don't know how many others are back there. Either way, we'll still have the machine gun to contend with. We need to try and use a couple of those new bazookas. I know they aren't very accurate but if we do get a hit that would finish off the machine gun anyhow."

"Dammit Shanghai, I want that machine gun. It will add a lot of firepower to the platoon. I've seen loose ammunition we could use lying all over the island."

"Yeah? Well I hope you're gonna carry it then 'cause I sure as hell don't plan to."

The lieutenant intervened by telling his platoon sergeant to get a rocket launcher team up to the firing point. He was on the 536 radio to the 1st platoon requesting that they send their bazooka man and his assistant over immediately.

"Sergeant, I want both bazookas up there side by side and flank them with two BARmen. Have the bazookas aim and fire as many times as it takes to knock that machine gun out. Each time the assistant gunners are reloading, have the BAR's open up. That'll keep the Japs' heads down and preclude them returning fire accurately. The range is less than 200 yards. With a little luck, those rocket launchers will take them out. I just hope the men have enough ammunition."

It took four rounds before the first rocket hit its mark. There were three additional Japanese bodies beside the badly damaged machine gun. The platoon sergeant was pleased as he considered that this new lieutenant might turn out to be all right after all. That is if he lasted long enough. Machine-gun fire was striking the Japanese position from the right flank. It was Easy Company; they were on the line and firing. They had gotten quietly into position without taking a casualty.

Word was passed that everyone was tied in on the line and they might as well prepare to go ahead and dig in for the night. They still had a couple of hours before dark and it would be a welcome break to dig in early. The men were told to get as much rest as they could as the terrain ahead was rough, rocky and all uphill. The next day would be a challenge but then, so far, every day had been a challenge.

Deadly Dave said, "I don't like digging in here. We're going to be vulnerable as hell. This is no place for a line of foxholes and we haven't even done a reconnaissance down to our front so we know what we are facing."

"Aw, quit your bitching Dave. We've still got a while before dark. Go ahead and look around if it makes you feel any better. One hole in the ground is just about the same as another."

Dave shook his head, "Y'know Chic, if I was a Nip and I wanted to take out a few Marines tonight, I'd use that draw in front of us as the perfect avenue of approach."

The draw provided excellent concealment; it was covered

with scrub bushes and small tropical trees.

Deadly Dave speculated aloud, "A column of enemy troops comin' from that area right across from us where we knocked out the machine gun position this afternoon could move down through that draw without bein' seen. They could follow it around to our front, then move straight up and pull a frontal assault on us after dark. They'd only have to cover about 40 feet after leaving the draw. We wouldn't even know they were there until they were attacking. If we knew what we were doin', we would surprise them by gettin' a concertina of barbed wire and stringin' it across our front just after dark so the little bastards would get hung up on it when they try to attack."

Chic asked, "Dave, what makes you think the Nips are smart enough to find us then do somethin' like that?"

"Easy, we shot two of their men from here, then we killed three more with the bazookas when we got their machine gun. It wouldn't take a genius to figure out that this is where we had to be firing from, it's the only logical place. They'll either deduce that we fell back or we're still here. We couldn't have advanced without them knowing it. They've probably been watchin' us dig in and are just waitin' for it to get good'n dark so they can attack."

Blackjack sounded disturbed, "Donahoe! What the hell are you and Yancey doin' digging in together? We've got two replacements by themselves over there next to Stahoviak and Mac. I want an experienced man with every one of the new men. Get your ass outa' there and send that new private, Pete something-or-other, over here to dig in with Chic. I knew you guys would be up to somethin' if I didn't keep an eye on you."

Donahoe asked, "How about getting' us some concertina wire so we can string it across the company front Sergeant?"

"Forget it Donahoe that stuff's too heavy and clumsy to carry up from battalion. We'll use it when we are in the defense. Right now, we'll be movin' forward first thing in the mornin'. If they'd wanted us to have barbed wire, they'd have sent it up to us. Now get the hell over there and dig in with that replacement."

Chic hated to lose Deadly Dave. He always felt comfortable with a BAR close by. The new man looked just like what he was; young, inexperienced and scared. Chic looked at him and said, "Okay Pete, here's the situation: There are no friendly troops out to our front so you can fire anywhere forward of where we are if you detect anything out there. That rocky ledge where they got the Nip machine gun shouldn't be a problem; the range is too far for effective night small-arms fire. The visibility will soon be reduced so we can't even see the ledge. They can't see us from over there and we can't see them. The clouds are closing in already and it will be raining soon so you can expect a really dark night. Battalion will put up plenty of flares for us if we need them.

"What I want you to watch out for is anyone moving through that draw down in front of us. It's covered with bushes and trees and could provide good concealment for an enemy tryin' to move in close to us before attacking. If it was gonna' be dry, we could hear them but if the rain continues it will be real hard to distinguish one sound from another. The sound of the rain covers other noises so you'll have to keep your eyes peeled for any movement. Have you got any questions?"

Pete hesitated for a moment then asked, "Chic, you don't really think the Japs are gonna try and attack us tonight do you?"

Chic answered, "Pete, that's what the Japs are supposed to do. If they think they can attack us and kill a few Marines, you can bet that's what they are gonna do. Our job is to be alert and kill them before they can get us. Now if you have any questions or if anything happens when you're on watch, wake me up. I'll take the first watch so you hunker down now and try to get some sleep. You may as well pull your poncho over you now 'cause the rain will be falling soon."

The tropical sun slowly immersed itself in the western sea as the darkness of the eastern horizon advanced steadily. The darkness soon conquered the cloud filled sky. The paleness of the moon rendered it somewhat insignificant for illumination and the heavy rain clouds completely obscured it intermittently throughout the night.

Chic quietly asked, "Hey Pete, do you hear somethin' out there?"

Pete replied, "I don't know. I don't think so but I really can't be sure. There were some faint sounds but it's probably just a couple of those damned jungle rats or some other little animals foolin' around."

There was concern in Chic's voice, "Like hell it is. It's gotta be Nips and they're comin' right for us. Better lock and load old buddy and don't forget what the gunny always says about closely aimed rifle fire."

POW, POW, POW! Pete was firing too fast. He was just a young replacement and he was scared. POW, POW POW! After the eighth round, the empty clip automatically ejected, "Pinnnng!" My God, he's fired off a whole clip of eight rounds already.

Chic asked, "Hey Pete, what ever happened to fire discipline? You've wasted a clip of ammo and told the enemy exactly where we are. Now, watch me and do exactly as I do and never fire two rounds when one will do. Be sure you can see what you are shootin' at. Dammit Pete, are you listenin' to me?"

Pete was not listening. At the age of 18 and with only two days in the company, Pete the replacement was dead.

Crouching in his foxhole with the body of a dead replacement, whose last name he didn't even know, the totality of the darkness and the discomfort from the drizzling rain spooked Chic. Would daylight ever arrive? There was a slight rustling sound to his front; he strained his eyes, ears and employed every instinct he had to determine exactly what and where it was. He tried to move the dead Marine's body out of his way but found it too heavy and awkward to move silently and his own mobility was so restricted in the narrow hole that he had to leave the body in place.

Again, rustling sounds to his immediate front. Why the hell weren't the men on his right and left firing? They probably wondered the same thing about him. He was kneeling on both knees now and leaning forward with his elbows on the dead Marine's back, using it like a sandbag. With his cheek against the rifle, he tried to get a sight picture. It was too dark for that. He would have to fire into the darkness purely by instinct. His safety was off and his finger was on the trigger, taking up the slack. Trembling with fear, Chic knew he must control the trembling and took in a deep breath. Wondering if it did any good, he inhaled again and slowly let the air out of his lungs. The fear certainly hadn't gone away but the trembling seemed to have subsided just a little.

He was about to kill a man he couldn't even see. A Jap who just kept coming closer and closer in the darkness. Patience, he must have patience. If he fired too soon, he'd miss for sure. He had to wait for the bastard to get really close so he could sense exactly where he was and hit him with the first round. He tried breathing deeply again and thought it helped a little. A faint light from a distant illumination flare revealed a dark object directly in front of him. Nothing had been there before! His finger slowly continued to squeeze and he was torn between exhilaration and cold, stark, fear. Suddenly, he saw flashes and felt the impact of a bullet and then another as they slammed into Pete's body under him.

Mother of Jesus, those rounds had to be meant for me!

If God had meant for him to survive why was he constantly being tested this way? His finger continued to squeeze. Blaam!!! He hadn't realized how loud an M-1 rifle could be. He had hit his target, he knew he had hit him - he couldn't have missed at such a short range yet, there were still scraping sounds and movement to his front. Out of the darkness of the night came the low-throated barking of a BAR over on his right. Donahoe! Good old Donahoe and his BAR! What a wonderful sound. Ross and Muldoon on the left joined in, then McLaughlin and others on the right opened fire. What had they been waiting for? Why hadn't they opened up sooner? Thank God they were firing now.

The dawn's early light revealed seven Japanese bodies scattered in front of their holes. One, armed with a pistol, was within a few feet of Chic's hole. So, that was it. Chic had known that no one armed with a bolt-action rifle like the Japs carried could have fired two rounds into Pete's body in such rapid succession. It had been an automatic pistol.

Chic planned on keeping the pistol as a souvenir as it had come so close to taking his life but when he heard that Deadly Dave Donahoe wanted it, he gladly gave it to him. Donahoe and his BAR had very likely saved Chic's life on more than one occasion.

Chic somberly emptied Pete's pockets and placed the contents in the dead Marine's haversack. It was only then that he learned that Pete had a last name, Andressen. He turned Pete's rifle and cartridge belt over to Sergeant Childs, the platoon guide, and took the haversack with Pete's personal effects to the new lieutenant. It was the lieutenant who had the responsibility of writing to Pete's next of kin. Chic was glad he was a Pfc and not a lieutenant.

Deadly Dave and Lucky helped Chic wrap Pete's body in his poncho and placed it on a stretcher. The three Marines sat down on the edge of Chic's foxhole. Lucky gestured toward the ledge where the machine gun had been knocked out and said, "You know; the Japs wouldn't have just put a heavy machine gun in that position for the hell of it. It had to be an outpost of one of their units. They may have a large defense up there in all that scrub brush and rocky terrain where we won't be able to see them until we are nearly on top of them. These seven dead Nips could have been a reconnaissance patrol trying to determine our strength and position. Those slopes look like a hell of a good area to defend and I sure don't look forward to trying to take 'em."

The company gunnery sergeant moved rapidly down the line passing the word.

"Prepare to move out. Get your gear together and man your loads. The 'Old Man' just got the word from battalion. He says we're going to be moving forward soon!"

Deadly Dave wasn't so sure about it as he said, "Jesus, we've gotta go down into that gorge and then climb up the other side. Its damned near a cliff it's so steep and it's probably riddled with caves. We're gonna have one hell of a time getting' up there. I wonder whose bright idea this was anyway."

Deadly Dave's eyes were glued to the area out to their front as he said, "I know you guys are going to think I'm cracking up or something but I really think I'm seeing something out there. Look over there where I'm pointing, about two hundred yards to our front. Do you guys see any strange movement?"

A runner and a lieutenant from battalion headquarters arrived with an important message for the skipper. The word was immediately passed for the men to get down and stay down until they were told to move forward. Large numbers of Japanese soldiers had been spotted moving toward us from the rugged slopes to our front. Deadly Dave had seen something out there.

The men lay in their holes prepared to move forward with one eye on the enemy's forward slope to the front and one eye on the sky as they waited for the promised close air support to appear.

Lieutenant Swift had his ANGR-9, usually called the Angry 9, radio to talk to the Corsair pilots. Some of our Marines were again assigned to crank the generator to give him power when directing the planes. As the Marines looked to their front it seemed almost as though a human wave was slowly rolling down the slope toward them. Lieutenant Swift called in the planes that had been circling overhead and the four of them peeled off one after the other firing their machine guns and significantly reducing the enemy force. In the opinion of the infantry Marines, these flyers were magnificent.

The word was soon passed "Move out!" and the Marines surged forward. The Corsairs had done a great job but there were still many Japanese alive who were able to fight.

The battalion moved forward and upward and the terrain became increasingly difficult as the elevation increased. Caves were a serious threat. Some were empty; some a haven for civilian refugees and others were heavily defended by dedicated Japanese soldiers. A defended cave could play havoc with the advance of a company of Marines and had to be neutralized. Ross and Muldoon were crouching behind the stump of a shattered tree beside platoon sergeant Black. Muldoon turned to Blackjack and in an exasperated tone asked,

"Sergeant, why the hell can't we get a flamethrower up here?"

Blackjack answered, "Cause there ain't any flamethrowers available to us right now, that's why. If we have to wait here until we can get a flamethrower we'll lose valuable time and maybe a few Marines. It could take a couple of hours and we can't spare that kind of time. We'll just have to take that damned cave out by ourselves and keep movin'."

Stripped of his pack and helmet and with a full cartridge belt as his only encumbrance, except for his M-1 rifle, Private Ross scampered gingerly up the steep rocky incline moving like a monkey.

Muldoon proudly exclaimed, "Lookit that little sonofabitch go! That man's got balls of steel."

When he had reached the height of the cave opening Ross slowed to a cautious crawl and started moving to his left. His M-1 rifle had been slung diagonally across his back to free both of his hands. In trying to unsling his rifle while balanced on a narrow ledge, he lost his footing and slid downward six or eight feet. He crawled back up until he was again beside the cave opening. Finding a narrow foothold he chambered a round then turned so he could point his muzzle into the cave opening and leaning back for protection he fired emptying a clip of eight rounds. He pulled his rifle back, reached into his cartridge belt for another clip, inserted it and this time took a step closer to the cave opening while firing into it. He emptied the second eight-round clip into the cave but 10 rounds were heard. This time the Japs were firing back!

Ross' body slid down a few feet below the cave opening and stopped. His rifle clattered as it slid and bounced all the way down.

Shanghai Pooley shouted, "Cover me! I'm gonna go up and get that kid! Has anyone got any grenades left?"

Muldoon answered his squad leader, "I haven't got any more frags left, Shanghai, but here's a "Willie Peter" that oughta get their attention. Wait a minute dammit! He's my buddy; I'll get the little bastard down myself. Gimmie back that grenade."

Muldoon was moving up as Ross had done minutes before but with much less agility. He stumbled once or twice and slid back some but he was going to get up to Ross no matter what it took. Muldoon found the same ledge Ross had been standing on when he was hit but Muldoon had an advantage, he was armed with a white phosphorous grenade. He bent the metal spoon up so it would fly free as soon as the pin was pulled, he didn't want the enemy throwing the grenade back at him, then he pulled the pin and cautiously lobbed the grenade into the cave's opening.

Billowing white clouds tumbled from the cave's opening as Private Muldoon cautiously inched his way down toward Ross' body. He could see fresh bloodstains on the left chest and shoulder of Ross' dungaree shirt. Muldoon slung his rifle and reached for Ross when he was startled to hear Ross' voice:

"Muldoon, you sonofabitch, what are you doin' up here?"

Startled but relieved, Muldoon answered, "I came up to retrieve your body but since you ain't dead I guess I can go back down."

"No dammit! I need help, the little bastards shot me. Help me to get back down." Ross was pleading.

"What's it worth to you?" Muldoon slyly asked.

"What do you mean what's it worth to me? Muldoon, as soon as I recover I'm gonna kick your ass right up between your shoulder blades. Now if you won't help me, get the hell outa here and tell someone else from the platoon to come up and get me before I bleed to death."

Leslie Muldoon looked at the man who had been closer to him than either of his natural brothers and winced at the blood saturating his chest and shoulder. He took Ross' right arm and put it around his neck and wondered how he would get him down without falling or sliding just as Weasel and Eddie O'Neill arrived to help. Ross was evacuated, the cave neutralized and the company moved on toward its next objective.

The company halted and the men moved off the narrow trail and blended into the tropical vegetation. They were out of sight of the enemy and for a change they were not under fire. At least not for the time being. Canteens were eagerly broken out and their precious contents savored sparingly. Water was never in plentiful supply. Most of the men sat on their helmets or stretched out on the ground hoping the halt would last for at least a few minutes. Weasel couldn't get over the superb performance of the Corsairs. He moved over by Fearless, sat down on his helmet and asked: "Fearless, how do you suppose we could go about gettin' ourselves transferred into aviation?"

"Gosh Weasel, I don't know but there must be a way. I guess we'll have to wait until we're out of combat. Then we can go to the first sergeant and ask him to write us a letter. The Skipper could sign it with an endorsement sayin' what good Marines we are and that we'd be a real asset to some aviation squadron."

"Aw hell Fearless, we could never get the Skipper to lie like that and you know it."

"Yeah I guess you're right Weasel but he might sign it just to get rid of us. Let's go see Chief and ask him how we could pull it off. He really knows a lot of things about how the Marine Corps works." Fearless answered.

"He should dammit, he's Old Corps. You know he's got three hashmarks," observed the weasel.

Chief looked surprised as he asked, "What's all this talk about you guys wanting to get into aviation? You're already in the best outfit there is. Don't you know that the infantry is considered the Queen of Battle?"

Fearless answered, "The Queen of Battle, my ass! The way this outfit has been gettin' screwed lately, I'd say we're more like the whores of battle."

Pharmacist Mate 3/c Drinkwine walked down the column and stopped beside Private Muldoon. Removing his helmet he put it on the ground and like many of the Marines sat down on it.

"Well I guess your phony buddy back at the aid station is playing his "wound" for all it's worth."

"What!? What the hell are you talking about you damn chancre mechanic? Ross was hit and hit hard, remember, I was the first one to get to him. I saw the blood all over his chest and shoulder myself. You know, I'm beginning to think old Fearless Frank Quinlan knows what he's talkin' about when it comes to you corpsmen."

Doc answered, "Fearless Frank's an idiot. Just wait until he needs a corpsman sometime. Yeah, your buddy Ross bled a little but it wasn't a serious wound. Remember that I'm the one who treated him. If it had been a direct hit, it may have killed him but I think a ricochet or a fragment of coral must have hit him. It just broke the skin and caused a lump and a little bleeding but it didn't penetrate very deep or do any real damage. The battalion medical officer is not going to tolerate that guy hanging around sickbay for more than a day or two, they need the space for other patients. He'll probably have a sore chest for a few days but he can still squeeze a trigger. Ross will be back soon, you'll see."

"Listen swabbie, Ross is a good Marine and if he was here

right now he would get up and knock you flat on your ass. I'd do it myself but I'm just too damned tired to get up and swing at you. I'll get you when I feel better, you can bet on that!"

The corpsman noticed that Muldoon's eyes were glazed and he was very flushed. His speech wasn't quite right, as he seemed to be almost slurring his words. He was nearly delirious.

"Here loudmouth, open up and stick this under your tongue. Maybe it'll keep you quiet for a while."

Muldoon dutifully allowed the corpsman to place a thermometer under his tongue.

"You been takin' your Atabrine tablets like you're supposed to?"

"Hell yes, can't you tell by lookin' at me? I'm all yellow from the damned stuff."

"How do you feel?"

"What the hell do you mean, how do I feel? I just told you that I'm too damned tired to take a swing at you. I'm weak as a kitten and my bones ache. Now get the hell outa here and let me rest awhile."

"How'd you like to see your phony buddy Ross?" the doc asked.

"Dammit Doc, don't call him a phony! What do you mean, how would I like to see him?"

"Well, he's just got a little scratch on his chest; you are a lot sicker than he is. I'm gonna get you sent back to battalion. You've got dengue fever."

The platoon sergeant, still acting as platoon leader, approached with the company executive officer. They had something to say.

"Okay men, listen up. We're going to be here for a few more minutes so if any of you want to break out a ration or smoke another cigarette, do it now while we're giving you the scoop. When we get the word to move out, we're going to be moving to the northeast, through those foothills. There's some pretty rough terrain up there and we're going to be moving uphill all the way. You men know what you're supposed to do. Just be certain you maintain an interval of at least six yards and don't close up, no matter what. Our ultimate objective is gonna be Mount Tapotchau but we won't be able to get up there for a few days. We've got to take those foothills first."

The troops watched as Doc Drinkwine assisted a shaky Private Muldoon in walking back through the column and they wondered just what dengue fever was. Before leaving the Mariana Islands, they would all know and they would wish they had never heard of it. Muldoon was first, but most of them would eventually become its victims.

* * * * * * * * * *

The World on Fire

21 June 1944

On the 21st of June there was increased enemy activity to the front. The Japs were sending out patrols with the intention of infiltrating our lines. One of their most effective tactics was to get small groups to infiltrate behind us and wait until after dark then attack our rear with small-arms fire and grenades. This could cause serious problems when the Marines shifted their positions and returned the enemy fire. It would leave our original front exposed or only partially covered. The enemies' main attack against our original front would then present a major challenge and, at times, would take us by surprise. This had worked for them during the first few days of fighting on Saipan but the Marines were now "street smart" as to the ways of the wily Nips. Only a few succeeded in infiltrating after the first couple of days but many died attempting it.

The day was spent probing the enemy area to our front with patrols and ferreting out their infiltrators and snipers to our rear. Our lines remained in place and did not advance on this date.

Privates Ross and Muldoon had gone on patrol in the morning to scout the area in front of their position and to eliminate Japanese snipers. They had the misfortune to help carry one of their wounded buddies back to the company area. Pfc Mike O'Leary had located a Jap sniper but the Jap was a better shot. Ross and Muldoon agreed that O'Leary was a good guy but they both wished that he had been a few pounds lighter.

The afternoon found them back at their positions or more accurately, back where their positions had been. An artillery round had completely destroyed Ross and Muldoon's foxhole while they had been out on patrol. Digging their new foxhole was vastly easier after having the ground softened up by the enemy shell. The Saipan sun was hot and Ross and Muldoon were tired after the morning patrol and especially after helping to carry O'Leary back. When they finished re-digging their foxhole they both laid down to take a break. Within minutes the squad leader detailed the pair to a carrying party and off they went to the battalion CP to carry water, rations and ammunition.

Back at their position, the weary men crawled into their hole and waited eagerly for nightfall, they craved sleep. In an adjacent foxhole, Fearless Frank and Wetzel the Weasel continued to fantasize about what a wonderful and safe life they could have had if only they had been in the air wing. They were determined to apply for transfers to aviation duty as soon as it could be arranged.

No one in Fox Company doubted that sleep would come easily on this night of 21 June 1944, they were all exhausted. Shortly after nightfall a new turn of events made them forget about sleep. They started to wonder if any of them would live long enough to ever see daylight again. A Japanese patrol had managed to gain access to the huge American ammunition and fuel dump, which had been established from Green Beach Two to the Charan Kanoa airstrip. The Nips were successful in blowing it, and themselves, up.

Stash, always one to look for humor at odd times, jokingly yelled "Fire in the Hole!" He became suddenly silent as the smile on his face was first frozen, and then completely vanished. His eyes opened wide and seemed to get round and large as he felt a strong wave of unusually hot air and the ground under him started to tremble and shake.

Corporal Jerden said. "Omigod, the chaplain was right. The Navy must have unloaded all the ammunition and explosives in the Pacific. I've never seen an explosion anywhere near as big as this!"

Sergeant Childs speculated, "That's because there's never been one as big as this. The whole damned island is blowing apart!"

Corporal Jerden had not been too certain about the chaplain's description of the ammo and fuel dump. He thought the Father might have exaggerated its size a bit to ease the men's concerns about the departure of the fleet. Jerden's eyes widened in disbelief as his eardrums were violently assailed and he realized the chaplain had been very conservative in his description. There could never have been such a huge explosion anywhere, ever before. Jerden would never again doubt the word of a priest.

Explosions rocked the island with an incredible fury and the pitch black of the night became a brilliant white. The blinding light of the multiple explosions turned the darkness into daylight. Heavy 55-gallon steel drums of aviation gas tumbled through the air as though they were weightless while others continued exploding with a terrifying frequency throughout the night.

A searing blast of heat scorched Chic as thousands of pounds of explosives ignited and went up in a giant fireball that rose high above the island. Chic lay motionless for a few moments attempting to gather his wits. His head hurt and hurt badly. Something had struck his helmet a terrible blow and caused him to have difficulty focusing his eyes.

Misery loves company and he quickly decided that he was miserable enough to need plenty of company. He knew he could not stay where he was. Dazed, but protected by the hole, he stayed where he had fallen only long enough to put a fresh clip of ammunition into the chamber of his rifle, then he bounded from the hole and promptly tripped over some debris. Glancing back he saw what his nose was already telling him it was what was left of a decomposing human corpse. Shakily getting back on his feet again and sickened by the stench emitted by the body being disturbed, he continued moving through the brilliant light.

Stumbling forward for a few more steps he was down again and still dazed. He was overwhelmed with the hopelessness of his situation. His principal means of protection, his rifle, the rifle that he prized so highly was of no value against the massive explosions that threatened to blow the whole island apart. Yet he could not relax his firm grip on the rifle. Useless or not, he was a Marine and it was a part of him.

Afraid to stand up, only to be blown off his feet again, he crawled rapidly toward where he knew two of his squad mates were dug in. Joining Big Ski and Little Ski in their hole, he immediately noticed that Big Ski was not himself. He was crying like a baby and trembling. Big Ski was scared, really scared and this was no act! Chic had seen Big Ski do some very brave things in the face of near certain death and yet here he was, reduced to the mentality of a scared three-year-old.

The island was rocked with violent explosions of every description. Ammunition and bombs that had been destined for Marine artillery and aircraft detonated with a force that rocked the island time after time. There were explosions of every size and type as steel shell fragments slammed loudly into the sides of tanks and amtracs. Little Ski mumbled,

"This has got to be what hell is like."

Chic and Little Ski looked at one another wondering what they could do for the trembling Big Ski as Little Ski exclaimed,

"If we should live through this, I hope I never have to hear the "National Anthem" again."

"Why's that Ski?"

"'Cause when they come to that part about, "The Rocket's Red Glare, the Bombs Bursting in Air," I'm gonna think about tonight and start shakin' and tremblin' that's why!"

"Yeah Ski, I guess we're getting a preview of coming attractions. When we die and go to hell, they won't even have to show us around. We will have already been there!"

"Hey Mac, ya got a light?" The trembling Big Ski was regaining his composure and sounded almost normal. There was a look of shock and disbelief on Little Ski's face as he replied,

"You dumb sonofabitch! The whole worlds on fire an' you want a match?"

Haltingly, Big Ski mumbled, "What happened? How did all of this get started?"

Little Ski's immediate reply was, "The Old Man thinks some Samurai sonofabitch must've gotten into the ammo dump with a flamethrower or somethin'."

Big Ski ended the conversation with, "Jesus, what a mess!"

The clouds overhead reflected vivid shades of pink, orange and a strange blue-white with constant flashes that resembled lightening. Looking beyond the bright clouds one could occasionally glimpse a bit of the actual sky off in the vast distance. It was still black. What a strange feeling, knowing that the night skies were still black. At least something had remained the same while the world was trying to blow itself apart.

The explosions continued well into 22 June as expended bits of steel plummeted earthward from time to time, whirring toward the ground with sickening thuds. There were ungodly whirring and swishing sounds as shards of steel and white-hot shell fragments sped mercilessly overhead. Shanghai Pooley assured the men of his squad that the war would not be postponed because the ammo dump had been blown up. The company gunnery sergeant made a good argument for carefully aimed rifle fire as he passed the word to all hands that if they were to run out of ammo because of the loss of the dump, they would fight with bayonets, K-Bars, or their bare hands.

The corps commander, General H.M. "Howlin' Mad" Smith had declared that we would commence a new all-out offensive on the 22nd. So that's why we hadn't advanced the previous day! The general probably believed he was giving us a break. He must've thought we'd be resting up for the big new offensive. Resting hell! We were exhausted and no one, American, Japanese or Chamorro had had any sleep. The Marines had to forget about their sleepiness and fatigue and the noise and spent pyrotechnics and the flying bits of steel. It was time to move out.

* * * * * * * * * *

Conquest of Tapotchau

22 -26 - June 1944

At 0600 on 22 June the Americans started "Howlin' Mad's" major offensive. Both Marine divisions were in the attack. The 2nd was on the left and the 4th on the right. They spent most of the day moving to the north and made excellent progress until reaching the lower slopes of Mount Tapotchau. Rugged terrain impeded their further advance and the 8th Marines had to bivouac for the night along the base of the mountain. When the offensive resumed, Army units from the 27th Division were committed to the center of the drive between the Marine divisions. Only light resistance was encountered at first but the attack never gained the expected momentum because of the brutally rough terrain.

The thickly growing tagnan-tagnan, and in some places rocks and gravel, and the sharply rising slopes proved brutal. The few existing trails were viewed with considerable suspicion as they may be mined, booby-trapped or covered by enemy fire. The gain of a few yards forward frequently was delayed by a sheer drop into a crevasse of several feet or some other nearly impassable obstacle that must be conquered. When the time came to stop for the night, the company was on an upward slope and in an untenable defensive position.

The company commander was far from satisfied with the position his company occupied. He knew his orders had directed that they advance as far as possible before stopping for the night, but his men were in an indefensible position. He requested permission to withdraw back off of the rough tree-covered hill so he could realign his forward elements for a night defense. The sun's descent into the west was accelerating. He wanted to hold back the darkness. Why didn't battalion answer? Surely they could see it was getting dark. In anticipation of the captain's request, the field music, Netherland, was again trying to raise battalion on the SCR-300 radio. Battalion's reply was not encouraging. The captain was told to wait until the Bn-6 could be informed of the request and his answer returned.

The Skipper advised each of his platoon leaders to stand-by in their present positions until permission could be obtained for them to fall back off of the wooded hill and dig in. They stood-by anticipating that at any moment the word would be passed to move back down. None prepared defensive fighting holes where they were. The afternoon sun was rapidly vanishing in the west and the eastern sky was ominously darkening. To hell with battalion! The captain was concerned for his men and had to make a decision. The enemy occupied the high ground and probably was established in several good defensive positions including caves to their front. He had to get his men out of there.

Before he could order the company to fall back to a proper defensive position, Netherland who had been jabbering on the radio to someone at battalion, interrupted him. He asked that they repeat the message for his commanding officer then he gave the handset to the skipper with a discouraging look.

One glance at his field music and the captain knew that he didn't want to hear what he was about to be told. The word from battalion was to wait until after dark, then pull the men surreptitiously back to defensive positions. The battalion commander did not want the men moving back down while it was light enough for the enemy to see them. Mission impossible, but orders are orders. After darkness, the word was passed for the men to start moving back down a few at a time.

When the Japanese opened fire, it was just as though a command had been given for a whole battalion to open up at the same instant. There seemed to be soldiers firing from behind every rock and tree on the upper heights of the wooded hillside.

The Marines kept firing and falling back in the darkness. Someone had the presence of mind to call for illumination and soon the world changed from near total blackness to various shades of black and white. The burning flares descended casting their eerie shadows as Japanese and American bodies moving downward through the rocks and brush were nearly indistinguishable from one another.

Some of the Japanese managed to infiltrate down into the Marine lines in the darkness and confusion. In the hand to hand fighting with rifle butts, bayonets, and ka-bar knives that ensued, many were slain. As were some Marines. The Americans could never understand the Japanese zeal not only to fight but the apparent eagerness with which many of them sacrificed their own lives. In an act of suicidal madness, some of the Japanese who were not killed by the Marines blew themselves apart with their own hand grenades.

By now, some Marines had stopped, turned to face the enemy and attempted to scratch out fighting holes in the ground for protection and from where they intended to keep fighting the Japs. To continue moving downward in the light of the flares was nearly suicidal. It is not the way of Marines to turn their backs on an enemy.

Ammunition was getting low. There was no means of re-supply and every round had to count. Flares came less frequently and there were fewer men moving down the rugged hillside in the darkness. What had been incessant rifle and machine gun fire was now only sporadic. An occasional blood-curdling scream on the wooded hill was an indication that a soldier of Nippon had suddenly and fatally encountered American steel.

Ammunition had gotten so low by this time that McLaughlin had to borrow a few cartridges from the Weasel. Mac inserted a clip in his M-1 rifle and started crawling back toward his own position as the moon started to gradually slip out from behind its cloud cover and provided a slight amount of light. Looking up, Mac was horrified to see something looming before him. As the light increased he recognized it as the shadowy form of a Jap soldier. Weasel's extra cartridges saved Mac's life - the Jap lost his.

There was no way to evacuate the wounded in the darkness, especially in such impossible terrain while under fire, so they had to lie up there with the dead. A Jap counterattack was expected at any time and the wounded men who could still fire their rifles were expected to do so. Chic Yancey was crawling forward to assist Mac McKeown, a badly wounded comrade, when he heard the whirring of bullets close overhead. He dropped back to the ground and lay there immobile while the bullets hummed dangerously close. When the fire let up, he squirmed around enough to see that McKeown had been hit again and was deathly still. He was probably dead.

Chic's movement caught the eye of the Jap machine gunner, who opened up as Chic froze.

He was in an exposed position and the only thing he could do was lie there as if dead and pray inwardly. He knew what it would mean to attempt crawling back down toward friendly lines — death at the hands of his own buddies, should the machine-gunner miss him. He didn't dare to move. Lord how long that night was! Somehow, for some reason known only to God, he was spared again.

Through that long night of terror he lay under the eyes of that watchful machine gunner aching with the pain that comes from long periods of total immobility. Hardly breathing for fear of being detected, he prayed all night long. He said every prayer he could remember and then he made up a few new ones. He did more than just pray that night; he learned to really pray—not just mouth the words—but to pray with his whole being.

The small-arms fire of the rifles and machine-guns had been bad enough but now the Japs had started using mortars. Chic had been motionless hardly willing to breathe for fear the Jap machine gunner would realize he was still alive and put a few rounds into him. Now the scenario had changed. With the mortar fire falling all around him, he had to move off of the bare ground and get into defilade. The machine gun was suddenly of secondary importance.

The explosion of a Jap mortar shell arrived with such a jolt that it lifted him off the ground. It was close up and personal. He was terrified for a second, and then his mind started to function again. A drifting flare overhead revealed a depression in the ground which was probably a large shell hole and he dove for it. Sure enough, the Jap machine gunner was still on the job. He fired a couple of bursts, which struck the ground close to where Chic had been.

The Butcher spotted the hole Chic was in and was crawling toward it from the other direction. The big corpsman was dragging a wounded Marine. Chic had to forget his fears and fire at that machine gunner before he spotted Butcher and his patient. He couldn't see the gunner but he knew about where he was and fired each round with a prayer that it hit its mark. Pulling his patient into the crater, Butcher started working his medical magic as other mortar shells burst around them.

The wounded Marine had a rifle-grenade launcher, which would be of no further use to him. Thank heaven; Chic Yancey still had a couple of grenades left. He grabbed the rifle, found the needed crimped grenade ammo in the Marine's cartridge belt and affixed his fragmentation grenade to the launcher device. Carefully aiming and firing in the direction of the machine gun position he knew his chances of eliminating the machine-gun had increased dramatically. All he needed to do was to get close with that grenade.

Butcher stuck a bayonet affixed to an M-1 rifle into the ground and taped a container of blood plasma to the stock. The precious fluid flowed down through a tube into the Marine's arm. Butcher then stuck a syrette of morphine into his patient's right arm and dutifully painted an "M" on his forehead with iodine. It was only then that Chic realized something was wrong with Doc Butcher. He had winced a few times and looked like he was hurting. He finally asked if Chic would give him a hand with something.

Then he removed his dungaree shirt and revealed a thin gash about four inches long that had been made across his back by a fragment from one of the grenades or mortar rounds. The slice wasn't deep but it had broken the skin and was bleeding and probably burned like hell. Doc handed Chic a gauze pad impregnated with alcohol and asked him to swab it clean then apply sulfur powder and put a piece of gauze over it and cover it with lots of adhesive tape so the dressing would stay in place. Putting his shirt back on and strapping on his war-belt, the big corpsman went back to caring for his patient. The alcohol must have burned fiercely but the Butcher hardly flinched.

The light from occasional flares and the pale moon was helpful but was often not sufficient to reveal the location of the enemy soldiers that were all around them. The waning hours of the night passed slowly with sporadic firing from both sides and Japanese mortar rounds continuing to fall. The damned Nips apparently had little regard for the lives of their own men as their mortars fell indiscriminately among friend and foe alike on those formidable slopes of the wooded foothills leading to Mount Tapotchau.

As the night wore on, the mortar fire and enemy activity slowly subsided until finally little more than an occasional moan from a wounded or dying man could be heard then finally, nothing. Silence engulfed the darkness of the killing zone.

There in the dark stillness of the jungle hillside, only a few yards from Chic's shell hole he saw a small red spot. It glowed brightly for a moment then subsided. A cigarette, it had to be someone smoking a cigarette. There it was again. Damn! A Marine would never do such a thing. He placed his hand on Butcher's shoulder and then pointed in the direction of the red glow. Butcher nodded his head and slowly, soundlessly lifted his BAR into his shoulder. Chic tapped him again and reached for his last fragmentation grenade clipped onto his cartridge belt and motioned that he was going to throw it. With an emphatic shaking of his head, Butcher signaled, no! The corpsman aimed his BAR and carefully fired a short burst. The automatic fire shattered the quiet stillness of the morning darkness. There was a light crashing sound that must have been a body striking bushes at it hit the ground.

"Doc, why didn't you want me to throw my grenade? There may be several of them out there and I could have gotten them all with a grenade."

"No way! That stupid jerk had to be alone. If he were with anyone else they would have known better than to let him smoke that cigarette. Besides, you couldn't see what you were throwing at. Your grenade could have hit one of these trees and bounced right back at us."

Daylight gave Butcher an opportunity to move forward and see what he had bagged during the night. Fearless and the Weasel cautiously moved forward with Butcher, rifles at the ready. The corpsman had shot a Jap officer less than 50 feet from his position. He was upset to find that the Japanese had stripped the body of valuables during the darkness. No Samurai sword and no pistol, his pockets had been cut and emptied and there was nothing of value on him. The little finger of his left hand was missing, freshly cut off. What in hell could that have been all about? Butcher made a mental note to talk to Shanghai and see if he could explain such a thing. He used his K-Bar knife to remove the insignia from his victim's collar.

Shanghai identified the red tab with a star and yellow borders and two yellow stripes as the insignia of a major in the Japanese Army. He further gave his opinion of what happened to the Japanese officer's little finger. It may be understandable to the Japanese but it was shocking and disgusting to Americans. Shanghai speculated, "The sonofabitch must have been on a personal reconnaissance checking out where our positions were. He should have let his men do the job. They would have known better than to smoke. Only a damned arrogant Jap officer would be dumb enough to be smoking a cigarette on a dark night while observing the enemy at close range."

Doc speculated, "Yeah, arrogant or very nervous or maybe just plain stupid. He may have been all three."

After treating their wounded and locating and moving all the dead down to an assembly area the men concentrated on cleaning their weapons. Ammunition, water and rations were soon distributed and a unit of C-rations was wolfed down by each hungry Marine. Canteens were quickly drained and refilled. The company commander moved from platoon to platoon chatting with the men and encouraging them. He told his Marines that the terrain ahead was rough and rocky and all uphill. The day was going to be a challenge. So far, every day on the damned island had been a challenge. The anticipated order soon came as Gunny Littleton bellowed: "Prepare to move out! Get your gear on and standby. We've got a lot more of that high ground to take so it ain't gonna be easy". More cave-pocked hills and steep crevasses awaited the battle-weary Marines who had known for days that their mission would ultimately be to assault and capture Mount Tapotchau. Chic had failed to be impressed by Mount Tapotchau, he asked, "Weasel, when we were stationed in California did you and Fearless ever get up to the mountains? You know, like the High Sierras?"

"No Chic, the farthest we ever got from Camp Elliott was to Los Angeles. Fearless knew a lot of girls in L.A. and we just never thought about going anywhere else except there or to San Diego once in a while if we got weeknight liberty. Why do you ask?"

"'Cause I grew up in California that's why and I've been up to the High Sierras. They are real mountains, in fact some of them are thousands of feet high. All this talk about the great Mount Tapotchau is a lot of bunk. Compared to the mountains in the Sierra Nevada range, any puny bump on the ground the size of this 1,550-foot Mount Tapotchau wouldn't even command enough respectability to be called a hill."

The commanding voice of Platoon Sergeant Black terminated their conversation. "Okay you men, knock it off and move your butts down into that covered ravine where the lieutenant is. He wants to talk about our mission."

Chic mumbled half to himself, "Yeah, I guess he's gonna remind us again about how formidable Mount Tapotchau is. Then he'll probably tell us we've gotta go up there and take it on the double before some other outfit accidentally stumbles up there and stakes out a claim to it. Wake me up when we get to the top of the hill will ya? I'm so sleepy I don't even know how far I can walk."

No one on the island of Saipan, Japanese, Chamorro or American had slept during the fuel and ammunition dump explosions on the night of 21 June and certainly no one in Fox Company had gotten any sleep on the night of the 22nd.

The men, deprived of much sleep since D-day and totally without sleep during the past 48 hours felt numb.

The lieutenant told his men that the corps commander, General Holland M. Smith had ordered a major offensive. It had started at 0600 yesterday, 22 June while the huge ammo and fuel dump was still exploding. The 8th Marines had a major role to play in the offensive. We were going to take Mount Tapotchau. The 2nd Marine Division would be on the left and the 4th Marine Division on the right. The 8th Marines would be on the right flank of the 2nd Division. We would have to maintain contact with the left flank of the 4th Division. The regiment made excellent progress when they moved out. The two battalions up and one back moved forward at a good clip reducing what enemy positions they encountered. And then they encountered a new enemy, the slopes of Mount Tapotchau. The brutal terrain slowed down and finally completely stopped the regiment's forward movement.

The next morning when the offensive resumed, Army units

from the 27th Infantry Division were brought into the line and positioned between the 2nd and 4th Marine Divisions. Only light resistance was encountered at first but the offensive never gained the expected momentum because of the brutally rough terrain.

As they moved north the regiment made slow, tortuous but impressive progress. There was uneasiness among the men. Fighting for their lives in such a miserable environment was bad enough. Having part of the Army's 27th Division on their right to "protect" their flank was another matter. When Marines go in harm's way, they prefer to have other Marines covering their flanks. It was not long before the right flank of the 8th Marines was left exposed. The Army unit had dropped back and lost contact with the regiment. Later in the day, elements of the Army's 106th Infantry Regiment were re-located and contact was temporarily reestablished.

It had been one hell of a morning with the right flank exposed to the enemy as the Marines attacked upwards frequently crawling on all fours through the thick vegetation over nearly impassible rocks and crevices. The going was very slow and laborious. When they received enemy fire from their right flank and had to neutralize it they often sustained casualties. When this happened there were many unkind expletives hurled at the non-existent Army troops who were supposed to be tied in to the right flank.

In a brief communication to battalion headquarters, the company commander reported that the unit from the 106th Infantry that was supposed to be covering our right flank was nowhere to be found. He further reported that the 106th must have been relieved by a Japanese outfit because they were on our right flank and they were doing an excellent job of covering us. They were also killing some of us.

At 1855 in the evening, the 2nd Battalion, 25th Marines from the 4th Marine Division was temporarily attached to the 8th Marines. The mission of 2/25 was to cover the right flank of the regiment and to re-establish and maintain contact with elements of the Army's 27th Infantry Division. There had been no recent contact with them. More than a few members of the regiment breathed sighs of relief. It was good to have brother Marines covering your flanks. It didn't matter what regiment or what division they were from, they were Marines and Marines were always there when needed, they could be depended upon.

The 8th Marines pressed on with their conquest of Mount Tapotchau. The jagged, craggy landscape was choked with heavy foliage. Time and time again the brutal terrain prevented them from achieving their goal. The fanatical Japanese defenders were often less of a hindrance than the terrain.

Deadly Dave asked, "D'you guys realize what it's gonna be like from here on up, tryin' to get our dead and wounded down from this God forsaken place?"

Lucky answered, "Yeah, I didn't think it could get any worse than it has been the last few days but you're right, from here on up, it'll be damn near impossible to get anyone out."

It was indeed nearly impossible to get the dead and wounded down. This Herculean feat was accomplished through the miracle of total dedication that the Marines had for one another. Bodies, wounded and dead, were passed gently from man to man down through the tangled growth and, at times, nearly vertical mountainside. The Marines struggled slowly onward and upward.

On 25 June, the regimental commander, Colonel Clarence E. Wallace, ordered one more attack with his three battalions and the 1st Battalion, 29th Marines. The colonel wanted a final push for the summit of Tapotchau with his three battalions getting close to the summit and encircling it then 1/29 moving through them up to the top, capturing it and setting in a defensive perimeter. With 1/29 holding the summit, the other three battalions were to carefully and methodically work their way back down driving the Japs out of their caves and crevices and either capturing or killing them.

Progress had been slow all morning as the troops could only move at a crawl over the tortuous ground. The numerous crevasses and narrow ravines provided Japanese riflemen and machine gunners with excellent concealment from which to harass or ambush the climbing Marines.

When they were near the summit, the 2nd squad found and followed a narrow, partially overgrown, trail. It presented a significant challenge, as it was extremely difficult to get a decent foothold anywhere. The Marines would advance three steps upward and slide back two.

Fighting his shortness of breath, Shanghai looked back down at his men and ordered, "Okay you guys, we're almost there, the top can't be more than a few yards ahead of us, just keep following me and stay behind one another on this trail and keep climbing. Let's move out!"

Fearless Frank looked up at the Weasel, who was right above him on the trail and exclaimed, "Did you hear that Weasel? Cheer up! The top can't be more than a few more yards ahead of us. Shit-house mouse, buddy we've only been climbing this sonofabitch for five days! You know what I bet? I bet we'll have to keep on climbing it forever 'cause, mark my words, this damned overgrown cliff don't even have a top!"

The advance halted for the men to take a badly needed break to catch their breaths just as a platoon-sized patrol from the old 2nd scout company, now called the division reconnaissance company, approached from below.

A voice from the patrol asked, "Hey Shanghai, how're you doing?"

Shanghai answered, "Fair dinkum *Cobber*. What are you doin' up here?"

The voice answered, "We're supposed to see if there really is a top to this damned rock. If there is, we're to go up and see what's going on."

Shanghai replied, "It's only a few more feet Herb, wait up and we'll go with you."

Sergeant Childs, the platoon guide, crouching on the trail beside Shanghai exclaimed: "Are you crazy Shanghai? You haven't got anyone's permission to go up there!"

Shanghai gave the younger sergeant a knowing look as he explained: *"Pongyo*, sometimes it's a helluva lot easier to ask forgiveness than it is to ask permission. We'll see you later. C'mon men follow me!"

The squad and the reconnaissance Marines struggled up the nearly vertical trail that led them the 20 feet or so through the heavy undergrowth to the summit. They were on top of Mount Tapotchau by 1100. For some reason the Japanese had leveled off the pinnacle on the very top of the mountain and had created a flat area about 30 feet in diameter.

Herb asked, "How the hell do you suppose the little bastards did this?"

"They must have done the whole thing with coolie labor by hand probably with picks and shovels. There's no way they could ever have gotten any earth-moving equipment up here." Shanghai responded.

"Yeah, it must have been a hell of a job to level this place. I wonder what they intended to use it for?"

Looking around, the men saw the island below them, they noticed no sign of the enemy on the summit and at the direction of Lieutenant Drake of the Recon Platoon they started back down the narrow trail. They had gone back down but a few yards to where the rest of the men were waiting when Shanghai had his squad stop and take a break. They were huddled beside the trail just below the summit.

The reconnaissance Marines were sent back up to secure and defend the summit. It was nearly dark when a column from the 1st Battalion, 29th Marines, led by Lieutenant Drake from recon and Major R. McC. Tompkins, the battalion commander, filed slowly past on their way up to the summit. They were plodding, sliding and practically clawing their way upward when one of the Marines asked, "Hey Mac, is it much farther to the top of this damned thing?"

Lucky answered, "Not much, you're practically at the top now".

The Marine asked, "Have any of you guys been up there yet?"

Lucky responded, "Yeah, we were all up there a couple of hours ago."

"What's it like?"

"Nice view. You can see the whole island. And you guys are lucky; we didn't see any Japs up there."

The Marine from the 29th said "Thanks Mac." And continued moving upward with the file.

Stash was sitting on a rock with his helmet in his lap and scratching his head as he exclaimed, "I can't believe it, after all the time and effort it took for us to get up here; now that we've arrived the damned place is like Grand Central Station! It's a good thing we didn't see any Japs up on top. With all those guys from Recon and the 29th up there, there won't be any room left for the Japs."

The idea that there were no Japanese troops on top of the mountain was accurate but there were plenty of them hiding just below the top on the northern slopes and in the caves that dotted the northern cliffs. Shortly after dark on the night of 26 June, at a little after 1900, large numbers of Japanese infantry started crawling upward until they were poised to swarm in a human wave over the northern side of Tapotchau's summit.

The Japanese had every intention of recapturing the mountaintop, no matter what the cost. As they came over the crest, the Marines' rifle fire slammed into them. Some, who were hit but not killed, detonated hand grenades blowing themselves apart, a common practice among the Japanese but a trait the Marines found impossible to understand.

The Battle of Mount Tapotchau has not been adequately recorded in the history books but to those who participated in it from the Division reconnaissance company, the 1st Battalion, 29th Marines and the 8th Marines, it was a significant event in the Saipan Campaign. Attempting to fight their way back up the cliffs and steep slopes in the dark in a valiant effort to retake the summit was a decided disadvantage for the Japanese. An even greater disadvantage for them was the fact that U.S. Marines were occupying and defending the summit.

Marine casualties on Saipan that grim 26 June 1944 were 22 killed and 119 wounded. An awful price to pay but infinitesimal compared to the horrible Japanese losses. Forever after Mount Tapotchau remained USMC.

At 0630 the regiment moved forward along the main ridge of Tapotchau. The 1st Battalion, 29th Marines was left to occupy the spine of the ridge while the other three battalions continued moving down the slopes. The rough and rugged terrain continued to be a tremendous hindrance to downward movement, which was made even worse by enemy fire.

The 2nd Battalion went down the western slopes clearing enemy emplacements whenever possible and routing them out of their caves hidden in the crevasses and ravines. When caves could not be cleared otherwise, flamethrowers, grenades and satchel charges were employed and the caves became tombs.

Early in the afternoon, a provisional rifle company was made up from division shore party personnel. They were sent up to Mount Tapotchau and relieved the 1st Battalion, 29th Marines. The provisional rifle company, now an infantry unit, was designated as security for the division observation post. The 1st Battalion, 29th Marines continued to fight their way along the ridge of Tapotchau's spine as the three battalions of the 8th Marines were fighting their way back down the treacherous slopes.

Chic now understood that the greatness of a mountain had little to do with its height. Even a mountain goat would have had considerable trouble getting up or down the cracks and crevasses, the gullies and cliffs and the tangled jungle vegetation that made up this impossible mass of coral. The 1,550-foot mountain that had so arrogantly risen up from the ocean's depths cloaked itself in miserable, nearly impenetrable, green vegetation and was called Mount Tapotchau. There were few mountains anywhere in the world that could compare with this one. It was a bitch!

Going down was equally as difficult as climbing up. The descending Marines continued locating and capturing or killing cave-dwelling Japanese soldiers as they slid, stumbled and fought their way back down the slopes of the miserable mountain.

*　*　*　*　*　*　*　*　*　*

Caves of Death

29 June 1944

Rations were consumed, ammunition and grenades distributed and canteens filled. The men knew they would soon be on the move again toward their four new objectives. When the word was passed to move forward they encountered the usual problems of clearing mines while taking sniper fire, dispatching enemy patrols that were probing to their front and clearing caves and other enemy obstacles. The two flamethrowers assigned to the company were highly effective in neutralizing caves. When they ran out of napalm they had to fall back to be recharged.

With the flamethrowers gone, a new cave confronted them. Shanghai had taught his men to look for signs of activity around cave entrances. Dutch Shute read the tracks and saw the obvious signs. The cave was now or had recently been occupied. He knew it was his turn but still, Dutch silently cursed the situation he was now in.

The tracks leading to and from were a dead giveaway. There had been foot traffic since the last rain and it had just rained last night. WP grenades sometimes worked pretty well, but there was no substitute for a flamethrower. With a flamethrower they could incinerate the damned Japs and not have to worry about survivors. Dutch had a white phosphorous grenade and a satchel charge to use on the cave. With his rifle slung diagonally across his back to allow free use of both his hands, Dutch worked his way as close to the cave's entrance as possible. Reaching across his chest to his left belt suspender ring, he unclipped the white phosphorous grenade that had been affixed to it. Grenade in hand, he pulled the pin and reaching his right arm back, prepared to throw, and then he froze.

There was concern in Blackjack's voice as he asked no one in particular, "What the hell is Shute doin' up there?"

Shanghai responded with, "I dunno, but whatever it is, he's havin' a helluva time doin' it. It looks like he pulled the pin on his grenade and now he's tryin' to put it back in."

A very nervous Dutch Shute was fumbling with the grenade. He was obviously trying to replace the pin and he was having some difficulty. Just as Dutch had been about to toss the deadly grenade in, he had heard what was almost certainly an infant crying. There was just no way he was going to be able to throw the grenade into that cave now. The faint sounds of a baby crying continued to come from somewhere within the cave.

What was he going to do now? He couldn't kill a little child and he sure as hell didn't want to risk going into the cave just to be killed. Perspiration saturated Dutch's forehead. He was praying and cursing simultaneously as he worked furtively to push the pin back in. He breathed a sigh of relief as the stubborn pin finally went in. Remembering that during their training someone had told them that if they were trying to get Japs to come out they should holler *"Dete koi! Shimpai shinaiday"*! Or something that sounded like it. He had no alternative so he shouted the only words in Japanese he'd ever heard except for *banzai*. He prayed that his pronunciation was correct. Or at least that it would be close enough to be understood and that the Japs would comply.

Concerned that if he failed and they didn't come out, he would still have the responsibility for clearing the cave. That meant killing a baby. He didn't know if he could go through with it. Moments after he had hollered into the cave, Dutch heard a soft, trembling female voice speaking in words that were totally unintelligible to him. A small, ragged woman exited the cave stopping to bow deeply every few steps. As she approached the dumbfounded Marine, she reached out toward him and placed a small child in his arms. At a complete loss as to what he should do next, he simply turned and started walking down the hill toward the men in his squad. The poor little woman followed close behind him, still pausing to bow from time to time.

Shanghai Pooley spoke softly in Japanese to the frail woman as he unscrewed the cap from his canteen and handed it to her. She seemed reluctant to drink from the canteen until Pooley spoke a few more reassuring words. Dutch handed the sobbing baby to his sergeant and Shanghai immediately handed it back to the woman.

A startled Deadly Dave asked, "Jeezus, where'd all these people come from?"

Unnoticed by the distracted Marines, six bedraggled native Chamorro civilians approached the surprised and embarrassed squad. They had quietly filed out of the cave after the woman with the baby.

The members of the squad had known that Shanghai could read Japanese but they were genuinely surprised at the fluency with which they now heard him speaking. Dutch had other things to think about. He was sitting on a felled coconut tree with his face in his hands and hoping that no one knew how close he had come to killing that baby and these poor innocent and defenseless Chamorro people.

A runner arrived from battalion escorting some replacements and a message for the company commander. The Skipper was to assign the new replacements as he saw fit and have the runner take the prisoners back to battalion. Sergeant Pooley was to accompany them. The battalion commander wanted Shanghai to work with the Bn-2 for awhile. Interpreters were scarce and good interpreters, except for Shanghai, were nonexistent.

Sergeant Childs, the platoon guide, approached the replacements assigned to the platoon and looking at a piece of paper the runner had given him, called out their names. Each acknowledged with a clipped response of "Here." Childs assigned the first four men to squads and then as he called "Jones!" he looked up into the face of one of the biggest, meanest, most unkempt men he had ever seen wearing a Marine uniform. He asked, "Where the hell did you come from and who are you?"

The response was quick and sure, "From the Marine Detachment aboard USS *Texas* and my name's Jones. Who wants to know?"

"Sergeant G. W. Childs, U. S. Marine Corps that's who. I'm the Platoon Guide and I want to know your name so I can properly introduce you to your squad leader, Shanghai Pooley who will probably decide to send you back to where you came from after he sees you. Why didn't you shave before you came ashore? You look like a bum. Get your gear and follow me, I'll take you over to the 2nd Squad and introduce you. Shanghai is certain to find you interesting. All of the other men in the squad have been properly broken in and Shanghai has been lookin' for a new challenge."

"I don't need no breakin' in. I've got more time in the Corps than most of these other guys and probably more than you, so get off my ass," snapped Jones.

Eyes flashing, Childs asked, "When did you come into the Marine Corps wise guy?"

"In June of '39, when did you come in?" shot back Jones.

Sergeant Childs's volume dropped a bit and he gave the appearance of being slightly crestfallen as he stated: "None of your damned business. What is your rank?"

Without hesitation, Jones snapped, "Private, so I haven't got anything to lose. Where do you want me to drop my gear? I don't want to fight anybody till I take off my pack."

As they approached the squad, Childs declared, "Poncho! This guy's name is Jones, he's gonna dig in with you till Shanghai gets back and decides what to do with him. Show him the ropes and see that he knows what's going on around here. If he screws up, it's your fault. When Shanghai gets back from battalion, introduce him to this seagoin' bellhop."

Poncho Gutierrez looked up at Jones with scorn. He was not impressed by Jones' size nor was he in the habit of welcoming new men into the squad. In fact, he hardly spoke to those with whom he'd been serving for two years.

Henry "Hashmark" Jones was a heavyweight when he was in the ring and he looked as though he should still be in the ring. He was big, he was ugly and he was bad. Poncho was not intimidated, Jones was. Hashmark Jones wasn't quite sure what it was about Poncho that told him to be very cautious in his dealings with this little Mexican who had been told to "show him the ropes." He soon started to find out. Jones casually asked Poncho what the leather bag on his cartridge belt was for. Poncho's dark, steely eyes looked at Jones in a piercing manner until Jones looked back, then they seemed to bore right into him. Poncho was not accustomed to talking, but he decided to invest a few words this time to insure that he wouldn't be bothered in the future.

Poncho reached down and untied the leather thongs that fastened the bag to his belt. He opened the bag and told Jones to cup his hands together. Then he poured out the contents of the bag into Jones's hands. Jones stared at his hands and their contents in horror and disbelief. He was holding a score of human teeth, several with dried blood still on them. All of the teeth had gold fillings. Poncho held the bag open and indicated to Jones to pour the contents back into it.

"Don't ever touch my leather bag or try to take any gold teeth unless you kill the Japs they come from yourself. All the others are mine. You understand?"

"Si Compadre, comprendo," Jones responded in his best Tex-Mex accent.

Poncho was staring at the big man's face again.

"You're a gringo, how come you're speakin' Spanish?"

"I'm from Juarez; I was raised on the border. I don't speak much Mex, just a little," said Jones.

Poncho shot back with, "In this squad, we speak American, you got that?" Jones had hoped for a moment that his little knowledge of border-Spanish would help to form a bond with Poncho but he could now see it was out of the question. Poncho was a loner, he was tough and he was not looking for any friends.

"Yeah I got it," Jones declared.

Hashmark Jones wasn't a typical Marine. He always looked like he needed a shave and his dungarees fit like an old potato sack. He had an unusually gruff voice, used crude language and looked upon others with scorn. The troops changed their opinions of Hashmark after the first close-up firefight he participated in. Hashmark Jones turned out to be every bit as tough as he looked and sounded.

Glancing at the small Marine standing beside Sergeant Childs, Fearless Frank exclaimed, "Good Grief, what is that?" The last of the new replacements was being assigned to the squad. This one was unusual enough to attract the attention of all hands. He appeared to be just a boy as he stood there with his large, curious eyes looking out from under the rim of his helmet. His dungarees hung loosely on him as though they were a couple of sizes too big. Actually, it wasn't that the dungarees were so big; it was just that this Marine was so small. He had a pale, young, Irish face that radiated innocence and seemed to ask, "Why am I here and what am I supposed to do?"

Corporal Jerden asked: "What's your name boy and how old are you?"

"Private Kevin Mulcahy, Sir and I'm seventeen" (He was not a very good liar). Sergeant Childs decided that Chief, being an older, wiser Marine, would be the one to assign Mulcahy to. Chief could take Mulcahy under his wing until he could get his bearings and Shanghai decided what to do with him. Chief looked at Kevin Mulcahy and said "Kid, you look like an altar boy." The lad looked up at him and replied, "I was an altar boy but for the last couple of years, I've been singing with the choir. Are you Catholic?"

"No, I'm Pima," said Chief.

"I've never heard of Pima, what kind of a church is that?" the kid innocently asked.

"It ain't a church kid, it's a tribe. I'm a Pima Indian."

"Gosh, Sir, I've never talked to a real Indian before. I would never have known you were an Indian," declared the kid.

"I'll be damned! You're the second person I've met who doesn't know what an Indian looks like – and the other guy was an Irishman too. Your name is Mulcahy, his name was O'Malley. My God, that was over 13 years ago. He was the guy who recruited me into the Corps back in Saint Louis. He thought I was a Spaniard. O'Malley didn't know a thing about Indians. I wonder what ever happened to old Sergeant Dan O'Malley....?" mused Chief.

Chief started right off calling the youngster "Choirboy" and soon thereafter all that served with him referred to Private Kevin Mulcahy as "The Choirboy." Pure and decent and, in spite of his exposure to the Corps and to the "raggedy assed Marines" he always gave the impression of being an innocent kid. The youngest of four brothers, he had followed the other three into the service. His family assumed that Kevin would return home after the war, enter a seminary and eventually become a priest. He had always thought so too until he'd gone through Marine boot camp and then met Peggy Coughlin, after that, he wasn't quite so sure.

Corporal Jerden shouted, "Chief, send that little kid back with the ammo and water detail. We've got to put some muscles on him."

Chief responded, "Choirboy! Get your butt up to the company CP. You're goin' to a party."

"A party, Sir?" queried the choirboy.

"Yeah, a workin' party. Now git! An' don't forget your rifle. Marines don't go anywhere around here without their weapons," declared the Chief.

The Choirboy was like a little puppy dog, he followed the raggedy assed Marines around desperately wanting to be accepted as one of them. Whatever he was asked to do, he did cheerfully and quickly. Choirboy was the perfect private. He volunteered to go on every working party, and always helped others dig their foxholes or clean their weapons. He willingly shared everything he had with the others.

Hashmark Jones and Kevin Mulcahy did not seem to know each other when they joined the company, even though they had arrived with the same replacement draft. The two privates were opposites and presented quite a contrast. The worldly Jones, big and burly with his unshaven face and deep, gruff voice looked much older than his 24 years. Kevin Mulcahy was the smallest man in the company, claiming to be seventeen, he hardly looked fifteen. His soft, timid voice, childish enthusiasm and eagerness to please marked him as one of a kind. He and Hashmark Jones were both assigned to Barnsmell Nesbitt's fire team.

Barnsmell had asked to have Hashmark assigned. He needed a BARman to replace Malone who had been killed. To Hashmark being a BARman was just fine. He was bigger and stronger than most Marines and the BAR provided him a better chance to kill Japs. Being in Nesbitt's fire team also provided Hashmark with an additional benefit, it meant that he would not have to dig in with Poncho. Kevin Mulcahy was the rifleman in Nesbitt's fire team. When Jones and Mulcahy were side by side, the contrast was almost humorous. There was nearly a foot difference in their height.

As the company moved into the pockmarked hills with their proliferation of caves and crevices it was slow going. A single cave in the right location could delay a company of Marines for an unacceptable length of time.

The lieutenant voiced his displeasure, "Dammit Blackjack, that's three rifle grenades so far and not a one of them has made it into the cave opening. There's got to be a better way. We can't wait for them to get a flamethrower up here from battalion."

"Yeah Lieutenant," the platoon sergeant replied, "There's got to be a faster way to get those bastards." Pointing to a Marine crouched nearby he shouted, "Runner, get Sergeant Childs down here!" The sound of boondockers scraping on gravel was heard and the runner was off at a trot.

Blackjack could hear Childs kicking up coral stones as he half ran and half slid down to the platoon CP. The movement was enough to arouse the Japs who fired a couple more poorly aimed rounds at the fast-moving sergeant. Blackjack asked,

"Childs, your squad is closest to that damned cave, do you think you've got anyone who can get in close enough to lob in a 'Willie Peter' and then toss a satchel charge in there?"

"I dunno Blackjack. It's a bitch of an area to approach. We'd take all day trying to sneak through that jungle on the right and we sure as hell can't approach over that jagged coral rock on the left. We'd have to go right up the middle. It would be rough going and we'd be exposed the whole way," said Childs.

"Well, select a couple of 'volunteers' give them some 'Willie Peters' and Mark-II's and take this satchel charge along with you. Tell them to approach as best they can from the front and we'll try to keep the Nips busy with rifle fire directed at the entrance. Do you see that rocky protrusion just this side of the cave?" asked the lieutenant.

"Yeah sure, I see it, Sir."

The platoon sergeant spoke next, "Well *Cobber*, tell who-ever you send up there that when they start to move around or over that ledge, we'll have to cease firing to keep from hit-ting them. From that point on, they'll be on their own and they'll have to move fast. Tell 'em to throw in the white phos-phorous first to blind the Nips because when they throw in the satchel charge they've got to take their time and be damn certain it goes all the way in. If they screw up *Cobber*, you will have two less men in that rag-tail squad of yours. Now get the hell out of here and neutralize that cave!"

Childs responded, "I wish Shanghai was here, it's his damned squad. Lieutenant, how long is he going to be takin' it easy back in the rear echelon anyhow?"

"As long as the battalion intelligence officer wants him I guess. They've got him talkin' to a bunch of Nip prisoners at the CP," said the lieutenant.

Blackjack looked at Childs with a grin before speaking then said, "It's about time you earned your pay as an NCO. Leading that squad oughta' be a snap for an old salt like you."

Childs said, "If you weren't the platoon sergeant Black-jack, I'd kick your ass. Just remember, when we get back to Wellington you're buyin' the steak and eggs and all the bloody brew I can drink."

Blackjack responded with, "By the way Childs..."

"Yeah?"

"Semper Fi Buddy."

Childs grumbled, "You sonofabitch!"

It took Sergeant Childs a lot longer to get back up to the squad's position than it had taken him to come down. Once up there, it was only four of five minutes before two Marines could be seen stealthily moving toward the cave's entrance. Platoon Sergeant Black and the lieutenant could see that Childs was the lead man with Private Eddy O'Neil following cautiously behind.

Blackjack had known Childs would do it himself. It was just what he had wanted. Childs' chances of success were as good as anyone's and probably a hell of a lot better than most. He'd been with the company since Samoa and had proven himself in combat on Guadalcanal and Tarawa.

The sergeant spun around and dropped. He'd been winged in the arm and it was serious enough to cause him to drop his rifle and fall prone. Eddy O'Neil continued moving toward the cave entrance. "Corpsman up!" shouted a voice from among the Marines.

Butcher didn't need to be told to go. Like most Navy corpsmen with Marines, he operated mostly on instinct. Whenever someone yelled "Corpsman!" he was already on his feet and running. He didn't run fast, he was too big and too clumsy for that but what he lacked in speed, he made up for in courage and dedication. If the Japs poked their heads out of that cave-opening they would see him running right up the middle with no protection. He was an easy target; they could kill him with one carefully aimed round.

"All right you guys cover the Doc and be damned sure those Nips don't get a shot at him. I don't care if it takes every round you've got!" shrieked Blackjack.

The order was unnecessary. Marines take care of their corpsmen, it is an unwritten law and an unmistakable trait among warriors who have been baptized in blood. They understand the true meaning of brotherhood.

There was no way any Nip soldier could approach the opening of that cave from the inside without being shot multiple times. The first platoon automatically started laying down a base of rifle fire as the men of the second platoon moved forward like a wave surging ashore on a sandy beach. A squad of riflemen surrounded their corpsman as he ministered to his patient. The other two squads emptied clips of M-1 ammunition into the jagged coral opening until they noticed a very brave and very scared Marine slowly inching his way toward the cave from the right side. He moved cautiously until he was inches from the opening.

Billowing white smoke poured out of the cave. Private Eddy O'Neil had succeeded in lobbing a white phosphorous grenade into the cave and for added insurance he threw in two fragmentation grenades followed by the satchel charge. The company could move forward now. The smoking cave opening would not pose a threat to any more Marines.

"Ya know Fearless, if old Eddy O'Neil was in the Army, he'd probably get a Navy Cross or somethin' for what he just did," exclaimed the Weasel.

"The Army don't give out Navy Crosses you dumb-ass. They've got their own medals," retorted Fearless Frank.

"Well, I'm sure they would have given him somethin'. The doggies are very big on handin' out medals. It took a lot of guts for ol' Eddy to move up there under fire until he got to the cave entrance," quipped Weasel.

"He was just doin' his job dammit. He's a Marine. By the way have you heard how bad Childs was hit?" asked Fearless.

Weasel answered, "Doc Butcher says we were wastin' our time tryin' to help that guy, he's a tough Marine. It would take a hell of a lot more than a little flesh wound in the arm to put him out of the action. Doc says he wasn't wounded seriously. It was just a flesh wound with some loss of blood. Sick Bay will probably be sendin' him back to the company for duty before long.

Blackjack and the Chief looked at one another with some measure of relief. The bond between Old Corps Marines is a close one and they had already lost far too many friends. They would both be glad to see Childs return. Meanwhile, Corporal Al Jerden assumed the duties of acting squad leader.

The attack on "the four pimples" resumed early on the 29th in the form of probing actions by platoon-sized patrols. The regiment needed to find a route to get tanks into this area to effectively reduce the enemy positions in the hills. When encountered, Japanese defensive positions continued to be attacked with flamethrowers, satchel charges and grenades and were gradually but effectively neutralized or eliminated.

Early on the 30th, two of the hills were taken and a suitable means of ingress was finally available for the tanks. Once they were in place and opened fire, it was only a matter of time before the Four Pimples were ours entirely and the 8th Marines, minus the 2nd Battalion, were headed toward Tanapag Harbor, their next objective.

In the afternoon, Fox company's skipper told his Marines that the battalion had been assigned another special mission. The battalion was being detached from the regiment and was to be attached to the 2nd Marines for the assault on the city of Garapan.

The men were aware that Garapan was the capital city of the Mariana Islands. This was to be something new and different; they had never before fought in a city. The battalion was designated as the reserve element for the 2nd Marines during the assault and capture of Garapan.

* * * * * * * * * *

Garapan

30 June 1944

The conquest of Tapotchau was over. The mountain was ours but the price, paid in Marine blood, had been high. There were several missing faces when the new lieutenant was introduced to the platoon. The men waited in anticipation to hear what their future held. Before briefing them on their next objective, the lieutenant brought them up to date on what had been happening during the days they had spent ascending and securing Mount Tapotchau.

The men were relieved to learn that the fuel and ammunition lost in the massive explosions when the dump was destroyed on the 21st were rapidly being replenished. They felt like cheering when told the results of the Great Marianas

Turkey Shoot. The "Mud Marines" felt great pride and affection for the U.S. Navy and those gallant Navy and Marine pilots who had been so successful in virtually destroying Japanese naval airpower. The score was astounding.

The lieutenant reported that the war in Europe was going well. The Army had made great advances since landing in France on 6 June. The troops looked at one another in astonishment; they had almost forgotten that the Army was fighting a war in Europe.

The new lieutenant advised his men that the battalion would follow the 2nd Marines through what remained of Garapan eliminating holdouts and snipers and rendering whatever assistance the 2nd Marines may need. The lieutenant mumbled something about being glad to be aboard but his voice was all but drowned out by Gunnery Sergeant Littleton as he directed, "Alright Men, get your gear on! We're movin' out! You liberty hounds will be happy to know that we are bound for the big city of Garapan. Take the city and then, if there's anything left of it, check with me. I'll let you know what time Liberty Call will be sounded."

Garapan was a native Chamorro village when first discovered by Ferdinand Magellan in 1521. Since that time, it has been built up and developed by the Spaniards, the Germans and the Japanese. Garapan's known history covered a period of well over four hundred years, it had long been the capital city of the Mariana Islands.

The mission of the 2nd Marines was to locate and eliminate snipers and Japanese military holdouts that may have been hiding in what remained of the buildings. Not much was standing that could help to identify Garapan as a city when the 2nd Marines moved through what was left of it. Naval gunfire, air and artillery had done their job well. There was little left beyond the bombed out shells of buildings and the usual debris of war.

There were piles of rubble scattered everywhere. Among the few buildings still identifiable were the Japanese jail and the walls of an old bank supposedly built by the Germans. The ancient Spanish-built Catholic Church still had most of its walls intact but the roof had been destroyed. Over what remained of the altar was a large (life-size) crucifix on which the face of Jesus Christ had been shot away. In this war nothing was sacred, and nothing was immune from destruction.

A wizened little Spanish priest, Father Pio, and four tired nuns appeared from somewhere. None spoke English but some of the men had taken high school Spanish and the Chief was fluent in Spanish. Poncho's first language was Spanish but he rarely spoke to anyone and certainly no one thought he would be inclined to speak to a priest.

After a brief conversation with the Marines, Father Pio showed them a well behind the church. It was the first really fresh water any of them had tasted since leaving Hawaii. Father Pio explained that unfortunately, there were only three natural springs on the island. Fresh water would continue to be a problem throughout the campaign.

Having passed through the devastation of Garapan, disposing of snipers and taking a few ragged and hungry prisoners, the 2nd Battalion was detached from the 2nd Marines to rejoin the 8th Marines.

The company turned eastward and was advancing up the slopes of the foothills. As they moved toward a grassy rise flanked by trees and heavy brush, Chic Yancey was developing serious reservations. He had been fortunate in surviving the campaign thus far.

Combat was one terrifying experience after another. Casualties had been high and there was little reason to believe that things would improve any time soon. He was often afraid and fear could be a worse enemy than the Japanese. Each Marine had to cope with fear in his own special way.

Shanghai was talking like he always did, showing no emotion and being very professional. He made it sound like a routine training exercise. If it was up to him he would never assault the damned hill in this manner, Chic knew it had to be someone else's idea. He told himself, "Shanghai must be following orders. He just wouldn't have us do a thing like this if it was up to him."

"Alright, when I give the word, two of you guys start running. When they've gone 10 paces, I want the next two men to take off! Don't stop and don't slow down, just get up there! The 1st squad is taking off right after the 1st platoon and then we'll follow right behind the 1st squad."

Steely fingers wrapped firmly around Chic's upper arm. The words were spoken softly, the sergeant hardly moving his lips. "Listen asshole! If you want to start making tactical decisions for this lashup, I suggest you get a college education first and then go to Quantico and get a professional education and then come back out here wearing a pair of gold lieutenant's bars."

Chic turned to look up into the steady eyes of Shanghai Pooley, his squad leader. He had no way of knowing that the CO was on a tight schedule to get back to the regiment and reluctantly had to move to the objective very rapidly. Nor did Chic have any way of knowing that Shanghai, along with Platoon Sergeant J. B. Black, had quietly advised the new lieutenant that it would be unwise to move up the exposed slope in the manner prescribed.

The lieutenant chose to ignore the sergeants' advice but he had heard Chic's comment and glared his disapproval. No words were necessary. Chic had made an immediate and lasting enemy of the new lieutenant.

The 2nd Platoon was squatting down in the bush at the bottom of the clearing. Chic watched the 1st Platoon struggling up the slope. The men were faltering - it was too far to run up such a steep hill with packs, rifles, helmets and a full unit of fire. Big Ski put his hand on Chic's shoulder.

"You'd better give the new shavetail a wide berth buddy. He's not the type to let a Pfc complain about his tactical decisions and get away with it. He's got your number but good - it's written all over his face."

Chic, squatting on his haunches beside Big Ski, took a long drag of his cigarette. He inhaled deeply then exhaled a stream of smoke and stood up, field stripping his butt. The 1st squad was moving now. The 2nd squad was ready. Shanghai once more admonished his men to stay dispersed keeping at least 10 paces between runners. Pooley and the Reverend Corporal "Riverboat" Brown took off. The next two were Fearless and the Weasel. The lieutenant glared at Chic, pointed and then indicated it was time for him and Mc Laughlin to move out by snarling, "Okay loudmouth, shove off!"

Chic heard Big Ski mumble, "Good luck buddy!"

It wasn't too bad at first, then Chic noticed McLaughlin

falling back a couple of paces. The heat and tremendous humidity were depressing. Chic found it increasingly difficult to breathe. He yelled at Mac to keep up, as they passed a couple of spent men from the 1st Platoon lying in the grass trying to catch their breaths. Soon Chic found himself fighting to keep moving and maintain his speed. He felt as though there were twenty-pound weights fastened to each of his feet. His lungs were bursting as he exclaimed to no one in particular.

"Damned cigarettes!"

Pushing as hard as he could, Chic was slowing noticeably. He could feel himself staggering. He couldn't let himself stop and give that damned lieutenant the satisfaction of knowing he couldn't run all the way up.

Chic's heart was pounding so hard it throbbed loudly in his ears but it was his lungs that were really a problem. He couldn't get enough air - couldn't catch his breath. He swore to himself that he would never smoke another cigarette. Chic stumbled and was down - exhausted. He could feel Mc Laughlin huffing and gasping for breath right behind him. As Mac started coming up to pass on Chic's right, he urged, "C'mon Chic, on your feet! Don't let that damn lieutenant see you on the deck!"

The light machine gun that started crackling out of the dense bush on their left was well concealed by the jungle foliage. Pow-pow-pow-pow-pow!!! Chic, lying flat on the ground was jerked up and spun to the right violently! It felt like his shoulders had been torn from his body and then it felt like a tank had run over his back. Mac was screaming and someone down in the rear was yelling for a corpsman. Chic didn't know if he could move his arms – the pain was awful. Now shouts from above, "Corpsman! Corpsman!"

Chic's head turned to the right and he saw McLaughlin. Mac's legs were bloody and he was crying like a baby. His fists were beating on the ground — there was no movement in his legs. Corporal Kinney and two other Marines from the 1st platoon who were just a few yards up ahead - lay dead on the grassy slope.

The "Butcher" was lumbering up the hill in a superhuman effort to get to the wounded Marines. A good corpsman, he always seemed to be nearby when needed. Butcher handled fear as though it didn't exist. His placid face and unassuming manner seemed strangely out of place amid the intense stress, death and destruction of the battlefield. His face looked almost angelic when he was tending the wounded under fire. All the Marines knew that when the war was over and the Butcher realized his lifelong dream of becoming a surgeon, he would be a very good one.

The men of the 1st Platoon lay prone on the grassy slope. They were firing sporadically at the treeline on the left in hopes of getting a lucky shot at the unseen enemy. Some started coming back down to help move the casualties. The 1st and 2nd squads of the 2nd platoon still attempting to move up stopped - and took up firing positions. There was little cover or concealment on the grassy slope. All hands were now directing their fire into the jungle where they thought the machine gun was located.

Two very brave Marines from the 1st platoon crawled toward the treeline on the left flank. They lobbed hand grenades into the bush until the Nambu was permanently silenced. Mac was carried back down on a stretcher. Doc Drinkwine later said all five rounds that had gone through Chic's pack had gone through Mac's knees as well, shattering the bones and inflicting severe damage. He would later lose both legs. Chic's haversack had only slowed down the bullets that found their way into Mac's knees.

Chic's pack was ripped apart. There were puffs of white cotton in what had, moments before, been an olive drab, canvas haversack. The mess kit was mangled, as was the toilet kit. The head of a toothbrush had disintegrated and tufts of bristles were scattered throughout the pack. Miraculously, Chic's New Testament and Prayer Book, gifts from his mother, had been wrapped tightly in waterproof plastic and were undamaged. Chic lay on the slope waiting for his breathing to normalize and wondering if both his arms were broken at the shoulders. Deadly Dave Donahoe, good old Donahoe, was helping to get the shoulder straps off Chic as he gently removed what was left of the pack. The Japanese machine gun had been silenced now and the troops were again moving up the slope. This time they moved just inside the treeline and with great caution.

If Chic still had a pack he couldn't have carried it. His shoulders were bruised and burning. No blood, no lacerations, but lots of pain. Chic was getting used to pain, it seemed to go with being a Marine. The new lieutenant was reassigned to the 1st platoon. Their lieutenant had been seriously wounded and evacuated and the 2nd platoon was not lacking for leaders, they still had a number of strong NCO's left. Chic somehow felt that the company commander sensed how they felt about the lieutenant and moved him for the mutual good of all concerned. Yet, in fairness, it had not been the lieutenant's decision to move up the open slope. He too had been following orders.

As the 2nd Battalion rejoined their regiment, they found themselves in a virtual hornet's nest once again. On July 2nd, the entire front of the 2nd Battalion and part of the 1st Battalion, 29th Marines was raked by enemy machine-gun fire from caves in a coral-limestone hill complex. Tanks and flamethrowers were employed against the enemy's fortified emplacements but intense enemy fire stopped any attempt to completely overrun the hill.

Neutralization of the strongpoint did not occur on this blistering hot afternoon. Detaching from the hilly terrain in which they had been fighting, the 8th Marines had been directed to attack and seize the Tanapag Harbor area. As the regiment left for Tanapag, Fox Company was left behind to contain the Japanese in their coral and limestone emplacements. Orphaned, the company set about the task of methodically reducing the Japanese emplacements.

The day had been hotter than usual, the sky cloudless and nearly white in its brightness. Time passed as the Marines kept the cave entrances in their rifle sights and watched for even the slightest movement. Each platoon leader noted the location and identification of the dead. They would be recovered as soon as the objectives were taken. Carrying parties strained mightily as they moved the wounded back to safety over the rough hilly terrain and returned carrying rations, water and precious ammunition.

The sun grew misty, as the day grew old, until it gleamed in a pale sky like a white pearl high in the heavens. Then it gradually descended into the west and dusk came early followed by a gray, starless night. Far into the dark quiet hours the men lay motionless, waiting and wondering. They listened intently for the slightest movement from the enemy positions to their front. Nothing significant occurred throughout the night except a bombing run by a single Japanese plane.

With the dawn, there was movement by each of the opposing forces but Fox Company had the advantage.

The Japs were well dug-in but they were no match for a company of hot, sweaty, pissed-off Marines who had been left behind overnight by their regiment and were armed with flamethrowers, rocket launchers, satchel charges and grenades. The Japanese caves and bunkers soon became tombs.

The regiment, minus Fox Company, had successfully reached the sea and seized Tanapag Harbor by 1300 on the 4th of July. Later, on the afternoon of the 4th, Fox Company proudly reported that the enemy emplacements had been reduced and the threat no longer existed. The company was ready to rejoin the battalion for its next objective.

Shanghai wondered what Poncho could be up to. He was not in the habit of initiating conversations but here he was, perched on the edge of Shanghai's foxhole and looking as though he wanted to say something.

"What is it Gutierrez, what's up?" queried Shanghai.

"Sergeant, its Choirboy. Unless you want me to go over the hill, keep that little kid away from me! He gives me the creeps always sayin' his rosary and prayin' all the time," and then Gutierrez added, "He even tried to get me to pray with him. Dammit Shanghai, if I wanted to be a Jeezus freak, I'd of joined the Chaplains' Corps."

Shanghai was scowling as he addressed Poncho. "Poncho, you wouldn't make a pimple on a chaplain's ass. I won't have Mulcahy dig in with you again — you might be a bad influence on him. You should have been glad to have that kid for a foxhole buddy; he's probably the most decent guy you could ever team up with. Now shove off and get back to your position!"

U.S. artillery was firing an impressive Independence Day barrage that seemed to employ every gun on the island. It was the Marines' way of celebrating the 4th of July. The artillery fire wasn't just fired in celebration; it was fired at selected targets including the command post of Lieutenant General Yoshitsugu Saito. General Saito and several members of his staff were wounded during the big Independence Day Shoot.

Most of the 2nd Marine Division including the tired 8th Marines went into reserve late on the afternoon of the 4th of July during the artillery barrage. It was to be a badly needed break. Foxholes were dug and water, rations and ammunition had been brought up. The terrain in front of the company's position dropped off sharply for about 30 feet. It was nearly a cliff. A good position to defend since the flanks and rear were covered by the rest of the battalion. It was still daylight. C-rations were consumed and foxholes improved as much as conditions permitted.

Fields of fire had been carefully chosen for the heavy 1917A1 water-cooled machine guns that had replaced the 1919A4 light, air-cooled machine guns. The men were taking advantage of this brief period of being in defense, to relax. Some re-read the letters that had been nearly memorized. Mail call was not sounded often in combat and letters had to last for several readings.

Deadly Dave and Stash had gone over to where the 3rd platoon was dug in to have a smoke with Ross and Muldoon and to wait for it to get dark. Ross and Muldoon had been reassigned to give the 3rd some experienced men until they got more replacements or until their med-evaced casualties started coming back to duty. Lucky Lane and Chic Yancey were sitting on the edge of their hole with Chief looking down on the terrain to their front. It was nearly twilight. As usual, they paid little attention to the singing and harmonizing going on over in the 3rd platoon's area.

Poncho called over from his hole, "Hey you guys, Chief, Chic, listen!"

Poncho was not one for small talk and almost never spoke unless it was important.

"Listen Dammit!"

Ross, Muldoon, Stash and Deadly Dave always sang when they could get together and had nothing better to do. They generally started by singing "The Raggedy Assed Marines" and then went on to tunes they could harmonize with. It was old stuff, but Poncho obviously wanted them to hear something else. Lucky Lane, Chief and Chic strained to listen. Then it dawned on them what Poncho had been hearing.

Intermingled with the familiar voices of their buddies, then rising above them in volume and quality was another voice. This one was new to them. Lucky chuckled, "I never thought of Poncho as a music lover. An undertaker maybe, or a Mafia hit-man, but not a music lover."

Poncho admonished, "Quiet Lane! Knock it off!"

It was the beautiful Irish Tenor voice of Private Kevin Mulcahy, the choirboy. His wonderful voice rose above the others and the moving words and music of "Mother Machree" brought a lump to Chic's throat. Then, a succession of many other old favorites. The other singers tapered off and soon quit singing altogether before Choirboy had even finished "Mother Machree," Private Kevin Mulcahy, the choir boy, had finally come into his own.

As silence crept over their position and darkness descended upon them, the sounds of that fine tenor voice lingered in their memories and reminded them of home and of better times in that wonderful land so far across the sea.

The 2nd Marine Division's break as the corps reserve was to be short-lived. General Saito's *Gyokusai*, the great Saipan Banzai charge was launched on July 7th. The 2nd Marine Division, including the 8th Marines, came back into the front lines replacing the Army's shattered 27th Infantry Division, and entered the final drive against the remaining Japanese forces on Saipan.

The 2nd Battalion was to move through the mountainous area east of Tanapag. It consisted of a canyon winding between steep cave-studded cliffs. Jungle growth and erosion by tropical rains helped to keep many cave locations hidden from view.

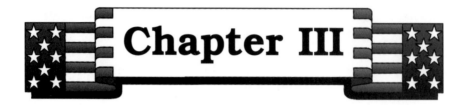

Chapter III

The Canteen and the Crucifix

East of Tanapag - 9 July 1944

The great *Gyokusai*, perhaps the largest in history, was finished, as were more than forty-two hundred Japanese fighting men. Most organized resistance had ceased to exist. Only scattered groups of Japanese fighting men were left. They were armed but practically devoid of effective leadership. Their senior officers had either died fighting or had taken their own lives. The Code of Bushido did not permit surrender. These were the conditions that prevailed on Saipan Island that steamy hot July morning in 1944.

The regiment was pushing north up the beach and had wheeled inland through the mountainous area east of Tanapag. Jungle growth and erosion by tropical rains helped to keep many of the caves in the steep winding canyon hidden from view. The regiment started moving through the jungle-covered hills in a wide arc that was designed to bring it back toward the sea a few miles south of Marpi Point. The battalion was moving on a jungle trail that was little more than two ruts worn in the ground by oxcart wheels.

Three weeks of combat had been almost too much for Chic. The teenaged warrior was overtaken by the powerful narcotic effect of a high fever and extreme fatigue. As the column continued moving cautiously forward he felt as though his own movements were in slow motion. It took all of his powers of concentration to focus on continuing to walk forward with the column.

As he trudged along in the lengthy, winding column of men he had the same thought over and over. He wanted to stop, sit down in the shade, relax completely and drink water, lots of cool, clear water. Not this damned smelly, contaminated, Saipan water but real water, the kind of sweet, cool water he remembered from back home. He was hot, he was thirsty and he was fatigued beyond description. He slowly, clumsily removed his canteen from its carrier on his web belt and started to unscrew the cap. Before he could take a sip of the precious water, something within him said "to hell with it" and the canteen slipped through his fingers onto the trail. Instinct had now taken over and he kept moving forward on that alone. He knew he couldn't continue to walk much farther. Doc Drinkwine was up the line a short distance. Chic wanted to catch up with him but he was too weak to move faster and he felt himself staggering. Whitey Shultz grabbed his arm, "What's wrong with you Chic? Have you found some Nip sake that we don't know about?"

"Of course not Whitey. I was just tryin' to catch up with Doc. I think I need some medicine or something, I feel terrible."

"Hey you guys, pass the word up for Doc to fall out and come back here. Something's wrong with Yancey."

During a halt in the movement, "Doc" Drinkwine informed the only officer nearby, Mr. Yoakum of the 1st platoon, that Pfc Yancey was having difficulty walking. His temperature was 104 degrees and his blood pressure was dangerously low. Dengue fever, rampant on Saipan, was continuing to take its toll.

The lieutenant told Doc to put a casualty tag on the young Marine and lay him beside the trail in a small clearing. Battalion headquarters was right behind Fox Company and the battalion aid station would be along any minute. They could pick him up and get him back to the rear. The company moved on.

Chic's head was throbbing with an awful pain and he felt

very nauseous. Doc and Whitey Schultz had put his pack under his head and laid his rifle by his right side. His helmet was beside his left shoulder. He wanted to watch his platoon and company as they moved by but he could not keep his eyes open.

As he lay back, the fingers of his right hand gently closed on his rifle's stock. Rifles were high and holy things to Marines and they were much respected. A Marine without his rifle felt naked. Chic's last conscious thoughts on that early Saipan morning were of his rifle. How secure he felt lying there in the warm sun with his right hand gently clasping the rifle's stock.

He hoped the battalion aid station wouldn't come along too soon. He didn't want to be moved. The headache and nausea were too severe and the bones in his arms and legs hurt like they were broken. No wonder Doc had called dengue "Broken Bone Fever." Chic just wanted to lie where he was. Time passed as the delirious Marine was intermittently racked with fever or trembling with chills. Most of the time, he slept. It was a sleep induced not only by the sickness but brought on by three weeks of hard fighting and near exhaustion.

The tropical sun acted as a tranquillizer. He was totally oblivious to events around him and he no longer heard the jungle sounds or the sporadic firing up where the point of the column had been. Battalion headquarters, with the aid station, had taken another route!

Regaining consciousness did not come easily. It was painful and confusing. The blows were to both his right and left sides and hurt. They were inflicted on his ankles, knees, hips - everywhere from his rib cage down. One painful blow followed another. He fought through the delirium and forced his eyes open. He could hear human sounds but could not discern what they were.

The searing white hot sun was directly overhead. Something dark was shading him - it was all around but the sun continued to burn into his eyes from an opening in the center. Huddled dark forms began to take shape. They were human, no details, just dark forms. The fingers of Chic's right hand groped for his rifle - it wasn't there! His arms had been moved, they were now outstretched. Suddenly, he was fully awake and terrified. The dark shadowy forms above him were wearing *ryakubo* the peaked visor caps of the Japanese Army!

The chills and fever were momentarily forgotten. Terror replaced all other emotions except for the pain periodically being directed to his legs and hips. Images became more distinct as he saw the source of his pain. The Japanese, wearing their split-toed rubber and canvas *jikatabi* shoes were kicking him. He knew they would kill him and wondered why they hadn't already done so.

The kicking stopped and he could sense one of the forms moving closer. He could smell him! Suddenly, a canteen was thrust at his face. He tried to reach for it but did not have full control over his hands. The man pushed the canteen up to his lips. He was hot and dry and his lips were parched and swollen like large blisters. As the canteen was pushed against him he felt his blistered lower lip split and warm fluid trickled down his chin. His heart was pounding so hard that each beat seemed to move his whole body. He was scared! He was also dehydrated and tremendously thirsty.

The canteen pressed against his lips and hurt. He wondered what was in it. The Japanese were capable of terrible things - they hated Americans. Was the water poisoned? Was it actually water? Could it have been urine? The temptation to drink was powerful but he knew better - Japanese soldiers would never give an American Marine a drink of water.

He looked up, vainly trying to see the man's face. The sun was too bright. As the form bent over him, a strange thing occurred. A beaded chain fell from around the soldier's neck and there - dangling from it in the blazing sun - was a cross. It hung there for a moment turning slowly in the bright sunlight. Chic squinted and through narrowed eyelids could now see a crucifix! This soldier was wearing rosary beads and a crucifix - he must have stolen it from a dead Marine! Or, was it possible that this Japanese soldier was a Christian?

The water was warm, it tasted awful, and it was crawling with God knows what - but it was water. Chic felt some of the water spill out of the corners of his mouth and run down his chin and neck. This was upsetting; he didn't want to lose a drop - especially since this was probably going to be the last drink he would ever have.

His hands trembled as he attempted clumsily to screw the top onto the canteen. He failed and tried again. There was no understanding or compassion in the faces of the Japanese. They stared arrogantly with no attempt to hide their feelings of hatred and disgust.

Again, he tried to feel for the M-1 rifle he knew should be at his right side. He wasn't thinking of shooting anyone, he just wanted his rifle. It was as though a part of him was missing; a Marine and his rifle should never be parted.

Chic now realized his helmet and pack were also missing. It was about this time that he got his first lesson in Japanese. The word was *Oy*! It was said gutturally and with emphasis. Loosely translated, it meant something like, Hey!! This was followed by *suware*! He wondered what that meant? This was followed by kicks to the ankles and legs and then rough hands pushed him into the sitting position. Thus the word *suware* (sit) was learned.

The Japanese soldiers moved in a single file. There were no scouts out and no flank security. Chic wondered why they had taken him with them. How long did they think he could keep walking? It was obvious that the Japanese did not give a damn how sick, weak or exhausted he was. When the sickness and fatigue was so overwhelming that he felt he couldn't take another step, he had only to think of the consequences. When they moved, he moved. He wondered at the stories he had heard in training about the great Japanese jungle fighters. These soldiers were not at home in the jungle, in fact, they seemed to know as little about it as he did. One noteworthy difference was their discipline. Chic was impressed with their discipline and with their complete disregard for danger.

They moved slowly and laboriously through the jungle. Chic moved with them as if in a trance and most of the time, he was. Rest breaks were welcomed as the terrain was rough and the jungle paths overgrown with tagnan-tagnan and all manner of vegetation. During one break, a soldier offered Chic some cold rice which he carried in a small wooden box. The rice was rancid and stunk but the Nips gulped it down. Chic's appetite vanished with the first mouthful. The taste was as bad as the smell. It smelled something like shellac. He attempted to size up his captors. At first there seemed to be a large number but eventually he realized that there were only nine. They were under the command of *Gunso* (Sergeant) Suzuki, the Christian. Chic thought again of the crucifix and wondered. He had never heard of a Japanese Christian, but then, he had never heard much of anything about the Japanese until they bombed Pearl Harbor.

The column moved through the thick jungle in a single file, Chic near the center. At one point they watched as a platoon of Marines passed nearby in a burned out cane field. The Marines were in a tactical formation out in the open. He thought about moving up through the clearing where Mac had lost his legs. It had only been a week or so ago but now seemed like it had happened in a different lifetime. These Marines were doing something just as foolish as his outfit had done.

The Japanese stood frozen, Chic wanted to yell or make a break. Whatever he did would surely have resulted in dead Marines. The Japanese had the advantage of concealment while the Marines were moving outside the tree line in the open.

The Japanese soldiers were oblivious to Chic's condition. They each had problems of their own. When his chills started they just prodded him to keep moving. He wondered why they hadn't killed him - what did they want? Most of the time, *Gunso* Suzuki ignored him. When he did try to talk, communication was nearly impossible as he spoke only Japanese and Chic only English. When the other Japs slapped or kicked him, Suzuki did not interfere. Their hatred of Americans was very strong and very obvious.

Why did they want to keep him alive? He fantasized about what might happen when they got to their destination. Was it possible they didn't realize he was only a Pfc? Would they torture him for intelligence information? Information that he did not have. What could he tell them except for his name, rank and serial number? He knew absolutely nothing that could be of value to the enemy. Perhaps he should contrive something, tell them something that would throw them off. No, if he tried it, they would know he was lying. It would make the outcome worse.

Chic felt like a zombie, moving but having so little control, he was virtually unconscious. They kept moving and as they did, he noticed the strain was as great on them as it was on him. One, who seemed to be the youngest, had to be assisted in walking. They all were sick, hungry and exhausted. The dressings on their wounds were filthy and had obviously not been changed in days. There was caked dried blood on some of their bandages and parts of their uniforms. He thought they must be in great danger of infection. He couldn't help feeling a twinge of respect for them.

During a break, they drank from a stream. There were very few streams on Saipan and Chic was grateful they had found this one. They filled their canteens. Chic was permitted to fill the canteen Suzuki had given him. When they moved out, just a few meters upstream was the cadaver of a Japanese soldier. His head and right arm were under water. Most of the flesh had been eaten or washed away leaving the submerged skull and bones exposed. The part of his body that was out of the water was bloated, disfigured and discolored as were most of the dead bodies that littered Saipan.

Chic was horrified and became violently ill but kept moving as he vomited up the contaminated water he had just drunk. The Japanese were impassive. They continued moving. Chic was hot and sweaty and was so dizzy at times he couldn't walk without falling down. One of the soldiers gave him a limb to use as a walking stick for support. He tried to stay close to this fellow, thinking he would be more compassionate than the others, but when he started to fall behind, he was kicked with a vengeance. The hatred in his erstwhile benefactor's eyes was quite apparent.

If the Japanese were not near the entrance to a cave, when the tropical monsoon rains poured down, they just squatted and waited for it to end. Some held large banana leaves over their backs as umbrellas. Chick tried to eat the tiny green bananas but soon learned what Suzuki and his men already knew. They looked at him in disgust as he spit out the totally inedible green fruit.

There were piles of snail shells beside some of the trails. Chick had heard somewhere that the snails on Saipan were edible when cooked and poisonous when eaten raw. He wondered just how hungry a man would have to be before he would attempt to eat them. They were huge slimy creatures, many of them more than three inches high. They left a nasty trail of mucus wherever they went. Chick's hunger pangs were coming more frequently now but he didn't think he was ready for the giant snails.

As darkness was descending, they came to a clearing where he was pushed to the ground and one of his captors barked *"Suware!"* He sat. The soldiers made tea and consumed more of their rancid rice. Chick was given a small portion of the rice on a leaf. The odor of the rancid rice gagged him, he could not swallow it. He had found two wild limes earlier and had slipped them into his pockets. They were his evening meal.

Chic thought about his squad and the men in his platoon and wondered if they missed him or if they merely thought he was with the battalion aid station. Too fatigued and ill to remember or care about the contaminated water, he raised the Japanese canteen to his lips and drank from it and then leaned back on the ground and was asleep.

* * * * * * * * * *

Ghost of the Samurai

Rain falling in the darkness interrupted his uneasy sleep. He longed for his poncho, now the property of "Shoes," a pock-marked little Japanese. Shoes was the only one who was wearing *henjoka*, leather hobnailed shoes. The other Japanese soldiers all wore rubber and canvas split-toed *jikatabi*. The rain brought on more chills and trembling. It seemed to him that the symptoms of his dengue fever would never end but dengue was not his only source of discomfort. He had multiple bruises from his hips to his ankles made by his captors' kicking. He wondered if Shoes had not been responsible for most of his bruises. The rains stopped but the chills and pain did not. There was little sleep in store for him this night.

It was odd not having a rifle or any means of defense. The Jap with the long face and horn-rim glasses, who looked like a cartoon character, had Chic's M-1 rifle cradled between his knees. The little stocky one who had trouble walking and appeared to be every bit as sick as Chic, was lying flat on his back snoring uneasily, his right arm outstretched, his hand clutching the carbine rifle that was usually strapped diagonally across his back. *Gunso* Suzuki, in addition to his sword, had a regular .25 caliber Arisaka rifle like most of the others.

The Japs were well armed but had no rations except tea and that horrible rancid rice that even they seemed to have trouble getting down. Their uniforms had obviously not been changed in days and, in fact, they didn't appear to have changes of uniform. Only three of the nine were wearing packs and one of them had belonged to Chic before his capture. The Japanese soldiers were skinny, hungry, and dirty and although hostile towards him, showed no apparent interest in engaging in further combat with the American forces.

They were searching for something or someone, looking in every crevasse in the cliffs and in every cave they encountered. Chic surmised that their main interest was in finding food and supplies and a good source of potable water but they were seeking something else as well. Possibly they had families who were displaced by the fighting or perhaps they were looking for other members of their unit who may have survived the big *banzai* attack. He worried that they may be seeking an officer or someone in authority to turn their prisoner over to. He further worried that Suzuki somehow seemed to know where he was going and what he was doing, he had a mission.

Twice today, he had seen Suzuki make the sign of the cross. Once when they were passing a family of dead Chamorros lying beside the trail, and again in the heavy bush beside the stream where the dead soldier was lying partially in the water they had drunk. Yes, Suzuki really was different. The crucifix he wore was not just ornamental. His faith had to be sincere.

Looking at the little band of Japanese soldiers lying there asleep gave the impression that there was no war at all - they just looked like a bunch of dirty, ragged coolies sleeping like babes. He wondered why they were fighting this war. Why did they care so much about killing Americans that they would willingly sacrifice their own lives? Could they really believe their Emperor was God?

They were positioned in a wide circle in a rough clearing, with Chic in the center. He couldn't believe they hadn't tied his hands or tried to restrain him in some way. They must have understood how sick and weak he really was. For the time being, escape was out of the question.

Chic had seen a couple of his captors get up and walk over to the edge of the clearing into the heavier vegetation to relieve themselves. He thought, maybe if he could just do that, they wouldn't notice. He could then melt into the jungle - they'd never know he was gone until after daylight when they were fully awake. These thoughts kept running through his mind. He wondered if he did melt into the jungle, just how far he could go. They had walked all day and his legs and thighs ached. He knew the Dengue fever had severely weakened him and he was delirious much of the time. Would an escape attempt mean certain death? Or would it give him a chance for survival?

A third Jap got up and walked over to the edge of the clearing to relieve himself. He walked back to where he had been sleeping, scratched his filthy body and lay down to resume his sleep. Chic had to try. Slowly, cautiously, he raised himself up on his knees then tried to stand. He was very stiff and sore but managed to get on his feet. The canteen - now his only possession, was tied to his belt. As he cautiously approached the edge of the clearing, his eyes darted from one prone body to the next. They all seemed to be sleeping. The moon was peering through a gap between the clouds and lit up the area with an eerie glow. When Chic had finished, he felt a strange sense of euphoria - he was a prisoner, and yet he had just gotten up and walked to the edge of the clearing. He sensed no awareness or movement from his captors.

The clearing, now bathed in moonlight, was quiet. Chic, still standing, looked his captors over cautiously, slowly. They seemed to be reclining just where they had been before, but no, one was missing! There were only eight sleeping bodies. Who was gone? What had happened? He hadn't been aware of any movement, hadn't heard anything. Chic wondered if he was dreaming or delirious.

At the far end of the clearing was a slight rise. There in an open space between the trees, was a motionless form. It seemed to be the figure of a man but with the moonlight behind it, it was shadowlike and silhouetted. As Chic stared the shadow became more pronounced and took on a form that appeared like a man standing in an arrogant pose with feet apart, one hand on his hip, the other hand on the hilt of a sword extending out from his side. It was like a scene from an old Japanese movie.

Chic shivered, and decided that he must be delirious; he was seeing a Japanese ghost. He stared at this specter of an ancient Samurai warrior. He could see the shadowy form until a dark cloud crept across the face of the moon, decreasing the light and rendering the Samurai nearly invisible. Then, a flash of lightening accompanied by a loud crack startled the young Marine. Suddenly, the ghostly Samurai was back still standing motionless. He was bathed in light for a fraction of a second while the lightening flashed. A tiny brightness sparkled for a brief moment; it was something around his neck, a reflection. It had to be the crucifix. The ghostly Samurai was Suzuki.

Except for the *ryakubo* (peaked Army cap) he was wearing, his stance and his shadow did make him look like an ancient Samurai warrior. He seemed to be looking over his troops as if to protect them from the elements and from the enemy. It was a strange scene, this ghostly Samurai standing, glaring at his sleeping troops and at their prisoner, who was on his feet and at the opposite end of the clearing.

It had been a bizarre experience, having lasted only seconds, yet it was somehow frightening. Was he being given a message of some kind? If so, he could not comprehend its meaning. All thoughts of escaping into the darkness of the jungle were erased from his mind. Suzuki was a paradox - a contradiction in cultures. Was he the ancient Samurai warrior or the modern, compassionate Christian soldier? Perhaps he was neither, but then again, he may be a little of both.

Another flash of lightening, the brightness lasted a bit longer, and the truth could be plainly seen. All pomp and dignity was stripped from what just seconds before appeared to be the silhouette of a Samurai. The light revealed a poor little Japanese sergeant, ragged, dirty and tired.

What could be in this man's thoughts? Was he thinking of his men and what was to become of them? Perhaps he was thinking of his family and his home in Nagasaki. Maybe he thought of the defeat of the Japanese forces and the loss of so much of what he loved and believed in. Perhaps he was thinking that with this American prisoner, he would have a means to surrender. A bartering chip, to get good treatment for his men, perhaps even to keep them alive. His thoughts about life and death, especially death, were bound to be different from the other Japanese. He was a Christian and probably not as inclined to embrace death for the Emperor as enthusiastically as the others.

Chic slowly returned to his former position in the center of the clearing and as he sat down, he saw Suzuki resuming his position between two of the others. He had many thoughts and questions in his mind but they were soon washed away by the raindrops which started gradually and were soon a deluge. One thought remained uppermost in his mind. If he had tried to make a break for it, could he have been successful. This heavy rain surely would have masked his retreat through the jungle. He wished that he had felt strong enough to have plunged into the bush and just kept going. He prayed for strength and wisdom and hoped for another opportunity.

* * * * * * * * * *

The Captive

The rain subsided and finally stopped entirely. It would soon be morning and the mosquitoes would diminish. This would be a signal for the flies to awaken and feed ravenously on anything, animal or human, alive or dead. Throughout the night Chic had vainly waited for daybreak. He had finally given up after the rain stopped and allowed himself to doze off. It seemed like only moments later, when he heard the first sounds of his captors muffled jabbering and wondered what they could be saying. Some of their words were beginning to sound familiar but they still had no meaning to him.

Suddenly, it was full daylight. How he wished he had been able to relax and sleep during the long night! Now it was too late. He sat up and tried to rub away some of the pain in his legs while watching the Japs for a clue as to what was going to be expected of him before they started pushing and kicking. He opened the canteen and drank slowly and carefully. It was as though he had expected them to take it away from him. It wasn't until much later that he remembered the bloated cadaver in the water where he had filled the canteen. His thirst was great and his willpower waning. It no longer mattered if the water was safe or not.

They were soon on their feet and moving once again, a continuation of the previous day. At one point, shortly after they had gotten started, there was a commotion up near the head of the column. It was around a bend and Chic could not see what was happening but he sensed it was something serious. If only he could understand Japanese.

The two nearest him resented his interest in what was happening up ahead. They made him squat, oriental style, with his feet flat, facing the direction from whence they had come. Not an easy task for an inexperienced occidental. He was not permitted to turn his head to the left or right. It seemed so childish, like many of the things the Japanese did. They knew he couldn't see around the bend and they certainly knew he couldn't understand what was being said. Kurihara, the tallest of the group of ragged soldiers, finally told him to get up and move out.

"Ishoni koi! Ikki masho! Hyaku!"

When they rounded the bend in the trail, Chic was appalled! There, lying beside a shattered tree was the youngest looking member of the group, the one who had been so weak the day before. He was spread-eagled and was obviously dead. They had simply laid him there on the ground. No poncho to cover his body, no respectful burial. One of the others now had an extra rifle slung across his back. They moved through strangely familiar terrain, up hills and down ravines, all jungle covered, and then occasionally they would break out into unexpected clearings denuded of vegetation by shells and bombs, and pock-marked by craters in the shattered coral. It reminded him of being with his platoon during the assault on Mount Tapotchau. Some of the trails they crossed were so familiar he knew he'd been on them before.

He wondered about the prospects for his longevity as they moved down a jungle trail that was narrow and winding. As they descended, there would be an occasional break in the trees and bushes sufficient to permit Chic to glimpse briefly at the sugarcane fields below. Suzuki gave the signal for them to halt. Considering the vast differences in their cultures, it was a surprise to Chic that the Japanese used many of the same military arm and hand signals as Americans. Something or someone had gotten Suzuki's attention. They squatted in the trail and waited.

Slowly winding their way up from a lower elevation another column was approaching on the same trail. As the distance closed, Chic could see that they were refugees. Japanese civilians and maybe Chamorros, he still had difficulty telling them apart. They were a bedraggled lot indeed, pitiful to behold and showing great fatigue but still on their feet and climbing up the jungle trail.

Suzuki stood up and waited as the other column approached. The old man in the lead bowed in a courtly manner to Suzuki who returned the salutation in kind. They spoke, but only for a few moments, then both bowed again and resumed moving. Surely Suzuki had warned him that there was nothing on that trail. Whatever they sought, their quest was futile. Unless, they were seeking their enemy, possibly for medical help and to surrender. Chic had been told that Japanese soldiers would not permit their civilians to surrender. He had seen evidence of this.

As they passed the other file, they were so close that they would occasionally brush against one another. Chic noted that they were mostly women, children and older men. All were filthy dirty, and were carrying bundles tied up in cloth, which he surmised was all that was left of their worldly possessions. Some had dirty bandages covering their wounds. A few had open sores and wounds seething with living maggots. He had seen maggots consuming many dead bodies, but had never before seen them in the wounds of living people. He was to learn later that those disgusting maggots could well have saved many lives by keeping wounds clean and preventing gangrene.

The women had their babies strapped or tied to their backs. Some children were also carrying babies on their backs. The infants and children appeared to be oblivious to the flies that were all over them. Chic marveled at the Japanese children. They were obviously hungry and in great discomfort from their sores and wounds yet none were openly crying. He detected a few whimpers and saw tears on some dirty cheeks, but no audible crying. The column was passed now, but it would not be forgotten. The thought of those poor human derelicts enduring such pain and suffering would live in Chic's memory always.

They were adjacent to the cane field now, just inside the tree line. As Chic gnawed on a broken piece of sugarcane attempting to extract a bit of energy from the sweet juice, he was besieged with flies. They were all over him and the cane. He tried to blow and brush them away, but, they were the most persistent flies he had ever encountered. The flies bothered him especially when they gathered at the corners of his mouth. Brushing, wiping and blowing them away hardly helped. They always returned in seconds.

He had never imagined that there could be so many flies anywhere on earth. Nor could he have imagined, before his Saipan adventure, that there would be an island on this earth a mere twelve miles long with over 30,000 dead humans to provide such ideal breeding conditions for the flies.

The little band stumbled into a clearing where the remains of two small buildings were grim reminders of the devastation of war. A small observation plane flew over and Chic was again reminded of the futility of his plight. If only he could communicate with that plane. There was no way. It circled a couple of times and was soon gone.

Suzuki called a break and before squatting, Chic spied two small ripe tomatoes under a vine. He picked one up and gratefully wiped off the ants and dirt. On the bottom was a large rotten spot but the famished Marine was not discouraged, the rest of the tomato was delicious as was the second one, which he gulped down hoping his captors, in their own quest for food, wouldn't notice. He saw chicken feathers scattered around the ruins, but obviously someone had gotten there before them. There was no living livestock only the bloated, very ripe, carcass of a carabao, lying where it had been tethered while still living. The Japs were preoccupied with some small watermelons they had found. They were only about the size of grapefruit, but still seemed ripe enough to eat. Chic had been told to sit and was not permitted the luxury of foraging for food. He wondered if any of the Japs would share scraps from their melons with him but soon realized they had no such intentions.

It came as a complete surprise! Chic had so divorced himself from the role of a combat Marine that he now only thought of himself as a captive. In his pre-occupation with his aches and pains, the symptoms of dengue and self-pity, he'd forgotten about the real world and the war he had been so much a part of until two days before. Why couldn't he have realized that the airplane was an artillery spotter? It didn't take him long to remember that he was now with the enemy. The shrill shriek of incoming artillery was not what he had expected nor was the accuracy of the first round. It was almost on top of them. Suzuki was screaming commands and the Japs were moving. They moved surprisingly fast for men who were starving and on the brink of exhaustion.

Chic was on his feet hoping to outrun the second round which was now screaming toward them. He started to run downhill in the opposite direction from his captors but, almost immediately, ran into a roll of rusty wire and was sprawled on the ground when the second round detonated. Thankfully, it was a few yards away. Someone, jerked him to his feet and half pushed, half dragged him into the tree line. They were soon back on a trail winding through the tagnan-tagnan.

As they stumbled on, Chic silently uttered prayers of thanks. He was grateful to be alive. How could the Japs have risked their lives to save him, their enemy? They were in great jeopardy of being killed by that artillery themselves and they obviously hated his guts. Could it be that their pride and ego was so great that they would risk their lives to drag him back rather than have him escape from them? What could possibly be their motive for keeping him alive?

The rocky cliffs of Saipan's treacherous terrain were very difficult for the haggard, little band of half-starved, defeated warriors to negotiate. Having an ill prisoner did not help their situation. The cliffs harbored deep crevices and there were numerous caves. The intense pounding of naval gunfire and artillery had exposed many but some were still well hidden by the lush vegetation and the natural folds.

Many Japanese had sought refuge in the caves and they had been sealed in by the naval gunfire or artillery or had been burned alive by flamethrowers. The caves they had entered for refuge often became their tombs.

Winding down the narrow trails of the cliffs was treacherous. Climbing back up was slow and extremely fatiguing. Footing was unsure. Chic began to see the advantage in the split-toed rubber and canvas *jikatabi* shoes most of the Japanese wore. Suzuki was in and out of several caves on that second day. He seemed to be searching for something or someone.

As they approached some caves, it was obvious that there were dead entombed in them - the stench of death was overwhelming. There were bodies and parts of bodies in front of the entrances to some of the caves. Chic could see that it would be futile to search the bodies for food. That had obviously already been done. Many had their pockets cut open and the contents of their packs were strewn about helter skelter. Nothing of use had been left.

On one occasion, Suzuki sent two of his men into a well-concealed cave that he had just inspected. They emerged with a large sake bottle of water and a covered wooden bucket. Chic knew instinctively that the bucket contained rice. What he didn't know was that in their pockets were flat tin cans. When the cans were produced, Chic could read the large lettering on the labels. It was in English. They were 'Formosa' brand and contained crabmeat.

He prayed that they would share with him this nourishment that was so badly needed. Chic was given a scoop of rice on a green leaf. It was about as much as might fit in a tablespoon. Two small twigs sufficed as chopsticks. The young Marine savored every grain and made it last as long as possible. The rice was cold, but not rancid, it was edible and to someone starving, it was delicious. There was to be no crabmeat for the captive.

At the conclusion of this welcome repast and as the Japanese were all squatting and smoking, Suzuki barked something in Japanese at the one called Nakamura. He untied a little white rag and took a cigarette butt from it. Nakamura lit the butt and handed it to Chic. Chic bowed his appreciation for the gesture as he'd seen the Japanese do but he was too sick to appreciate the cigarette. As he smoked it he remembered his vow never to smoke another cigarette. It seemed so long ago, that awful day on the hill when his pack was shot to pieces and Mac had lost his legs.

Chic was becoming obsessed with escaping and tried to make plans. If only they had given him a little more of that rice, he could have saved it for after his escape. He had done his best to stay alert while they were moving and to look for signs that would help guide him back to friendly forces, but the fatigue, hunger and dengue fever combined to play tricks on his memory and to dull his sense of reasoning. One thing he could not lose sight of; he knew that he must get away soon if he wanted to live. He loved life and was not ready to give it up.

*   *   *   *   *   *   *   *   *

ALONE!

Silence! Darkness, none of the jungle sounds were emitted from the creatures of the night that he knew were out there. The only discernable sound was the pounding of his heart. He finally understood the expression, "The silence was deafening." Saipan was quiet. It was the first time he had been aware of complete silence since arriving on the Island so long ago. He couldn't remember ever wishing for the noise and inconvenience of rain or artillery until now. Now that he needed the sounds of war or nature to help cover his escape, they just weren't there.

One of the Nips was snoring erratically. He started and stopped and made noises with his throat. Oh God! Chic thought, he's sure to awaken the others with that racket.

The crunching of twigs was very distinct, then Chic heard the footsteps. One of his captors was up and walking. He grunted and walked over to the tree line. Chic thought the sound of his urinating would waken the others.

Chic had to do something. He sat upright, then got to his feet. It hurt like hell he was badly bruised. When he got up, he was devastated. He saw that all of his efforts at crawling so carefully had only resulted in moving him a couple of feet, not even a full yard. If Kurihara had looked right at him, he wouldn't have even noticed that Chic had been crawling toward freedom. There had been so little progress.

He walked over to the edge of the clearing, about ten feet from Kurihara, and tried to relieve himself. Was he foolish to try this? No! The Japanese apparently found it acceptable for him to do just what they themselves were doing. His life depended on what he did now. Kurihara walked back to his spot and Chic started back to his but, after just a couple of steps, he stopped and lay down. Still in the little draw that put him in a slight defilade but several steps closer to the edge of the clearing.

He thought to himself that this had been the smartest thing he had done. It got him closer to his objective. He didn't dare move for a very long time. His intense fear of being caught never waned or subsided. He was scared. But, he knew it was now or never. If discovered, his captors would surely kill him. If he didn't get away now, he would die from weakness and hunger. All day, he had been having hunger pangs.

He kept crawling, slowly, carefully, he just had to make it! The night was so still he could hear himself breathing. He could hear his arms and legs brushing across the ground as he moved them slowly ever forward toward the darkness and hoped-for safety and he could hear tiny twigs being crushed under his weight. These were very slight sounds, but in the imagination of the terrified young Marine, they were amplified a hundred-fold.

Suddenly, the stillness of the night was shattered by small arms fire. Suzuki and his men were sure to be awakened by the firing and were certain to spot him. He couldn't just rush back and lie down as though he'd been there all along. His imminent discovery was all the more tragic because he was so close to the edge of the clearing.

When the firing started, he froze. Thoughts of survival rushed through his mind. What could he do? He knew that if he tried to spring up and run like hell eight rifles would be firing at him simultaneously. His heart sank as he heard a Whooosh! and a pop. It was a flare. Someone down there somewhere below this jungle plateau was engaged in a firefight and needed illumination. He didn't dare move. His heart was pounding furiously and he again thought of rushing forward, come what may.

It was still the rainy season, why couldn't it be raining to mask the sounds he might make while escaping. No such luck, but the flare was not close, it was probably a quarter-mile away, still it added light to the very dark night. The firing tapered off, then stopped.

His movements were painfully slow and deliberate as the night wore on. One of them was up. Chic didn't dare to look, but he heard him distinctly. Someone on the other side of the clearing was moving around and walking. He muttered something under his breath. It was Japanese and Chic couldn't understand it but he thought it was cursing. Maybe the little bastard had stubbed his toe.

Now, another voice in Japanese and this time it sounded more familiar. Something like *"Damate nasai yoh!"* Chic had heard it before and thought it must mean, "Knock it off!" What an awful time for two of the Japs to get into an argument. He kept edging closer to freedom. As he crawled by Suzuki he could see the sergeant's face. Suzuki was sleeping soundly and his rosary beads were around his neck. The crucifix hung out where Chic could see it. It reminded him of the first time he had seen it, a welcome glimmer of hope in the blinding sunlight. It was right after that when he had been given that first precious drink of water. In his mind, the cross and the canteen would forever be related.

Why had they kept him alive? He couldn't know what it was but curiosity was gnawing at him. What had they in mind for him? What value could he have been to them? The young Marine would never know because he was either going to escape or he was going to die trying.

He must have been about 15 feet into the heavy bush when he realized that there was no trail. He was crawling through a maze of low growing shrubbery that was nearly impenetrable. It was, among other things, the dreaded tagnan-tagnan.

He was making precious little progress. For a while the element of fear was so great that he hardly felt the pain in his arms and legs. There were new pains now, his knees and elbows burned like they were on fire. They had long since been worn raw and were getting worse by the minute.

Chic was out of breath and his heart was pounding so loud that he thought his captors would hear it. But no, they were not his captors. Not anymore, he was away from them and they wouldn't hear his heart pounding but they would hear twigs and brush rustling if he tried to move too rapidly. He was up on his knees and hands now, creeping. He didn't dare try standing upright as yet.

He could not identify the sounds, but assumed they were made by rats and birds and whatever other creatures infested the depths of Saipan's jungle on a hot, steamy, July night. He noticed that it was getting much darker. The rain clouds must be gathering again but he didn't even bother to look up at them. He simply decided that the will to live was stronger than any other instinct and made himself keep going.

When the rain started to fall, he listened intently for any voices or sounds from the clearing. The rain was sure to awaken Suzuki and his men and they would find him gone. As close as he was, and moving so slowly, they were certain to locate him. He had to move faster.

His knees and elbows reminded him that there was a limit to how much pain a human being could endure. Both arms and legs were wet with blood now and when the cloth of his dungarees pulled away it smarted painfully. A considerable amount of the skin on his elbows and knees had been worn or scraped off.

The rain was falling harder, just what he had been hoping and praying for. He rose to a standing position and tried to walk. It was a slow laborious process, one step at a time. The twisted, tangled scrub bush was nearly impossible to get through. Every few steps, he would bump into a larger bush or tree and have to work his way slowly around it. It was very dark. Chic knew that he would have to get around to the far side of where the clearing was as he distanced himself from Suzuki's men. The firing had been down in that area and firing meant friendly troops. It could also mean enemy troops and extreme danger. He kept praying as he moved.

The distant firing started up again and this time he could detect the "pow-pow-pow" of a Browning automatic rifle. Whoever was doing the shooting was depressing the trigger for too long a time. Long bursts were not the way a real professional BARman would employ this fine weapon. He thought about Deadly Dave Donahoe and how he would caress his BAR firing short bursts of two and three rounds. Short bursts, but deadly.

He was trying to walk upright now and stiff legged because bending his blood-soaked legs was extremely painful. It just didn't work. If he was going to get through the jungle, he would have to use his legs as they were intended. More importantly, he was going to have to use his head. He had to find a trail. There was no way out of the terrible maze, except via the trails through the *tagnan-tagnan.*

He knew Suzuki couldn't find him now. It was too dark, and the rain was coming down heavy. They couldn't hear him. Unless he got turned around and stupidly blundered back into their clearing.

A few bursts of fire, which sounded like it was from another BAR, broke the silence. Then, another grenade. There was something going on down below him. It seemed to be on a lower elevation and it wasn't far off. He got back onto his feet and started forward holding his trousers out from his legs so the blood wouldn't keep sticking to them. A flash of lightening gave him some light for a moment but what he saw gave him no encouragement.

There were just trees and brush, in all directions and it was very thick. He kept forcing his legs forward one at a time. He had to keep moving and get to where that firing had come from. Suddenly, the ground under his feet was gone.

It was as though a dozen wildcats were scratching him all at the same time as he plunged rapidly downward. His buttocks bumped on what felt like very hard rocks as the downward momentum increased. There was no more brush scratching him, just bumps and the scraping of a very hard surface. The sound of pebbles and gravel plunging downward with him and the terror of realizing that he had gone over what was undoubtedly a cliff.

When he ground to a stop, he was facing forward, his hands outstretched. The heels of both hands were raw, bloody and burning. He could feel the dirt and gravel in his latest wounds. His knees were so painfully sore and bloody that he dared not kneel on them to get up. He rolled over, sat up and then tried to get on his feet. Slipping on the muddy ground he realized that he was out of the bush. Looking up through the darkness and rain he saw that he had come a long way down and he had done so very rapidly.

Suzuki and his band had no chance of finding him now. He hurt all over, he had hunger pangs, he was delirious with fever and sickness, and he was almost completely exhausted. But, if only he could stay alive, he was free!

" Halt, who is there!!?"

Chic froze, and his heart danced wildly within his breast, thank God, it was an American voice. There was the sound of a bolt slamming forward to the receiver of an M-1 rifle.

"Help me!" Chic called.

"Jack, did you hear that?"

"Yeah, a goddam Jap speaking English".

"What's the password you sonofabitch?"

Chic responded weakly, but with as much force as he could muster, "I don't know the password. I've been gone for a few days, the Nips had me but I got away."

Chic could hear other clicking sounds and knew it was M-1 rifles being taken off safety. The sound of bolts going forward told him that rounds were being chambered - they didn't believe him!

"Sergeant, get over here quick! I don't know how many of 'em are out there but one of 'em speaks English real good. Thinks he can fool us."

"Get the lieutenant up here and knock it off Jack! What if he's an American?"

"Hell Sarge, he ain't no American. What would an American be doing coming in from that direction? And he don't even know the password. Let's kill the bastard."

Chic yelled as loudly as he could, "I don't know what the password is now, but a couple of days ago it was 'Lala Palooza Lou.' No Nip can pronounce that and you know it! Now let me come into your position, I really need help."

"Throw your weapon out here and do it carefully!"

"I haven't got a weapon, I told you the Nips had me."

"Who won the World Series last year?"

"How should I know? I don't even remember who played in the series. I was too busy fighting in this damned war." Chic immediately thought of Hand Grenade Harrington and how he might have handled such a question. Harrington could have told them who won the series in each of the past 30 years - and then Chic remembered that Harrington, like so many others, was dead.

"Lieutenant, I told these guys he was a Jap. Let me open up before he throws a grenade at us. I know that's why he wants us to let him in closer. He's gonna try and kill us. Let's get him first."

Chic was sobbing and praying. He hadn't anticipated this. He firmly believed that all he had to do was tell them he was a Marine and everything would be all right. It was the lieutenant's voice now and he spoke with some authority.

"How do we know you're who you say you are?"

"Please, are you the lieutenant?"

"Yes."

"Lieutenant, let me talk to you please, I'm sick, and I'm hurt real bad, I'm a Marine!"

"All right you men, hold your fire, I believe him."

"Geez Lieutenant, you're gonna get us all killed. That guy is a Jap. He don't even know the password!"

"I said, hold your fire and I mean it. Put that rifle down Jack!"

Chic could see someone approaching him from out of the shadows. It was an American and he had a pistol in his hand.

"Over here sir, I don't think I can walk much farther."

"All right you men, get a medic up here now and tell him to bring a stretcher! We've got to get this guy back to battalion right away, he's got blood all over him!"

As Chic drifted in and out of consciousness, he was aware of some things going on around him but only vaguely. They had given him water and some pills. Someone had put dressings on his legs and arms and they had removed a stretcher from a jeep ambulance, lowered it and were now shoving it back in. Whoever was on the stretcher was covered with a blanket. He was going to have the privilege of riding on the top. The other stretcher contained a dead body. They were shoving his stretcher in now and he tried to get a look at the man by his right shoulder. Chic told himself he would never forget that voice.

"Hey Mac, is your name Jack?"

"Yeah, it is. Why?"

"When this war is over Jack, you'd better get your ass out of the Marine Corps just as fast as you can, because if you don't, I'm gonna find you, and when I do, I'm gonna kill you. Do you understand me?"

"No! What the hell are you talking about? I've never seen you before in my life. You must be crazy, I'm no goddam Marine! This is the 105th Infantry."

The jeep ambulance was moving now and Chic, try as he may, could not get a good look at the face of the soldier standing back there in the moonlight. The one who had been so intent on shooting him while he was trying to re-enter friendly lines. The soldier whose name was Jack.

Chic awoke on a folding cot under a mosquito net. Two Army medics were standing nearby looking at him. He motioned to them and asked for a priest. One nodded and walked away. The other medic pulled the net up and felt his forehead, then stuck a thermometer in his mouth and proceeded to take his pulse.

"Hello there, how do you feel?" It was an Army chaplain.

Chic responded, "Hello Padre, how long have you been here?" Oh, not long, you are a pretty sick soldier."

"I'm not a soldier. I'm a Marine Father, a U.S. Marine!" "Well son, its just the same, we're here to do our jobs and get this terrible war over with and go back home."

"Father, I'm a Protestant." "I know you are." "How'd you know that?" "I looked at your dogtags." "Father, if somebody is wearing rosary beads around his neck with a crucifix, does that mean he is a Catholic?"

"Well it certainly can mean that, why do you ask?"

"What about the Japs Father?"

"Oh, there are lots of Japanese Catholics and the natives here on Saipan, the Chamorros, most of them are Catholic. I've heard there was a beautiful Catholic Church here in the town of Garapan before we started bombing and shelling."

Chic thought it wise not to tell the priest that he had seen and been inside the shell that remained of the church in Garapan. Or that the face of Christ on the large crucifix over the altar had been defaced by gunfire.

"Father, I saw a Jap wearing a crucifix!"

"Of course, there's nothing unusual about that. There are many Catholics in Japan, especially in Kyushu, the south-ernmost island. That's where Nagasaki is located. I guess Nagasaki could be called the Christian capital of the orient. There is a large Protestant community there too."

Chic thought to himself that if he lived until the end of the war, as unlikely as that may be, once they invaded Japan, he just may go to see this Christian capital. Nagasaki, the place where Suzuki was from! The priest was still speaking but Chic did not hear him, he was asleep.

"I'll see about getting you some new fatigues son, there really isn't much left of your old ones."

Looking at the medic, the chaplain asked, "By the way Shapiro, what is he doing with that Japanese canteen?"

"Well Father, he's delirious or asleep most of the time but when he is awake, he says some pretty bizarre things. Claims he was a prisoner of the Japanese, that he escaped. Doctor Levy's going to see if we can get a psychiatrist to talk to him. He sure sounds to me like he needs some kind of help, maybe a straightjacket would be a good start when he recovers from the dengue fever."

"Well, since you mentioned it, I thought I detected a bit of hostility in him when I referred to him as 'soldier'."

"You know Father, it's kind of strange, but all of our Marine patients seem to be sensitive about that. It's almost as though being a Marine is like being part of a religious order or a cult of some kind. I think they're all a little crazy."

BED REST

Chic's cot was the last one in the tent but he noticed that no one ever entered or left the tent at his end. When the air-raid siren sounded, the medics would help hustle him and the other patients all the way to the far end of the tent, or ward as they called it. Just beyond the far end of the ward, someone had dug a large ditch for the patients to use as a common air-raid shelter.

He lifted the mosquito net and got out of his cot then pulled the tent flap back and stepped out into the sunlight. Right in front of him was a little concrete enclosure with a wall about 3 feet high and 9 inches thick. He sat on the little wall in his skivvies and looked things over. It was a rectangular enclosure about 6 feet long by 5 feet wide. The floor of the structure appeared to be dirt but with all of the recent tropical rains, it looked pretty muddy. July was the beginning of the rainy season on Saipan. If someone were to throw a little dirt in there to cover up the mud it would make a fine foxhole.

The sun was hot and Chic was still very weak so he left his seat on the wall of the concrete foxhole and moved back into the hospital tent. It was only about 10 feet from the foxhole to his end of the tent.

He planned to escape just as soon as he felt strong enough, and he decided he'd better start getting ready right now. He lifted the mosquito net and crawled into his cot. He would rest just a little while then get up again and try on the clothes the chaplain had Shapiro bring him. They were neatly folded under his cot.

Chic was soon up and getting dressed. He was weak, but could not waste time by just lying around. He looked, and couldn't believe his eyes! The clothes the chaplain had sent him were brand new U.S. Army fatigues. They were a much darker green than Marine herringbone dungarees and were cut entirely different. He put them on and immediately was uneasy. He felt like an imposter! He'd never worn an Army uniform before and somehow just couldn't feel right about it. He had to sit on the edge of the cot, he was still weak. He called to a medic who had just finished changing the dressings on a patient a couple of cots down from his.

"Hey medic! Where's Corporal Shapiro? "

"He's off! You can't expect us to be on duty twenty four hours a day can you?"

Chic answered half to himself.

"No, I guess not, only Marines do that. Look Buddy, I've got a problem and I need your help."

"Yeah, what is it?"

"Well, the chaplain had Shapiro get me this set of fatigues and my boondockers are under the cot, but he didn't bring me a cover or any socks and my socks are completely worn out."

"What's a cover?"

"A hat or a helmet! What the hell do you call it in the Army?"

"A hat or a helmet."

"Oh. Well, I'm sorry. I guess I expect everyone to speak Marine."

"Yeah, you guys are really a bunch of kooks! I've never had a Marine patient yet that was normal."

"Well, anyhow pal, do you think you can find me a pair of socks and a cover? The doctor told me just this morning that he thought I should be going to chow with the ambulatory patients."

"I'll see what I can do about some socks but you don't need a hat."

There was no field music to sound chow call in the Army hospital, they just quietly passed the word that anyone wanting to go to chow could do so. There was no formation, just stragglers. Chic watched some of the patients at the far end of the ward and followed them at a respectable distance. He decided to watch the others and see where the messhall was and do just as they did. No one wore a cover to chow.

The messhall turned out to be another hospital tent just like the ones the wards were in. Solid food tasted pretty good for a change. Chic's jaw actually felt tired just from chewing. The hot coffee was great. It tasted even better when he realized that it was his first cup of real coffee in a month. His last cup of coffee had been aboard ship on the morning of D-day, back on 15 June. Since then, all he'd had was the powdered coffee that came in K-rations and C-rations.

By the time Chic finished lunch and got back to his cot in the ward, he was really bushed. The treatment was working, he knew he was rapidly healing but he had a lot of strength to regain. They said a movie was going to be shown in one of the other ward tents but Chic fell asleep and missed it. He was up early and ready for morning chow. When Doctor Levy made his rounds, he found Chic all dressed and waiting.

"Just where do you think you're going young man?"

"After you finish checking me over I'm going to morning chow Doc."

"Medic, can't you people read a chart? I've prescribed bed rest for this patient. He's been through a lot and is in a weakened condition. If we expect the treatment to work, he's going to have to get plenty of rest."

"Doctor, I'm sorry, but he told the ward corpsman yesterday that you said he should go to the mess hall for his meals."

"Oh, I see. Well then, I don't suppose we'll need these charts anymore will we? Just ask the patients what the physicians have prescribed."

"Doctor, I'm really sorry. It won't happen again."

"Shapiro, you know how the Marine patients are. These kids have got to be a little crazy before the Marines will even take them. They're all like that."

When the doctor and his group were near the far end of the ward, Chic slipped out his end and walked around to the front on the outside. He had to step over several tent pegs and guy lines. He walked the short distance to the messhall tent and entered for breakfast. On his way back, Chic was feeling smug about going to breakfast and yet he was apprehensive as to whether he'd be found out. He was passing the second ward tent when he heard a shout, "Hey Yancey! Chic! In here, it's me, Eddie O'Neill!"

He entered the ward tent and noted that every patient was wearing a cast of one type or another. He spotted Eddie right away and saw that he had been badly shot up. Chic put a cigarette in Eddie's mouth for him to take a drag. Not because Eddie had asked for it, but because that's what he had seen done in the movies. The good guy always lit up a cigarette and put it between the lips of a buddy who was badly wounded or was dying.

"What happened to you Eddie?"

"We was ambushed Chic. The day after you went to sickbay. They told us the island was secured and we'd just be doing a little mopping up, so we cut the big patrols down to platoon size and really got our ass waxed. We ran into a pretty good-sized Jap position over by Marpi Point. Mortar fire hit me twice. The first time it wasn't so bad, just hurt like hell, but the second time I blacked out and didn't know anything until I woke up here.

Chic, you've got to help me. I know I'm hurt bad but these damned doggies don't know what they're doing. I think they want to amputate my right leg. Chic, help me get out to one of the Navy's hospital ships. They'll be able to fix me up and send me back to the States, I know they can. I can't let these guys cut my leg off."

The cigarette had fallen out of his mouth and was on his chest. Chic quickly brushed it off and noticed a red mark where it had started to burn Eddie. He hadn't flinched. Chic assumed he was on some pretty strong painkillers.

Back at his cot in the ward tent, Chic was confronted by an irate Shapiro who informed him that from now on, he would stay in bed and follow orders, "Or else." Whatever that meant. "Dammit Shapiro, I didn't mean to get you guys in any trouble. I just thought Doctor Levy would be pleased at how fast I was healing with all the wonderful care I was getting from you and the other medics. Look buddy, I really think of you as a friend. I appreciate all of the swell care you've given to me. Why, maybe after I get out of here, I'll even give you some of my Jap souvenirs. No, not that; don't even look at that canteen! It stays with me. I was thinking about a Jap flag or maybe even a Samurai sword or something. My outfit is right up where all of the good stuff is you know."

"Don't do me any favors, the only souvenir I want is an honorable discharge."

"Shapiro, you doggies are lucky we are officially at war with the Japs, 'cause if we weren't, we'd have plenty of justification for declaring war on the U.S. Army and don't you forget it. You're lucky you have a friend in the Marine Corps."

"Yeah, who's that?"

"Me, dammit. I told you before I think of you as a friend Shapiro. Say, by the way, you know that Marine patient over in the ward just before you get to the mess tent? His right leg is in a big cast from the waist down. He was hit by mortars a couple of times. Name's O'Neill, Private Eddie O'Neill."

"What about O'Neill?"

"Well, I was just wondering about him. He's a friend of mine and it looks like he got hit pretty bad."

"Well, I guess I could go over and look at his chart or maybe talk to the ward corpsman. I'll let you know after my watch."

"Thanks Doc, I'd really appreciate it."

Strange, Chic thought, I really would appreciate it. Old Shapiro isn't such a bad guy after all.

Shapiro was back and was gently shaking his young patient.

"Yeah, what is it Doc, more medicine?"

"No, I'm off duty. You wanted to know about that Marine patient, O'Neill."

"Oh yeah, sure. What did you find out Doc?"

"They're going to move him out to a hospital ship in the morning. They have better facilities for amputations than we do. If you want to see him again, you'd better do it tonight. He'll be moved down to the beach for evacuation early in the morning."

"Thanks Doc, I really appreciate the information."

The pain and anguish felt by Private Eddie O'Neill, USMC, could easily be seen in his facial expression.

"Hey Eddy, whatta ya think? They're moving you out to a hospital ship in the morning."

"Oh Chic, its you. A hospital ship? Back to the Navy Docs? Oh gee, that's great. I'm so thankful. I knew that if I stayed here much longer, these damned doggies were gonna cut my leg off. I'll really be glad to get out to a hospital ship. Chic, it's the only way I'm gonna save my leg."

"Yeah Eddie, the Navy will take good care of you. Maybe you'll even know some of the corpsmen when you get out there."

As Chic walked back to his ward, he felt depressed and guilty for not telling his friend why he was going aboard the hospital ship. The air-raid siren sounded and all was forgotten.

Pandemonium! Patients, medics, technicians and even some of the medical officers scrambled for their crudely dug community holes. Chic was knocked aside by the rushing horde. He was close to the trench near the front of his ward that served as an air-raid shelter. He quietly stepped in and hunkered down. Things were safer and more orderly up on the front lines. He'd had it with this place! He wasn't going to put up with this. The crowd reminded him of what Blackjack, his platoon sergeant, called a 'Chinese fire drill.'

"Washing Machine Charley" flew over, dropped a couple of bombs and continued flying through a remarkable display of tracer rounds, which filled the sky. It was soon over. Washing Machine Charley continued on his way and presumably returned to wherever he had come from. Every antiaircraft artillery piece on the island and aboard all the ships present had been firing at that lone aircraft which Chic assumed was a Japanese bomber. This was not one of the prouder moments for Navy, Army and Marine antiaircraft artillerymen in the greater Saipan area.

Chic silently vowed to himself that he would never again be trampled while attempting to enter the air-raid trench. In fact, he determined never to enter that trench again. There were safer places to withstand an air raid. His bruises and abrasions could not easily withstand the patients that were wearing casts and were inclined to bump and jostle whoever got in their way.

As Chic was returning to the ward following the air raid, he noticed packs, belts, helmets and other assorted field equipment piled on the ground between two tents. Barnes was assisting a patient who needed someone to lean on. Chic came alongside and took the patients free arm and put it around his neck, taking some of the weight off Barnes.

"Hey Doc, what's all that 782 gear doing piled up on the ground?"

"What's 782 gear?"

"You know, those packs and helmets and things over there."

"Oh, that's just a bunch of stuff waiting to go to salvage. There'll be a truck along to pick it up in a day or so."

"When guys come in here, don't they get to keep their 782 gear?"

"Not if they die or get sent out to a hospital ship or are flown out. What would they need that old field equipment for?"

"Nothing' I guess, just thought I'd ask."

Chic made a mental note to pick up a helmet the next time he passed this way. Before they could get into the ward it was sprinkling.

When Chic got back to his bunk, he was out of breath. His strength wasn't coming back as rapidly as he hoped. He needed to walk more, to build up his wind. He tucked the mosquito net in around him and lay back to relax. The rain was coming down hard now and Chic liked the sound of it hitting the canvas. There were gusts of wind, and with the wind and rain together, the air seemed clean and refreshing. It had been a long time since Chic had consciously taken a good deep breath without somehow smelling decaying bodies or rotting jungle vegetation.

Water started dripping on the top of his mosquito net. He crawled out and moved his cot at an angle so the dripping missed it and fell to the dirt deck of the tent. He spotted a bedpan nearby and placed it under the leak. He felt relaxed and at peace and soon drifted into a sound sleep.

Chic sensed someone gently kicking the end of his cot to awaken him. He sat up immediately. Two medics were waiting to take his vital signs and give him more medication. One was Barnes and the other one was new. Chic thought to himself how nice it was to be awakened gently by someone's boot on your cot. He would never forget Suzuki's men kicking him. The little bastards didn't have to do that. But then, he thought of the alternative. They very well could have stuck a bayonet through him.

He was glad to be alive and healing. Secretly, he knew that he would always love life more than anyone could imagine. He'd had some close calls that made him appreciate life very much.

It was morning and Chic had returned from breakfast. Doctor Levy did not make his usual rounds. Another doctor came instead, an Army lieutenant colonel. When they were approaching Chic's cot, he heard a medic say,

"Here he is doctor; this is the patient Doctor Levy was telling you about."

The lieutenant colonel doctor insisted that Chic take off his fatigues and submit to a thorough examination of his legs and hips. The doctor seemed to be duly impressed and made some notes then he asked,

"Do you expect me to believe these bruises were made by the Japs kicking you?"

"Yes sir, that's what happened."

"What about all these cuts and abrasions, what happened here? Did the Japs claw you with their fingernails?"

Chic sensed that the doctor was trying to be funny or didn't believe him. He was hurt and angry at the same time.

"Doctor, when I got away, it was very dark and it was raining hard. I had to crawl through some really tough jungle - then I fell over the edge of a cliff through some *tagnan-tagnan*, which scratched the hell out of me. It was in the dark, and frankly, I'm surprised I lived through it. I prayed more that night than I had anytime before in my life. Then, when I finally found an American position, one of your Army men tried to shoot me because I didn't know the password. I'm sorry if the Colonel doesn't believe me, but that's what happened."

"I do believe you son, I believe you. You've had a terrible experience but you're going to be all right now, you just need plenty of rest. Those bruises will be fading away before you know it. We'll take good care of you here."

"Yes sir, thank you sir."

He didn't buy it. Army officers were not to be trusted, they didn't talk or act like our Marine officers. Chic knew he was healing and soon he would be able to make his escape from the Army. He lay back on his cot and dozed off. When the air-raid siren went off, Chic was sleeping soundly. He awoke with a start and got to his feet - still groggy.

* * * * * * * * * *

The Concrete Foxhole

"Oh no, Washing Machine Charley again! Half the United States Army will try to fit into that oversized foxhole beating their way in with casts and crutches. I'm not going to let some character club my bruises with his cast. I've got the best foxhole on the island all to myself."

Still in his skivvies and with no time to spare, Chic noted all the others had already evacuated the ward. He quickly hobbled out his end of the tent to his concrete foxhole. He sat down on the wall and turning, threw his legs over. Thud! Thud! Thud! This time, Washing Machine Charley wasn't kidding. His bombs were dropping close! Without hesitation, Chic slid into the foxhole.

What a surprise! When his feet hit the deck, they just kept going down. The 'floor' was warm and had the same consistency as soft mud, but with a very strong odor. When his feet hit bottom, the warm ooze was nearly up to his armpits. Chic had experienced plenty of unusual things in the Marine Corps, but this one was really different. His heart was beating so hard it hurt. He was completely out of his element and felt near panic. He was afraid to take a step because the soft 'mud' might swallow him up. He didn't want to drown in the stuff and he didn't want to admit to himself what it really was. He just wanted to think of it as mud. As the odor assailed his nostrils, he fought to keep his hands and arms above the muck and mire. His arms were getting heavier by the second.

Finally, the all clear sounded! It seemed like hours had passed. He wanted desperately to lower his throbbing arms, now covered by big blue-green flies. He repeatedly called for help but his pleas were unheard. 'Oh God, what have I gotten into this time? No one has come out of my end of the tent since I got here, they always use the other end. I'm completely alone in this pit with no way out.' He ran his hands along the concrete but it was completely smooth. Nothing to hold on to and the top was about two feet beyond his reach. "Help! Help! Down here! Help!" It was all to no avail.

He was desperate. He was tired, alone, his arms ached and no matter how he yelled no one seemed to hear. When he did holler, his voice bounced off the four smooth concrete walls with a strange hollow sound that almost had an echo. The flies were biting his arms, the top of his head and the back of his neck. He kept brushing them from his face. Oh God! He thought, I got through boot camp and combat. I got shot and recovered. I got captured and escaped and now the Army's got me in a 'shit-pit' and they're going to let me drown in it. Why did I ever have to be sent to a damned Army hospital?

Chic prayed and he hoped. There seemed to be nothing else he could do. He thought, "Dammit, I'm a Marine! I'm going to come through this just like I have everything else."

As bad as everything else was in his concrete foxhole, the acoustics were pretty good. He sang a couple of songs which were not complimentary to the Army. His voice sounded much better than it had back home in the shower but singing was not his forte. He never could carry a tune. He bellowed out, "Awn, hup, treep! Treep fow ya left!"

Counting cadence was something a Marine could do. If they couldn't hear his calls for help, maybe they'd hear him counting cadence. He felt like an idiot. The only way he could be saved was by being heard. He was really tired. He thought his cadence sounded pretty good, but still, no one heard him. He couldn't go on forever. "From the Halls of Monte-zoou-ma, To the Shores of Tripoli!" He belted out "The Marine's Hymn" in the loudest voice he could muster - singing and praying that someone would hear it.

"Corporal Shapiro! Get over here. Your Marine friend has gone completely batty!"

It was one of the medics.

"We need a derrick to get the damned fool out of this old cistern and we need a straight jacket to contain him after we get him out."

"Oh my God!"

It was Shapiro's voice.

"He's up to his armpits in crap and he's singin' "The Marines' Hymn!" Nobody is gonna believe this, not even the psychiatrist."

"Shapiro, you dumb doggie, get me outta here!" Chic was pleading.

Shapiro thought, "Well, at least he's coherent."

The sergeant asked, "Okay Shapiro, just how do you propose to get him out of there?"

"What do you mean me? You're a sergeant! How are you going to get him out?"

The sergeant replied in a stage-whisper intended for Chic to hear, "I say we do ourselves a favor and leave him in there. We've got too many of these crazy Marines around here as it is."

"When you Army pukes finish your vaudeville act up there, get me outta here and do it fast. I can't stand up any longer and there's no feeling left in my arms!"

The sergeant, becoming concerned, barked, "Barnes, find a ladder and hurry up about it."

"Okay Sarge, but where?"

"I don't care where, just go somewhere and find a ladder and bring it back here fast. Otherwise, this damn fool Marine is gonna die."

The sergeant looked around the immediate vicinity and found an old length of bamboo. Holding one end, he reached over the concrete wall and lowered the other end to Chic.

"Okay, hold on to the end tightly and Shapiro and I will pull you out. Just don't get near us when you are out. Shapiro!!"

Corporal Shapiro was nowhere in sight. Chic grabbed the bamboo but his arms would not support his weight sufficiently for him to be pulled up. By now, there were several Army people watching - from a distance. Their curiosity was obvious but the smell was not pleasant. Shapiro was back with a heavy Manila hemp rope. He and the sergeant tied it in a noose, which they passed down to Chic. He placed it around his chest under his arms and they hoisted the unfortunate Marine up and out of his concrete foxhole.

Two of the Army personnel hosed Chic off. One held and aimed a hose while the other pumped a portable water tank. Chic was then marched unceremoniously to an outdoor shower, which was supplied by a 55-gallon drum on a wooden overhead platform. Shapiro reappeared with clean skivvies

for Chic and stated,

"My sergeant says if I have anything further to do with any of you Marines, he's going to put me in the stockade for the rest of the war. Do you know what that means?"

"Sure" Chic replied and then explained, "Your Army stockade is kind of a mild version of our brig. It would really be a good deal for you Doc. You wouldn't be any worse off than you are in this damned place and if they make you a prisoner, you won't have to stand any more duty. And do you know what else? As a prisoner, you won't have to go into combat. I'd definitely take him up on it if I were you."

The look on Shapiro's face indicated that he now fully realized that Marines actually were crazy. He was glad he was going off duty and wouldn't have to be near this madman.

When they marched Chic back to the ward, he could see that a couple of Japanese prisoners were shoveling quicklime into his concrete foxhole. He was very glad to lie down and was thankful for the slight anonymity provided by the mosquito netting. He was now well known to the staff and patients alike and was not enjoying his popularity.

After evening chow, while walking back to the ward, Chic reached into the pile of field equipment and found a steel helmet. He wished it had a camouflaged cover but it did not. He put the helmet on his head just as it started raining. Good, he thought, maybe they'll think I just want it for a rain hat.

Chic had now acquired all the items he would need to make his escape. He could sense impending new adventures and knew his escape from the Army was imminent. He walked back to the ward with a feeling of exhilaration softly whistling "The Marines' Hymn."

* * * * * * * * *

Marine Gunner

The medic stated, "It's nearly Oh four thirty hours."

Chick smiled to himself. In the Navy and Marine Corps, it was simply 0430. He would soon be back where people could tell time without always saying "hours". Believing that the best time for him to make his escape would be while it was still dark, he slipped out the back end of the ward tent for the last time. He worked his way close to the dirt road where the jeeps and trucks would be moving after daylight. In spite of some continuing weakness he felt greatly relieved finally making his escape.

There was a two-man security post less than 100 yards from the hospital compound. Chic watched the two Army sentries with interest and wondered if he should toss a couple of pebbles near their post to scare them awake and make them more alert, but he decided against it. If he had to run to escape, he was too weak and wouldn't make it. He stealthily circumvented their post and continued on his way to freedom. The rain didn't bother him.

Daylight streaked across the sky like a rocket and to Chic, the sky, the sun, the clouds and everything he beheld seemed somehow beautiful. He had never thought about the sunrise being beautiful before but this time it was different. He was free and he would soon be back with the Marines having new adventures. He was walking on the side of a road recently topped with crushed coral. There were lots of puddles from the rain, but it was slacking off now and would soon stop.

The first vehicle to come into sight was a jeep being driven by a Marine. The driver stopped and asked Chic what he was doing walking down the road without a weapon and where he was going. Chic tried to explain that he had just escaped from the Army and had to get back to his unit. Marine Gunner Gene B. Robinson was not buying it.

"Sonny, it appears to me that we have a problem here. First of all, I doubt very much that you are a Marine. Why are you wearing Army clothes, including an Army helmet? And, no self respecting Marine would be without his weapon on Saipan. Not even in a rear area like this unless he was a deserter or crazy, or maybe both. Get in! We're going to take you someplace and get this straightened out."

Chic had seen but had not recognized the tactical marks on the jeep so he asked the gunner what outfit he was with.

"I'm a bomb disposal technician with the V Amphibious Corps. Now suppose you tell me what outfit you're with. I know a soldier when I see one!"

"Dammit Gunner! Don't call me a soldier, I'm a Marine! I'm in the 8th Marines. I got separated from my outfit and wound up in an Army hospital. It was awful, I've had enough of the damned Army and I just want to get back to my outfit. That's all"

"Where are your Marine dungarees?"

"They were all ragged and bloody and the doggies took them away from me. An Army chaplain got this outfit for me. He didn't know I was going to use it to escape."

"What about your outfit? What battalion are you in and who's the CO?"

"I'm in the 2nd Battalion and the new CO is Major Chamberlain. It was Colonel Crowe, but he got hit a couple of times the first day."

"I knew Jim Crowe, served with him in France and Germany right after the big war and again in China. He was one fine Marine, sure am sorry he's dead."

"He isn't dead Gunner. We all heard he was dead too, but after a couple of days, a strange thing happened. Major Chamberlain who is now the CO started getting radio messages from him, from USS *Solace*, the hospital ship. He had somehow gotten an SCR-300 radio aboard that ship and he was trying to take over and command the battalion by radio.

"Sounds just like Jim, he wouldn't give up command easily, that's for sure. But the professor will make a fine battalion commander. I knew him in Iceland when we were in the 6th Marines and we called him the professor then too. For a Reserve, he's a pretty good Marine officer. Tell me kid, what was Crowe like?"

"Well sir, he could chew ass better'n any officer in the Marine Corps. He had sharp eyes that could bore a hole right through you. Nobody ever lied to him 'cause he would've known it and he would probably have killed them. He has a big chestnut colored mustache; it's waxed and comes out to points. He always keeps it looking sharp, even in the field. Gunner, I really am a Marine and everything I'm telling you is true. Look, I've still got my dogtags, read 'em."

"No kid, I don't want to see your dogtags. You've made a believer out of me; you couldn't know all this if you weren't one of Jim Crowe's Marines. I believe your story. Now we've got to find out how to go about getting you back to your outfit, wherever they are.

"You know, about that Army uniform you're wearing, that's really nothing new. After we'd been in France a while in 1917, they made us turn in our Marine greens and we all had to wear Army uniforms for the rest of the war. Some of us started drilling holes in our steel helmets and putting our Marine emblems on the front so everyone would know just who we were.

"Of course, there was a big stink over the Marine emblems and we got accused of defacing government property. I guess they wanted to court-martial a few of us to set an example. But you know Chic, before the Army could bring charges against any of us every Marine in the brigade had the eagle, globe and anchor on his steel pot. And I mean from the commanding general, old Johnny Jingle-Britches himself, right down the chain of command to the last private in the rear rank. That's the way it was in the 'Old Corps'. Marines were a close-knit outfit and they really stuck together. A man's rank didn't mean nearly as much to him as being a Marine did."

Bouncing along in the jeep at daybreak and listening to the old gunner reminisce was like a tonic for Chic. He hadn't ridden in a jeep since first coming overseas. When his battalion went anywhere, they generally walked. That's what the infantry was all about.

"Looks like someone's in trouble," the gunner was indicating a 2½ ton truck off to the side of the road and headed in the opposite direction.

"No one stops along here unless he has to. There's still plenty of well-armed Japs all over the island."

As Chic glanced at the truck, the driver was just closing the hood. He noticed with satisfaction that the tactical marking stenciled on it was a yellow rectangle, the mark of the 8th Marines. As they pulled over to the side, Chic exclaimed, "Hey Gunner! They're from the 8th Marines."

"Need any help Mac?"

"Not now Gunner, I've finally got it running okay. Thanks just the same."

It was Chic who spoke next.

"Hey Marine, where're you headed?"

"I'm just taking a load down to Graves Registration at the Division cemetery then I'll be going back up to the 8th Marines. That is, after I slosh out the back of my rig with water to get the blood washed out."

"I need a ride up to the Second Battalion."

"Sure, I know right where they are. I'll be glad to take you over there after I drop this load off. You'll have to ride on the outside until we offload. We got hit last night and the back's full of dead Marines."

The gunner reached back into the jeep and retrieved something that he handed to Chic. "Here kid, you don't want to forget this, I know souvenirs mean a lot to you young fellows."

It was Suzuki's canteen.

Pfc Jim Yancey turned and looked at Marine Gunner Robinson. The older Marine stretched out his hand, Chic took it and as they shook hands, their eyes met with a steady, honest appraisal of one another. Marines of two generations, standing beside a truck filled with the bodies of their dead, on a battle scarred island in the middle of the Pacific Ocean. Chic sensed that this was an important moment in his life. As the young Marine and the old Gunner gripped hands in a firm shake, the torch was passed. The older Marine spoke softly, "Take good care of our Marine Corps son."

"Aye, aye, Sir."

Chic stepped back one pace and gave the gunner his sharpest salute. Marine Gunner Gene B. Robinson returned it in kind, got back into his jeep and moved on. Chic thought to himself what a strange thing for him to have said. "Take good care of our Marine Corps."

*   *   *   *   *   *   *   *   *   *

The first sergeant greeted the delegation and suggested that the company commander might wish to listen to what may prove to be of some interest to him. Chic glanced at Captain Barrett but, as usual, the skipper's granite face revealed nothing. First Sergeant Stewart had a few choice words for Yancey's ears and he started with, "Well, there goes another perfectly good Muster Roll shot all to hell! Just how are we going to explain it this time Skipper? I've never had to perform so much administrative sleight of hand in official documents over one clown before in my entire Marine Corps career. In fact, another entry with Yancey's name on it may just be the end of my career! And maybe yours to boot Captain. After all, as the commanding officer you sign these fictitious works of administrative legerdemain.

"Pfc Yancey, what I am alluding to is the fact that we ran you on the Muster Roll as sick, evacuated to battalion. We then received inquiries from battalion as to who and where you were. They had no record of you being checked into sickbay. There was concern at battalion that our record keeping was below par and left something to be desired. There was also a great deal of interest in Lieutenant Yoakum's decision to leave one of his Marines alone and sick in the jungle.

"The battalion sergeant major and I were able to work things out and get the first muster roll back from regiment and re-do it after conducting an extensive search for you. Not only the company muster roll, but the battalion muster roll as well had to be completely re-written just to get you off of it as a medical evacuee and run you as missing. The sergeant major has other things he would like to have his clerks do besides reconstructing muster rolls to suit the particular 'status of the day' of one of our Pfc's.

"You may be flattered to know that the United States Marine Corps has initiated two, not one mind you but two, investigations into your case. One was to determine what the hell happened to you when you vanished from that trail in the jungle. You were supposed to wait for the Battalion Aid Station and had been so instructed. The other was to determine if Lieutenant Yoakum was derelict in the performance of his duties by losing a Pfc rifleman. The investigation of the lieutenant was terminated by a Jap land mine.

"Now suppose you start right at the beginning and tell us as much as you can about your adventures, including where you have been, how you got there, and why you are masquerading as a soldier. I would like to know why you have no rifle, pack or personal gear except for a damned Jap canteen. When you finish, I'll make a recommendation to the Skipper here, which may be anything from patting you on your little pointed head to slamming your worthless ass in the nearest brig! After I've made my recommendation the Captain will make a decision as to just what we are going to do for you, to you or with you. Now sound off! And it had better be good."

Chic reluctantly told the whole incredible story. He covered everything except his escapade in the concrete foxhole which he didn't dare relate to anyone.

When Chic had finished his tale, the first sergeant looked at the company commander and waited for him to speak. The captain's face still looked as though it had been chiseled from granite as he glanced at the first sergeant, who simply stated, "Hell Skipper, you know what my recommendations are."

Captain Barrett looked at Chic and spoke slowly and distinctly, "Yancey, I'm sending you back to your platoon. We need all the experienced riflemen we can get. In the meantime, Shanghai will see to it that your platoon guide finds you a rifle and I understand your platoon sergeant has some influence with battalion supply (Blackjack's brother Milt was the battalion supply sergeant).

"He will arrange to get you some dungarees and an issue of 782 gear. I'll inform the battalion commander of your story and see if he wants us to draw up the charge sheet on you or if they would prefer to do it at battalion. You may have to reimburse the government for your lost rifle and equipment and at the end of your enlistment you will likely have to make up for the lost time. You at least showed enough initiative to escape from the Army and come back to us so I'll see if I can talk the old man into letting you keep your Pfc stripes."

Chic felt nauseous in the pit of his stomach, his knees were shaking and he had a strong compulsion to blurt out that he was a good Marine and hadn't done anything wrong. Somehow he was able to maintain control of himself long enough to mumble the expected, "Aye, aye, Sir. Thank you, Sir".

In turning to leave, Chic was almost certain that he detected an ever-so-slight smile briefly start to crack the granite veneer of the captain's face. And just for the slightest moment, he even thought he saw a twinkle in the captain's eye. Briefly, he even thought the captain winked - but that was totally out of the question, he would never do such a thing. It had to have been Chic's imagination. The Skipper glanced at the first sergeant and snapped, "Top! Get someone over at battalion who knows what he's doing and find out just who is supposed to be running that Army hospital! I think the Marine Corps is entitled to a full explanation of why they didn't respond to our queries about Yancey or at least report that they had him as a patient. Then see what you and the sergeant major can do about the muster roll entries on Yancey. Just run him as present for duty and that's it."

Chic walked back to the platoon's position with Blackjack and Shanghai. Shanghai told Chic to put his gear in the hole he was sharing with Chief. The three of them would be in the same foxhole for the next couple of days then turning to Chief he said, "Chief, keep an eye on this bird, I don't want him getting lost in the damned jungle and joining up with the Japs again. Meanwhile, Childs is finding him an M-1. When he gets the rifle, give him some ammo and take him out in front of our position and have him test fire it and zero it in."

Chief and Chic came back into the line from firing a few rounds and found Stash Stahoviak waiting with dungarees, a camouflaged helmet cover and a full issue of well-worn 782 gear. Stash handed Chic a Memorandum Receipt Book and said: "Here Chic, you've got to sign a 734 slip for this stuff. You know the Marine Corps never parts with anything without getting a signature on a memorandum receipt.

Chief, who seldom spoke unless it was necessary, scowled at Chic and said: "Kid, I don't know how many haversacks the Marine Corps has issued to you but that's the third one you've gotten since you've been in this squad. You'd better start taking care of your equipment or you ain't going to be able to afford to get out when your enlistment is up. You know you've got to reimburse the government for all those haversacks."

Chic knew that Chief had seen his first haversack shot full of holes when Mc Laughlin lost his legs on the hills above Garapan and he would soon learn that the Japs had taken the second one away from him when he was their prisoner. Stash was grinning from ear to ear as he and Chic realized that the stoic Chief actually was attempting humor. It was the first time any of the men had witnessed such a thing.

Chic removed the Army fatigues and put on Marine dungarees and a change seemed to come over him. He knew now that he was really back. Glancing down at his left breast pocket, he looked at the USMC and the Marine emblem stenciled in black. He had learned in Boot Camp that the U.S. Marines were the only military service in the world that always went into combat proudly wearing their Corps emblem over their hearts. He had remembered it but it was just another tradition and really didn't mean much until now. From this moment on that stenciled Marine Corps emblem over his heart would have tremendous significance.

It was Chic's first night back and he was on watch.

"Chief, I've got some movement out to the right front. Its about 20 yards out! Look over there and tell me if you see anything."

"Sure, two big rats, I was watching them earlier when I had the watch. Don't worry about them; they're just looking for chow. As long as they are moving around out there, you know there's no live Japs close to them. Watch your left front that's the most likely avenue of approach. Now, how about telling me how you stayed alive when the Nips had you?"

"Okay, if you want to hear it, but there's not really much to it. They were hungry and sick and I think most of the fight had gone out of them. They were mean as hell but at least they didn't try to kill me. They must have been trying to find an officer to turn me over to. I guess they would have killed me soon if I hadn't gotten away when I did.

"When the Japs moved through the jungle, they didn't have anyone out on the flanks and the point man was just the first guy in the file. They didn't really move tactically and they were noisy. They were starving yet they didn't know what might be edible and what wasn't. In fact, they didn't know any more about surviving in the damned jungle than I did and that's sure not much."

"You need to talk to Shanghai. Tell that to him. He can probably tell you why they kept you alive and what they were going to do with you. He knows a lot about the Japanese and he is always studying and trying to learn more. As far as I'm concerned, he knows more about the Nips than anyone else in the regiment does and maybe in the whole 2nd Marine Division.

The gruff voice of Shanghai Pooley cut through the darkness as he asked,

"Why don't you guys shut up and let a man get some sleep! Chief, for an Indian that's supposed to be so quiet, you are certainly destroying your reputation tonight. Hell, if you two are going to talk about me, you should at least do it when I'm not around to listen to you."

Chief showed no emotion but Chic was embarrassed. He thought Shanghai had been asleep. Chic was also consumed with curiosity. He hoped he would be able to talk directly to Shanghai sometime and find out about his adventures in China. The old sergeant was reading Chic's mind. He looked at him in the dim light of the moon and gently said: "It's a long story kid and I try not to think about it anymore than I have to. Chief gives me more credit than I deserve when he says I know a lot about the Japanese. If I really knew a lot about them I wouldn't be here tonight and I sure as hell wouldn't be a buck sergeant. I can't tell you why they let you live. I can't even venture a guess why they didn't kill you. I'll tell you one thing though; you are damned lucky to be alive. The soldiers we've been fighting here on Saipan are in the 31st Army. Before being assigned to the 31st, many of them were in the Kwangtung Army in China and Manchukuo - and they are brutal sons-of-bitches. They would probably get a great deal of pleasure out of slowly torturing you to death. Just in case you haven't heard, they have had lots of experience torturing and killing people. You'll learn a lot more about that when we get back to China"

Shanghai continued, "As far as jungle fighting is concerned, I've heard the same propaganda as you have but I never put much stock in it. Most of them have never seen a jungle before. Remember their experienced troops were in China for a long time. It gets colder than a well digger's ass up there. The ones I've talked to have only been on Saipan a short while. They were more concerned with preparing defensive positions and learning to repulse an amphibious assault than they were surviving in the jungle."

Chic was impressed with Shanghai's knowledge of their

Japanese adversaries. He asked, "Sergeant, how do you know they are in the 31st Army or that they served in China?"

"Hell that's easy, I've been talking to them. We need all the intelligence information we can get and there's no better source than Japanese prisoners. You see kid, once they have been captured; their lives are over as far as they are concerned. There is no greater disgrace for a Japanese fighting man than to be captured by the enemy. Once we have them, they've got nothing left to lose. They don't expect to ever go home and they don't feel they owe Japan anything because the Japanese consider them dead. I haven't met one yet that wasn't willing to answer questions if he was treated right and given food and a few cigarettes. Now both of you shut to hell up and let me get some sleep!"

Chic thought about what Shanghai had said. He wanted to understand the Japanese. He sincerely wanted to know what it was that made them so different. Chic could not help feeling respect for their bravery and discipline but he also felt considerable contempt for them. Every U.S. Marine he had ever known wanted to live. The Japanese, for some reason, seemed intent on dying for their Emperor.

Chic had much to think about during his turn at watch on that first night back with the platoon. It had been an eventful day starting with his escape from the Army hospital and meeting Marine Gunner Robinson. He had re-entered a world where there were no longer medics to supervise his every move. No more doctors to look at his wounds and bruises as though he were some kind of a freak. Unfortunately, there would no longer be the opportunity to sit down at a mess table to eat hot Army rations.

The harsh blue-black clouds had spread themselves over a soft peach- colored sky vainly trying to hold back the dawn. They gradually separated, fell back and were consumed by daylight. It was morning on Saipan.

"Where the hell do you think you're going?" demanded Shanghai.

"I'm going on patrol with you guys. I'm back in your squad, remember?" was Chic's response.

Shanghai scoffed, "Yeah, I remember. Life has just been too good to me lately. Listen kid, and get this straight. I'm not going to have some "sick-bay commando," just back from a leisurely vacation in a doggie hospital hold this squad back if we get in a firefight or if we've got to go through rough terrain or climb one of those damned cliffs. You are assigned to stay here and maintain security on our gear.

Get yourself back into shape so you can do the job the Marine Corps is paying you to do. When we get back this afternoon, I'll take you out for a little run. I'll decide then whether you are an asset or a liability to the squad".

Life in the field had its drawbacks but at least it was the rainy season. They could take a shower simply by soaping down just before a rainstorm then standing out in the open and letting the rain wash off all the soap. There was usually more than adequate rain to do the job. When he stripped down to wash, Chic got considerable attention from the others. His bruises went from his hips to his ankles and were various shades of purple and blue with some tinges of brown and green. Suzuki and his men may have saved Chic's life but they left marks on him that made him understand what low regard they had for him. The marks would last for weeks.

The next night was uneventful and passed slowly. Eventually, it was time to awaken the sergeant for his watch. Chic wanted to stay awake and talk to Shanghai and ask him about many things, but it would have to wait for another time. As soon as he curled up at his end of the hole, he was asleep.

It was morning in the Marianas and Muldoon asked the same question that all the men had been asking every day.

"When are we gettin' outa' this damned place?"

The answer, which had been the same every day, came from Ross.

"The word is that we'll be leaving to go aboard ship any day now. The music says it may even be tomorrow. We're supposed to land on Tinian sometime this month. Besides, what are you bitching about? You never had it so good!"

*   *   *   *   *   *   *   *   *   *

Shanghai's Secret

Chic was glad to be back to duty and plodding along on the trail with his buddies. Looking to the right and left he glanced up from time to time making certain there were no Nip snipers overhead. An enemy could be very close and yet remain unseen in the jungle. Periodically, the point men would shift positions and two fresh men would rotate up. It was important to keep sharp men on the point, men who could be relied upon to remain constantly on the alert.

Corporals Jerden and Riverboat Brown usually traded off bringing up the rear. Fearless and Deadly Dave had just come off the point and rejoined the main body. Fearless asked Dutch Shute to change places with him and when asked why, he replied:

"Cause Butcher's back there, that's why. I don't want any damned swabbies walking behind me."

"But Fearless, Butcher's a corpsman! He's one of us."

"I know he's a corpsman you dumb ass! And don't kid yourself about corpsmen, they're the worst kind! You never know when one of them is gonna reach out and stick a needle into you or give you the wrong kind of medicine and screw you all up. I'm tellin' you Dutch, you shouldn't trust those guys and believe me, the Navy doctors they work for are just as bad."

"What! How can you say a thing like that Fearless?"

"Well Dutch, just think about it for a minute. Those Navy doctors go to school for years and they are supposed to be professionals. Doesn't it seem strange to you that what they do after all that time is still called practice?"

Fearless Frank was probably the only Marine in the Fleet Marine Force who despised Navy corpsmen. It was an obsession he seemed unable or unwilling to overcome.

Walking along with his rifle cradled in his arms and thinking of nothing in particular, Chic started sizing up his lot in life. How fortunate he was to still be alive. So many of the old hands were gone now. Who would be next? He thought about Tinian, the next campaign. What would it be like? The Japanese over on Tinian Island had certainly had plenty of time to prepare their defenses and they knew the Marines would be coming soon. Would they have blockhouses and bunkers like Tarawa? How many more of his buddies would be killed or badly wounded?

"Why do we have to take the damned island anyway?"

He was thinking out loud now and Epstein answered, "You mean Tinian?"

Obviously he was thinking of the same things as Chic. They probably all were.

"Yeah, it's only three miles across the channel. Why couldn't we just pound it with artillery from Saipan and by-pass it entirely. We've got Saipan dammit! Why do we need another island just three miles away? We've already lost enough guys taking this damned place!"

Riverboat Brown was not an old Corps Marine, he was a replacement, but he was a corporal and as such, he had to occasionally assert himself.

"No wonder you guys are still privates. Did you ever consider that if we didn't need Tinian, we wouldn't be taking it? Did you ever notice how flat that place is? There are no mountains or hills on it. That island could be made into a huge airfield. We could station our big bombers over there, you know, like the B-17's and the B-24's. They could maybe fly all the way to Japan and blow the hell out of the Nips. If we did something like that, then we wouldn't have to take any more islands. We could drop enough bombs on the Japs to end the war. It could be over in just a couple of more years or so."

Riverboat's idea was preposterous, the only way we were going to defeat Japan was to take the China Coast and then stage enough men and equipment there to invade Japan. It would take years, at least until 1948. All the men knew it would take years to get to Japan. All the men that is, except Riverboat Brown. They had been keeping their voices low as they talked, but not low enough. Shanghai was upset. After halting the patrol, he quietly let it be known that the next sonofabitch that uttered a sound was going to get his butt kicked. The patrol resumed in silence.

Back in the company area the men's nerves were on edge. No one was looking forward to hitting another beach. The nights were all the same. Once in a while a few lost Japanese soldiers would blunder into the company's area while out foraging for food or supplies and a minor firefight would ensue with the usual results. Chic's strength had returned quickly after his escape from the Army hospital but he continued to stay in the foxhole with Shanghai and the Chief.

The first sergeant's voice announced, "Okay, all you guys that are Catholic, the chaplain's comin' up here to hear your confessions and after that, he's gonna say mass."

Private Kevin Mulcahy looked up at the priest with deep respect and told him that when he sang in the choir back home in his parish the choir director would occasionally have him do a solo. The priest thought that was nice and casually asked Choirboy if he'd like to sing one during mass today. Mulcahy looked down for a moment then he looked up at the priest and modestly said he would like to try.

"What would you like to sing Kevin?"

"Please Father, would it be alright if I sing the 'Ave Maria'?"

"Do you think you can do it?"

"Sure Father I can do it, you'll see."

Private Kevin Mulcahy did sing the "Ave Maria" that day and it was one of the most remarkable things that happened outside of combat. Bone-tired, muddy Marines sitting on the ground in their dirty, sweat-soaked dungarees with their rifles close beside them listened intently. His voice was clear and true and without any accompaniment he just stood there and sang. He sang it so beautifully all that heard him were spellbound. With memories of home and family and of better times haunting them, some calloused warriors wept silently.

*   *   *   *   *   *   *   *   *   *

On one particular dark and quiet night, Shanghai had just finished discussing with Chic the reasons why they couldn't stake out an area in the jungle overnight to ambush the Japs. He seemed to agree that Chic's ideas would work but in spite of his feelings, it could not be done without the permission of the officers. It was not to be. Shanghai looked at Chic and quietly said: "You've wanted to know about my interest in the Japanese for a long time. I guess the only way

I'm going to keep you from asking so damned many questions is to go ahead and tell you the story.

"You may not like what you are about to hear and it may surprise you to hear it but you asked for it. If you ever tell this to anyone else I'll kick your ass right up between your shoulder blades and I'll never forgive you. I want you to know that I have not discussed this with anyone since my court-martial. I didn't think I would ever be able to talk about it again, but its eating me up inside and you seem to be interested. I just can't forget what happened.

"I was given a bum rap, I was reduced in rank, lost my security clearance and was transferred out of China, yet I did nothing that any other Marine would not do under similar circumstances. This sure as hell isn't going to be what you had expected to hear, but I believe you really want to know so here it is."

He talked all through his watch and through Chic's watch. When the time came to call Chief, they let him sleep. It took the whole night, but the sergeant related his moving story just as it had happened. Chic was thankful the night was dark, too dark to look Shanghai in the eye. He knew the salty old sergeant was deeply moved and from the sound of his voice, there had to be tears coursing down his cheeks part of the time. Though Shanghai may never have told anyone the story before Chic could sense that he had re-lived it a thousand times. He was haunted and tortured by his memories. The salty sergeant and the young Pfc sat in their foxhole and while the Chief slept they watched the darkness fade away.

Heavy blue-black clouds had spread themselves all across the tropical skies vainly trying to hold back the dawn. They gradually separated, fell back and as the rising sun climbed slowly up out of the east the shadowy specters of the night vanished. The brightness of the sun illuminated the island of the dead and once again it was morning on Saipan.

This night would not be spoken of again yet neither of them would ever forget it. Shanghai felt relief in at last having told another person the story of what had befallen him. He had spoken of exciting times while learning his craft studying under the brilliant Major Sullivan and his associates in Asiatic Fleet Headquarters. He spoke of the interesting contacts he had made in the international community and his frequent voyages to Japan and trips to remote parts of China. He also spoke of the great love that knew no bounds and how it had filled his heart so completely and brought him the greatest happiness imaginable.

Paradoxically, it was that same love which caused the tragic consequences over which he had no control. He spoke of his lost love as one who knew he could never love again. Chic tried to understand but he had never been in love. He knew he could not reveal Shanghai's story yet he would never forget it. Few men are privileged to share the innermost secrets of another. When Chic had heard Shanghai's tale, he realized how tragic and unfair life can be. In the Corps, there is a time worn verse that describes Shanghai's life:

"And when he dies and goes to heaven,
To Saint Peter he will tell
Another Marine reporting Sir,
I've served my time in hell."

God must have something very special in store for Sergeant Shanghai Pooley.

* * * * * * * * * *

The Deception

At dawn on a hot July morning as the men were finishing their C-rations and preparing for the day's patrol, Shanghai directed that all empty ration cans, cigarette butts, papers and trash be put into two empty sandbags. They were taking them along.

There were familiar signposts along the trail: scarred trees partially denuded by previous firefights; decomposing enemy bodies in grotesque positions and varying stages of decay; and a multitude of footprints. Some of the prints were left by bare feet and some by Japanese Army hobnail boots. Others were made by the rubber and canvas split-toed *jikatabi* shoes most Japanese soldiers wore and some were made by U. S.

Marines' boondockers. Some of the footprints were old and some were fresh. Shanghai showed considerable interest in footprints.

An hour into the jungle there was a ravine where a small stream trickled past the opening of a cave. This cave had been the scene of a firefight the week before. It had previously served as a Japanese unit headquarters and supply point. The entrance, when covered with vegetation and camouflage, was nearly invisible. This was no longer the case. Fragmentation grenades and white phosphorous had scarred, burned and exposed the face of the cliff and the cave's entrance. This spot held a strange fascination for Shanghai.

As the troops entered the ravine, the sergeant studied the Japanese footprints. He placed the squad in covering positions and directed Whitey Schultz and Deadly Dave Donahoe to scatter the trash from the two sandbags on the ground beside the stream. He then went up to the cave's entrance where a wire had been stretched to support the camouflage, which no longer existed.

Shanghai gently removed an American Flag from his haversack and almost reverently attached it to the horizontal wire so it covered the cave's entrance. He and Chief opened their packs and broke out a dozen empty sandbags. He had two of the men fill them, cautiously and silently, while the rest of the squad remained alert and ready to open fire. As the bags were filled they were placed neatly across the cave entrance, two courses high. They created the appearance of a fortified position.

The sergeant built a fire inside the cave and put some green twigs on it to cause smoke. He punched some holes in a can of C-ration hash and carefully placed it on the fire, upright. The squad resumed its patrolling.

They had been on the jungle trail about 10 minutes when the sergeant halted his patrol and had the men rally round. He gave them the word. They were not going to continue on routine patrol. They would proceed back to the cave by a different route. If anyone told the new lieutenant or the company commander what they were up to he (Shanghai) would "kick your ass 'till your nose bleeds." The troops knew that when Shanghai said something, he meant it. His secret would be safe with them.

The sergeant explained to his men that since the enemy had found the cave a good location for their command post and supply point, they would think it logical for the Americans to do the same. In order to convince them of the presence of a number of Americans, scattering fresh trash that was strictly American in origin and creating a number of fresh footprints seemed the logical thing to do. Placing the sandbags across the front of the cave would give the impression that the Marines had spent some time improving the position and intended to stay there.

Suspending the flag over the entrance was Shanghai's special touch. He had served in China and remembered that every Japanese headquarters he had ever seen was marked by their flag. Since American troops rarely ever carried their flag in the field, this one was sure to give the impression that whoever was using the position must be a very important person, perhaps even a general. If any Japanese troops see their old CP cave now, they will be certain to assault it.

The squad was deployed in good firing positions in thick vegetation. They were on two sides of the ravine looking down at the cave entrance and the trail, the most obvious route of approach.

The whole area now had the appearance of an occupied American position. Possibly an important headquarters with the flag, the smell of food cooking and the multitude of American footprints created when Shanghai had put up the flag and when Schultz and Donahoe scattered the empty ration cans and other trash around the area. The two men who had filled the sandbags each had to make a trip up to the entrance with every bag and then return to fill the next one. If Chic didn't know better, he would have estimated by the footprints that there were at least 30 Americans in and around the cave. Most of the old Japanese prints had been walked over and were obliterated.

The flag over the cave's entrance hung brightly but still as death. There was no breeze and there were no jungle sounds - the heat was stifling. Finally, the first signs of life - mosquitoes. Soon they were all over the squad. No one dared move. The hours seemed like days. All of the jungle sounds slowly returned. Insects and reptiles crawled and squirmed. A giant iguana feasted on flies. The troops wished he would go after the damned mosquitoes. No one moved. A wisp of grey smoke drifted out of the top of the cave's entrance and proceeded up the face of the cliff. The burning C-ration hash smelled a lot better than it usually tasted.

Jungle birds soared from tree to tree and chattered at nothing in particular. Several landed on the wire suspending the American flag. One of the birds relieved itself and the excrement ran down one of the bright white stripes. Shanghai audibly sucked in his breath - he obviously had the bird in his rifle sights. Shanghai's finger was on the trigger but he exercised great restraint. He was a very patriotic Marine and didn't take lightly to birds crapping on his flag.

As though they sensed Shanghai's anger, the birds flapped their wings and took off as one. The usual jungle noises built up to a crescendo and suddenly stopped. Silence. Nothing stirred except the infernal mosquitoes. The iguana was frozen in place, the smaller lizards had vanished, the birds were all gone. It wasn't Shanghai's anger that disturbed them, it was the new intruders.

Seven Japanese soldiers filed silently down the lonely trail into the ravine. Their leader saw the flag and stopped. He quietly motioned them to get down. They did so, but too late. They were already in the ravine and were bunched up. The column of prone bodies had little room in which to disperse. The quiet stillness was broken by a gentle gust of fresh air.

A breeze seemed to come up from nowhere and Chic wondered if somehow his sergeant hadn't pre-arranged this with God. Chic heard him whisper softly, *"kamikaze"* (divine wind). It was the first time Chic and the other young Marines had ever heard the expression. Later in the war, they would wish it had been the only time.

The previously immobile flag was now fluttering in the cave's entrance and the Japanese, seeing the sudden movement and believing there to be someone inside the cave, opened fire. As their bullets struck the coral face of the cliff in and around the cave's entrance, they kicked up dust spots which must have seemed like smoke from return fire. The Japs quickly reloaded their bolt-action Arisaka rifles and continued firing as they slowly inched forward.

Finally, one of the Nips who had worked his way around to the right side of the cave's entrance detonated a grenade primer and threw the grenade into the cave. The American flag jerked and fluttered wildly for a moment and then it was still. It hung limply, tattered and torn, filled with numerous small fragment holes.

The Japanese soldier was dead. Shanghai did not like his flag being desecrated. When Shanghai shot the first Jap, it was a signal to the squad to open fire. The seven dead soldiers lay in their firing positions - none had returned the squad's fire. They couldn't have known from whence it had come. They had all been exposed in the open low ground facing the cave and Shanghai Pooley had positioned his men in the thick foliage on the high ground.

Shanghai was a professional. He had served his apprenticeship as a jungle fighter in Nicaragua. In 1937, while an noncommissioned serving with the Fourth Regiment of Marines in Shanghai, he had developed an intense dislike for the Japanese military. This was due to several incidents, not the least of which was the sinking of the United States Gunboat, *Panay*, on the Yangtze River. As the squad filed back to the company area through the damp musty trail, smelling of rotting vegetation and reeking of death, the men felt somehow that their accomplishment had been worthwhile. There would be seven less Japs to deal with on future patrols. This was a good score. On most days they had only been getting one or two and sometimes at the cost of a dead or wounded Marine.

The men felt it had been like shooting fish in a barrel. If only the sergeant had let them strip the Japs of souvenirs. He had been firm in cautioning them not to approach the enemy dead and they had obeyed, even Poncho, whose obvious disappointment showed in his face. It had been an effective deception. The squad maintained silence. When shipmates had asked about the patrol, Shanghai's men indicated it was just the usual routine.

Shanghai informed Blackjack and Childs that he'd had all the men "test fire" their weapons in the jungle and thus a resupply of ammunition would be needed. He also mentioned that he had a pretty good idea where he could find some "Nips" on his next patrol. He'd seen some signs.

The squad did not go on patrol the next day. It was their turn to carry water, ammo and rations from battalion up to the company's position.

They marveled at the equipment available to the headquarters personnel and looked longingly at the tentage and semi-permanent covered holes. It must be neat to be in the "rear echelon" and live like this. There were plenty of expeditionary cans of water, cases of rations and even a couple of trucks and some jeeps in the battalion CP. Everything was pretty well dispersed but still, this area would have been a very inviting target for enemy artillery prior to the island being secured.

On the following day, the squad moved out at dawn charged with a bit more enthusiasm than seemed normal for a routine patrol. Everyone was curious but they tried not to let it show. The Marine Corps was a close-knit brotherhood. If an NCO, especially an "old Corps" NCO, told you to keep your mouth shut, that's just what you did. Sharing in a secret helped to bind the squad even closer than it already had been, if that was possible.

As they entered the bush, the familiar stench of decaying bodies assaulted their nostrils. They wondered what their squad leader had in mind. Would it be another deception or just a routine patrol?

The squad moved through the jungle trail in a column formation. They were getting close to the ravine and the unlucky seven, when a rustling sound was heard. It got louder and finally exploded into what sounded like a full company of Jap infantry coming at them from the right flank.

All rifles pointed to the right and all-hands were in firing positions. Not a word had been spoken. Only Shanghai had maintained his position, standing calmly in the center of the column facing to the right, but with his rifle still at sling arms.

"All right you meatheads, who do you people think you are? Frank Buck the great white hunter? Don't you men know a pork chop when you see it?"

In a clearing to their right (now their front) scurried a small pig. Its four legs were moving like lightening in what appeared to be four different directions. It crashed madly, and very audibly, into the heavy bush and was gone. Whitey Schultz exclaimed, "My God, I thought an animal would be better co-ordinated than that. That boar made more racket than a herd of wild elephants."

Shanghai Pooley calmly explained that it wasn't a wild boar, it was a domestic pig. He was forced to live in the jungle due to the complete devastation around him and he was probably suffering from "combat fatigue." He had to be terrified at the thought of 10 big, ugly Marines all pointing loaded rifles at him. The patrol moved on, somewhat embarrassed but nevertheless relieved.

As they approached the ravine, Shanghai had them disperse more widely than before and he moved slowly, obviously exercising more caution than he normally would in a familiar area. He motioned his men silently up to the high ground one at a time.

They were all on one side of the ravine this time, in heavy vegetation. The concealment was excellent but moving quietly was difficult. The men wondered at all the stealth and secrecy. After all, the Japs were dead. They could see all seven bodies just where they had been two days before. The troops were proud of their squad leader's deception. They had really fooled the enemy.

The sergeant moved slowly and very quietly from man to man briefly explaining that something was not right. When they had left the seven bodies, all had been in firing positions - prone. Now, they lay on their backs, someone had turned them over and frisked them but left them where they had fallen. None of our other patrols had been in this area yesterday. The sergeant was convinced, someone was trying to deceive the deceiver.

The squad remained silent and motionless as the jungle sounds gradually returned. They had obviously invaded the domain of the insufferable mosquitoes once again and would need to call upon considerable self-discipline to remain frozen in position.

Except for the non-human jungle inhabitants and the enemy dead, the squad seemed to be alone.

"Cover me, I'm going down to get what's left of my flag. I want to plant it on the Emperor's palace when we get to

Tokyo."

Shanghai slipped stealthily down into the ravine and as he moved out into the open to cross the little stream, a metallic clicking sound emanated from somewhere inside the cave.

The Nambu machine gun spit forth its fiery staccato from the shadows of the cave. Shanghai was on the deck rolling for cover before the first round left the muzzle of the Nambu. Six M-1 rifles and three BARs poured a volley of fire into the mouth of the cave but it was Shanghai's WP grenade that dislodged the sole remaining enemy from within.

A Japanese soldier ran screaming out of the cave, fell, rolled to the flat ground and tried to claw his way to the stream. It all happened in but a few seconds as a piece of the white phosphorous burned through him. By the time he reached the little stream he was dead. Shanghai searched him and the cave, and found nothing he thought would be of interest.

The seven bodies from the earlier patrol contained no documents or material of intelligence value. The Jap rifles were broken, disassembled and the parts scattered in the jungle. One had a Luger pistol but the holster was impregnated with body fluids and could never be properly cleaned. Bodies decompose fast in the tropics and decomposition was already well along here. Poncho had a look of satisfaction about him as he patted the small leather pouch that hung from his cartridge belt. The squad moved out cautiously - this time, when they got back, they would report killing eight of the enemy.

* * * * * * * * * *

THE DUEL

The squad was on another routine patrol. The men were carrying their rifles at sling arms. The squad rarely moved through the jungle at sling arms, but this time there may have been a bit of over-confidence. Enemy activity had been minimal the past few days and the island had been officially secured for some time. Saipan was beginning to feel like home now that the Marines knew they would be leaving for Tinian in just a few days.

Shanghai was always teaching. He had read the tracks and shown them to the two point men. "You had better learn to read the obvious signs if you expect to stay alive and accomplish anything worthwhile when you are on patrol. If you've got any questions that I haven't answered, ask Chief, he taught me most of what I know back in the jungles of Central America when most of you were still wearing diapers."

The Chief chuckled quietly to himself as he thought of Shanghai's way of always trying to give credit to others. He hadn't taught Shanghai a damned thing about reading tracks. They had both been green recruits newly arrived in Nicaragua when they learned tracking in order to stay alive. Members of the Nicaraguan Guardia Nacional, had taught them. Chief knew that Shanghai thought he would have credibility with the troops because he was an Indian. He also knew that Shanghai was aware that in spite of his heritage, he didn't know the first thing about being an Indian. He had left the reservation at an early age and had never returned. Most of what little Indian lore he knew, he had gleaned from books and movies.

Shanghai had the men's complete attention as he spoke, he was teaching as usual, "There are signs that someone has been moving around here. There aren't many of them, just one or two. Look at the footprints. Footprints are not always a nice clean outline of someone's shoe or foot on the ground. Be realistic, look for something sensible. Do you see those little broken twigs? Okay, they're fresh, do you see that? Someone has stepped on them and crushed or broken them under his feet. The broken twigs are on the trail right? You don't see any of them off the trail or under the bush. Now, look at the dirt and the rotting vegetation on the ground. Do you see how it has been disturbed here and there? About the same distance between the turbulence on the ground as a short man's stride would be right? Okay, now, look at the trees and bushes. Look up and see if anything is disturbed, fragile things like small branches and twigs. They may indicate to you that it was a man. Do you see that little broken branch? Now see here? There's a couple more broken in the same way. That gives you a pretty good clue that it was a man or something just as tall as a man and if you'll look closely, you can see the direction he was moving in. Now if there had been a lot of foot traffic around here, the rotting vegetation and dirt on the trail would be churned up much more than it is. This indicates that there has only been one or two. Someone has used this trail in the last couple of hours. They're probably hiding out around here, close by. Get those rifles off your shoulders, insert a clip of ammo and stay alert."

Deadly Dave and Epstein were the point men. They entered the clearing first then stepped aside and waited for the others. Shanghai stepped into the clearing and automatically sensed someone's presence. His attention was riveted to the little lean-to shack at the far end of the clearing. He was about to meet his destiny.

As the men filed into the little clearing, they fanned out to the sides. They all looked at Shanghai who had stopped at the top end of the clearing and was standing with his feet apart and was facing down toward the little lean-to. It seemed as though the whole thing had been rehearsed. It was like a dream, it just couldn't really be happening. But happen it did. There were two rows of Marines, facing each other. The men looked at their sergeant and then, almost casually glanced down in the direction of the lean-to.

Ross was closest to it. He was the shortest man in the squad but one of the most effective. His buddy, Muldoon was standing next to him as always. The two were inseparable. Shanghai hollered something in Japanese and then waited. He yelled something else then waited again.

Ross spotted him first and sprang into action. He whipped his rifle around and went into a crouching position with his muzzle pointed right at the lean-to shack not more than 20 feet from him. Shanghai's voice rang out loud and clear,

"Hold your fire! He's mine, I've got him!"

There, at the lower end of the clearing was a Japanese lieutenant climbing out of the lean-to in full dress uniform. How he managed to look so neat and clean in the steamy hot jungle was a mystery. This was apparently the moment he had been waiting for. He was about to die for his Emperor and wanted to do it in style.

The lieutenant stood up in front of his little shack facing

the Marine sergeant as though the rest of the squad wasn't even there. He didn't glance to the left or right, just stared at Pooley. It was Shanghai's voice,

"All right you guys, steady now, don't any of you move. This one's gonna be mine!"

Again, Shanghai spoke in Japanese, almost softly. The lieutenant responded with a sneer and a grunt. Then he reached up with his left hand and loosened the flap on his holster. Slowly and methodically he reached across his body with his right hand and drew his pistol from the holster on his left hip. He stood there for a moment, pistol in hand pointing down. He stared at the Marine sergeant. Shanghai was moving at about the same speed as the lieutenant as he loosened his holster flap with his right hand, then dropped his hands to his sides.

They stood there looking very much like a couple of characters in an old western movie. Then it happened! Shanghai had given his adversary the advantage. The Jap's pistol was in his hand, and Pooley's .45 was still in its holster. The Jap raised his pistol, taking aim just as though he was on a firing range. Shanghai drew his pistol and in what appeared to be one smooth movement, raised his arm, aimed and fired. The Japanese lieutenant had gotten his wish. He died instantly. Shanghai was still teaching as he said, "Men, don't ever underestimate your enemy."

A stream of blood was coursing down the front of Shanghai's dungaree shirt.

"The little sonovabitch shot me."

Shanghai unslung his haversack with some difficulty then gently sat down, before any of the awe-stricken Marines could react. He placed the pack between his knees clutching it and laid back.

"Corpsman! Corpsman! Get up here Doc! " It was Chief's voice. He had been the closest to Shanghai and the first to realize he had really been shot. This was the first time anyone in the squad had seen Chief show any visible sign of emotion when someone had gotten hit. Which, until recently, had been fairly often. Now here was Shanghai, shot in the belly in a duel with a damned Jap when the island had been secured for days. It just didn't seem fair.

Chief wondered who was going to hold the Corps together when this damned war was over? These kids didn't understand about the real Marine Corps, they were just part-time help. In for the duration of the war and then back to civilian life. So many of the real Marines, the old timers, were gone now.

Poncho did an immediate inspection of the Japanese officer and disappointment showed on his face that indicated to the others that the Jap had no gold teeth. Lucky and Stash checked the lean-to in hopes of finding a Samurai sword but found nothing but the Japanese officer's dirty field uniform and some small personal effects. As Chic looked at the body he noticed that the one medal the Japanese officer was wearing was the China Incident War Medal. The only Japanese award he could identify. Shanghai had told him what it was.

Shanghai lifted his head and asked that someone get the Jap's pistol for him. Epstein already had it. He took it out of his pack and sheepishly put it on the stretcher with his squad leader who made some remark about what a great training aid it would be when he related the sea story of his duel with a Jap officer.

Corporal Jerden asked about the camera he knew was in Pooley's pack, The sergeant answered,

"I'll take good care of it '*Cobber*' don't you worry. If you want copies of any of the pictures, you guys will have to come and see me."

Then he spoke in a lower tone, "I'm beginning to think this wound is gonna be good enough to get me all the way back to the States. Its starting to hurt like hell. Hey Doc! Are you gonna give me a syrette of that morphine or not?"

The remorse started to set in immediately. Ten well-armed Marines and a corpsman, any one of whom could have easily blown that Jap away — and none of them did a thing. Shanghai would be sorely missed, not only by his squad, but by the whole company. He was a very special Marine. They all hoped he would be returned to duty soon. The squad would not be the same until Shanghai came back.

Chief placed his big hand on Corporal Jerden's shoulder and looked him squarely in the eyes.

"You're senior, so you are in charge. Now listen to me carefully and get it straight. I'm taking the point. Follow me. I want everyone ready and alert. There'll be a round in every chamber. Don't screw up. You know I don't talk much. Watch my arm and hand signals and do just as I indicate. We are going Nip hunting and we are not securing from this patrol until we get at least three Japs for Shanghai. Not even if we have to stay out here all night. Any questions?"

"Hell no Chief, I'm with you."

Corporal Jerden looked over his squad.

"All right you men, listen up! Chief is going to be on the point. Little Ski, I want you right behind Chief. Watch him and relay his signals back to me. Poncho! You and Stash will go next. The rest of you guys follow me and be damned sure to watch for my signals. All right, lock and load. I want a round in every chamber. We are going to kill us some Nips for old Shanghai. Okay Chief, move out!"

* * * * * * * * * *

Ticket to Tinian

Corporal Jerden moved from hole to hole briefing his men and making certain they all knew, and repeated back to him, the sign and countersign. The sign was; little Louie lost his lollipop, and the countersign; the little girl is licking the lollipop.

A disgusted Fearless Frank asked, "Who the hell thinks up these stupid passwords anyhow?"

Stash answered, "Someone back at corps headquarters who is a hell of a lot smarter than any of us."

Fearless said, "I can't believe those childish noncombatants in the rear echelon can't think up something a little more Marine-like than that."

"Well *Cobber*, you know they've gotta have words that we can all pronounce but that the Nips can't pronounce. That's why there's always a lot of L's. Besides, it wouldn't be fair if it was Marine-like. You know there's an Army division on this island. It has to be suitable for them too," Corporal Jerden answered.

"Okay Corporal, I guess that explains it," said Lucky. "The doggies can relate to Louie and the little girl licking lollipops. I'm more concerned about relating to having enough ammunition and water to make it through another day."

Corporal Jerden confessed to Stash, Lucky and Fearless that he would be glad when Shanghai returned from the hospital and took over the squad again. In the meanwhile, he advised them that he intended to run the squad just like Shanghai had done. They had all better get used to him "kickin' ass" whenever it was called for. "Friendship ends where duty begins." He moved on to the next hole occupied by Deadly Dave and Big Ski and checked their fields of fire, questioned them on combat procedures and imparted the sign and countersign where he got basically the same comments and questions as before. The men would all be glad when Shanghai returned. No matter how difficult a situation they found themselves in, Shanghai always knew how to handle it.

The new lieutenant and Blackjack briefed Jerden on the area where the squad was to patrol. He marked his map and asked a few pertinent questions while drinking a cup of K-ration soluble coffee. When the time came to move out, he'd made a decision.

"All right men, when we move out, I want Choirboy and Lucky up on the point."

He quietly admonished Lucky to be alert and keep his eyes open. The Choirboy didn't know what to look for; he'd never been on the point. Lucky would be a good teacher for the kid. Choirboy's eyes sparkled. He was filled with pride and anticipation at having finally been thought qualified to be on the point. He knew he could do a good job. The patrol moved out.

Lucky had been exposed to much of Shanghai's wisdom and had learned well. He handled himself on patrol like the professional he was. He sought tracks on the ground that may indicate a tripwire, booby-trap or a recent enemy presence. His eyes were constantly roving from one side of the trail to the other and he often looked up for signs of snipers overhead. They moved cautiously forward in a steady, drizzling rain, on a tree-lined trail that was mostly mud.

Choirboy nervously reflected on the responsibility that had

been thrust upon him. The lives of all the men behind him could well rest in his and Lucky's hands. Shanghai had never trusted him to take the point. Now that Corporal Jerden had given him this responsibility, he could not let the squad down. If there were any Japs along the trail, he knew that he must be the first to spot them.

Lucky Lane suddenly lurched forward uttering a muffled "Damn!" and dropped into the mud, falling flat on his face. The Choirboy had not heard a round fired. He knew that something was desperately wrong but he could not identify what. Overcome with fear and with his heart beating fiercely he dropped to one knee and started firing into the heavy foliage. Emptying his first clip of eight rounds, he inserted another and resumed firing.

Lucky shouted, "Dammit kid, what in the hell are you doing!?"

"I'm tryin' to kill the Japs, Lucky. What did they do to you? What did they hit you with?" asked the Choirboy.

"They didn't hit me with anything dammit! I tripped on a big root, probably from one of those damned banyan trees while I was lookin' up through the rain to see if there were any Jap snipers in the trees."

The squad would see to it that Choirboy would never be allowed to forget his first "firefight" when he expended two clips of perfectly good M-1 ammo at the phantom enemy. The patrol moved on with two new point men.

Little Ski asked, "Hey Stash, do you see that cave opening up on the left of the trail?

Stash answered, "Yeah, I sure do. We'd better hold up until we can get the word back to Jerden. We've got to check it out. Look at the deck Ski, it's been used a lot, you can see the tracks."

Ski responded with, "They're pretty obvious aren't they?"

"Yeah, we can't take a chance on moving past it or trying to bypass it. The Japs in there are probably just waiting to blow us away. Let's get a man up there to take it out like we did the last one."

"Okay Stash, whose turn is it?" asked Ski.

Corporal Jerden was now the squad leader and he decided that this would be a good time to assert himself.

"Never mind whose turn it is, I'm in charge here. Big Ski, I want you to get up there and check it out. How many grenades do you have? Have you got a WP or thermite grenade you can lob in there?"

Big Ski approached the cave with considerable trepidation. He knew it was now or had recently been occupied. The tracks leading to and from were a dead giveaway. WP Grenades had been working pretty well if we could just get them into the caves without getting Marines shot in the process. Grenade in hand, Big Ski edged carefully toward the entrance then suddenly stopped.

"What's that dumb bastard doing up there?" asked Jerden.

Ski had stopped dead in his tracks as he had heard a baby crying.

Ski shouted, *"Detekoi, Shimpai Shinaide*! We need Shanghai up here! When are those chancre mechanics at sickbay gonna send him back to us?"

Big Ski knelt down beside the entrance to the cave thinking about Dutch Shute's experience with the Chamorro mother and her little baby that he had almost killed with a grenade just a couple of weeks ago.

Jerden, still unaware of what his man was up to, thought "Oh God! He's gonna get killed for sure now. He's kneeling right in the entrance."

Big Ski slung his BAR over his shoulder and reached out with both his hands. As the curious and very nervous Marines watched a small naked child not more than two years old padded out of the cave directly toward him and ran right into his outstretched arms. Folding the child in his arms, the big Polack stood up. A young woman with a baby strapped to her back emerged from the cave bowing repeatedly. The look on her face told a heart-rending story. It was plain to see that she fully expected to be killed by the American barbarians.

He reached his hand out to the young woman to help her down but she was petrified with fear and would not dare to touch an American devil. She cautiously followed until they were down on the trail where she kept bowing, fearful tears silently staining her dirty cheeks. Corporal Jerden arrived to see what was going on and as soon as he saw the stunned look on the young mother's face he knew she had lost her desire and perhaps her ability to smile. Glancing back up at the cave's opening he exclaimed: "Riverboat! Get some of your men up there to help those people!"

"Ohmigod, will ya look at that? There must be a whole family of 'em and they're carrying someone out of there all wrapped up. It turned out to be an elderly, deceased family member, a woman; who would have to be buried very soon. Among the 11 souls who emerged were two Japanese soldiers in uniform who came out with their rifles slung over their shoulders and their hands up. They gladly relinquished their rifles in exchange for cigarettes and a drink of water. From the looks of the "soldiers" they couldn't have been more than 15 or 16 years old. They were possibly Chamorro boys who had been pressed into service by the Japanese.

Once back from the patrol, the men learned that there was a big meeting going on back at the battalion command post. The men were eager for the officers to return so they could confront the field music, and find out what was going on. They lit heat tabs, warmed water in their canteen cups and brewed C-ration coffee.

As they drank their coffee and smoked cigarettes the men reflected on the campaign to date and wondered when they would have to make the inevitable landing on Tinian. They knew it was going to be soon. The danger from the Japanese on Saipan was diminishing with each new day. As the tropical sun beat down on them the men's conversation soon turned to the continuing challenges they faced on this miserable Island of the Dead.

The heat of the sun caused the men to sweat profusely. Sweating caused raw skin, heat rash, fungus infections and weakness in general. It also made one very thirsty. There was never enough of the smelly, foul-tasting drinking water. Sometimes the men could look out in almost any direction and see a vast expanse of water. It was the beautiful blue Pacific Ocean or the Philippine Sea stretching as far as the eye could see. The vision was cruel and misleading. Salt water is blue and it's beautiful, but it isn't much good for anything except floating ships. It is especially not good for drinking. Fresh water was the second most cherished commodity on these islands of death. Ammunition was the first - and to Marines, the most important.

"How miserable can a place be?" The troops were constantly plagued by "jungle rot" fungus infections in their ears, under their arms and on their feet, especially between the toes. Heat rash that itched and burned only got worse when baked by the sun and nourished with human sweat. Dengue fever always seemed to keep at least one or two members of the squad barely able to function. The men dreamed of food, real food not just K-rations and C-rations. The rations were adequate for a week or two but they were too small to be filling, too rich and lacked variety. In time, the three choices in C-rations, Meat & Vegetable Stew, Meat & Vegetable Hash and Meat & Beans, became very monotonous. The men lost strength from lack of proper nourishment. (*Later in the war, the C-ration menu would be expanded to afford a greater variety.*)

In the daytime, flies were everywhere. During one of the intelligence briefings while still aboard ship the men had been told that the Japanese had actually imported the flies from some exotic place in New Guinea, to aid the sugar crops. The flies are supposed to eat some little parasite that destroys the sugarcane. Well, they'll never have to worry about importing flies again with a bonanza of more than 31,000 dead humans and scores of dead water buffalo and horses for the flies to dine on and use as a haven for breeding. Saipan is assured of the world's most bountiful crop of those nasty little blue/green flies forevermore.

Each evening as the sun descended into the west and was gradually swallowed up by the sea, the men occupied their holes and restlessly waited for darkness. With darkness, the millions of flies gradually diminished and eventually they were gone. Then, with the darkness a new intruder appeared - the mosquito. At first there would only seem to be one or two buzzing around. It was only a slight annoyance but was still disturbing. As the night wore on, the little cannibals were joined by their friends and relations and as their numbers grew, they massed for the attack. Pacific Island mosquitoes were voracious. They took great delight in biting ears, eyelids, nostrils, necks and hands. They would attack any part of the human anatomy that may be exposed. They were everywhere and nothing seemed to discourage them. They had a particular affinity for the mosquito repellent that would occasionally be issued to the troops.

Most Marines wore old ragged, faded dungarees. They ate K-rations or C-rations because that is what they were issued and because there was simply nothing else to eat. The combat-wise Marines made a point of picking up and saving any loose ammunition that was lying around after a firefight, never knowing when a few extra rounds might make the difference between life and death.

The officers were returning from the briefing at battalion and the men looked forward to getting the music's opinion of what was going on as soon as he could conveniently slip away from the skipper. The voice of Blackjack blasted them into action as he proclaimed, "Okay men, listen up. Mail call! You guys in the 2nd platoon, gather round for mail call!"

One of the times that the troops looked forward to the most was mail call. Some were excited about it and could hardly wait to get that special letter from home. Some were apprehensive, not knowing what to expect after having been away from home for so long. The married men especially looked forward to getting letters of reassurance that everything was all right on the home front and being told that they were loved and missed. The lucky ones were those who had someone back home who could write a 'newsy' letter that was filled with information about what was going on at home with their friends and family but didn't dwell on the hardships the civilians had to put up with because of the war.

Deadly Dave Donahoe had a letter in his hand; it was probably from his father. His dad was a disabled veteran of World War I and wrote to him on a regular basis. They had done a lot of hunting and fishing together, especially since his mother died, and they were very close.

"Well Deadly Dave, I see you got a couple of big fat letters there, how's everything goin' on the home front back in Montana?"

"Not worth a damn! One of the letters was from my Dad's VFW Post. Dad gave them a Jap flag I sent home and he told them I was a big hero fighting for right and freedom and all that old stuff. You know how fathers are, he probably even believes some of it."

"Yeah, we know, he's just being proud of you, what's wrong with that?"

"Well, they elected me to be a life member of their Veterans of Foreign Wars post and sent me my membership card. I wish they hadn't done that. I'll be a member of that post as long as I live and with my luck do you know what's gonna happen if I live through this damned war?"

"No Deadly Dave and neither do you."

"Well, I can pretty well guess what's going to happen. With my luck, I'll make it back to the States and when I'm on my way to my first VFW meeting I'll probably get run over by a beer truck and be killed. So that tells you what I think of a life membership, you never know how long or how short a time it's for."

"Dammit Dave, that's no way to talk. If any of us get out of this war alive, we'll probably be declared indestructible. We may even live forever. Just look how much we've been through already and we're still here."

"Yeah, but it's a hell of a way to live. Golden Gate in Fortyeight. Listen Chic, not many of us are gonna get back. Look how many of our guys are gone already and its only 1944, the war probably isn't even half over."

"Dave, you're a damn fatalist. You've got to stop thinkin' that way and make up your mind that you've got to make it back home. You don't want to disappoint all of those good lookin' girls back in Montana do you?"

Fearless Frank and the Weasel were talking to Big Ski when Ski abruptly broke it off and walking over to Fearless, pulled him aside and spoke to him confidentially.

"Fearless, you know all of those girls you're always writing to?"

"Of course, I know them. Do you think I'd be writing to them if I didn't know them?

"Well, I was just wonderin' if you might have any extras that you don't need that you'd be willin' to share? I'd kind of like to have someone to write to once in a while."

"What!? What about Stella down in Wellington? I thought you were a one woman man. You told me you had made up your mind to marry her."

"Stella? Oh yeah, her. Well I'll tell you Fearless; I kind of changed my mind about her. She wrote me that she didn't think it would be a very good idea for us to write to each other anymore. It turned out that she had a husband in the New Zealand Army. He was on his way home from North Africa. I guess he was with the British Eighth Army or somethin'."

"Wow, Big Ski, I had no idea Stella was married."

"Yeah, Fearless, me too. I didn't know she was married either."

"Well Ski, I guess I could share a couple of pen pals with you. Gimme a cigarette then get something to write on and I'll give you a couple of addresses."

Private Ross folded up his letters and stuffed them into his dungaree shirt as he looked south across the channel and spoke to Muldoon.

"Take a look out there and tell me what you see old man."

"Hell, there's nothin' out there except a couple of Navy destroyers and that damned island."

"Yeah, that's it, the island. Do you see all that smoke over there?"

"Of course I see it; they've been poundin' that rock for days now and I guess you know what that means."

"Yeah, it means we've got a Ticket to Tinian."

"That's right and you know we'll all be on that train so you'd better hope our tickets are 'round trip'."

Chapter IV

Jig Day

Saipan – 24 July 1944

The young lieutenant looked at his Marines. They were a ragged, scroungy bunch and their pallor was almost as yellow as the Atabrine tablets they'd been taking for the past couple of months. Some of these men had been in the platoon for two years and were veterans of three campaigns. He had only been in the Marine Corps for one year. To him, the year seemed like a long time but he knew that to his men he was an outsider, just another replacement. The men were not ready to fully accept him. They had already lost too many lieutenants. He would have to earn their confidence and respect and prove himself worthy of being their leader. Looking at the skeptical faces before him he knew it may be one of the greatest challenges he'd ever have to face.

He wondered to himself if it would ever be possible for him to show these men in word or deed just how much he admired and respected them. When he had first been commissioned he had no idea of the relationship between commissioned and enlisted Marines. He knew that as an officer he would be in charge of enlisted men and that they would be required to obey his lawful orders, salute him and call him sir. He was experiencing twinges of doubt. Would he be able to lead these Marines in combat? Men who had served together and fought together and were perhaps closer to one another even than blood brothers? What he was experiencing now was completely unexpected. It was as though a great magnet was drawing him toward them and would not release him until he had somehow earned their respect.

He had never encountered a dirtier, more calloused, profane group of malcontents than these Marines who comprised his platoon. Yet, there was something magical about them. A feeling of close camaraderie bound them together. It was born of going in harms way repeatedly and giving and receiving full support from one another under the most trying of conditions. These men had together walked through the Valley of the Shadow of Death; they had crawled into the Jaws of Hell together and had survived. They were capable of accomplishing great things as a unit if properly led and motivated. Yet, the fact remained that they reminded him a little of a gang of hoodlums. How could he possibly want to be accepted by them? No one back home among his family or his friends at Princeton would ever understand the deep feelings he had for these men. He had actually grown to love them. They were his Marines.

"Okay men, listen up, this is the news you've all been waiting for. We had a briefing back at the Battalion CP a little while ago and I am now able to tell you that we are finally getting off of this cursed island. We'll have an early reveille tomorrow morning and then at daybreak we'll leave for the beach. We're going to go aboard ship, in fact it's LST 715, we'll get some real food and hot showers and we can survey all of your ragged or worn out dungarees. Most of you might even get to see a movie and you are all encouraged to write home. We'll be aboard the LST for two days to rest up, clean up, refit and get ready for the next campaign. This time there won't be a D-Day. As far as the Nips are concerned, the jig is up, so we are calling it Jig-day. Jig-day will be on 24 July and as you all know that is just three days from right now. That's when we go ashore on Tinian Island.

"And now for the good news. As you all know, traditionally our battalion, is in the first wave. This time it is going to be different. The 4th Marine Division will be in the assault waves.

We're going to land after they are ashore. But before I get ahead of myself, let me tell you all I know about Tinian and what you can expect.

"The campaign to soften up Tinian for our invasion has already been underway for some time. Massed artillery barrages are being fired the three miles across the channel from here and Navy and Marine air has been pounding the island from above. There is no question; the Japanese know we will assault Tinian soon. They've had an additional 39 days since the invasion of Saipan to prepare their defenses. They know we're coming and they've done a lot of preparing. Now men, if you don't mind my personal opinions, listen to this: "The most successful amphibious landing can be made only with some measure of surprise. I'm sure you are all thinking that it's highly unlikely that the U.S. forces can achieve any measure of surprise at Tinian after such a long softening-up period. Do you agree with me so far? Well men, unlikely or not, we are going to achieve a strong measure of surprise when we land on Tinian. In fact, we're going to shock hell out of the Nips. We're going to do it simply because of the characteristic Japanese preoccupation with the obvious."

The men were listening eagerly to their new lieutenant but they were weary from over a month and a half of fighting on Saipan.

"Here's the game plan and when you hear it, I'm sure you'll agree that our intelligence people have done a first class job this time. We know a lot about Tinian and its defenses. There are steep natural escarpments and cliffs almost all the way around this island providing good protection from any invasion from the sea. The island has only two obvious beaches that could be considered suitable for an amphibious landing. The best is at Sunharon, just west of Tinian Town in the southwestern part of the island and the other is across the island to the north on the eastern shore. Sunharon is by far the more likely landing beach of the two and so it has been softened up presumably for a landing. Much attention is being paid to it by naval gunfire and our Marine artillery based here on Saipan.

"Because Sunharon offers almost ideal landing conditions, the Japanese know that the Americans will consider it for our landing. Colonel Kiyochi Ogata, the Japanese commander on Tinian, has been taking defensive measures he thinks will be appropriate to defend Sunharon. The beach has been heavily mined as were the approaches to it. The Japanese have built underwater obstacles and installed a system of mutually supporting defensive positions designed to allow enfilade fire to cover every foot of the beach. While we were fighting on Saipan, time was being purchased for Ogata to continue strengthening his Tinian defenses. Our attack is clearly expected to occur at Sunharon. Are you with me so far? Okay, let's get into the Japanese commander's head and see if we can outguess him.

"Sun Tzu teaches that a good general never does what the enemy expects. Ogata may have decided that he had better consider the alternate beach over on the eastern shore just in case. It is not nearly as good a landing beach as Sunharon and we are expending a lot of bombs and shells on Sunharon. But, one doesn't know what the enemy may be up to. He knows we expect him to defend in force at Sunharon where we are concentrating so much fire. For that very reason he may think we are planning a surprise and will land on the northeastern shore beach? Ogata cannot permit himself to fall into a trap. He must defend Yellow Beach over on the east side as well as the Red and Green Beaches at Sunharon.

"Our American intelligence specialists assume that with so much attention being paid to the Sunharon beach by naval gunfire and artillery, the Japanese are going to think that in order to surprise them we have chosen "Yellow Beach". And yet, the Japanese could not entirely rule out Sunharon because of the amount of attention we are paying to it. Our planners decided to lend credibility to the possibility of a landing on Yellow Beach. U.S. planes and artillery from Saipan have started working over the beaches between Asiga Point and Masalog Point that's where Yellow Beach is. With a little luck, this may cause the Japanese to split their assets and establish a second line of defense in the northeast. If Ogata splits his forces, it will greatly favor us."

Pfc Epstein was following the lieutenant's every word, he knew what the lieutenant was going to tell them next. He had to show his intelligence by stating, "I've got it Lieutenant, we're going to make the Japs wonder which of the beaches we're going to hit and then at H-hour, with their forces split, we'll invade them both."

"Good try leatherneck, but that's not the plan. If its bad for the enemy to split his forces, why wouldn't it be just as bad for us to split ours?"

Epstein answered, but this time did not sound so sure of himself. "Well, because we've got two Marine divisions. The 4th could invade Yellow Beach and the 2nd could hit Red and Green beaches." The lieutenant went on, "You men all know that surprise is vital to the success of the landing and so Red and Green Beaches at Sunharon and Yellow Beach over on the northeast have all been ruled out. What's really going to happen is this: "Close to the northern tip of Tinian on the northwest coast and not far from the large Japanese Ushi Airfield is a very unlikely location for a landing. There are two narrow strips of sandy beach separated by a 1,000 yard area of rugged coral boulders washed by hard surf. This will present a significant challenge to a landing force. It is so unlikely that it could be suitable for an amphibious landing that it will come as a complete surprise to the Japanese when we actually land there. I think it may just surprise the hell out of a lot of very apprehensive Marines including some of you sitting right here in front of me.

"White Beach I, where we intend to land, is only wide enough to get two amtracs in side by side. If the Japanese guess what the 4th Marine Division is up to, the landing will turn into a bloody debacle. It's up to us to see that this doesn't happen."

Sergeant Childs had seen far too much combat to think a hair-brained scheme like this would work and he asked, "How the hell are we going to do that Lieutenant? If they are crazy enough to land on a beach that narrow how can we help them?"

"By subterfuge, Sergeant. In fact, instead of calling it Jig-day we should maybe call it Joke-day because on that day we are going to fool the hell out of the Japanese. We are going to mislead the Japs into thinking the American landing is going to be on Red and Green Beaches in the southern part of the island. The Sunharon beach is the only beach on the island that's really suitable for a landing and it's where they expect us to land. They'll never expect us to land two divisions of Marines on a beach so narrow it will only accommodate two amtracs at a time. So, just to reinforce what they already think they know, the 2nd Marine Division will go over the side, get into our landing craft and head for Sunharon. It will be exactly like a real landing with plenty of supporting arms; even the battlewagons will support us, except that when we get so close that we know they have been fooled, we're going to turn around and head back out to our ships."

Still skeptical, Childs asked, "What are we going to do after that Lieutenant?"

"After that, we'll go back aboard LST 715 and then later we'll disembark again and this time we'll really go ashore. We are going to follow right in behind the 4th Marine Division over White Beach I and fan out after we get past the beach." The lieutenant looked over his platoon trying to make eye contact with as many of the men as possible. "Alright men, that's it. You all know as much as I do about the invasion of Tinian island. Try and get some rest and check your gear carefully. You never know what you will need ashore or how long we'll be over there. So, be prepared for anything. That's all, carry on."

The lieutenant's briefing left his Marines wondering at the wisdom of having the 4th Marine Division land on such a restricted beach. They also wondered whether the Japanese would be fooled by their feint toward the southern beach. All hoped the joke would be on the Japanese and would not backfire on the Americans. The tactical concept for the landing on Tinian scared hell out of the veterans of Tarawa and Saipan.

Fearless Frank asked, "Okay you guys, what do you think is gonna happen when the 4th Division's first two amtracs get blown all to hell by the Nips?"

Corporal Al Jerden was not convinced that any aspect of the plan to take Tinian was going to work. He shrugged his shoulders and answered Fearless, "Well its pretty obvious that we can't use the same beaches 'cause they'll be blocked by our destroyed amtracs and that probably means that we'll go back over and land at Sunharon just like the Japs expect us to. Since they've got all those great defenses the lieutenant told us about, a whole lot more of us are probably gonna die."

The men were very glad they would not be in the assault waves on this operation. If the Japs were able to destroy the first two amtracs as they drove up the narrow beach they could cause a traffic jam of monumental proportions which could well result in the greatest beachhead slaughter of the war.

Fearless Frank Quinlan asked no one in particular, "Who the hell are the jokers that think these impossible scenarios up?"

Stash was pleased to answer with: "They've got a bunch of senior old Navy and Marine officers back at Pearl Harbor who drink to excess and stay up late at night playing games like, Who can think up the most preposterous scenario for a Marine landing? Whoever wins the game gets to propose his plan to Admiral Nimitz who is the Commander-in-Chief, Pacific Ocean Area. The admiral figures that he's had all these old senior guys workin' on the plan and they claim to be experts so it must have merit. He signs his approval and it's forwarded to us for execution."

"Yeah, execution is the right word for it Stash. We're gonna lose a lotta Marines on that damn beach. We shouldn't even try to take the island. I don't care what old Riverboat says about it bein' needed for an airfield for our bombers. We've got airfields on Saipan."

There was talk among the men as to what could be done while the 4th Marine Division was landing if the first two amtracs were destroyed on the beach. Would we then invade Sunharon after all? Some thought that a likely scenario. If the 4th Division troops were stopped by the Japs on White Beach, it would be disastrous for them and for all concerned. It could result in a serious blood bath.

Less than three miles across the channel from Saipan, Tinian was within artillery range. The 155's on Saipan had been firing on Tinian targets for days before the landings. Just prior to Jig-day, this pounding by Marine artillery was accelerated.

Deadly Dave looked at Fearless with an impish grin and asked, "Hey Fearless! How does it feel to be back aboard ship?"

"Oh man, that hot water and soap sure felt good. And did you see the chow; those swabbies were sure piling it on our trays. Man, this is really living. Are you goin' to the movies tonight?" asked Fearless.

"You bet. I think everybody in the platoon is gonna try and squeeze in. Have you heard what's playing?" asked Deadly Dave.

"No, but it doesn't really matter, anything is better than nothing." replied Fearless.

Deadly Dave was still grinning as he asked, "Fearless, how come you seem so happy to be aboard ship? I thought you hated the Navy?"

Fearless' innocent response was, "Naw, I never said I hated the Navy. It's the corpsmen I hate and because corpsmen are swabbies, I just naturally don't care much for swabbies. The Navy itself is okay. I like their ships and their chow and the fresh water, when we can get it. I like being underway too, as long as we're steaming toward the good old Golden Gate."

Stash piped up with, "Yeah, fat chance of that. Its not gonna happen for a long time, Buddy. Remember, Golden Gate in '48, Bread Line in '49."

24 July 1944

Time aboard ship passed all too quickly for the embarked Marines. Sleeping on canvas bunks was strangely uncomfortable to men who had become so accustomed to sleeping on the rough, hard ground. They had gotten the promised hot showers and real food and had new dungarees issued but now, the time had come for them to start earning their pay again.

The piercing trill of the boatswain's pipe and the mellow notes of a bugle were as welcome as old friends but the call to general quarters and the continuous loud barking of the claxon were no friends to the raw nerves of combat weary Marines. The ominous "Land the Landing Force" shattering the early morning darkness was a command they'd sooner not hear.

The men moved rapidly in single file down the steel ladders into the well deck, where they boarded the amphibious tractors that were to take them in toward the Sunharon Beach.

"Doesn't this outfit ever go anywhere in the daylight anymore?" moaned Riverboat Brown.

Al Jerden retorted with, "Shut up and move out of the way Riverboat. There's other people tryin' to get into this rust bucket and besides, if its dark and you can't see, that means the Nips can't see either and that's just the way I want it."

The 2nd Marine Division's mock assault on Tinian Town's beach must have been convincing. Wave after wave of landing craft heading for the beach came under fire from Tinian's defenders as the heavy 16-inch shells of the battleship *Colorado* rumbled menacingly overhead. Cruisers, light and heavy, and sleek destroyers pounded the Tinian coast with their main batteries. Wave after wave of landing craft moving toward the beach received an enthusiastic reception from the Japanese defenders as artillery, antiboat guns and heavy mortars opened up on the assaulting force with a vengeance.

The battleship *Colorado* shuddered under the impact of enemy shells hitting her from a battery of three 6-inch naval guns. She immediately returned fire and the duel was joined. Ultimately, the Japanese battery struck *Colorado* 22 times in a period of approximately 15 minutes. Ten of the 43 killed aboard *Colorado* were Marines and 32 Marines were among the 198 wounded. The skipper of the destroyer, *Norman Scott*, was killed along with 18 of his crewmen. Forty-seven more were wounded. The damage was severe enough to keep the destroyer out of action.

In the landing craft headed toward the beach, the Marines felt as though they were seeing a repeat of a bad movie but the sound was too loud and the bullets were real.

"Hell, *Cobber*, this is just like Saipan! The damned Japs still have plenty of artillery and they know just what to do with it," proclaimed Jerden.

"Yeah, and the lieutenant was sure right about them having good defenses on that Sunharon Beach. Damn! I thought we were supposed to turn around and head back to the ship," complained Deadly Dave.

"Me too, but maybe the 4th Division got clobbered tryin' to get ashore on that tiny "White Beach" and they've decided to send us ashore on Sunharon," worried Jerden.

Lucky Lane was not pleased with the prospect of going ashore at Sunharon and said, "If they do it's gonna be one hell of a bloodbath. Remember what the lieutenant said when he told us about their defenses?"

Riverboat Brown voiced his opinion, "I sure do and because of it I know they'll never put us ashore here. We'd be annihilated. If the 4th got torn up too bad, they'll probably try to land us on Yellow Beach over on the other side of the island."

A feeling of great relief came over the men as their amtrac slowed, then came about, and headed back toward that beautiful big grey LST out on the horizon. There were seven transport ships waiting to retrieve the fleet of amtracs, Peter boats, Mike boats and other assorted landing craft that had been made available for the 2nd Marine Division's amphibious landing demonstration. So far, Jig-day was working; the joke seemed to be on the Japanese. And to a lesser extent; on the men of the 2nd platoon who had initially been so skeptical of the plan.

* * * * * * * * * *

Ushi Point Airfield

Tinian – 25 July 1944

Once back aboard ship, the men were treated to a hot meal and were told they could relax. Some stretched out on their bunks and hoped they could see a movie later. The 2nd Battalion would not be going ashore until daylight tomorrow. Shortly after evening chow, a smiling Navy radioman came into the compartment to relate that he had just been listening to a broadcast by Tokyo Rose. She reported that the Americans had attempted to land on Tinian Island in the Marianas and were soundly defeated. Not a single American "boat" had managed to reach the beach. The American fleet had retreated over the horizon after suffering staggering losses at Sunharon Beach.

Lucky exclaimed, "Wow! I guess somebody really did know what they were doing when they planned our demonstration. Someone knows what he's talking about but it sure isn't Tokyo Rose. We must have fooled the Japs completely. I wish we knew how those guys in the 4th Division are doing."

Riverboat Brown had some poignant statements to make from the scriptures and he ended them with his usual, "Oh ye of little faith." He was the only man in the 2nd Platoon who had been totally confident in the plan from the start. He had predicted that the mock landing would be a success and would completely fool the Japanese.

Later in the evening, just prior to "Taps," Blackjack climbed down into the compartment and told the men to gather round. He and the other staff NCO's had just come from a briefing with the company officers and wanted to let the men know how things were going over on White Beach. The 4th Marine Division had landed, surprising the Nips and thus took minimum casualties. The 1st Battalion, 8th Marines had gone ashore right after the 24th and 25th Marines of the 4th Division. We were to follow them in at daybreak. So far, things looked good ashore.

Landing on a beach that had already been secured was a new and welcome experience for the men of the battalion. What a wonder it was to get ashore without losing a man.

Corporal Jerden observed, "We musta' really lucked out on this one Cobber. The Marines who landed here yesterday had one helluva fight on their hands. Lookit all them dead Japs lying around?"

Epstein answered, "Yeah, there must be hundreds of 'em. Ski, are you thinking' what I'm thinkin'?"

"I am if you're thinkin' that this is just gonna be more of the same old stuff. This pile of coral and sand ain't no different from Saipan. There may not be another Mount Tapotchau here but otherwise the terrain is just the same and that's not good. The Japs look the same too, except that so far, the ones we've seen are all dead."

"Yeah", Epstein replied, "They said at the briefings that the island was almost flat. I must really be getting' soft in the head. I was stupid enough to believe them."

"Yeah, me too," Big Ski agreed, "That's because from three miles away over on Saipan it looks kinda flat. I'll bet this damned place has just as many caves and steep cliffs as Saipan."

The conversation was terminated by the voice of Gunny

Johannsen barking "Okay men, get your gear on, we're moving out!"

The regiment moved northeasterly toward Ushi Point Airfield. They were to secure the airfield and then move to and secure the east coast - bisecting the island. As they inched slowly forward through the gnarled terrain and snare-like undergrowth the area was littered with Japanese bodies from the previous night's fighting. Caution was exercised lest we have a recurrence of what happened on Saipan when Deadly Dave lost his new assistant BARman, Dennis Brennan, killed by a "dead" Jap.

At first there was little opposition as they moved through the open country. Gradually, the opposition developed. It began on the left from among the coral formations just inland from the beach as the battalion moved north. Shortly before noon, they encountered a high volume of rifle fire from concealed positions in the craggy coral along the coast. The advance ground to a standstill. The 1st Battalion swung around and moved up on the left and with the increased firepower of the two battalions, side by side; they advanced on and destroyed the enemy positions. The enemy fire slowly diminished and finally ceased. They saw about 20 bodies but had no idea how many more there were. There was no time for counting the enemy dead; we had to keep moving north by east.

Corporal Jerden had a look of satisfaction as he stated, "You know *Cobber* that was really a good move the way the 1st Battalion came right up to help us and we all fired on those Japs as we were moving forward. I'm convinced the reason our casualties were so light was because of the heavy volume of fire we were able to direct at the little bastards. They didn't have a chance. It was almost like watching a movie. I've noticed a lot of times when there's other Marines involved how we all work together and support each other. I wish the Army could have supported us like that going up Tapotchau. If they had, a lot of our guys would still be alive."

"Yeah Al," Ski answered, "When the stuff hits the fan and the chips are really down and we need help Marines do work pretty good together. I guess its all part of that spirit of Semper Fidelis old Gunny Johannsen's always talking about."

Shortly after noon with the 1st Battalion on the left and the 2nd on the right, the regiment moved eastward to attack the built-up area around Ushi Point Airfield and soon they were moving across the airfield itself. Enemy fire was minimal and casualties light. It was almost nightfall when the weary but proud troops, already 200 yards beyond their objective, were told to halt and dig in.

Foxholes were completed, rations consumed and cigarettes were lit under ponchos as the men groused about life in general and the Tinian rain in particular. They watched and waited. Darkness was soon upon them and another adventure started to take shape. Something was burning between their position and the far end of the airfield. At first the men watched the glow of a fire and thought it must be a destroyed tank or a truck burning. Within minutes the glow increased in size and finally the large Japanese fuel and oil dump between their position and the airfield exploded and started burning. Soon flames were leaping high into the sky. The cloud cover overhead reflected the orange and crimson of the burning fuel.

Fearless shot a glance at Lucky and then nodded toward the flames and asked, "Hey Lucky, can you believe this is happening to us again? I never thought it would be possible. Just look how that stuff is going up!"

"Well Fearless," Lucky answered, "It could develop into something like that. I sure as hell hope it doesn't though. So far, I haven't heard anything that sounded like ordnance exploding, I think it's just the fuel dump but it sure must be a big one."

The lines of the 2nd Battalion had to be moved, they were too close to the burning fuel dump. Moving a battalion's position, even a couple of hundred yards, could be challenging under the conditions that prevailed. Japanese troops with a lust to kill were wandering all over the area on a pitch black night and a huge burning fuel dump with flames leaping high into the sky and were casting strange moving shadows over the battlefield. The movement was made in spite of the men being silhouetted by the flames as they again dug their holes in the rain. It was all accomplished under sporadic small arms fire but miraculously without casualties. The Japanese fuel dump burned throughout the night but with considerably less intensity than had the huge American fuel and ammunition dump on Saipan.

In a foxhole with Deadly Dave Donahoe, Choirboy sobbed that he really didn't want to kill Japs. "I just don't think I can do it Dave. I can't line my sights up on another human being and purposely squeeze off a round and kill him. You know the Commandments say, 'Thou shalt not kill."

Deadly Dave quietly answered the emotionally stressed lad, "Look kid, that ain't exactly what the Commandments mean. You shouldn't kill maliciously or just for the hell of it and you should always try not to kill innocent people, like women and children or old, sick people. But if some screwy Jap is runnin' at you with a bayonet screamin' *banzai* or if he's firing his rifle at you tryin' to kill you, then by God, you'd better shoot. You are not shooting to kill; you are shooting to stay alive. If you don't kill them someone else may have to do it for you, and by then, it may be too late for you. You will very likely already be dead."

"Dave, I don't think you understand what I'm trying to say. Just the idea of killing another man, of permanently depriving him of his life and of shattering the hopes and dreams of his loved ones is a terrible thing to think about. I just don't think I can do it. Why can't the Japs just give up and surrender to us, they must know we're going to win anyway?"

Deadly Dave Donahoe was always a patient man and he went on to quietly explain, "Choirboy, you've got a lot to learn about the Japs. First of all, they really don't think we're going to win the war. They think they are. They fully expect their Navy to come steaming up any day now and blast us off these islands. In the second place, surrender is not in their vocabulary. They don't understand the meaning of such a word. They will either die trying to kill you or they will kill themselves if you don't do the job for them. That's all there is to it, they really expect to die and you hope you don't have to die. So, for God's sake kid, be a good Samaritan and help the little bastards to achieve their goal. Kill as many of them as you can!"

The Choirboy was not convinced. He would anguish over whether he could kill another man or not; he would discuss it with others in the squad and he was destined to lose sleep over it.

Poncho

Tinian Island – 26 July 1944

Billowing clouds of black smoke from the oil and fuel dump fire still filled the sky but the flames were slowly burning down and would be out in a few hours. Men stirred in their foxholes. It was time to stretch, light up a cigarette and thank God the night was finally over. Water was sparingly poured into canteen cups which were only half-filled then placed over heat-tabs and soluble coffee powder taken from the C-rations was emptied into the cups. There was a little packet of four cigarettes in the C-ration cans and so it became routine for most of the men to light up their first cigarette of the day while their coffee was heating up.

Daylight found the battalion moving across reasonably flat terrain and through seemingly endless cane fields as they headed toward the east coast of the island. Enemy fire was sporadic and somewhat ineffective although a few casualties were sustained. They moved all the way to the east end of the island where the eastern cliffs of Tinian were vertical, dropping straight down into the churning sea 100 feet below.

On their feet again the men moved south. Replacements and mail were received. This was the largest draft of replacements they had gotten since landing in the Marianas; the company was brought nearly up to full strength. Southward movement stopped at 1700 and the men were told to dig in for the night. They strung barbed wire concertina along the front lines in preparation for whatever was to come after dark. C-rations, the only food available, was not very appetizing when compared to the hot Navy chow they had recently enjoyed aboard ship.

Jerden looked at Nesbit and asked, "Did you know the new lieutenant told Blackjack that we've covered 2,500 yards in just the last two days? We sure as hell couldn't move like that over on Saipan."

"The lieutenant said that, huh? Well, I guess he knows what he's talking about. He's a pretty good officer, at least he's the best one we've seen since Lieutenant Stacey. I wonder just how much farther the Nips are gonna let us move before they really clobber us."

"Don't even think about it, just pray that our luck holds."

When the men had completed their foxholes and insured that the barbed wire was securely in place they attached a few empty C-ration cans to the wire and placed a couple of pebbles in each can. This was their crude, but effective, alarm system in case any Japanese attempted to penetrate the barbed wire in the darkness. While the Marines waited for it to get dark, the strains of "Oh Maimie Riley," "I Don't Want To Be a Soldier," "The Raggedy Assed Marines," Over There," and, of course, "The Rose of Trallee," wafted over the platoon's position. Kevin Mulcahy's wonderful Irish tenor voice was always a delight to listen to. Someone remarked that it was too bad that Ross and Muldoon had been assigned to another platoon, their voices were missed.

Choirboy turned to Riverboat and quietly said, "Corporal Brown, Sir?

"You can just call me Riverboat if you want to kid. Everyone else does. Besides, I was an enlisted man once myself."

"Yes, Sir, thank you, Sir. Corporal, I wanted to talk to you about Platoon Sergeant Black's tattoo. You know the big dragon on his left arm?"

"Yeah Choirboy sure, what about it?"

"Well Sir, Platoon Sergeant Black is a very knowledgeable man. He seems to know just about everything. In fact, next to Sergeant Shanghai Pooley, he's probably the smartest man in the 2nd Platoon."

"Yeah, I guess you could say that. Why Choirboy, what's this all about?"

"Well Sir, it's that dragon. Why would such an intelligent man have something like that tattooed on his arm. He must know that there's no such thing as a real dragon. It's just a mythological creature."

Riverboat asked, "Have you ever been to China Choirboy?"

"No Sir, of course not."

"Well, Blackjack has. He's served in China twice and he knows a lot about the Orient and I guess that dragon reminds him of China. You know kid, of all the Marines I've met who served in China during the 1920's and 30's, they all seem to have very fond memories of it. Now as far as Blackjack's dragon is concerned, if he's been to China, and if he thinks so much of dragons that he paid to have one tattooed on him for life, and if he thinks they are real, who am I to say otherwise? I've never been to China.

"You know kid, in this life, everyone likes to be reminded of something about his past from time to time. When old Blackjack looks down at that magnificent Imperial Dragon, it brings back memories to him of his time in China. Now as far as I'm concerned, the only places I've ever been assigned to as a Marine are these damned Pacific islands and although I've got a lot of memories of it, they ain't very pleasant ones. I'm not stayin' in the Marine Corps when the war ends, if it ever does, I'm goin' back to Mississippi and work on the river. I'll have my own boat someday and do you want to know what my dragon's gonna be? "

Choirboy looked surprised and asked, "Surely you don't intend to get a tattoo, Corporal?"

"Naw, hell no. I don't need one. To remind myself of my time on these damned islands, I'm gonna have an extra salt shaker on the table at home and instead of puttin' salt or pepper in it, I'm gonna fill it with sand. Whenever I start to eat real food again, I'll just sprinkle a little sand on it to remind me of how much I enjoyed my time out here in these lovely tropical islands."

"Okay Corporal Brown, I know you are just kidding with me but remember what I said about dragons. They aren't real, there are no dragons."

Riverboat Brown had never seen a dragon but he was not so sure they didn't exist. He was not a well educated man but he was perceptive and he could read people. He knew someone who had been a truly great Marine, a teacher and a leader and all his men respected him. But for his many good qualities something was just not right. This man had a dragon, a personal dragon. He fought hard but could never seem to defeat the dragon that was within him. As he closed his eyes and hoped sleep would come soon, Riverboat Brown seriously wondered about Shanghai's dragon.

* * * * * * * * * *

It was morning in the Marianas. The sun rose fast over Tinian Island and the brightness and heat soon conquered all. It beckoned to the large population of maggots and flies to awaken. It baked the ground to a hardness that challenged every Marine's skill with an entrenching tool, no matter their determination and experience at digging foxholes. To the battle weary Marines, the coral seemed like granite. The stench of the dead hung over the area to their front like a pall and assaulted the nostrils and sensitivities of the most hardened combat veterans. The unpleasantness reminded the Marines that this was nothing but a continuation of their recent Saipan experiences.

Lucky exclaimed, "Look Dave, over there! In front of Riverboat and Stash's hole, two dead Japs."

"That was close; one of them is only about a yard out. Hell, that's bayonet range. Someone's moving around out there! Over by the dead Japs. Look he's crawling toward the one that's face up. My God, it's one of our guys! It's gotta be a Marine. He's wearing Marine dungarees," answered Deadly Dave.

"Riverboat must know him, he's standing up!" Lucky said, then hesitated a moment before continuing, "He may be wearing Marine dungarees but he's no Marine. That's Poncho!"

"Poncho?" Dave exclaimed, "Then shoot the son of a bitch! We can say we thought there were three Japs and one was still alive."

"Damn, I'd like to," Lucky groaned, "but everybody would know I did it on purpose. If I live through this war I sure as hell don't want to spend the rest of my life in the Mare Island Naval Prison. All we can do is hope the enemy kills him. I'm sure they will sooner or later, the greedy bastard takes a lot of chances."

Poncho Gutierrez was a non-Marine. He was one of those rare individuals who had gotten into the Corps but had never really become a part of it. Marines don't talk much about his kind. Fortunately for the Corps, there aren't many of them. One of the problems with Poncho was that he was the only Mexican in the company and the only one some of the troops had ever met in person. Several of the troops from back east just naturally assumed that all Mexicans were like Poncho.

This was unfair as hell to other Mexicans, there was only one Poncho Gutierrez.

At mail call, he never got a letter. To many Marines, this would have been devastating, but Poncho didn't seem to expect any mail nor mind not getting any. He was a loner and had certain personal habits that did not endear him to the troops. If there was such a thing as an outsider in the 2nd platoon, it was Poncho Gutierrez. He had been assigned to the 1st and 3rd squads at different times and it just seemed that this was the 2nd squad's turn to put up with him.

Poncho Gutierrez was a wartime Marine, not a professional. Some benevolent judge had determined he could save the taxpayers a lot of money if Poncho would join the service instead of going to jail. Poncho obliged the judge by enlisting in the United States Marine Corps. This was unfortunate for the Corps and some recruiter probably should have been drummed out of the service for complying with the judge's wishes. Poncho didn't say very much. He only talked when he had to, so it took the guys in the 2nd squad a long time to piece together his story. Of course, they never did find out what it was he did that caused him to come into the Corps instead of going to jail.

Poncho had lived under an assumed name. He did a couple of years in a reform school in New Mexico as a juvenile and when he got out, he took someone else's name and traveled with a carnival. He moved all over the southwest but never said much about it except that he'd been here and there. He was once pretty well off financially, and there was no doubt in anyone's mind that he expected to be that way again just as soon as he could get out of the Corps. When he got drunk, he used to talk about all the money he once had. He had worked in a mortuary for two years before getting fired. This was the one thing he could talk about. He truly enjoyed his work.

Marines generally became pretty calloused after they'd been in combat awhile and many became souvenir hunters. Japanese Samurai swords, pistols, flags and other such things were much sought after. Combat Marines with a few souvenirs to sell could always count on picking up liberty money from rear echelon personnel. Poncho laughed at the others. He wouldn't waste his time on Jap flags.

Poncho was a "gold digger." He almost surely had the largest collection of gold teeth in the entire Asiatic-Pacific Theater of Operations. In combat, he always carried a small, leather bag that had been refilled many times. The troops never learned where he stashed his treasure when the bag was full but Poncho always managed to find some place to put it and would again start out with an empty bag.

Poncho Gutierrez was very good at what he did and he would no doubt be rich someday. When it came to friendship, Poncho was poor indeed. Even the chaplain avoided him. His methods of extracting gold teeth would have made any self-respecting oral surgeon cringe. Whenever the squad was in combat, Poncho reeked with the smell of death. He simply couldn't pass up a cadaver, not even those that had lain out in the elements a day or two. The Marines of the 2nd squad were battle hardened, callused, and tough as hell and they could put up with just about anything but to them, Poncho Gutierrez was truly obnoxious.

During the fighting on Saipan Poncho had come down with a bad case of dengue fever. In order for the squad to keep up, the men carried Poncho's pack and at times had to practically carry him. This was done as a matter of necessity and not because of any great love they had for Poncho.

Lucky, Ross, Epstein, Muldoon or one of the others would open Poncho's C-rations for him and see that his canteen was filled whenever fresh water was available. Doc checked on him a couple of times each day and threatened to have him evacuated if his temperature didn't go down soon. He was able to walk, after a fashion, and moved with the squad but must have been delirious a good part of the time.

Chic was reminded of the time he'd spent stumbling through the jungle in a daze while over on Saipan. He'd had malaria and dengue or the Japs would never have taken him. He knew exactly how Poncho felt and if it had been anyone else but Poncho, he would have felt considerable compassion for him.

At night, the squad leader made sure Poncho was in a hole with at least two other men. He could not be depended upon to stand watches in his condition. After dark, when the troops were in their fighting holes, it was always 50 percent alert. Poncho was not the only member of the squad to come down with dengue fever, in fact almost everyone got it at one time or another. The only unusual thing about Poncho's dengue was that when he got it, the troops assisted him and treated him just like he was one of them. When Poncho was himself, the men wanted little to do with him.

Now, in spite of Poncho's antisocial behavior and his nasty habit of removing teeth from the dead, it has to be said that in a firefight, he held his own. He didn't volunteer for anything and he certainly wouldn't go out of his way to help anyone but when rifle fire was needed on a target, Poncho was always there to deliver it and with a high degree of accuracy. Poncho was tough, wiry, antisocial, and just about the best man to have with you in a firefight. In spite of his value with a rifle, the other men in the platoon could never quite understand or accept Poncho's passion for collecting gold teeth.

* * * * * * * * * *

The Charred Cross

Tinian – August 1944

Kevin Mulcahy wanted to be accepted by the other Marines and he did as much as he could to prove himself worthy. It was doubtful if he ever fully understood how much the troops actually cared about him. He was everyone's kid brother and there wasn't a man in the company who didn't enjoy kidding him about his size and exuberance or listening to his beautiful tenor voice singing the old Irish favorites.

Choirboy always volunteered to hump expeditionary cans of water, belts and boxes of ammunition and cases of rations. On patrol, he frequently volunteered to take the point without understanding the dangers or responsibilities of being on the point. Shanghai Pooley had never permitted Mulcahy to be on the point when he was with the squad. The kid needed experience and seasoning. He was an "eager beaver" and very naïve.

Choirboy finally got a break. The new lieutenant, upon

learning that Choirboy had never been assigned as a runner, had sent him to the company CP to pull a couple of day's duty as a runner and the company had sent him on back to battalion. An eager beaver like the Choirboy would make a good runner. While he was in the rear echelon, maybe he could even scrounge a couple of extra cans of C-rations to help fatten him up.

Fearless Frank Quinlan was overjoyed. Mail call had been sounded and Fearless had gotten a fistful of letters as usual. Mail call was a special time and everyone was intent on opening their letters and reading them for the first time. Most would be re-read many subsequent times until they were finally worn out or until the next mail call.

Choirboy missed mail call since he was back at battalion. He got a sizeable number of letters including four from a Miss Peggy Coughlin.

The platoon sergeant told the platoon guide to "hold his mail till the kid gets back tomorrow or the next day. We don't want it to get lost being sent back and forth. Mail from home is bound to make the little guy feel a lot better."

Word filtered down to the company that the Choirboy had met with immediate acceptance in the Battalion CP. Some of the runners had been relaxing by the battalion message center and Choirboy had started singing with a couple of the others. They say it sounded pretty good. The battalion commander who had been passing by even stopped briefly to listen to a couple of songs. When the singing stopped, the CO asked them to sing Smedley Butler's favorite song. Choirboy was embarrassed not only because he didn't know the song, he didn't even know who Smedley Butler was.

The lieutenant colonel squatted down on his haunches with the privates and taught them the words to, "Sweet Adeline." Then he had them sing it with him a couple of times. It was a perfect tune for harmonizing. When the CO moved on to more important matters, he admonished the battalion message center chief, Technical Sergeant Mahoney, to instruct the runners as to the importance of knowing about Major General Smedley Darlington Butler and his many contributions to the Corps.

*   *   *   *   *   *   *   *   *   *

Fatigue was evident on the faces of the tired Marines as they trudged along in a column beside a burned out cane field. An unrelenting sun; stark in its brightness, hot and merciless was beating down upon them. There was no breeze. The air was still. Heat waves rose up from the blackened sugarcane field. Two Japanese planes flew over side by side with two Marine Corsairs in hot pursuit. Except for the sound of the aircraft, now far off in the distance, a heavy silence hung over the "secured" island of Tinian.

In the charred cane field, a few yards off to the left sprawled the body of a dead Marine. He was spread-eagled, his arms outstretched. The ever present Tinian flies had invaded his open mouth and nostrils and his wide, unseeing, glazed eyes. A few feet from the body lay his cartridge belt. The canteen was missing, as was his poncho. The Marine's rifle was nowhere in sight. Damned Japs!

In the bright sunlight three of the men stepped forward looking down silently at the remains of their brother. They cast dark human shadows that stretched across the body and lingered for brief moments like ghostly spirits. Then, one after the other, the shadows slowly drifted away. Corporal Jerden loosened his cartridge belt and removed his folded poncho. With Donahoe's assistance, he opened it and gently placed it over the body of the young Marine.

A depressed Donahoe mumbled, "I just can't believe Choirboy is dead."

Jerden quickly responded with, "He ain't dead dammit! Don't you remember what Shanghai always says? No one is really dead until they are forgotten."

"Yeah, we know what Shanghai says, but why him? Why Mulcahy?" Chic asked. "He never did anything bad in his life."

As they rejoined the now moving column on patrol their eyes were filled with hatred and their hearts lusted for vengeance.

It was Riverboat Brown, the self proclaimed preacher who spoke up.

"We've lost a lot of guys and mostly all of them were good. Not as good as Choirboy maybe but still they were all pretty good guys. We all know that we are still going to lose a lot more before this war's over. This outfit just can't remain at full-strength all the time. So what you have to understand is that God in his infinite wisdom is just selectively pruning our ranks. He may have an important assignment elsewhere for Choirboy."

The men were not listening to Riverboat Brown. They each had their own thoughts and emotions to contend with.

As the patrol rounded a bend in the trail, Poncho turned to the squad leader and remarked that he had forgotten something and would catch up with the patrol in a few minutes. He then turned and retraced his steps back along the trail from whence they had come.

Corporal Jerden shot a quick glance at Lucky and said, "Lucky! Poncho's goin' back for somethin' he says he forgot. This is really unusual. Follow him and see what the sonofabitch is up to. I don't trust him."

Lucky's eyes flashed, "Who does? Choirboy didn't have any gold teeth did he? If that's what Poncho is going back for, I'll kill him."

"Not that I ever noticed. Aw, hell no! The kid doesn't have any gold teeth! Just follow Poncho and see what he does and be sure he doesn't see you."

Lucky Lane followed the trail and after the first turn, stepped into the jungle. From his concealed position he could see where Choirboy's body lay in the burned cane field. He observed Poncho heading right for Choirboy. Lucky clicked the safety off of his M-1 rifle fully intending to shoot the despicable Poncho if he disturbed the boy's body.

Poncho Gutierrez cut a length of vine and selected two broken lengths of charred cane from the ground. Lashing them together he fashioned a crude cross which he hurriedly planted by Choirboy's poncho-covered head. Kneeling beside the dead lad he reverently bowed his head and made the sign of the cross. After a few moments, he again made the sign of the cross, got up and quickly bolted back to the trail to catch up with the patrol.

Almost in disbelief Lucky Lane stared at the charred cross then stepped back out of the jungle onto the trail beyond the bend and sprinted rapidly to catch up with the patrol before Poncho could spot him.

Jerden asked, "What was the little bastard doin' back there

Lucky?"

"Oh nothing much, he just picked something up from the ground. Must have dropped it while we were all looking at Choirboy's body. He'll be here in a minute; I had to rush to get back without him seeing me."

Poncho's secret would be forever safe with God and with Lucky Lane.

The bedraggled squad returned from the afternoon patrol. They had taken Private Kevin Mulcahy's body to the battalion aid station. Sergeant Childs passed the word that he wanted to see all hands from the 2nd squad over by his hole as soon as they finished cleaning their weapons. The men were tired. Choirboy wasn't as heavy as the rest of the men but carrying his body in a poncho for a couple of miles was a chore. They had all taken turns carrying the corners of the poncho and were all equally fatigued.

Deadly Dave spoke, "Yeah Sergeant, we're all here, what do you want?"

Childs answered, "Riverboat has something he want's to say to the squad."

"Men, I've asked Childs to get you all together so I could remind you that even though we've all been moving under some pretty dark clouds for the last couple of months, it won't always be this way. If it's God's will, the sun will rise and shine again and for those of us who have survived, life will go on. Now y'all gather around and reverently bow your heads and I'll lead us in a prayer for Choirboy."

Hashmark Jones snarled, "What the hell do you think you are Riverboat, a damn chaplain or somethin'? I'm gonna go heat my C-rations, it'll be dark soon and I've got the first watch."

The Reverend Riverboat Brown, never one to be discouraged, drew himself up to his full 5'8" as he snapped, "Goddamit Hashmark, we live together, we fight together, and some of us are even gonna die together; so what's wrong with us worshipping almighty God together? Now shape up and bow your head you sonofabitch; we're gonna pray for Choirboy and you're gonna pray with us."

Riverboat Brown held out his Bible with his left hand, placed his right hand upon it, bowed his head slightly as was his custom and started praying and quoting from the scriptures. Some of the scriptures he quoted sounded like he had made them up as he went along but then Riverboat always did things like that and no one really seemed to mind. They all knew his intentions were good.

Hashmark Jones stood meekly with his head bowed and acted remarkably like a small child that had just been scolded. The other members of the squad were always amused at how this burly, non-conforming, fierce warrior readily agreed to whatever the small, slick-sleeved corporal directed him to do.

When Riverboat had finished praying for Choirboy, Sergeant Childs reminded the men of something Shanghai Pooley was fond of saying.

"Remember men, no one is really dead until they are forgotten. I think those of us that live through this damned war will keep Choirboy alive for a long time 'cause none of us will ever forget the little guy."

* * * * * * * * * *

Tinian Typhoon

28 July 1944

The men were accustomed to daily rain squalls, gusty winds and ominous dark clouds. After all, it was the rainy season in the Marianas. Occasionally a downpour would be such a gully washer that some even called it the monsoon season.

On the afternoon of 28 July, the fourth day ashore; the wind blowing in from the west seemed strangely different. It was not only the changing of the velocity or the dampness it brought, it just felt odd. Somehow it sounded different too, sort of a mournful moaning and then all quiet and then the same unusual sound again. The skipper was getting a transmission on the SCR-300 that advised him to move his company rapidly into the cover of the heavily wooded area on our right flank and have the men dig in. The skipper added his own admonishment to all hands to; "Take cover immediately and stay down!" The sky darkened as heavy swells and fierce winds commenced to batter Tinian's west coast.

"What the hell's goin' on *Cobber*?" asked Epstein with a hint of concern in his voice. He'd never seen bad weather build so rapidly.

Fearless Frank, no less concerned, answered, "How should I know, I'm just an enlisted man. I guess maybe God's pissed off at us again."

"Wow! He must really be mad this time. Lookit the sky."

"Shut up and start diggin' Epstein! It's almost on top of us." Fearless quipped.

There was a soft rolling sound sweeping across the island from the western sea. The sound grew louder as it moved closer and soon it had become a roar. It was frightening as the sky rapidly darkened and then it was upon us. The Tinian rains came down heavily, mercilessly, it came down in sheets and with a vengeance, until the island was awash. The wind blowing in from the west had increased in force and was whipping the rain along its path.

The area the company was in now was wooded, a part of the Tinian jungle. The Japs were forgotten as there was a greater threat now and the men did not have to be told what it was. Sergeant Childs waved his arms in a wide circle and motioned downward with his hands and yelled at the top of his lungs for the men to get down and dig in. He looked at Chic Yancey and Deadly Dave Donahoe and waved them down and then proceeded on to the other men telling each in turn where he wanted their holes. Yancey and Donahoe looked at one another. This was a new experience for them and they knew by the wild look in Childs' eyes that it was new to him as well. If they could move just 15 yards to their left there was a rocky ledge with an overhang they could get under. Neither of them thought the sergeant would know any different and at the time they really didn't care. They scurried to squeeze under the protection of the rock ledge and started digging.

The heavy rains poured down in sheets reducing visibility to no more than a few feet. Loud cracking and crashing sounds and heavy thumps were heard throughout the forested area. The cracking sounds were limbs being torn from big trees and many whole trees were being smashed down by the force of wind and the weight of the terrible downpour. Nothing else could be heard above the loud howling of the wind and the cracking and crashing of falling trees and the constant pouring water. It was a typhoon, a real honest to God typhoon! Chic and Dave had never been in a typhoon before and if they survived this one, they hoped never to be in one again.

The rain was changing. It had been coming nearly straight down but now they noticed it was falling at an angle and the angle was becoming more acute. It was soon nearly horizontal! The wind had increased tremendously in force and was whipping the rain horizontally along its path.

The seas surrounding Tinian had changed to a dirty gray-blue as the winds mounted and the waves boiled over one another and grew into larger, uglier masses. The roaring surf forced all beach operations to shut down. One of our LST's broached and went hard aground on the Tinian reef where it would remain until mid-August. An LCI washed up on the reef north of White Beach 1. The two pontoon causeway piers that had been established at White Beach became victims of the rough seas. The pier on White Beach 1 broached after its anchor chains parted; shortly thereafter the pier on White Beach 2 broke into two parts.

Brutal winds accompanied the deluge. As the winds increased in velocity the rains diminished enough to permit some limited visibility. As the Marines dared to glance into the violence roaring across the earth, diverse objects could be seen flying at great speed. Corrugated roofs of buildings appeared from nowhere and sailed along with uprooted trees. From somewhere a steel 55 gallon drum appeared tumbling through the air as though it was weightless.

The deafening downpour seemed determined never to end - then, suddenly, as though the great power that released the deluge was exhausted, it stopped. It was over.

Foxholes were filled with water, cans of rations were floating; everything was utterly soaked through and through. It had been a breathtaking experience. One had but to look at the great number of large trees that had been uprooted or broken like twigs to understand the magnitude of the typhoon. As the men started assembling Sergeant Childs stared at a fallen tree and muttered, "Oh God, I'm sure this is where I told Yancey and Donahoe to dig in!"

They enjoyed the sergeant's concern for a few moments as they freed themselves from their rocky lair and crawled out to approach the other men.

Marines, who thought they would be safe as long as they stayed down in their holes, were scattered throughout the woods. It took time to round the dazed company up. Many claimed to have no idea how they got to where they were when found. Some, who were the worse for wear, may have even envied the cave-dwelling Japanese, at least for the moment. If we weren't fighting the Nips, we were fighting the damned elements. We had a pretty good score against the Typhoon, it was over and we still had all our men, some were the worse for wear but all were alive. It wasn't always easy being a Marine.

* * * * * * * * * *

The Gringo Bastards

They were facing terrain that was fairly flat for about 2000 yards. Then it rose in an abrupt, jungle shrouded steep slope up to a wide plateau. Along the island's east coast the rise was so steep that the men were at a loss as to how they would be able to conquer it. Even in the center the rise was steep enough that the one crude road up had to follow a series of hairpin turns. Near the west coast the cliff became somewhat gentler and was easier to climb. Intelligence estimates indicated that there were somewhere between 1800 to 2300 Japanese fighting men contained in this area. The Marines knew that they would have to pay dearly to take what remained of Tinian as its steep cliffs and terraced plateaus narrowed down from Marpo Point in the east to Lalo Point at its southern extremity.

Anticipating considerable resistance from the Japanese, the Corps commander had issued his most detailed operational order since Jig-day and disseminated a special naval gunfire annex. The battleships *Tennessee* and *California* and the cruisers *Louisville*, *Montpelier* and *Birmingham* and several destroyers would direct their combined firepower against the cliffs and wooded plateaus. The destroyer *Monssen* was assigned in direct support of the battalion. The warships threw a total of over 615 tons of shells into their targets. During this heavy bombardment by the Navy and by Marine artillery, the men were instructed to stay in their foxholes and keep their heads down. No friendly casualties were desired - and none resulted.

The cliffs were an easy target for the naval gunfire and artillery but the shrieking and whining of the shells overhead from midnight until "move out" time at 0830 was nerve-wracking to say the least. Word was passed that the engineers from the 20th Marines in the 4th Marine Division had found and cleared 45 mines from the area. This was supposed to be good news to the "Mud Marines" but it had a somewhat sobering effect on them as Barnsmell Nesbitt speculated, "If the engineers found and cleared 45 mines around here then it stands to reason that they didn't clear any of the mines that they haven't found. That task my lads has been left to us as we tiptoe through the tulips. I strongly suggest that you bastards keep your eyes open and step gingerly."

Barnsmell's advice was unnecessary. All hands were highly alert and keenly observant as they moved upward toward the southern reaches of Tinian Island.

The high southern plateau which continued generally flat and open to the coastal cliffs at Lalo Point on the island's southern extremity seemed to be their ultimate objective. The men learned that the two Marine divisions had captured four-fifths of the island. It was now 31 July, Jig-plus 7 day. My God, it felt like they'd been here seven weeks, not days. The Japanese forces were compressed into the southern fifth of the island they were now facing. There was nowhere left for them to withdraw. The Marines knew that the big showdown fight to the death could not be far off.

The word had been passed that Fox Company was needed. They had to get up to the plateau somehow. There seemed to be no other way than to just start climbing. As we moved up the steep draw, the 3rd squad was moving on our right and the 1st squad was to bring up the rear. It would have been a great position to defend but we were assaulting. The few trees nearby had been destroyed by naval gunfire and artillery. The sun was almost directly overhead and it was hot. The draw was littered with rocks and boulders and honeycombed with limestone caves large and small.

The going was slow and laborious. The advance was made one step at a time. The troops had to be careful where they stepped or they would start small rocks rolling down on the men behind them. They moved hunched over using the weight of their rifles to help them maintain the momentum necessary for the constant movement upward and forward. The men were hot, tired and thirsty. The trail they were on had obviously seen a lot of use but it was difficult to tell how recent that use had been. Other than the usual discarded debris of combat, there were no immediate signs that there were any enemy troops nearby.

That damned snap and hissing sound was all too familiar to every man in the platoon. It was the unmistakable sound of a Jap grenade over on the right. The grenade was thrown from one of the cave openings and bounced and rolled down the trail. When the grenade detonated, it did so with a vengeance. The platoon was in a very vulnerable position. There were some large rocks and boulders that provided cover only for a few. The area was nearly devoid of trees and shrubs so other than the rocks, there was little concealment. All forward movement came to an abrupt halt. Men cringed behind boulders in the blazing sun and wondered if they had climbed into the jaws of hell.

The trail they were on could not really be described as going up the face of a cliff, it is more accurately described as two cliffs comprising the walls of a deep crevasse and fanning out from the narrowest point at about a forty-five degree angle. This torturous terrain was cut by nature into a limestone hill and was pockmarked with numerous small caves. Which cave the grenade came from was anybody's guess? Not knowing which caves the enemy was in made it difficult to decide just where to take cover.

Big Ski and Little Ski chose the wrong rocks to hide behind. Unknowingly, they were exposed to a well-concealed enemy. The telltale rapid staccato chatter of a Nambu filled the air with several short bursts. Big Ski and Little Ski had been on the point going up and thus were in the top position. The squad was strung out five to 10 yards apart all the way down to where the 1st squad had started up. Big Ski and Little Ski were screaming for a corpsman. They had both been hit. Doc Drinkwine had tried to respond but as he attempted to run up the trail, he encountered a Japanese hand grenade.

The grenade hit Doc right in the chest causing him to fall backward and roll and slide down for perhaps 50 feet. The indomitable corpsman sustained multiple lacerations and was bleeding from the head but the grenade did not detonate. It was a dud.

Chief spotted the cave out of which the Nambu had fired. The big Indian stood up and emptied a magazine from his BAR into it. Then he too was hit. A bullet creased his back horizontally from shoulder to shoulder. Not a serious wound, but one that would keep Chief out of action for some time.

There was a clatter coming up the trail. It was Poncho. His helmet was bouncing up and down and rattling noisily as he ran up the steep incline. He jerked his helmet off and threw it down into the ravine. The loss of this noisy encumbrance seemed to give him momentum.

As he approached the first cave he stopped long enough to reach into the gas mask pouch he had slung over his shoulder and take out a fragmentation grenade which he armed and gingerly threw into the cave opening. Three of the caves came to life simultaneously. The Japs seemed to have a surplus of ammunition that they were trying to get rid of all at once.

The enemy fire, though great in volume, was not carefully aimed. Poncho moved up to the next opening and dropped down in front of it. It was hard to tell if he'd been shot or had purposely hit the deck or both. The wiry Mexican was back on his feet and running toward the cave's entrance. He lobbed a white phosphorous grenade into the cave.

As the heavy white smoke billowed out of the cave, screams could be heard from within. Poncho was in front of the third cave and emptied a clip from his M-1 rifle into it. Shots came back at him. He was hit, spun around and slammed into the side of a large boulder just beside the cave's entrance.

Still on his feet, he took out his remaining grenade, pulled the pin, let the spoon fly and stepped in front of the entrance again and threw the deadly missile in almost at the moment of detonation. Machine gun fire was pouring out of the cave but as Poncho's final grenade detonated, there was an immediate total silence from within. All firing in the ravine had stopped. All that could be heard was muffled sobbing from within the one smoke filled cave and the voice of Big Ski pleading for help. Little Ski was already dead.

Gunnery Sergeant Johannsen and the new lieutenant got to Poncho first. He had multiple wounds. They wanted to help him but didn't know where to start. He seemed to be bleeding all over. The big gunny lifted him up and held him in his arms.

"It's okay Poncho, we'll have a corpsman up here right away. You were really great but what on earth made you do it?

"What do you mean, what made me do it, Gunny? I had to do it! This is my squad. These guys are my friends, my family. They saved my ass plenty of times when we were in firefights. I love these gringo bastards and no damned Japs are gonna shoot them up and live to tell about it. Not while I'm around."

Blood was trickling out of one corner of his mouth and both of his nostrils. He looked up as the gunnery sergeant cradled him in his arms but his eyes were glazed over and there was no pulse. Poncho was dead.

Slowly, quietly and without anyone even noticing the change, Private Poncho Gutierrez had become a United States Marine. His citation read in part, ".... He gallantly gave his life for his country." But the Gringo Bastards knew better. He had given his life for the 2nd platoon and for the Marines who were the only real friends and family he'd ever known.

* * * * * * * * * *

Night of the Dragon

31 July/1 August 1944

The company continued its precarious task of climbing up to the plateau. Slowly, carefully and without taking additional casualties they moved forward and upward. The climb to the top of that cliff was challenging and required teamwork but the men of Fox Company were up to it. Chic was thankful to have finally made it but he and the others were thinking about those who didn't make it. Chic would miss Big and Little Ski and Chief and for some unexplainable reason he wished he could see Poncho again and talk to him. He wanted to call him "Marine" something he'd never called him before. And he wanted to say thank you to the brave little Mexican who had probably saved many of their lives while sacrificing his own.

Once they had gotten up onto the plateau the men were positioned in the company's defensive perimeter. Each platoon was responsible for one third of the area. The command post was to be near the center. The company gunnery sergeant was with Blackjack and Sergeant Childs as they carefully selected their men's positions and checked for likely avenues of approach and the most effective fields of fire. The company commander and the lieutenants would be along later to inspect and question the men to be certain they understood the tactical situation and knew their duties and responsibilities. A jeep had somehow managed to negotiate the winding, narrow dirt road and arrived up in the company area pulling a trailer loaded with concertinas of barbed wire. This time, an unbroken ring of barbed wire would completely surround the company perimeter. It was to be laid about 30 yards out in front of the holes. The Japs would have a hell of a time if they tried to penetrate that wire.

A few more vehicles were actually able to use the narrow road with its many hairpin turns to get up to the plateau. Two half-tracks and a jeep ambulance had already made it up and another jeep towing a water buffalo was slowly negotiating the sharp turns. Other vehicles were attempting to follow. Arrival of the vehicles meant an adequate supply of water, rations and ammunition, at least for the time being.

The platoon prepared their positions and dug in. They had more effectives than usual in spite of the losses they took while climbing up. Blackjack was again in command of the platoon.

Blackjack personally took over supervision of stringing and anchoring the barbed wire. He had stripped to the waist and was working right alongside the men and showing them exactly what he wanted done. Platoon Sergeant Jack Black always found a certain amount of pleasure in removing his shirt. There, emblazoned on his left arm was the dragon. One of the young Marines would always ask to see the dragon dance and Blackjack would promptly consent proudly displaying his remarkable muscle control which did cause the dragon to appear to be moving.

The men had all seen Blackjack's tattoo on the inside of his left forearm. It went all the way from his wrist to his elbow and was indeed magnificent. Blackjack was very proud of his tattoo; he claimed it was done by the master of all tattoo artists in Peking, China. It was an Imperial Dragon. He seemed to know a lot about dragons and other mysteries of the Orient. Whether it was Imperial or just a run of the mill dragon had something to do with the number of talons on the dragon's feet. Blackjack's dragon had five talons. He'd had the tattoo for years, but I still don't think old Blackjack ever took off his shirt without glancing down and admiring that dragon on his left arm. Blackjack had served in China before the war and as far as the troops were concerned his years of service, the unique tattoo on his left arm, his colorful language and his time on the Old Asiatic Station all contributed to his reputation among the troops as a character. He was also an extremely competent NCO.

Blackjack's brother Milt was the battalion quartermaster sergeant. It was unusual having brothers in the same outfit, but the way they played their game, you'd think they were in separate services. The old-timers all knew that they were close but the two of them put on an act that made it look to the troops like they had nothing to do with each other.

Milt was the battalion supply sergeant; he rated wearing two flat bars under his three chevrons which indicated that he was a quartermaster sergeant in supply. Milt was senior to Blackjack by one rank, but he was in the rear echelon, way back at battalion headquarters. Blackjack took pleasure in pointing to the one rocker under his Platoon Sergeant's chevrons and then to Milt's two flat bars. The rocker indicated an NCO of the line in the Marine Corps of those days and the flat bars marked Milt as a specialist. Blackjack kidded Milt about being a noncombatant. Blackjack knew that if the war had not come along quite so soon, his brother would have completed college and probably would have become a commissioned officer in the Marine Corps Reserve.

A week before the big *Banzai* attack on Tinian, the 2nd platoon had been brought up to nearly full strength. The new lieutenant was now broken in to the point where the men respected him and they were beginning to like him and trust in his judgment. They did not think of him as a 90-day wonder. He was a lot like the regular officers they used to have. By the night of the attack they had lost the lieutenant and six Marines but that still left the platoon in pretty good shape. The new replacements were adjusting to life in the field under combat conditions as rapidly as could be expected. They listened to words of wisdom from the old salts in the outfit. The old hands knew that only a part of what they were telling the new men would be understood. By the time the new men realized most of what they were being told was true and was important, it would be too late.

Uncertainty and fear is normal and is expected in replacements just joining a veteran combat unit under fire. Over confidence is rarely found in replacements but when it is, it can lead to serious consequences and may well result in Navy crosses of the unwanted kind, the type made of wood.

Blackjack sent Chic with Sergeant Childs, the platoon guide and three other men, one from each squad, on a working party up to the CP. They made two trips and brought back ammo, water and rations. When they got back the second time, they were glad to see that Blackjack and the men had just about finished positioning the barbed wire concertina across the front of their position. The first and third platoons had done likewise and were securing the concertinas together so the company area would be completely encircled with barbed wire. The foxholes were about 30 feet back from the wire so all would have clear fields of fire from their foxholes, past the barbed wire 30 feet away and down to the treeline below. If they had to be dug in on a hilltop, Chic figured they had at least done all they could for their defense.

There was a natural avenue of approach in a draw that looked as though it conveyed most of the water off the hill whenever it rained, which was often several times a day during the rainy season. This was the rainy season. At the bottom of the draw, just into the heavy bush and out of the line of sight, about 75 yards away was a section of two 37 millimeter cannons from Weapons Company. The troops always welcomed the 37's. They were a formidable weapon, especially when employed against ground troops and firing canister.

As night approached, the men always tried to put the finishing touches on their foxholes, deepen them if light lasted long enough, coordinate their position with the others around them and re-check their fields of fire. Chic was the assigned runner and he was glad to be digging in with Blackjack. He was a professional who could always be depended on. Besides, it made him feel like an old salt to share the hole with his platoon sergeant. Chic and Blackjack had developed a special relationship after Chic's escape from the Army hospital on Saipan. Blackjack was the first staff noncommissioned officer that Chic had ever called by his nickname right to his face. Chic was very proud of his friendship with this salty old Marine.

The night started like any other night in combat. The men didn't like the position they were occupying but it was where the company had been told to dig in so the troops tried to make the best of it. The ground had been all chewed up by artillery but still had a few trees left on it. Several yards down below their position the trees and bush were still pretty thick. The company CP was near the top but couldn't be seen from the 2nd platoon's position because of the irregular contour of the ground.

Platoon Sergeant Black did not like the heavy treeline below their position; it afforded too much concealment to anyone wishing to move toward them.

Overcome by ignorance and a false sense of security, Chic

pointed out to Blackjack that even if anyone did succeed in getting through that jungle, they would have to move a long way up the fairly clear terrain to get to the barbed wire which they would then have to cross before getting into the company's perimeter. The old-timer looked up at the sky and then glanced at Chic. "Lad, I thought you'd been in the tropics long enough to know better'n that. Just look at that sky. It's going to rain like hell tonight and there won't be enough visibility to see a star shell flare if it goes off in your hand."

There is no substitute for knowledge and experience. Blackjack had been right again. Chic had been overseas for more than a year now, but this was the darkest night he could remember. There had been many pitch black nights in the islands but none darker than this. How could Blackjack always anticipate such things? Within minutes after darkness fell, the holes on their right and left were invisible.

Chic was glad they had used salvaged lengths of old Jap communications wire to run from one foxhole to the next. Jerking on a length of wire was a crude means of communication but better than none.

"Chic, when's the last time you put new batteries in that 536?"

"Yesterday afternoon. Don't you remember? You made Childs swap those doggies a Jap flag and cigarette case for them. "

"Yeah, I remember. I just wanted to be certain you put the new ones in. Have you tested it today?"

"Sure, and you're not going to believe this Blackjack, but it actually worked."

"Keep it dry and close by, we're liable to need it before Mother Nature decides to turn the lights back on."

Shafts of moonlight would occasionally penetrate the thick black clouds above as they juggled for position in the dark tropical sky. This would afford a little visibility but not much. The clouds would invariably drift back together and pour down rain again. So far it had been a miserable night - but it would get worse.

There was much firing and a hell of a clatter over on the far side of the plateau. The Japanese had gotten into the Marines' positions and killed some men and captured two of the vehicles that had made it to the top earlier. Major Chamberlain, the Professor, had come up to the plateau earlier in the afternoon and had remained. He now organized a group of volunteers and launched a counterattack against the Japanese. The Professor yelled "Let's go!" and they swarmed forward with rifles blazing and recaptured the two vehicles and killed a number of the enemy.

Monsoon rains in the dark of night have a way of distorting sounds even to the experienced ear of the most seasoned combat veteran. With the torrential rains came gusts of wind that created many sounds of their own. Blackjack grimaced through clenched teeth that he could hear the screams of a banshee. Chic didn't know for sure what a banshee was but he could hear the screams too and many other bizarre sounds to boot.

Blackjack regretted having the troops affix empty C-ration cans to the barbed wire. Generally it was a good idea but with such heavy wind and rain, it simply added to the many other disturbing sounds in the night.

Snap! Hisss! Thud. "Oh God, it's a grenade! Where did that thing come from? "Down Chic, its close!" The two hunkered down in a foxhole partially filled with water and silently prayed during the moments before detonation. Two more grenades were thrown in rapid succession. There was no need for the two Marines to communicate. They both knew the grenades had been thrown from above them and bounced and rolled down a few feet before going off. There were enemy troops within the company's position! With the exploding grenades, the heavy rains miraculously subsided and became a steady drizzle. A nuisance, but certainly not as blinding as it was before.

"*Banzai! Dai Nippon, Banzai!*" From down the hill came the reports of the 37's. They were firing for all they were worth, and at that particular time, they were worth one hell of a lot. There was movement all around. Most of it came from our own positions, the Japs had infiltrated during the deluge and no one was able to see or hear them until they threw their first grenades. The Nips were screaming and hollering like the devil himself was after them. We knew the devil was in their outfit, but up until now we hadn't been certain whether he was after them or was leading them.

Chic strained to focus on the dark forms moving about but it was impossible to tell friend from foe. He and Blackjack knew the old hands would not leave their holes. They were not sure how the replacements would react. Blackjack tugged on the comm wire leading to the holes on their left and right and they had tugged back so he knew those men were staying down. Blackjack worried aloud that if fire were directed at the nearest sounds, friendly troops were sure to be in the line of fire. Rifle fire started sporadically and soon became incessant. Most was coming from the right flank over by the third squad's area. The sounds were muffled by the drizzle and sounded like strings of Chinese firecrackers being set off.

Chic had the 536 out and was jabbering.

"Fox Six, Fox Six, this is Fox Two, Come in Fox Six, Come in Fox Six. Can you hear me Fox Six, over?"

Obviously, Fox Six was occupied with other pressing matters at the time.

"Okay Chic, that's enough! The Japs are gonna hear you and they'll be all over us in a minute."

Fox Six had started the 60mm mortars firing illumination shells. They put them up as fast as they could drop them down the tubes. The pop and swishing sound of the flares descending was a welcome sound but the flares swinging back and forth from their parachutes cast eerie shadows that played tricks on the eyes and, at best, gave poor illumination.

Platoon Sergeant Jack Black didn't want to believe what he thought he saw and what he was hearing, but he knew it was real. Part of his platoon including the 3rd squad was moving in a skirmish line just above them, from right to left, firing as they moved forward. Corporal Thompson was in the forefront, urging the men to "Follow Me!" He was only doing what he had been trained to do back in the States. He must have thought he could drive the screaming enemy back from their position.

Thompson was such an impressive leader that the men had actually gotten up out of their holes and followed him into the face of the banzai attack. Except for his total lack of combat experience against the Japanese, Thompson had all the attributes of a superb combat leader. What a shame, Blackjack thought. Thompson could have been so good if he'd just lasted a little longer so we could train him to fight the Japs.

There were forms moving all over the muddy hillside, but none remained standing. There were more grenades and there was sporadic rifle fire. Blackjack couldn't determine the fate of his heroic men but hoped that some who participated in that foolish counterattack had survived. The rain again increased in intensity and in direct proportion, the visibility decreased.

The scream was loud, profane and chilling. It emanated from Blackjack. The scream was accompanied by unintelligible foreign sounds from another person. The enemy had found their foxhole.

Chic was terrified! Someone was moving towards him from the right front and was only a few feet away. Blackjack was standing up beside Chic on the left and was engaged in what Chic thought was hand to hand combat. He could feel Blackjack but could barely distinguish the murky form of his attacker towering above.

Chic didn't want to fire for fear of hitting any of the survivors of Thompson's attack. He had no way of knowing yet that none had survived. He yelled at the top of his voice.

"Halt! Who is it? Halt you sonofabitch!"

He was hoping to hear an American voice but did not. Chic fired.

He was trying to make out his enemy to the right front that he could sense but not see and glance at Blackjack's plight at the same time. Nearly paralyzed with fear, what he saw would live on in his memory always as a superhuman feat of strength and courage. A Japanese soldier, standing on the edge of their hole had driven his bayonet down into Blackjack. The bayonet went into Blackjack's left upper arm and penetrated all the way until stopped by the muzzle hitting bone.

In a bizarre but remarkable feat, Blackjack reached across with his right hand and grasped the Jap's rifle by its upper hand guard and pulled the rifle all the way back, extracting the bayonet from his own arm. The little Jap was still holding onto the rifle and was driven back and knocked down by the force of the powerful Marine's actions. His hands released their grip on the rifle as the powerful Marine swung it in an arc over his head with his right hand. The rifle struck Chic a glancing blow, knocking him nearly out of the hole, and came down solidly on the by now prone Jap. The moon was floating out from behind the black clouds and revealed Blackjack wielding the rifle with bayonet still attached as a club using only his right hand and literally beating his assailant senseless.

Thank God a corpsman had finally responded to Chic's pleas and was treating the unconscious platoon sergeant. Neither the corpsman nor Chic realized the seriousness of Blackjack's wound at that time.

The 37's continued to pound away but they were firing much slower now, and small-arms fire continued throughout the night with lessening intensity. Flares were still going up occasionally but did little good with the heavy cloud cover, rains and wind. When the flares or a shaft of moonlight did permit a brief bit of visibility, prone forms could be seen throughout the company area. Friend and foe were indistinguishable from one another. Chic knew there were a lot of them. He couldn't discern any movement but hoped some of the Marines were still alive.

"How many men did we lose in the night?" Chic asked.

Lucky Lane answered, "I don't know, but we must've lost a hell of a lot. Most of 'em I guess."

Stash was in Chic's foxhole where Blackjack had been. His buddy had been killed and he had left when they were helping the seriously wounded up to the CP. He couldn't get back in the hole with his best friend's body so Chic had called him over to stay with him. There was a dead Jap just above Chic's side of the hole. His arm was hanging down into the hole. Chic and Stash didn't notice until daylight that the dead Jap's hand still held a grenade.

31 July 1944

Daylight revealed many horrors. Counting the living was faster than counting the dead, there were fewer of them. There were now 14 effectives in the 2nd platoon. They were "walking wounded" but could still carry on.

The company commander wanted a brief situation report

of what had gone on in the 2nd platoon's area and the first sergeant needed a report of the killed, wounded and effectives by name ASAP.

The captain stated, "Let the men know that the dragon died last night but Platoon Sergeant Black is going to make it."

Chic wasn't sure he fully understood but none the less he answered, "Aye, aye, Sir, the men will really be glad to know Blackjack is going to make it."

As he moved out, Chic asked the Top what the captain had meant about the dragon dying last night. The Top answered, "You know how Blackjack used to flex his muscles and make the dragon on his left arm dance?"

Chic answered, "Sure, I've seen him do it lots of times."

"Well, you won't see it anymore; the battalion surgeon had Chief Reynolds call the Skipper on the EE-8 about an hour ago. He told him Blackjack's left arm had been taken off right above the elbow."

Chic tried to run back down to the platoon area but quickly found that he couldn't run. He'd gotten some grenade fragments in his legs during the night and his left knee was bandaged too tightly. Doc had been busy treating far too many serious casualties throughout the night for Chic to bother him about a tight bandage. He limped back to the platoon.

As Chic moved through the company area, he thought about all the things that had happened in the night. Those 37's over on the left had really saved their butts. They had piled up over 40 dead bodies in front of their position. Only two members of the 37's platoon survived. Blackjack wasn't the only one who'd lost an arm. The lieutenant in command of the 37's had put a web belt tourniquet on his shattered arm and continued to fire after his men had been killed or wounded and his position was surrounded. The arm was now useless but the lieutenant was still alive. He ought to get a medal for the night's action.

The rear echelon pogues from battalion headquarters had actually formed up a platoon of noncombatant cooks, bakers, clerks and quartermasters and tried to come up that winding road to help reinforce the company. They didn't make it all the way but a couple had died trying. Not bad for headquarters people.

Chic saw the men laying bodies in rows under some shade. Most were already covered up with ponchos. Knowing that some of his best friends were lying there, Chic stopped to pay his respects and reflect on his own mortality. Three 2½ ton trucks had come up from somewhere and the poncho wrapped bodies were being gently placed into them. A chaplain was checking dogtags and making some notes. He must have come up with the trucks.

The chaplain knelt beside a body that Chic immediately recognized as Corporal Thompson. Only Thompson could countercharge a Japanese banzai attack across a muddy hill during a monsoon in the dead of night, be riddled with bullet holes, fall dead into the mud with the rain beating on him all night and still look like a Marine. What a loss! He had to have been one of the best DI's the Marine Corps ever produced.

Right next to Thompson, the body was covered with a poncho but Chic could see the light blonde hair sticking out of one end. This had to be Whitey Schultz. He was the only man in the company who's hair was that platinum blonde color. It was Schultz who had put Chic's pack under his head and tried to make him comfortable back on Saipan just before Suzuki and his men came along.

As Chic stood mesmerized by the dead who only yesterday were his friends and buddies, he noticed the company first sergeant lifting a poncho and staring down at an old friend. It was Milt Black. Milt had organized and led the relief column up from battalion headquarters to help reinforce Fox Company. The battalion supply sergeant had given his life proving to his brother that in the Marine Corps, there is no such thing as a noncombatant.

Blackjack had lost his platoon, his arm and his brother all in one bitter night during the "Most perfect amphibious operation of World War II".

*　*　*　*　*　*　*　*　*　*

Cat & Mouse Game

Tinian – 1 August 1944

Following the Night of the Dragon on the Tinian plateau the battalion was relieved by the 3rd Battalion, 6th Marines. The 8th Marines, including 3/6, pushed on with their attack toward the coast. A little time was needed for the 2nd Battalion to reorganize, dress their wounds and mourn their dead. The men were proud of their victory on the plateau but in achieving it they had again been badly mauled.

While reorganizing, assigning billets to newly joined replacements, restoring gear and cleaning weapons, the men found themselves in what had once been a peaceful meadow surrounded by high ground on three sides. The sky was a bright blue with a smattering of puffy white clouds drifting slowly by.

The men looked at one another in astonishment as the beautiful, rich notes of a trumpet came wafting down from on high. It was soothing and relaxing to men who had known the sleeplessness and terror of combat for so long. The tune was Hoagie Carmichael's "Stardust" and it brought fond memories of the States and home and happier times to every man in the battalion who was fortunate enough to hear it. The young captain playing the trumpet was from an adjacent company. His name was Hoffman and he was destined to be one of the survivors who would continue to serve in the Corps. Years later when Major General Carl Hoffman retired from the Marine Corps, he was still playing his trumpet but never as beautifully as he did on that sunny August morning in 1944 in the meadow on Tinian Island.

Up on the high ground, the regiment was pushing to the southeast in an effort to reach the cliffs overlooking the water. The 2nd Battalion's respite did not last long. They were needed up on the plateau as backup for the 1st Battalion. By 1500 they were back up on the rim with the rest of the regiment looking down the precipitous rocky slopes and in so doing they could see their future. None wanted to believe it but there it was, right below them. The Marines had gone as far as they could. There was nothing left of Tinian Island but the Jap infested cliffs. Unfounded rumors placed the remaining Japanese military strength at approximately 1,800.

Patrols were sent down the dreaded cliffs to reconnoiter but what they were about to find had already been guessed at by the men. The cliffs were a honeycomb of deep crevasses and natural caves. Rifle and machine-gun fire announced that there were still plenty of Japanese fighting men on the island and they would have to be eliminated cave by cave. It was going to be a long, dangerous finale to what some thought of as the perfect amphibious operation of the war. To the men's great surprise, the island was declared secured at 1855. It was Tuesday, the 1st of August 1944.

On Wednesday and Thursday, the 6th Marines were confronted with large numbers of Japanese and Chamorro civilians who approached bearing white flags and desiring to surrender. They'd had enough of combat. Tragically, many others could not bring themselves to surrender and leapt over the cliffs to their deaths. It was a repeat of what had happened on Saipan. They had been so brainwashed by the Japanese Army and had such a great fear of and hatred for the American Marines that they were convinced that the Americans would rape them and then torture them to death. Rather than face such a horrible fate many chose death by suicide.

With Tinian secured, the 4th Marine Division departed for their camp on the island of Maui in Hawaii for further training. In another six months they would again make history by landing on the black volcanic sands of Iwo Jima and staining them red, blood red. The 2nd Marine Division, minus the 8th Marines soon left Tinian and returned to Saipan. The Japanese improved their defensive positions and waited.

The 8th Marines was strung out in a long line on a plateau overlooking the sea. It was in the Southeastern corner of the island near Marpo Point. As we sat in our holes and looked out to the southeast past the edge of the cliff into sheer nothingness, we realized that we were just 30 yards from nowhere. The land simply dropped down forming a cliff that ended in the choppy sea far below. It may as well have been the end of the earth. To our rear was a strip of jungle behind which we could look up and see another steep cliff.

It was back to daily patrolling. Many of the patrols went down the nearly vertical cliffs while others searched the jungle covered plateaus. The patrols that went down the face of the cliff were dangerous but they nearly always yielded a few Japanese who were willing to die or to surrender. Either way, the Marines were prepared to accommodate them.

The U.S. Navy was on station at daylight every morning. A PC (patrol craft) would come in as close to the cliffs as it could in reasonable safety and blast the face of the cliff first with music and then with exhortations in Japanese for the cave dwellers to come out and surrender to the Marines. The 78 rpm records they played were the latest hits from the United States. The morning reveille concerts always started with "Oh What a Beautiful Morning," followed by several popular tunes which often included: "The Trolley Song," "Drinkin' Rum and Coca Cola," "Chattanooga Choo-Choo," "Comin' in on a Wing and a Prayer," or "White Cliffs of Dover." Following the concert and the announcements, a warning in Japanese was given telling the people just how long they would have in which to come out and surrender to the Marines. When the time was up, the ship would open fire with its main battery.

There is no doubt that the Navy saved countless Marines lives by systematically blasting the caves in the cliffs around Marpo Point. As soon as the ship ceased firing the Marines would clamber down the cliffs to the cave entrances and attempt to neutralize them while their occupants, if any, were still dazed from the naval gunfire.

Muldoon grumbled, "This cat and mouse game is a helluva way to fight a war. The little bastards are down there just waitin' for us to go down the cliff so they can kill us and here we are waitin' at the top to kill them if they try to come up."

Ross responded, "Yeah Muldoon, it sure is a cat and mouse game. If they don't come up the cliff they're gonna starve to death and if we don't go down and get 'em we are gonna stay in this damned position for the rest of the war. And the way they've been feedin' us, or failing to feed us, we are probably gonna starve to death too."

The Marines didn't know how many Japs there still were. They only knew that they had to continue going after them until there was no longer a threat to the Americans on the island. Of course, the Japs didn't know how many Marines there were. If they had, they may well have decided on another *banzai* attack. Their mission was simply to kill as many Americans as they could while waiting for the Japanese Fleet to return to the Marianas to retake the islands.

Behind us was a narrow strip of jungle and another cliff rising high above the jungle plateau we were on. Battalion headquarters had devised a practical way to move our dead and wounded up the cliff and deliver cans of water and cases of rations and ammunition down to us. It was a modification of the old Navy Breeches buoy. A wire basket, known as a Stokes litter, designed for carrying the bodies of dead and wounded was "appropriated" from a Navy ship and rigged with a cable. Some enterprising soul up at the battalion CP had determined that he could affix the cable on to the bumper of a jeep to provide the power for operating the special "elevator". This became our means of receiving ammunition, water and rations and for getting our dead and wounded up the high cliff above us.

When the men were not out on patrol there was little for them to do but man their positions and wait for any Japanese that might attempt to leave the protection of their caves or climb up the cliffs. Most of the time was spent grousing. There were often discussions about how they would have preferred to be fighting the Germans in the war in Europe where the enemy was not inclined to *banzai* attacks and may even surrender rather than committing suicide. They fantasized that there might even be an occasional chance encounter with a grateful or friendly French or Belgian girl. But alas, the war in Europe belonged to the U.S. Army, the lucky devils. They resented and sometimes spoke disparagingly of General Clifton B. Cates and his ridiculous comments about the Tinian campaign.

Gunnery Sergeant Carl Johannsen was walking the line and chatting with the men as was his custom. He overheard the men of the 2nd squad griping about General Cates.

Johannsen was an old-timer who had fought in France during the First World War. He stopped and addressed the men of the 2nd squad.

"What's with you people and General Cates? I doubt if any

of you guys have even met the general. You sure seem ready to condemn him.

The gunny snapped, "What do you mean talking like that? And what's this "enjoyed himself" supposed to imply?"

Lucky answered, "Didn't you see the *Newsweek* article that old Stash got at mail call Gunny? Here, listen to this. Gimme that magazine Stash!" And Lucky Lane read:

"Admiral Raymond A. Spruance, commander of the Fifth Fleet in the Western Pacific, called the landing on Tinian on the 24th of July the most perfect amphibious assault of the war. It was certainly less costly in terms of Marines' lives than the Saipan landing which preceded it. After a series of suicidal Japanese counterattacks, the Marines rapidly drove south across the island."

"And then it says, 'Major General Clifton B. Cates, who commands the 4th Marine Division on Tinian, reported that the fighting was different from most any that we had experienced because it was good terrain....it was a good clean operation and I think the men really enjoyed it.' "

Lucky went on, "In my opinion, to the men who fought and bled in these damned campaigns, none of them was "....a good clean operation" and none of us "really enjoyed it!" The view may have been slightly different from the comfort and safety of General Cates' division command post than it was from our muddy foxholes."

"Where the hell else would you expect to find him if not in his CP? After all, he is the commanding general of a division comprised of some 20,000 men. I think there is something you men need to know about him."

Lucky Lane spoke up, "Gunny, the only thing we need to know about that general is why he wasn't up on the plateau with us on the night of the dragon when the Japs pulled that last banzai. I'd like to have seen just how much he would have "enjoyed" himself with dead Marines all around him and those slant-eyed, suicidal bastards trying to run him through with a bayonet."

The old gunny stroked his chin and said, "Well, Son, that may very well be so but don't sell the old general short. I think he has a pretty good idea of what combat is all about. By the way, Deadly Dave, if you and Stash have the time I'd like to tell you and Lucky a little story."

The Marines always had time to listen to the Old Gunny's stories.

"Well lads, this is about a young Marine lieutenant that I knew back in France during the first World War. It was near Soissons in the Aisne-Marne region. Without realizing it, the 6th Marines had run head-on into a German corps counterattack and all hell was breaking loose. We were virtually surrounded and were outnumbered nearly thirty to one.

This young lieutenant reported to regiment by field message and his report read something like this:

"I am in an old abandoned French trench bordering on road leading out from your CP and 350 yards from an old mill. I have only 10 men left out of my company and 20 out of other companies. We need support but it is almost suicide to try to get it here as we are swept by machine-gun fire and a constant artillery barrage is upon us. I have no one on my left and only a few on my right. I will hold."

"What do you men think about a message like that?"

"Damn Gunny, he was in a hell of a spot," declared Chic. "Did the lieutenant or any of his men get out alive?"

"Yep, he managed to bring the remaining men back, but it wasn't easy. I've never failed to be impressed by that message and I've always thought pretty highly of the lieutenant. Just in case you lads are interested in knowing more about him, his name is Clifton Bledsoe Cates and he is currently the commanding general of the 4th Marine Division."

The subject of General Cates was soon dropped as the men sheepishly busied themselves with other things. They had to clean their weapons, check ammunition and prepare to go back out on patrol.

The cat and mouse game continued as the men peered over the cliffs watching and waiting for their quarry to show themselves. The days became weeks and each morning the Stokes litter basket came down the cable with cans of water and boxes of rations and ammunition. The basket was sent back up the cable, too often containing the body of a dead or wounded Marine. For the company and the rest of the regiment, the world had shrunk. It consisted only of the long line of foxholes on the plateau along the edge of the cliff, the cane fields and jungle along the plateaus or the face of the cliffs themselves with their proliferation of deadly caves and crannies. This was the playing field for the cat and mouse game.

* * * * * * * * * *

The End of the Earth

The men ate their meager C-rations and prepared for another night on the plateau. During this rainy night there was no enemy activity noted in the company's area of responsibility. The men clad in their helmets and ponchos and armed with entrenching tools, were busy enough battling the elements.

The rains finally stopped but the heavens over the palisades were still black and filled with heavy clouds. Suddenly, the massive dark clouds were edged with a hint of silver that slowly changed to orange then seemed to burst into a golden yellow and finally, the dawn broke so fast you could almost hear it. Chick thought of Kipling's, " Road to Mandalay."

"Where the dawn comes up like thunder out of China 'crost the bay."

Muldoon said, "Y'know *Cobber*, sittin' in this damned hole on this strip of flat ground with that cliff droppin' off like it does and nothin' else out there but the rough sea way down below and the sky up above makes me kinda feel like we've come to the end of the earth. What a hell of a place for the Marine Corps to leave us. This is the most depressing place I've ever seen."

* * * * * * * * * *

It is a time-worn truth in the Marine Corps that when a man is so good as to be considered irreplaceable, he is often replaced by someone who surprisingly is just as good as and sometimes better than the irreplaceable one. The troops did not think the Corps had anyone who was good enough to replace their Company Gunnery Sergeant. When the new

Gunnery Sergeant, Carl Johannsen reported aboard back on Saipan the men viewed him with scorn.

Muldoon remembered the first time he had seen Gunny Johannsen. He had commented, "Lookit that old white-haired sonofabitch! How could anyone think he can keep up in a rifle company like ours?"

Ross had foolishly agreed, "Yeah, I hear he's a retread. He retired and got out of the Corps and now, because of the war, they let him come back on active duty. He'll never be able to keep up in this outfit. He's just too old."

It was not long before the men were wondering how on earth they would ever be able to keep up with the old white-haired gunny. In less than a month, he had become a Fox Company icon. He was tough, he was dedicated and he was bright and best of all, he had a brand of leadership that made the men respect him and want to be like him. He could climb the cliffs like a mountain goat and was at home in the jungle or on the plateau. When the men questioned the gunny about his prior service in the Marine Corps they were surprised to learn that he had served on the Mexican Border in 1916 and had later served in France during World War I. He was not an Old China Hand like Blackjack and Shanghai, but when he related his combat experiences from France, the men were more than a little impressed. Gunny Johannsen was a welcome addition to the company.

In one particular respect, Gunny Johannsen was like Shanghai. He was always teaching. He knew the men would soon be headed for another campaign and he knew there were replacements among them who had little or no combat experience except what they were now getting on the palisades. It was his responsibility to see that they were trained and educated for whatever was to come.

"The old gunny strolled down the line where he could talk to his men. It was an evening ritual with him. Each night when the men were settling in and waiting for darkness, he walked the line. He always had a number of comments to make and occasionally asked a few pertinent questions. The men were never really sure whether he was testing them or just making conversation. They liked listening to the old gunny. No matter what he was talking about the men always managed to glean something of value from him that would be helpful.

The battle for Tinian had been officially over for some time but combat never really ended for the 8th Marines. There were still plenty of hostile Japs on the island and it was the regiment's responsibility to kill or capture them.

The end of the war was a frequent topic of conversation. The often used saying "Golden Gate in forty-eight.....," didn't sound very optimistic but it must be remembered that the Marines of World War II had all lived through the Great Depression which was just ending as the war began and they fully expected to return to a country that was financially ruined by the huge expense of fighting the biggest war in world history, thus, "Bread line in forty-nine." On the palisades and cliffs, the cat and mouse game continued.

It was oppressively hot on Tinian Island that September afternoon in 1944. We had recently returned from the afternoon patrol and had cleaned our weapons and inventoried ammunition. A group of us sat and sprawled casually waiting for the blistering sun to drop below the western horizon and the conversation revolved around memories of recent combat and the wonders we had seen and done.

Most of us had only been in the Corps for a year or two so it didn't take long for us to run out of wonders and memories. The conversation soon changed to stories by Colonel John W. Thomason about life in the Old Corps and other books we'd read and of movies we'd seen like "The Singin' Marine" and "To the Shores of Tripoli."

Gunnery Sergeant Carl Johannsen was the oldest Marine in the company and the only one who had fought at Belleau Wood. When he had heard enough from the youngsters, the old Gunny leaned back on the ammunition crate he was seated on, gave us what might be described as a benevolent scowl then he uttered words that went something like this:

"Back along the fields of Flanders, Up at Buddha's gilded dome,

"To the stormy rocks off Hatteras or the frozen shores of Nome

"By the glow of Moana Loa, on that isle of golden dreams,

Long the bleak plains of Siberia to the sunny Philippines.

Raging storms and shifting ballast, typhoons rising in the west.

Golden silence of a dead calm, when the seagulls ride the crest."

His eyes swept across the group of young Marines and he scowled again as he looked at them and said:

"Lads, There are no books or painted pictures or no movies on the screen that can quite approach the memories of an old U.S. Marine.

"So why don't you boys just settle down now! With a little luck, perhaps some of you may live long enough to have some memories of your own someday."

And the old gunny passed on down the line of fighting holes looking in on and chatting with the rest of his men.

Tinian had lasted a long time for the 8th Marines. The balance of the 2nd Marine Division was back on Saipan and the 4th Marine Division had returned to Hawaii. The mission assigned to the 8th was simply to capture or eliminate the remaining Japanese forces and protect the thousands of Americans arriving on the island.

Daily patrols were conducted and almost every day the Japanese would lose a few men and the Marines may have one or two killed or wounded. This was repeated day after day, week after week causing the men to wonder who was going to run out of troops first. The 8th Marines was now the only U.S. infantry unit left on the island and it was anyone's guess how many Japanese fighting troops were left.

It was an unpleasant and tedious task for a regiment that had already fought its way through some of the toughest island campaigns in the Pacific but it had to be done by someone. If there was a good side to it, it was the experience and realistic training the newly joined replacements got. This played an important role in shaping them up for the next big campaign. The men resented this assignment and yet they somehow felt a sense of pride that it was their outfit that had been called upon to do it. No one bothered to tell them so, but they knew they were an elite regiment, perhaps one of the best in the Corps. This distinction sometimes cost them dearly as they were to learn again the following year during the greatest air, land and sea battle in history. Once again, while operating independently from the rest of the division.

The Japanese they were after now were the smart ones. They were highly skilled at evading detection and at staying alive. They knew how to live off the land, forage for food and hit their enemies where and when it was least expected. The other Japanese on Tinian were either dead or had been captured. Long after the island had been secured this handful of renegade Japs were causing casualties among the non-combatants. There were thousands of U.S. personnel arriving on Tinian. Navy Seabees and Army engineers worked around the clock in an unprecedented effort to turn the island of Tinian into what would soon become the busiest airfield on earth. The Japanese remaining on the island had to be dealt with by professionals. In July through October of 1944, the 8th Marines, experienced, battle-hardened and bloodied, were as professional as Marines get.

* * * * * * * * * *

Return to Saipan

25 October 1944

As they rode across Saipan they saw Quonset huts and strong-back tents. In some of the camps there were generators for electricity This was almost like Stateside living. Much of the rubble of combat had been cleared away and the whole island was buzzing with activity. The convoy of trucks lumbered on around the base of Mount Tapotchau and across the island as the Marines wondered what their living quarters would be like.

As some had expected, the camp was as far from civilization as it was possible to get and still be on the same island. They could not detect the odor of putrefied human flesh. Saipan really had changed: it was no longer "The Island of the Dead." It was now simply, "This damned place!" It was oppressively hot and the musty odor of rotting vegetation in the jungle was offensive but it was so much improved from what they had been accustomed to when last they were on Saipan.

The convoy stopped on a long slope that had once been a cane field and the battalion disembarked. Pyramidal tents, it seemed like hundreds of them, neatly lined up on a slope that had been cleared of all vegetation. It was almost a guarantee of some interesting adventures when the rains were heavy, and the hillside became a massive wash. Old hands wondered why they had not left some of the trees for shade from the blistering tropical sun and to help control erosion. The tents, neatly lined up in long rows, were an inviting target to enemy aircraft.

The battalion messhall was part Quonset hut and part tent. The troops really didn't give a damn what it was as long as they could finally get good rations. This was too much to hope for. It never happened. One of the duties to be performed by the messmen before chow was to set out and fill the G.I. cans with water. They filled the immersion burners with kerosene and placed them into the cans. One of the cooks would attempt to light each burner and was generally successful after a few puffs of smoke and some popping although there would occasionally be a loud report or explosion and another burner had to be found. The cook was usually unscathed.

The immersion burners were put into galvanized iron garbage cans that had been filled with water that was brought to a boil. There were three such cans lined up about 10 feet apart. The first can had soapy water for washing and the next two had clear water for rinsing and sterilization. The troops approached in a column of files holding their messkits by the long meat can handle. The meat can cover, knife, fork and spoon had slots for hanging them on the handle of the meat can. The mess kits were plunged into each of the three G.I. cans in succession and were thus washed and sterilized. The men shook them off as they approached the chow line and after air drying them for a minute or two, assembled the meat can and meat can cover and put the knife, fork and spoon into their dungaree shirt pocket. Holding their open messkits out in front of them they were now ready for whatever the cooks and messmen were about to ladle into them.

Their first encounter upon reaching the chowline was their friendly Navy corpsman who placed a yellow Atabrine tablet into each man's hand then watched suspiciously as they tossed them into their mouths, grimaced and swallowed. It was a bitter pill to take but not nearly so bitter as the Quinine tablets they had been taking a year before. The Atabrine was thought to be a deterrent to malaria and dengue fever. Malaria was non-existent on Saipan and practically all of the men had already suffered through at least one bout of dengue by now. Nevertheless, the Navy Medical Department was looking after the needs of the Marines and Atabrine consumption was as mandatory as taking salt tablets.

Once they had cleared the line the men had the option of sitting on benches at the wooden mess tables or going elsewhere. Elsewhere meant sitting on the ground to eat so most opted for the mess tent and benches. It was prohibited to take any type of food back to their quarters as that may present a health hazard or attract exotic tropical island critters of unknown origin. Considering the quality of the food, the men would have been reluctant to take it back to their tents even if it had been permitted.

The blackest day in the history of the 8th Marines came during the "hunger strike." The troops were fed up and certainly not with food. While the Army and the Navy were being fed B-rations and food that was almost as good as they would have gotten back home in the States, the 2nd Division Marines, five months after their assault landing on the bloody beaches of this island, were still eating leftover combat rations and whatever the mess personnel could scrounge up for them.

Most of the men were thin and gaunt. Even the replacements who had appeared to be well-fed when they first arrived, were losing weight. At first everyone took it, feeling that they had come here to fight a war, not to get fat. As time wore on with the constant training and patrolling, the monotony of the same old meager rations grew difficult to tolerate.

There was never quite enough food and what there was may have been nutritious, but it certainly wasn't up to the usual Marine standards of quality and quantity. The deplorable conditions that prevailed in the battalion messes of the regiment were a command problem and had to be addressed by the regimental and battalion commanders. The company grade and battalion staff officers were so consumed with supervising the patrol activities, training the troops and planning for the next operation that they may have overlooked Napoleon's admonition that an army travels on its stomach. If the food is good, men will put up with a lot. If it is bad, attitudes and performance are sure to suffer.

In the 8th Marines the food, and there was very little of it, had been of poor quality. No one intended that it be called a 'hunger strike,' someone simply said it. It was repeated by others and it stuck. The men just wanted a dramatic way of forcing their superiors to be aware of a serious problem that had heretofore gone unresolved. When the men were marched to chow they filed past the serving line without holding up their messkits to be filled. After clearing the line, the men quietly went back to their company areas. There was no demonstration and there were no threats and no one failed to perform his duties. The men were hurt and simply wanted someone up the chain of command to know about it and if possible, take corrective action.

In the 2nd Battalion, the new CO called a meeting of all the NCO's. They assembled on the side of a hill that had rows of sandbags placed so men could sit on them like an amphitheater. In the evenings this "Sandbag Cinema" was used to show movies. The new lieutenant colonel told his NCO's that he knew the chow was substandard and that he was looking into it and would take whatever action he could to see that things improved. He then issued a direct order to them that they would all go to chow and that they would hold out their messkits to receive food and then they would eat the food or there would be hell to pay. The "Needle" had nothing further to say and the NCO's were dismissed. With all the NCO's grudgingly going to chow and eating, the hungry troops could do nothing but follow suit. The unsuccessful "hunger strike" was thus concluded and the new battalion commander had achieved his first questionable victory.

There was some discussion among the men as to how "Jim" Crowe, their old battalion commander would have handled the situation. No one could be certain but all knew that he would have taken immediate corrective action of some type, even if that had meant a raid on an Army supply dump. Crowe would also have given the NCO's a pep talk that would have boosted their spirits and would have found its way back to the junior enlisted Marines who also needed some spirit boosting.

Lieutenant Colonel Henry Pierson "Jim" Crowe was a flamboyant and colorful character and a natural leader. His battalion missed him. Combat Marines didn't give a damn about morale, they considered it an Army word. Marines had esprit de corps, it was their hallmark and the foundation for the tremendous pride they had in their Corps. No other service could even come close to having the esprit de corps shared by all Marines. From time to time, someone would try to come up with an exact definition of esprit de corps but it just couldn't be done. It was beyond definitive explanation and actually was a somewhat elusive term as its definition may change at times according to the prevailing situation. At one time, esprit de corps could mean a deep and abiding love for and pride in the Corps shared by every member of the command. At another time, it may have a somewhat different connotation as explained by Pfc Fearless Frank Quinlan, who stated:

"Esprit de corps is what brings us all together in a real tight brotherhood in which we defy any outsider to say or do anything about the Corps or anyone in it. This esprit is the result of all of us being uniformly crapped on repeatedly by everyone and everything since we got into this damned outfit.

"If you want an example of what I'm talkin' about, let me remind you of what we've shared: The unbelievably tough training we went through; then living six deep on those damned transports for 40 or more days at a time with only two lousy meals a day; going through the hell of amphibious landings against heavily fortified beaches; fighting and crawling our way up that damned Mount Tapotchau and then fighting all over the damned island and its bastard offspring, Tinian and then being sent back to garrison this damned place and protect the "doggie" engineers and Navy Seabees while all along they are getting decent chow. And we are fed this slop and are training to go back into combat.

"Damned near half of the original outfit has been killed and the rest of us, except for a few replacements, have been wounded. But soon, we'll be going back into combat again. The Army and Navy are full of guys that have never heard a shot fired in anger but they're sending the Marines back in. Is there any one of you guys, just one of you, that can honestly tell me he's had a really decent meal anytime in the last year? Okay, now you know what esprit de corps is all about. We've got it because we're all in the same boat. We will always identify with one another. There ain't no other sonofabitch in this world outside of us right here in this screwed up outfit who has the vaguest idea how any of us feel about anything but all of us know just exactly how each other feels. We're in it together, we've got esprit de corps up the gazoo! Screw all the rest of them bastards out there! And by the way men, Semper Fi."

* * * * * * * * * *

Holiday Routine

November 1944

The monotony of training and patrolling was broken up by the numerous parties the troops were invited to. All of these came under the general heading of working parties. This went on for six days each week and then some benevolent soul back at higher headquarters who had a warped sense of humor and a vivid imagination decided to call the division's redeployment from Tinian to Saipan "Rest Camp." It was declared that there would be 'Holiday Routine' on Sundays.

It had been a long war for the raggedy assed Marines. Some knew they would not survive, all hoped they would. None felt heroic, but they had seen the horrors of war and knew it had to be fought by someone. It had to be won.

Marines wondered if the American people understood what they were experiencing. There were many inconveniences on the home front including shortages and the rationing of many essential items. The war in Europe made the headlines daily. Newspaper clippings from home told of the great advances being made by the Allies in Europe. No one seemed to give a damn that 3,100 American fighting men had been killed on Saipan. To the folks back home, it was just another remote island campaign.

There wasn't a Marine in the Pacific who hadn't wished that he was fighting in the European Theater. In the Pacific, it was a different kind of war and certainly a different enemy. No one who had not experienced, first hand, the devastation and carnage of combat in the Pacific, or the fanaticism of the Japanese would be able to truly understand or appreciate just how horrible it was.

When the U.S. forces landed at Normandy, they could look forward to fighting on land against a civilized enemy who may, if the situation became hopeless, surrender. When the Marines landed on a beach in the Pacific they could look forward to sustaining casualties while fighting a tenacious, fanatical enemy whose sole purpose in life was to kill them and who would actually take their own lives before surrendering.

Many Marines dreamed of fighting their way across Europe where there were cities, towns and villages and where the people spoke languages that were recognizable. Some Americans may even be welcomed as liberators.

During holiday routine the troops were permitted to wash clothes, write letters, clean their weapons and gear or just sit around playing cards, shooting the breeze or generally taking it easy. Tent flaps were nearly always rolled up unless there were serious rain squalls and the men could talk to one another between tents after dark, a movie may be shown. There was little regimentation and the men delighted in having a whole day off nearly every week unless they were on guard or mess duty.

They talked a lot about food and what they looked forward to eating when they got back to the States. There was also much talk of past conquests and accomplishments and plans were laid for elaborate liberty if ever the war really did come to an end.

They lied to one another about the many beautiful women they had known intimately, then realized that during their long ordeal in combat and on short rations, they had seldom thought of sex. This was easily explained by the "sea lawyers" who stated that the government didn't want them thinking of sex and thus had put liberal doses of saltpeter in their meager rations.

A few may have believed this, but most knew that they had been just too damned scared and hungry to think of sex. Survival had been uppermost in the minds of the men who really fought the war.

The first sergeant was only kidding when he repeated the old Corps saying, "There'll be liberty for all hands, but no liberty boats!" After all, it was a well known fact that in 1944, there simply was no place for tired, hungry, battle-weary men to go on liberty on the island of Saipan. It was also strictly forbidden for anyone to leave their area without being properly checked out.

Another old Corps saying was, "Tell it to the Marines!" You can tell it to the Marines but there is always a small percentage who never get the word. So it was that our young warriors decided that there must be something more exciting than cleaning their weapons, doing their laundry, writing letters and playing cards all day on Sundays.

Any old-timer will tell you that you can't leave young Marines alone and unsupervised for a whole day once a week and not expect them to get into mischief of some sort. It is only natural for young troops to seek adventure or excitement.

The first sergeant had instructed the company clerk to make up a check-in, check-out sheet in compliance with a recent division order. There was still a lot of enemy activity on the island and no one was permitted to leave their area without checking out. It was also necessary for them to be accompanied by an armed NCO. The company clerk made up the sheet, attached it to a clipboard and handed it to the first sergeant. The "Top" ascertained that there were spaces for "departure time, destination, and nature of business and estimated time of return."

The company commander was going up to the regimental headquarters area to coordinate something with operations. "First Sergeant."

"Yes Sir, Skipper."

"I've got to go to a meeting over at regiment tomorrow at 0900. Will you see that the duty 'Music' gets the word and has the jeep ready in time?"

"You bet I will Skipper. You know you're going to have to

take someone else along in addition to the 'Music?"

"What do you mean I'll have to take someone else along?"

"Yes Sir, in order to comply with that new division order I showed you the other day. You can't check out of the area unless you take an armed NCO with you. That leaves both of our field music's out. I'll get Gunny Paul to ride 'shotgun' for you."

"Okay Top, let the Gunny know we'll need him. It sure seems like a waste of manpower to take an NCO when the musics have been assigned to me as bodyguards."

Field Music First Class W. Max Netherland had been standing beside the company clerk pretending to be going through a stack of papers while covertly listening to the conversation. He was grinning like "the cat that ate the canary." The first sergeant knew what he was thinking and wanted no part of it. He and Gunny Paul had both known and served with Netherland in New York, while assigned to the World's Fair detachment back in 1939.

"Top, if you've got just a moment, I'd like to speak to you on a matter of importance that just might save manpower for the Marine Corps and enhance our efficiency here in the company."

"Music, save your breath. We are not going to make you an NCO so you can ride shotgun for the 'old man.' You know that as a company, we rate two field musics. Field music privates or field musics first class, that's all."

"You also know that they rate a field music corporal up in battalion headquarters and one field music sergeant in regimental headquarters. Now, if you think you can do a better job than the ones they've already got, go ahead and write a letter to the Commandant of the Marine Corps and request that he appoint you to whatever rank you think you can 'con' him into. Just remember one thing Netherland, I knew you on your first cruise, so don't think of using me as a reference because I promise you that if anyone asks me about you, I will tell the truth, the whole truth and nothing but the truth! That will not help you.

"Now do like the old man said, and be sure to have that Jeep on line tomorrow morning by 0845."

"Okay, Top, I'll be here with the Jeep."

"Oh, by the way Max, you'd better take along a couple of extra clips of ammo, just in case." The field music would have taken along extra ammunition without the first sergeant having to remind him. The first sergeant seemed to forget sometimes that they had been privates together back in '39. He may have wound up as a music but he was as good a Marine as anyone else in this damned outfit. He wished the top and the skipper would recognize that fact. Netherland was not just an ordinary, run of the mill field music. He was a man of many talents and vast experience.

After leaving the Corps upon completion of his first cruise, he was employed, among other things, as a sidewalk reporter in Chicago and was doing very well at it until this damned war came along and changed everything. He was a man of great initiative and imagination and was convinced in his heart that he would really strike it rich someday. He was not, as the first sergeant and the other staff NCO's thought, just a phony con artist.

The idea of a check-in, check-out log appealed immensely to the wily music. The log was used during the week by those few officers and staff NCO's who had to go somewhere on official business. It was not intended to be used by the privates and Pfc's of the 2nd squad and their associates. They reasoned that since there were no formations on Sundays, and since they were allowed to straggle to and from chow, what there was of it, and since they had no official duties to perform, unless they were assigned to guard duty, their absence from the area would not be missed.

They hadn't had any real freedom or liberty since leaving New Zealand back in November 1943. Their time at Camp Tarawa on Hawaii certainly didn't offer much in the way of liberty. They just had to try and get away for awhile and get their minds off the constant training and patrolling and what was to follow after they embarked for the next campaign. Maybe they could even find something edible on this damned island. Practically no one else ever mentioned having a desire to leave the company area on Sundays. There was just no place to go.

Each Sunday, a different one would enter the name of a fictitious brother and, under nature of business, they would write "Visit to Sergeant (here they would enter the fictitious name of the fictitious brother of the week) to coordinate military activities," and off they'd go. The fictitious brother was always listed as "Sergeant" as it seemed much more appropriate to "coordinate military activities" with a sergeant. If the first sergeant or anyone in company headquarters had ever taken a good look at the log, they may have been surprised to see that on Sundays, there were always two pages. The top page was for the officers, and others really having official business to check in and out and the second page was used exclusively by the raggedy assed Marines in hopes that no one would turn the page and find it. If there had ever been a serious problem, they could have pointed to the second page and proven that they had in fact been legally checked out.

This administrative sleight-of-hand was possible through the auspices of Field Music First Class W. Max Netherland, who always had access to the company headquarters tent. It was the mission of the company field musics to be the company commander's bodyguard, driver, radio operator and runner in addition to sounding bugle calls. It was perfectly normal for the musics to be in and around the company office at any time.

If anyone had known about these stalwarts checking out every Sunday to coordinate with the brothers of one another, they surely would have thought it remarkable that so many members of the 2nd squad had brothers in the Marine Corps on Saipan who were all sergeants and were serving in either the 2nd or 6th Marines.

After imbibing in bootlegged beer and some rather exotic "raisin jack," one time, in the boondocks behind the 3rd battalion's mess, the troops discussed the possibility of someone discovering the Sunday entries in the checkout log and perhaps having *Leatherneck* magazine or, *Pacific Stars and Stripes,* do a feature story on the men of the 2nd squad, nearly every one of whom had a brother who was serving as a sergeant in the other infantry regiments of the 2nd Marine Division. It was decided that if this was ever suggested, they would all go over to the other regiments, wherever they may be on the island, and attempt to find someone with the same surnames as theirs and immediately adopt them as their brothers. This minor problem having been solved, the troops got back to singing a few old songs and doing some serious drinking and imaginative planning for the next Sunday's holiday routine.

*　*　*　*　*　*　*　*　*　*

Saipan Liberty

It was in anticipation of high adventure that they left the company area on that bright Sunday morning just after divine services. They had lied about their destination since they had no idea where they actually were going. All could sense that Corporal Grogan had little interest in going beyond the 3rd Battalion area, where he was acquainted with a cook who, for the right price, seemed to always know where one could find a card game and some bootlegged booze or locally produced "Raisin Jack." It was decided that the others would look around and maybe go for a hike. They would be back later and meet Grogan. Grogan was to wait for them and to insure his dependability, each invested a small sum in his hoped-for luck at cards.

Off they trekked down a winding coral road hopefully leading to the, by now, "civilized" part of the island. None knew what to expect or what they may find, but all knew they just had to get away from the dreary routine of training, patrolling, working parties and inadequate food. The evenings included old movies in the Sandbag Cinema, the outdoor theater. The routine was occasionally broken by an air raid, which sent terror through the men's hearts as every bomb sounded like it was falling directly on them. Of course none ever did, the Japs had more lucrative targets out on the B-29 airstrips and that's where the bombs were intended to hit. The air raids became less frequent as time went by.

As the men strolled along the road together one started singing the words to an Old Corps song they had all heard many times from some of the pre-war Marines. They were soon all singing it together. Somehow, men just seemed to move easier when they were walking along and singing a good marching song.

"As we go marching, and the band begins to p-l-a-y, You can hear the people shouting,

"The raggedy assed Marines are on parade.

"Hey! The raggedy assed Marines, the raggedy assed Marines, The raggedy assed Marines are on parade," etc.

They had gone through a number of verses when, one by one, their level of enthusiasm started to wane.

The sun was hot and the road dusty. In a short time, the four were soaked in sweat and caked with dust. The blazing sun gave no quarter.

Deadly Dave proclaimed, "We must be nuts to be out here like this when we could be lying under a tree somewhere in the shade. Whose idea was this anyhow?"

There was no time for the guilty party to answer. A 2½ ton truck had rolled around the curve and spotting the four Marines, stopped. They jumped into the back and yelled their thanks to the driver and his "shotgun" assistant driver who proceeded on their way. Riding in the bed of the truck provided a welcome breeze which helped to dry the sweat and added to the hypnotic effect of just passing through this island for which they had fought so long and hard. Many of their comrades had paid with their lives for the ride they were now enjoying.

As the truck rumbled along the road, a large dust cloud was generated and held their attention as they marveled at the luxury of riding in the back of a truck moving so swiftly. The billowing dust clouds rose up with a vengeance, but always remained behind and never quite caught up with the moving vehicle. This lone moving truck created a wake of dust greater than a whole company of infantry marching on foot would have generated. While riding along and enjoying the breeze they again spontaneously started to sing "The Raggedy Assed Marines."

The island had changed remarkably. It was now an American base garrisoned by many support troops. The Army and Navy presence was everywhere. There were Quonset huts, strong-back tents and even some makeshift barracks. Troops living in these areas had many conveniences such as the Marines had not enjoyed in months. The driver stopped for them to disembark near the beach in an area that seemed to be the busiest part of Saipan Island.

What a transformation, they couldn't get over it. There was traffic on the new roads and in the water. Boats were coming and going between the ships and shore with supplies and personnel. Strolling down the beach like tourists, they were outsiders. This was their beach; it was their island. They had fought like hell for it. But now, there were other Americans here, lots of them. They were engineers, Seabees and Army Air Forces. There were all sorts of support personnel who looked right at home on the island, working like beavers, and seemed oblivious to everything around them except the work they were engaged in.

The troops got into a conversation with a sailor named Olson, the coxswain of one of the boats waiting at the beach and found that he was from USS *Orion*, (AS-18), a submarine tender that was 530 feet long and displaced 9,250 tons.

That didn't mean much to the Marines but then they learned that Olson was from Milwaukee. Shute's home town! Dutch Shute immediately started talking to Olson and found that they had grown up just a few blocks apart. They had never met each other before, but when you are young and thousands of miles from home and someone starts naming streets and schools and theaters and even knows a few bars you've gone into and been thrown out of for being underage, its like meeting a long lost friend or relative. Thus began a new adventure for a handful of raggedy assed Marines.

Olson, "The Mad Viking" proudly took them out to his ship to look around. None had ever been on a submarine tender before. It was like a mother hen to a flock of chicks, or in this case, submarines. They went up the accommodation ladder, rendered the double salute and stepped onto the quarterdeck. The Officer of the Deck was a grizzled old Navy Chief Warrant Boatswain who returned their salutes then beckoned them over to one side of the quarterdeck. They lined up at attention but he quickly put them at ease.

What are you Marines doing aboard this ship and what do you want?" An apprehensive Deadly Dave answered, "Oh, nothing sir, one of your coxswains just brought us aboard to look around, that's all." Then the inevitable question from the old

Boatswain, "What outfit are you men with?" Dutch answered, "We're in the 2nd Marine Division Sir." "How long have you been with them?" Dutch continued, "Oh, some of us a year, some a couple of years, Sir." The boatswain queried, "Were any of you at Tarawa?" Dutch answered, "Yes Sir."

The boatswain had a concerned look on his face as he asked "Did you ever know anyone in the 2nd Marines?"

"Yes Sir, we've worked with them. They were on our flanks at Tarawa."

The old Boatswain had a strangely forlorn look about him as he softly asked:" What about a Corporal by the name of Curtis. Michael T. Curtis, Jr. USMC, did any of you know him?"

The troops looked at one another and finally decided that none of them knew Corporal Mike Curtis. Chic thought he detected a tear coursing down the old man's cheek as he changed the subject, asking, "How long has it been since you boys have had a hot shower?"

Chief started to answer that they hadn't had a hot shower since first going ashore on Saipan six months ago. The 15th of June, last year. Donahoe reminded him that they had gone aboard an LST for some good Navy chow and all got hot showers and fresh dungarees two days before landing on Tinian, that would have been the 22nd of July.

Chic answered for the others. "Sir, we all had a hot fresh-water shower about five months ago."

Olson had arrived on the quarterdeck and as he approached them the old sailor looked at him, returned his salute, and said, "Coxswain, take these men below and get them hot showers and a hot meal. Then show them around the ship and give them whatever they want."

"Yes sir, Mr. Curtis."

"Remember what I said Olson, whatever they want." "Aye, aye, sir!"

The old sailor looked very sad with tears running down his cheeks. Chic had never seen an officer cry before, not even in combat.

Olson took them below to one of the crew's berthing compartments where he borrowed towels for their showers. Fresh water showers, steaming hot, and with real soap! What a luxury! It was difficult to believe they had gone so long without hot water.

When they emerged, Olson was gone and so were their dungarees. Several crew members crowded around offering to share their Navy dungarees with the now clean Marines. All had questions about the Marine Corps and especially about fighting the Japanese. It turned out that nearly every sailor in the compartment had a friend or relative or knew someone who was in the Corps.

They were escorted to chow in the crew's messing compartment by a group of their newfound friends who couldn't seem to get enough of their "war stories." The troops couldn't believe their eyes or their palettes. Chicken. The Navy was having chicken! Who cares if the potatoes were powdered or the green beans came out of a can? This was real chow! It was hot and it was good. They were invited to go through the line a second time. Without the slightest hesitation, all of them did.

After chow, the raggedy assed Marines, still attired in Navy dungarees, were taken on a tour. USS *Orion* was a fighting ship boasting four 5 inch guns, eight 40 millimeter cannons and twenty-three 20 millimeters. She had extensive repair facilities for submarines and the troops were awed when they saw the different shops and facilities which seemed nearly capable of building a ship from scratch. What impressed the troops most was a chief storekeeper who sent one of his third class petty officers to get the keys to the "Geedunk" and had him open it for their Marine guests. It was unbelievable, simply unbelievable. Here they were guests on a beautiful, clean ship of the U.S. Navy. They'd all had wonderful hot showers and great Navy chow and now, the "geedunk" was being opened just for them.

As a general rule, powdered ice-cream mix doesn't resemble real ice cream very closely. However, when you haven't tasted ice cream for eight or nine months, the cold mixture is just great.

Back in the crew's compartment, "The Mad Viking" had a surprise for the raggedy assed Marines. Their dungarees had been laundered, starched and pressed. Even their leggings had been washed. This was almost too much for the weary

Marines to believe, but it was really happening. Olson couldn't get enough of their war stories. They had been invited into the CPO's Mess and were having slices of chocolate sheet cake and good old Navy coffee when they first heard the term used. Someone referred to them as "Our Marines." They couldn't have been more flattered.

The Chiefs were a salty lot but treated the young Marines like special guests. The "Mad Viking" was made to wait out in the passageway while they were in the CPO's Mess. This reminded them of their own lowly rank and made them realize that the Chiefs were granting them a very special privilege. Juniors referred to all CPO's as "Chief." In the Marine Corps, one could be called "Chief" even if he were only a private, simply by being an Indian.

The Chiefs asked as many questions about combat ashore as the crew and showed a sincere interest which the troops appreciated. The CPO's valued Jap souvenirs as much as did the seamen and thus the raggedy assed Marines were invited to return aboard anytime they wished.

The Navy was treating them so well that the troops felt they should share one of their secrets with the crew. They confessed to having manufactured a number of Jap flags themselves and showed the sailors just how it was done. With the facilities aboard this wonderful ship, almost anything could be made.

A chief quartermaster told them he had access to parachute flares and thus to white silk. He was going to get a couple of his sailors to start making flags and would let the raggedy assed Marines check them over for quality and comparison to the real thing when they next came aboard. The raggedy assed Marines promised the chief they'd bring a couple of authentic Japanese flags aboard with them as samples when they next returned.

*   *   *   *   *   *   *   *   *   *

The Cemetery

They had come ashore with full packs and full stomachs. They'd had a rewarding afternoon aboard USS *Orion* and another happy Sunday excursion was coming to an end. They were on the west side of the island walking down a road paved with freshly crushed coral. They had hopes of spotting a vehicle bearing the tactical marks of the 8th Marines so they could bum a ride back to camp before the inevitable rains started. As they walked along, Deadly Dave mentioned that he'd been talking to a couple of submarine sailors just back from a combat patrol. He asked the others if any of them had ever heard of an island called Oaky Nawa or something that sounded like that. None had, not even the music.

The threatening sky had darkened and was becoming gloomy. It was overcast with an occasional shaft of bright sunlight penetrating the dark clouds and sending its gleaming golden-white diagonal pillars of light earthward. A small side road appeared on their left. It had also been freshly paved with crushed white coral. Over the little road a white wooden arch had been erected. The letters painted on the arch silently proclaiming "2nd Marine Division Cemetery".

It drew them like a magnet and without speaking a word they automatically turned into the cemetery and slowly strolled through its neat rows of countless white wooden crosses.

Lucky exclaimed, "Look at all these crosses! I didn't realize we had that many guys killed. And this cemetery is only for our division, there's got to be another cemetery for the 4th Division Marines somewhere around here and one for the 27th Army Division." With some trepidation, he continued, "Come on, let's walk through the rows. Maybe we'll find some of our shipmates' graves."

The names were stenciled in black on the white wooden crosses. Many had but a single word stenciled across them, UNKNOWN. Chic lamented, "I've been in lots of cemeteries before but this one is really different. All these guys were alive just a short time ago, most of them were young just like us. I didn't expect to see so many graves of Marines all at one time.

We are really lucky, every one of us, to still be alive!"

Netherland, the Music, was by far the most worldly of the group. Once he recovered from the shock and oppressive sadness that enshrouded this hallowed place, he reverted to type. The Music was a hopeless con-artist. Even in this place of sadness, he saw opportunity. "Listen you guys, and hear me out. I've got a really good idea. Its not like the others, this one's sure to be a winner. Just think of all the people back in the States who would like to have a picture of their special Marine's grave. If only we had a camera.

"I'll bet I could get access to the lists of next of kin of all these guys. There are thousands of them here! We could provide a real service to all those grieving mothers, wives and sweethearts. We wouldn't even have to charge very much. Just enough to cover expenses and of course make a small profit for ourselves. We could type up nice letters explaining that we will photograph the grave with the name showing and then include another shot of the whole cemetery for a very reasonable fee. You know, we could take a shot with that archway as the main focal point so they could read the, 2nd Marine Division Cemetery, that's painted on it. Damn! I wish old Shanghai would hurry and get back from the hospital so we could use his camera. There could be really big money in a deal like this."

The other three looked at one another in disgust, then they looked at Netherland. He was always coming up with a scheme to make himself rich or famous. This time he had crashed to a new low. This was more than the others would put up with. The tone of Chief's voice was very serious as he admonished, "Music, you dumb-ass, there's no way Shanghai will ever let you or anyone else use his camera and you know it! He, even more than the rest of us, would find your money-making scheme of photographing these graves so repulsive that he would probably kick you right square in the ass if he ever heard about it." Chic spotted a cross with a name he knew. It was Corporal Thompson, John R. USMC who had been killed in that last big *banzai* on Tinian during the Night of the Dragon when Blackjack lost his arm. Soon all were recognizing names of men they had known.

Chief spotted the grave of one of his old shipmates, Easy

Company's former top sergeant, Williams, Harry "B" First Sergeant, USMC. Donahoe exclaimed, "Look you guys, its Borgen, you remember Borgen, the kid from Erdahl, Minnesota?"

They found Pfc's John Boyd, Rick Byers, Bill Ameneira and then they saw a cross with Lieutenant Freeman's name on it and a Star of David with Bronson, Jerome. Jerry Bronson, the first man in the outfit to die on Saipan. He lost his head before he could even get out of the amtrac just prior to our reaching the beach. Poor Mac, Shanghai had made him give Bronson's bloody dog tag and a little Star of David to the amtrac crew before he could go ashore. Shanghai didn't want one of his men to be buried as an Unknown. Less than a week after that, Mac had lost both his legs, shattered by machine-gun fire.

Donahoe knelt down in front of one of the graves and made the sign of the cross. The others looked at the name stenciled in black on the white wooden cross and froze where they stood. They found it hard to believe what they were seeing, but it was clearly spelled out - Pooley, Paul (NMI), Sgt. USMC.

"So that's why Shanghai never wrote to anyone." Lucky said in a somber voice, "He's dead. How in the hell can he be dead? We all talked to him after he killed that Jap lieutenant. He was hit but he seemed like he was alright. The Navy even sent him out to one of the hospital ships to recover."

Chic couldn't hold back the feelings that welled up within him. Warm tears coursed down his cheeks as he silently prayed for the soul of the man who had taught him so much about how to stay alive and how to be a good Marine. He had respected Shanghai as much as he did his old Drill Instructor, Corporal Thompson, who had been killed in that last *banzai* attack on Tinian, or Platoon Sergeant Jack Black, who lost his left arm the same miserable night. He hoped the others wouldn't notice the tears. Crying wasn't very Marine-like. Besides, if Shanghai was alive he'd say it was a sign of weakness.

A gentle rain started to fall and the raggedy assed Marines were glad of it. It gave them a reason to leave the cemetery. Their feelings of sorrow and depression were a heavy burden. They vowed, each to the other, to return someday when they could find transportation and a little more time.

It was on this Sunday afternoon in late 1944 that Chic Yancey first realized that combat-hardened Marines, among the toughest fighting men in the world, are also among the most sentimental.

*　*　*　*　*　*　*　*　*　*

Blood Brothers

Mess call had just been sounded and chow bumps would follow in 3 minutes. The men grabbed their messgear from the nails on which they hung beside their cots and fell in on the company street. As they marched at route step up to the battalion mess, knowing glances were exchanged between the raggedy assed Marines. They had something important to discuss.

The food, as expected, was bland and unappetizing and the portions were not generous. As the men filed out of the chowline into the large mess tent they found bench space alongside Netherland, the field music, who was nearly finished eating. Netherland generally managed to be first in the chowline when he was assigned as the duty bugler and had to sound mess call and chow bumps. They sat side by side or across from one another. There were cautious glances to be sure no unauthorized personnel were listening.

Chic was looking forward to the next Sunday's adventure as he asked, "Our company's got the guard this week. Do any of you guys have the duty Sunday?"

Fearless Frank looked disgusted and disappointed as he confessed to being on duty the day they had planned another special liberty excursion.

"Music, dammit can't you do somethin' about the guard roster? You've got access to everything that goes on in company headquarters. I don't mind pulling the duty any other time but standin' guard on Sunday is against my religion. Just ask old Riverboat. You know he's a Baptist minister, or says he is. He'll tell you that one of the Ten Commandments says that Sunday is a day of rest and relaxation and special liberty. You are not supposed to stand the duty on Sundays."

"Good try Fearless, but no cigar. There is no way that I, or anyone else, can alter that guard roster once the first sergeant approves it. I'd rather try conning the Commandant of the Marine Corps himself than to negotiate with that sonofabitch."

Fearless responded, "Yeah, I guess you're right Music. You know him better'n anyone else around here. I heard you guys served together in the Worlds Fair detachment back in '39, you and Gunny Paul."

"Yeah, I guess he was in the detachment about the same time as me. I didn't know him or Paul very well, just saw them a few times that's all."

Fearless continued, "What were you guys then? What were your ranks?"

"The rank grabber was a Pfc and Gunny Paul and I were privates."

Fearless sounded confident as he said, "Well hell, you guys must be old buddies then. I'll bet you could put in a few good words for me."

"Forget it, Fearless. One good word from me and your ass will be grass in this outfit from now on. We are not friends, we have never been friends and we are never going to be friends. Now knock it off and make up your mind to stand your duty like a Marine. I pull more duty than any of you guys and you never hear me bitchin' about it."

Fearless couldn't resist reminding the music, "Of course, not because you don't really stand any duty at all, you just blow those damned bugle calls every once in a while and I might as well remind you that your bugle sounds as flat as a pancake."

The Music shot back with, "Look, you wartime warrior, you ain't even a real Marine so I shouldn't expect you to understand this but you don't blow a bugle, you blow your nose. You sound a bugle. You sound calls on a bugle. So the next time I sound a call on my bugle, you go blow your goddam nose. Okay? Now the next thing you need to know is that the United States Marine Corps didn't send me out here to entertain you bastards. They put me in this outfit to sound calls so you'll know what to do and when to do it. If they ain't musical enough for you, why don't you write a letter to the Quartermaster General of the Marine Corps and tell him you don't approve of these damned brown plastic bugles they've sent out to the FMF. They are flat as hell and they're never gonna get any better until we get back to the states or someplace where they start issuing real brass bugles again."

Quinlan was disappointed and he'd had enough of the Music. He addressed his remarks to the others, "I guess you guys had better go without me on Sunday. I've got a position of great responsibility guardin' the company shitter and a bunch of old tents. I'll go with you the next Sunday. By that time this damned field music noisemaker may just be in the brig for disturbin' the peace with his little plastic horn."

Corporal Grogan was going to be unable to perform his essential duties as armed NCO chaperone on Sunday due to a slight absence occasioned by him receiving five days in the brig.

With Grogan in the brig, it became necessary to find another "Responsible NCO". It was a disgusting state of affairs when a half-dozen privates couldn't even think of a single NCO in the entire company that could be trusted. They were all honest. It was decided that if they couldn't find a dishonest NCO then they would at least have to find one that was naïve enough to believe what they told him. Riverboat was a Baptist minister! Surely, that could work in their favor. There were few similarities between Corporal Grogan and Riverboat Brown except that they were about the same height which was totally immaterial. Grogan was corrupt, Riverboat was naïve, that was material!

Riverboat Brown was voted unanimously as successor to Grogan. Riverboat was another unlikely but colorful character who was well liked by all hands. He alleged that he had been a riverboat captain in civilian life and why he chose the Marine Corps instead of the Navy was never revealed. The size of his riverboat was never revealed either, but most of the men got a kick out of his stories and just imagined that his boat was a huge, lumbering side-wheeler plying its trade up and down the Mississippi, with Riverboat at the helm intermittently quoting from the Holy Bible and cursing like a sailor in his heavy Mississippi drawl.

Having Riverboat along only posed one serious problem, he really wanted to go along! He was not amenable to being left at the 3rd battalion mess to play cards and sip raisin jack as Grogan had happily done. After all, as a Baptist minister, Riverboat could do neither of these things, except on very special occasions. How would the raggedy-assed Marines keep their secret if an NCO were to know of their coveted liberty activities?

It became necessary to have an important council of war after dark on Saturday night. Riverboat was duly sworn to secrecy and since he was a very devout Christian the men believed they could trust him. He loved to quote the Bible on various occasions although there was some question as to the accuracy of the quotations. Chief wasn't as sure about him as the others were and he stated that if Riverboat was going to be taken into their confidence and trusted with their secrets, he should be a blood brother.

Chief wanted to take his Ka-Bar knife and cut their arms and mix their blood, making them blood brothers just like the Indians in the Old West used to do. Actually, Chief didn't know much about real Indians or the Old West, having left the reservation when he was quite young, but he had seen this mixing of blood done in the movies one time and was quite impressed by it.

None of the raggedy assed Marines had had anything to drink since the Sunday before, so the idea of mixing their blood didn't have the appeal it normally would have if the blood contained a sufficient amount of alcohol. Thus, the whole idea of blood brothers was dropped and Riverboat Brown had to be accepted on his own merits.

Riverboat was sworn to secrecy and as they were about to return to their tents it was revealed that he knew of a truck driver over at regiment who was making a run down to the beach early the next morning. They had never before departed early in the morning but were grateful for a ride and gladly accepted. Riverboat left to arrange it. Walking up to the motor pool early in the morning with the armed Riverboat bringing up the rear Chic casually mentioned to Dutch that it must look a little like a detail of prisoners being marched somewhere by an armed chaser. Dutch shuddered and muttered something about how he hoped it was not a prophesy of things to come.

It was the first time they had gotten down to the beach so early and they hoped they would be able to find a boat headed out to USS *Orion*. Sure enough, one of the first boats they spotted had AS-18 painted on the hull. The coxswain waved them a cheery 'hello' and bid them come aboard. They were soon all headed out to their favorite ship. While underway, Deadly Dave explained to Riverboat the mission of USS *Orion* and he called Riverboat's attention to the submarines tied up alongside her. She was like a mother hen with her chicks nestled around her. They soon arrived alongside, climbed up the accommodation ladder, rendered the double salute and stepped onto the deck.

When they arrived on board the chaplain was just about to start conducting services topside. The weather was nice and there were more men at church than could have fit on the mess decks where divine services were often held. *Orion* had three submarines tied up alongside and the congregation was greatly expanded by the presence of many of their crewmembers. Chic reasoned that submarine sailors, like infantry Marines, led a very dangerous existence and thus perhaps took their religion a bit more seriously than those not required to go in harms way so frequently.

During the course of the service, the chaplain commented that he was glad to see that "Our Marines" were back on board, and in time for church. It really made the men feel welcome especially when there were so many other visitors on board from the submarines alongside. Riverboat heartily approved of the chaplain and of *Orion* and its friendly crew of "bluejackets." He was convinced, temporarily, that he had fallen into good company when he decided to accompany the raggedy assed Marines on their adventures.

* * * * * * * * * *

Peaches on the Beaches

Another Sunday adventure was coming to an end and the men were on the quarterdeck preparing to go down the accommodation ladder. As they were going over the side, one of the bluejackets hollered, "Hey Marines, come back again next Sunday. We have chicken every Sunday!"

The men sensed that this bluejacket's sincere invitation reflected the feelings of the rest of *Orion's* crew. The sailors wanted to hear everything that happened ashore. They could see the intriguing island crowned by Mount Tapotchau and partially covered by jungle vegetation but they could only guess at the adventures that transpired beyond their view. The raggedy assed Marines would have gladly traded places with any of them. They'd had enough adventures to last them a very long time. The Marines promised to return every Sunday and they intended to keep their promise. Wondering, as they did, if the sailors had any idea how much it meant for them to be aboard that wonderful ship with its hot showers, good food, laundry, barber shop and friendly sailors.

Olson put them ashore right in the middle of an area the Army had been using to stage incoming supplies. Right on the beach were scores of pallets, piled high with food and all manner of things which were of interest to young, hungry Marines. There were pallets of canned peaches and fruit juice. Spam! They had all heard jokes about Spam but had rarely seen it served in a Marine mess. The Army may have had too much of it but to Marines, it was a delicacy!

The raggedy assed Marines couldn't believe their good fortune. They felt like kids in a candy store and wished there was a way to carry back enough to feed the whole battalion. They set about carefully selecting just those few delicacies that would fit in their packs. In the meantime, they decided to devour a couple of cans of peaches right there on the beach so they wouldn't have to carry them.

"Halt, you guys or you're dead!"

It was a U. S. Army guard with an M-1 carbine pointed right at them. He looked scared enough to shoot if they should try and make a break for it. They wisely decided to humor him. He had an AN/PRC 536 radio which he used to call for a backup. The Marines felt confident as they looked at one another and smiled. They had 536's and knew that they almost never worked. If the batteries weren't dead, something else was usually wrong. The one this doggie was using looked just like theirs, but there was an exception, his worked!

How could the Army get radios that worked when they were guarding peaches on the beaches? The Marines couldn't get them in combat where lives depended on effective communications.

A personnel carrier driven by a corporal and a Jeep arrived on the scene simultaneously. An army lieutenant leaped out of the Jeep with a drawn .45 in his hand. The guard explained to the lieutenant and the corporal how he and his trusty carbine had single-handedly captured these four hungry United States Marines stealing the army's supplies. He was obviously trying to talk the incident up to the level of a Silver Star Medal when Deadly Dave reached up to brush a fly from his right ear. The guard's eyes widened and there was an audible click as he took the carbine off safety.

Chic thought the lieutenant would give the soldier hell, but instead, it was the corporal who did the talking.

"You men get your hands up on top of your heads where we can see them! Keep them there until we get this all sorted out. There'll be no more moving and you'd better start showing a little respect to the lieutenant here. Atten- shun!!" Somehow Army commands just didn't sound like commands did in the Marine Corps but the raggedy assed Marines decided they had better humor these rear echelon commandos so they all instantly assumed the position of attention.

That was not exactly what the corporal had in mind. He wanted them to stand at attention, but with their hands still on their heads. This may have been a normal procedure in the Army but the Marines had never encountered it before. When they stood at attention, their hands were at their sides with thumbs along the seams of their trousers. They all dutifully placed their hands back on top of their heads while wondering how they would get out of this mess.

Now this Army lieutenant was crafty. He was not just some

run-of-the-mill 90-day wonder. He was obviously very con-
scientious. He was, no doubt, a highly trained and skilled
officer and had possibly even graduated somewhere in the
top ninety percent of his class at OCS. He was a little reckless
in waving his pistol around but the troops knew that he was
doing it just for emphasis and to show that he was really in
control of everything.

A rather lengthy interrogation followed during which the
troops dearly wished that the lieutenant or his corporal would
realize that they posed no serious threat to the security of the
U.S. Army on Saipan and tell them to put their hands down
and maybe even let them stand at ease. This was not to be the
case.

The lieutenant wanted to know who they were, where they
had come from, what they wanted and who their immediate
commanding officer was. He cleverly deduced that they were
not from one of the combat Marine units stationed on the
island. Those troops were dirty and unkempt and looked like
"something the cat dragged in." At least these four recalci-
trants were wearing clean uniforms. It suddenly dawned on
the raggedy-assed Marines, that of the more than twenty-
thousand Marines on Saipan, they were probably the only
ones on the whole island who were wearing clean starched
dungarees! Bless the United States Navy!

Chic responded to the lieutenant with: "Sir, we're seagoing Marines off USS *Orion*. You can see her from here. She's
moored right out there. Please don't send us back to the ship,
they'll court-martial us for sure. You just don't know how the
Navy hates us poor Marines. Captain Archibald Henderson is
in command of the MarDet and he is really an old Corps mar-
tinet. He'll crucify us if you send us back to the ship on report. Please Lieutenant, give us a break."

The desperate Marine's plea to the lieutenant fell on deaf
ears as he turned to the pistol wielding corporal who had
driven the weapons carrier.

"Corporal Custer, I want you to personally escort these
men back to their ship and turn them over to their commanding officer, Captain Henderson. Tell him I'm preparing a statement and will send it out with the charge sheets. Be sure and
check with their first sergeant and get the correct spelling of

all their names and their ranks and serial numbers for me. I want everything to be correct so the charges will stick. Put all this in writing if he wants it that way and tell the captain that this sentry, What's your name soldier? and I, will be only too glad to come out to the ship in person and appear as witnesses against them if he should feel it necessary."

"Now, you men, climb into the back of that truck and sit still. I don't want any talking or moving around until Corporal Custer tells you to get out and get into a boat so he can take you back to your ship. You are all on report and I hope you receive the maximum punishment. The canned peaches you were stealing are the property of the U.S. Army. Custer, be sure and report back to me as soon as you return to the beach. Alright Custer, go ahead, move out!"

Custer! The corporal's name was Custer! Chief could hardly contain himself. He almost never cracked a smile but this time, he was grinning from ear to ear. He mimicked what he thought an Indian in the movies may sound like as he stated, "Him Custer, me Injun. Who you think gonna win?" As the truck went bouncing down the beach, the troops knew what to expect. Deadly Dave Donahoe and Private Dutch Shute looked at one another grinning. They were trying to decide who would make the first move. Donohoe was faster, he climbed around the outside of the moving personnel carrier and slid in beside the astonished driver. Custer, with both hands on the steering wheel, was starting to brake as Donahoe reached over, opened the corporal's holster flap and withdrew the pistol.

"Wow, Custer, it must be pretty nice being in the Army. In the Corps, we don't usually get to carry a pistol unless we're a machine-gunner or an officer or some kind of a big shot. This pistol is really sharp."

"You fool, you guys are under arrest! Give me my pistol back before I add that to the charges we're preferring against you!"

"It wouldn't be wise of me to do that Custer. You see, I came up front here with the sole intention of kicking your ass. It wouldn't be very bright of me to kick your ass if you were armed. On the other hand, if I keep your pistol, I may lose my temper while I'm whipping you and there may be some temptation to shoot you. The only logical alternative corporal is to get rid of the damn thing. They're too dangerous anyhow."

With that, Donahoe, having removed the magazine and pulled back the slide, threw the pistol as far from the, by now halted, vehicle as he could. Deadly Dave Donahoe looked at the soldier and snarled, "Just remember 'Bigshot' all of us Marines have killed men we wasn't even mad at! Frankly, you'd be very easy to get mad at, I don't like you."

The corporal's eyes opened wide and his face took on an ashen hue. He knew the penalty for losing his weapon. He had to find it. He must get it back. What was he to do with this obviously insane Marine sitting beside him. What about the other three in the back of the truck? How could he control them if he didn't have a weapon?

Actually, the other three Marines were not in the back of the truck. Not any more they weren't. As fearful thoughts raced through the unfortunate soldiers mind, Chief was placing a stranglehold on him. Chief firmly removed the corporal from his vehicle and half dragged and half pulled him down the beach.

Corporal Custer, AUS, was invited to recline on the beach, face down! His pistol belt was promptly wrapped around his ankles and firmly secured while his hands were being strapped behind him by use of his web trouser belt. Just to insure that nothing further would call unwanted attention to the four "Seagoing Marines," they sacrificed one of the oranges given to them aboard the submarine tender. The orange, when placed in Custer's mouth and securely wrapped with an extra Jap bartering flag made an excellent gag which was tied securely behind Custer's head.

Free of the Army once again. Chic was beginning to feel that their troubles were over when he saw Dutch behind the wheel and heard the vehicle's engine revving up. Transportation back to camp, compliments of the U.S. Army. But no! Dutch jumped from the vehicle as it picked up speed while heading directly into the lagoon. The truck ran until the engine compartment was nearly covered by water then it sputtered to a stop.

Chic was awestricken as he asked, "What the hell have

you done Dutch? We've got to get back to camp!"

"I knew you guys would want to take that truck and if you did, we'd get caught for sure and we'd really be in trouble. Requisitioning a couple of cans of peaches is one thing, but stealing an Army truck is an entirely different matter. The doggies have got enough charges against us as it is. Now let's find a vehicle headed away from here and bum a ride before the tide comes in and gives Corporal Custer there a bath."

The four Marines ran up the beach and through the neatly stacked pallets and piles of U.S. Army supplies waiting to be loaded onto trucks. As they dodged into the tree line a few yards inland from the beach they noted that there was now a crushed coral road. The road roughly paralleled the beach just a ways inland from where the battalion had landed back on 15 June. It had only been a little over six months ago but seemed like an eternity. They ran to the left and were soon in recognizable terrain.

Up ahead of them was the rubble of what used to be the city of Garapan. It was from this area that the Jap *banzai* attack had come on the second night ashore. The 6th Marines had taken the brunt of that terrifying onslaught. They moved past some of the burned-out hulks of Jap tanks. It was hard to believe this was the position where they had spent that first agonizing night and where so many of their shipmates had been killed or wounded.

Everything was different now. There were Army and Navy units all over the beach area. It suddenly became obvious that every outfit on the island did not have holiday routine on Sundays like the 2nd Marine Division. There was much work in progress. The troops hoped their officers would never find out about all these Army and Navy people working just like it was another weekday. They had come to value their Sundays off and always looked forward to new adventures.

They knew the Army would be looking for them as soon as Corporal Custer or his partially submerged truck was discovered. They had to move fast and somehow get transportation back across the island. Chic knew that if they stayed on the roads, the army was sure to catch them. If they left the roads, there was no possibility of getting a ride back to the 8th Marines' area. They had to chance it, so they started up a winding coral road toward higher elevation and just after rounding a turn, they saw a quonset hut with a small sign in front indicating that they were in friendly territory.

It was a bomb disposal unit from the V Amphibious Corps. There was the same tactical mark that Chic had remembered seeing on Marine Gunner Robinson's jeep. Chic announced, "Hey you guys, we're really in luck! I've got a friend in this outfit. He's a Marine Gunner. Old Corps, like Gunny Johannsen. I know he can get us a ride back. He's even got a jeep of his own. Those doggies will never catch us now."

As the four approached the hut, they noticed a Marine unloading some gear from a truck. The truck bore the tactical mark of the V Amphibious Corps Bomb Disposal Unit.

Hardly able to hide his enthusiasm, Chic said, "Wait here you guys and let me see if they know how I can find the gunner."

Chic rushed over to lend a hand. "Can I help you with that stuff Mac?"

"Sure, if you don't mind, thanks. Where'd you guys come from and what are you doing here?"

Chic replied, "Oh, we're from the 8th Marines. We were on our way back to our outfit and just wanted to stop off and say hello to a friend."

As they carried the equipment into the hut, Chic looked around. He knew they would all know the gunner, but Chic hoped he would be here in person. He spotted a khaki cap hanging from a peg and noted with satisfaction that it bore the bursting bomb insignia of a Marine gunner. A Master Sergeant sitting at a field desk looked around and asked, "Who've you got with you Larsen?"

"Oh, he's from the 8th Marines. There's three more of 'em outside."

"What can I do for you men?"

Chic felt a surge of pride as he answered, "We're here to see Marine Gunner Robinson, he's a friend of mine. Is that his cover hanging over there?

The Master Sergeant gave Chic a compassionate look and stated, "Yes, that's Gunner's cap. My name's O'Leary, this is Gunner Robinson's field desk. At least it was until yesterday. He's dead. Some of those damned Jap holdouts rigged a bangalore torpedo as a booby trap and his jeep detonated it."

Chic's knees were suddenly weak and he felt sick." The bastards! He was really a good guy. I wish I could have seen him again while he was alive."

"How well did you know him?"

"I only met him once, but I feel like I knew him very well. He did me a big favor. He really helped me at a time when I badly needed help. I had just escaped from the Army hospital and he got me a ride back to my unit. I needed someone to believe me and he did. My story was pretty strange but he trusted me. I liked the gunner a lot. I was hoping to get a chance to talk with him now that we're back from Tinian and let him know everything turned out alright."

"Well kid, I've known Robinson for eighteen years and I've never met anyone I respected more. He was a real professional."

Chic replied with, "Sergeant, do you think he had a feeling he was gonna get it? Did he say anything to you that indicated he thought he might not be around for long?"

"No, of course not" the sergeant answered, "What ever made you ask such a thing?"

"Oh, it was just something he said to me when we were saying goodbye. I knew he was a real professional and he knew that's what I wanted to be. He said something that sounded kind of strange. He said, "Take good care of our Marine Corps son." It was as though he knew something was going to happen and he was kind of turning things over to me. I told him I would. My Gosh, I hope I can keep my word. No one can be as good a Marine he was."

"So you're the Marine that the Nips caught back in July? Gunner told us about finding you down on the beach road and giving you a lift. He got a big kick out of you telling him you escaped from the Army. He said he should have done the same thing when he was over in France during the first War. Gunner said he was going to go up to the 8th Marines someday now that they're back on Saipan, and look you up. I guess he didn't make it."

"No, I guess he didn't, but one thing is for sure. I'll never forget him! I'll bet old Gunner is in his full blues now, standing formal guard mount up there when they post and relieve all those Marines who are guarding heavens' streets."

* * * * * * * * * *

The Flag Incident

The Marines felt at home on this wonderful ship. It was almost like being back in the States for a short time one day a week. Although they dreaded the thought this, like all good things, would sooner or later come to an end.

Mister Curtis, the ship's boatswain, had heard that the Marines were back aboard. He made it a point to find them and let them know that he wanted to speak with them privately, before they left the ship.

The "Bosun" was not a happy man. It seems that there had been a series of strange and bizarre events during the past week or so that had always somehow caused him to think of the Marines.

The world's only floating flag factory had been established. The Chief Quartermaster allegedly assigned two young volunteers, a quartermaster and a signalman to operate it out of the ship's flag locker. The chief went into mass production. Wanting to find a quick way to dry and age large numbers of the newly made flags, the young sailors had attached them to halyards and ran each batch of them up the signal masts for a few minutes while the red paint was drying.

It was only a short time after they had started drying the flags from the masts that the admiral invited Commander Jonathan Lucas, the ship's captain, to come over to his cabin for a chat. The admiral appeared to have little or no interest in Japanese souvenirs. He did seem to Commander Lucas to be ill. Lucas noted that the admiral's face was flushed and his hands were trembling. He looked awful. In an innocent act of compassion Lucas stated: "You'd better sit down Admiral." The admiral snorted, "What the hell do you mean telling me to sit down? This is my cabin and you are here at my request and by God I'm the one who will determine if anyone is to sit down".

With that the admiral promptly sat down. He stared at the commander through narrowed eyes.

"You're not regular Navy are you Lucas?"

"No Sir, why do you ask, Admiral?"

"If you were a regular officer, you'd be standing at attention."

Commander Jonathan R. Lucas, USNR, came clumsily to attention wondering just what the hell was going on.

"I assume you came into the Navy just for the war and intend to leave it as soon as this mess is over. Am I correct?"

"I've spent the past 13 years in the Naval Reserve Admiral, but yes, you are correct. I'm looking forward to getting back to my firm and to my family as soon as this war is over."

The admiral asked Commander Lucas to explain why he had apparently gone over to the side of the enemy and taken his ship and crew with him. The stunned Lucas had no idea how to respond until the admiral informed him that *Orion Maru* formerly known as USS *Orion*, of the American Navy, was flying a Japanese ensign. Not only was she flying a Japanese ensign but the whole damned ship looked like she was rigged in "Dress Ship" for Emperor Hirohito's birthday party or some other festive Nipponese occasion but instead of the usual colorful signal flags, all of the flags were Japanese meatballs.

A rumor was rampant among the terrified Filipino stewards in the admiral's mess that the admiral was seriously contemplating putting the captain in irons, flogging him with a cat-o-nine-tails, hanging him from the yardarm, court-martialing him as an enemy agent or all of the above.

The admiral was interrupted by a radioman entering the cabin and placing a handful of dispatches on his desk. He snatched them up and ignoring Commander Lucas who was still standing at attention before his desk read those that were annotated "Operation Immediate." He scribbled his initials on some and handed them back to the radioman and then something caught his eye. It was on top of the other regular priority messages still on the desk and he noticed the name USS *Orion*.

The admiral felt a cold chill creeping up his spine. Ohmigod! Nimitz was back at Pearl, he couldn't have already learned of the *Orion* incident. Or could he? The admiral held the message in trembling hands as he started to read it, fully expecting to learn that he was being relieved of his command. To the admiral's amazement it was a hearty "Bravo Zulu" extended to the captain and crew of USS *Orion* for sustained superior performance in support of ongoing submarine operations and was signed by the Commander in Chief Pacific Ocean Area, Fleet Admiral Chester Nimitz.

Commander Jonathan R. Lucas, USNR, was permitted to return to his ship with an admonition that if the slightest infraction of regulations or departure from naval custom was noted on his ship at any future time, there would be hell to pay. He silently wondered if the admiral hadn't been working too hard lately or could it be that the admiral was truly a man completely devoid of a sense of humor. Recalling the look on the admiral's face and the sound of his voice, Jonathan Lucas had his answer.

Following his return to the ship, the crew noted a decided change in Captain Lucas. The two flag-making sailors were already residing in the ship's brig and a chief petty officer was going up before the mast on Monday morning. Something about being involved with the seamen who were caught illegally manufacturing Japanese flags. And doing it with US Navy parachute-flare silk! Mister Curtis was concerned about the possible consequences of enemy flags being flown from a U.S. Navy vessel in time of war. He was concerned about the ship's captain being in "hack" and nearly losing his command for flying not one, but a score of enemy flags.

One of his best coxswains, Olson by name, was apprehended attempting to slip over the side under cover of darkness, clad in Marine dungarees. It was obvious that Olson was jumping ship to join the Marines for their next operation. Olson had been caught and was not going anywhere but Mr. Curtis fervently hoped the Marines' next operation would be soon.

So, that's where the missing items of clothing that were "lost" in the ship's laundry had gone. The "Mad Viking" was secretly "ratholing" them for his own use.

Since befriending the raggedy assed Marines, Chief Warrant Officer Curtis' Navy career which spanned a period of thirty-two exemplary years had been on a downhill slide.

Mister Curtis had one final incident to report to the raggedy assed Marines. It seems there was an occurrence on the beach last Sunday wherein a small band of Marines were placed under arrest by the Army for stealing rations. They subsequently escaped and drove an Army truck into the lagoon. The NCO who had been placed in charge of the Marines was found on the beach, tied hand and foot. It took an Army searching party nearly an hour to find the corporal's pistol which the Marines had hidden in the sand on the beach. The identities of these renegade Marines remained unknown.

An Army second lieutenant, heavily armed as was his bodyguard, had come aboard looking for the Marines, who by some strange quirk of fate, just happened to have told the lieutenant that they were from the Marine Detachment, USS *Orion*. That was the last straw! Of course no one informed on them. The Navy and Marines always stick together where the Army is concerned. The lieutenant was merely advised that USS *Orion* did not rate or have a Marine Detachment.

The captain had become very sensitive about Jap flags and had decreed, "Anyone aboard this ship who is caught in possession of a Jap flag will be instantly incarcerated in the ship's brig. They will be left in the brig until their trial by court martial which may be convened at some future time after we return to the United States following the end of the war! That is, if we win the damned war. If we should lose the war, they will be summarily shot!"

The raggedy assed Marines realized that their sordid past had finally caught up with them. This would be their last Sunday aboard what they had come to think of as the greatest ship in the Navy. Chic had a lump in his throat as he rendered the double salute and started down the accommodation ladder for the last time. He felt as though he was saying goodbye to an old friend.

The raggedy assed Marines lamented that they were now considered persona non grata on the greatest ship in the Navy. They would miss USS *Orion* and her crew and they would surely miss her chicken every Sunday. There couldn't be many other places on Saipan that had food as good as that aboard *Orion*.

On one of their subsequent excursions the raggedy assed Marines had a stroke of exceedingly good luck in discovering the Seabees camp. Seabees contended that they had the best chow in the Navy. The raggedy assed Marines had been told that the submarine service had the best chow in the Navy. The Marines determined that it was their patriotic duty to make whatever sacrifice was necessary or required to resolve this dispute among friends and determine the winner.

The food was wonderful. Everything the men had previously heard about the Seabee mess was true. When they asked why they had been allowed to enter at the head of the chow line the answer, from a grizzled chief petty officer, came as a surprise.

"It's just our way of saying thanks to you boys. A detail of our men including a couple of my bulldozer operators helped to build your cemeteries. There's over three thousand dead Americans on this island and most of 'em are Marines. What they saw they will never forget and neither will the rest of us. Compared to most of us you Marines are pretty young and we like to think of you as being like the kid next door back home. Some of you need to have your butts kicked once in a while but we still respect you. We saw what you went through fighting your way across those beaches. Marines are always welcome in our messhall."

* * * * * * * * * *

Operation Iceberg

Tanapag Harbor, mid-March 1945

The 2nd Marine Division boarded ship from the floating docks at Tanapag Harbor and steamed across 1200 miles of the Philippine Sea. Their destination? Okinawa. Most of the battalion was embarked in USS *Mifflin*, an APA. Marines were at home at sea and shipboard life offered certain advantages. The food was of much better quality but would still be of insufficient quantity for the perpetually hungry Marines. Mess duty, avoided whenever possible ashore, was often a pretty good deal when embarked. Messmen always managed to have sufficient rations for themselves and a few friends.

Now a part of the III Amphibious Corps of the Tenth U.S. Army, they arrived off Okinawa in late March 1945. The faint sound of aircraft engines grew in intensity as they moved closer to the huge convoy. Soon the snarling, whining, insistent roar of the enemy planes getting louder and louder was joined by the constant and repeated bang, bang, banging of the 20 and 40 millimeter anti-aircraft cannons. A score of ships were firing their 20's and 40's furiously and sending a curtain of steel up to pierce the sky.

The incessant firing caused the ship to tremble and shudder. When the deck was raked with machine-gun fire, a line of bullets traced a shattered pattern across the wooden hatch cover over hold #2. The men below looked up and saw the splintered holes in the cover overhead. Prayers instantly became more meaningful as Navy corpsmen quickly sought out and attended the injured.

Topside, ack-ack fire continued to fill the sky with orange tracers and ascending red balls of flame. The planes, hardly visible in the dimness of the early morning, were diving toward their targets. There was a loud thud and one of the engines was stilled! A blinding flash of light told onlookers that one of the Japanese pilots had hit his target.

We would later learn that it was USS *Hinsdale*, APA 120. The headquarters group of the 3rd Battalion, 2nd Marines had been aboard *Hinsdale*. Another Japanese plane dove into one of the LSTs in the convoy and disintegrated in a ball of flame. We were being introduced to the Divine Wind. The Japanese called them *"kamikaze."*

In what seemed a lifetime ago in the jungles of Saipan, Shanghai had used the term *"kamikaze"* and told his men it meant something like "Wind from the Gods." He had been describing a gentle breeze that caused an American flag suspended over the entrance of a cave to flutter. The moving flag played a key role in a successful deception. It was the first time any of the men had heard the term kamikaze and the sergeant had patiently told them of its origin and explained that it was the name given to the divine wind which had saved Japan from a massive Mongol invasion back in the Middle

Ages. None had expected to hear the term again. At Okinawa, they would wish they never had heard it. *Kamikaze* became a dreaded part of the Marines everyday vocabulary.

Sunday, 1 April 1945 was April Fools' Day and in the Christian world it was Easter Sunday. On Okinawa, it was to be the day of the American invasion. It had not been called D-Day this time but rather was dubbed L-day. The Japanese had a big April Fools' surprise planned for the U.S. forces and the Americans had a joke of their own to play.

The Japanese were going to let the Americans come ashore virtually unopposed and lull them into a sense of false security. When the U.S. forces moved south, they would encounter elaborate defensive positions that were nearly impregnable. It was here that Lieutenant General Mitsuru Ushijima, commanding the Japanese 32nd Army, planned to annihilate the American invaders.

The American's April Fool surprise involved the 2nd Marine Division. The division's mission was diversionary, a demonstration. They were to execute a feint landing as they had done at Tinian.

On Easter morning, after a suitable period of softening up by air and naval gunfire, the word was passed to "Land the Landing Force!" The men of the 2nd Marine Division went over the side and into their landing craft.

The Division staged their massive demonstration off the Chinen Peninsula in southeastern Okinawa. The plan was to make the Japanese think it was the main landing. The entire 2nd Marine Division was involved as wave after wave of landing craft started for the beach.

The Japanese were aware that this was an excellent landing beach but Ushijima had gambled that the Americans would come ashore at a place less obvious. He had guessed right but at the time of the demonstration, the Japanese weren't so sure. Twenty thousand U.S. Marines approaching the shore in hundreds of landing craft with heavy covering fire made a pretty convincing argument that the landing was real.

The landing force approached the beach drawing significant enemy fire and then at the last possible moment turned back and returned to their ships. The men's joy at being returned to the safety of their ships was short-lived as the intensity of the *kamikaze* threat was increasing significantly.

The plan for the actual landing seemed to be working as the invasion force went ashore virtually unopposed. By sundown on that April fool's day, the U.S. forces had secured a beachhead four miles wide and nearly two miles deep with virtually no opposition. It was a remarkable day.

The lack of effective enemy opposition must have been quite a surprise to Lieutenant General Simon Bolivar Buckner and his staff and a sense of false security may have influenced their planning for the immediate future. It was a great relief to the fighting men but they would not have felt so relieved had they but known that Lieutenant General Ushijima's April Fool's plan was working like a charm.

The 2nd Marine Division reenacted their landing demonstration on 2 April with somewhat less enemy fire directed at them from shore positions. Gunnery Sergeant Carl Johannsen thought they would try again on Tuesday the 3rd and surprise the Japs by actually landing. He believed this would have been an excellent area at which to land as it would have forced the Japanese commander to split his forces and fight the Americans to their south as well as to their north.

The men listened attentively to the gunny's theories and silently thanked their lucky stars that the commanding general of the Tenth U.S. Army didn't have the benefit of the gunny's opinions. They were satisfied to remain aboard ship for a while longer eating hot Navy chow and sleeping in canvass bunks.

Leaning against the ship's rail, the battalion sergeant major chomped down on his cigar and reinforced Johannsen by stating: "Gunny, this is the most stupid thing I have ever witnessed. Those dumb bastards need us ashore not out here floating around like sitting ducks. What the hell can Buckner be waiting for?"

Johannsen replied, "I don't know much about Buckner Sergeant Major but every time someone mentions him I can't help but think about his last command and what happened to them on Kiska."

"Oh yeah, what was that?"

"Well Sergeant Major, don't you remember reading about the Kiska campaign in the news? After a massive naval bombardment, Buckner had 35,000 of his U.S. and Canadian troops storm ashore on Kiska island in the Aleutians. Twenty-one of his men were killed in the firefight. I'm sure the casualties would have been higher if there had been any enemy forces on the island. That should tell you something about Buckner's leadership and the kind of training his men got."

The surprised sergeant major responded, "Wow, if it had been a Marine general he would have been sacked for sure! But instead of relieving Buckner, they've promoted him and given him command of the whole Tenth Army?"

Gunny Johannsen asked, "Are you beginning to see my point Sergeant Major?"

"I sure am, and I'm also glad I'm a Marine."

As each day passed the men of the 2nd Marine Division waited for the call to go ashore. Marines adjusted well to shipboard life when they were going somewhere but just steaming in circles off an island where their brother Marines were fighting gave them an uneasy feeling. The uneasy feeling was greatly exacerbated by the growing number of *kamikaze* planes.

The first really big *kamikaze* raids came on 6 and 7 April with nearly 700 planes participating. Three-hundred and fifty-five of them were *kamikaze* suicide planes. *Kamikaze* raids of this magnitude presented a serious threat to troops embarked in the Navy's transports. The 2nd Marine Division either had to be put ashore on Okinawa or be gotten out of the area.

The gunny made no attempt to hide his disgust as he said to the sergeant major, "General Buckner must be filling a job vastly beyond his capabilities or he is in serious need of psychiatric treatment. At the very least, he needs a new staff, and most of them should be combat experienced Marines. I can't believe what those Army sonsabitches are doing. They've got us all right here and they must know they are going to need us. Why in the hell don't they put the division ashore now before the Japs blow us out of the water? And once they get us offloaded, they'd better send all these transport ships somewhere to a safe haven damned soon."

The scuttlebutt drifting down from "Officers' Country" paralleled Gunny Johannsen's sentiments but may have been expressed in a more genteel manner.

The gunny passed the word to the men that they had better be prepared to go ashore on a moment's notice; possibly in a matter of minutes, not hours. It was simply too foolhardy to keep a division of twenty-thousand Marines afloat on ships in Okinawan waters under constant threat of the *kamikaze*. Besides, even the Army must know the division would sooner or later be needed ashore.

Expecting to land at any moment, the men were totally unprepared for the 10th Army's next move. On 10 April, the convoy carrying the division was sent steaming back over the Philippine Sea to Saipan. A feeling of relief swept through the troop compartments. Thank heaven the convoy had successfully evaded the *kamikazes* and Japanese submarines.

On 13 April, as the convoy was making way toward Saipan the shrill whistle of a boatswain's pipe sounded alerting the men to a forthcoming announcement. "Now hear this, now hear this. All hands, that is all hands, knock off all ship's work. Maintain silence throughout the ship, that is, knock off ship's work and maintain silence throughout the ship. The captain has an important announcement."

"This is the captain speaking. Men, it is my sad duty to inform you that the President of the United States is dead. More information will be promulgated to you as it becomes available. I repeat, President Roosevelt is dead."

The boatswain's pipe screeched again followed by the announcement: "All hands carry on, that is, all hands carry on. Resume ship's work."

Chic, who had been walking across the deck was frozen in his tracks. The President was dead. The world had suddenly changed. A strange feeling came over him and he felt almost as though he'd lost a member of his own family. He was deeply saddened and was sorry for all the times he had said disparaging things about President Roosevelt. He hadn't been a big supporter of Roosevelt, but the man was the President of the United States. It was almost like hearing that someone had burned an American flag. He found the sad news hard to believe. Stash stepped up beside Chic and asked:

"Who the hell is Harry Truman?"

Chic responded, "Beats me, I don't think I've ever heard of the guy. Why?"

* * * * * * * * * *

The Night March

17 June 1945

There had been rumors that the 2nd Division would be returning to Okinawa. This did not come as a surprise to Gunny Johannsen. The men knew that the gunny was right when he said they should never have left. Someone heard that they were only sending one regiment from the 2nd Division. The men knew instinctively that it would be the 8th Marines. They had previously been detached from the division to mop up and secure Tinian. Now, it looked like they were going to be detached again. No one wanted to go back into the horrors of combat but the men did feel a sense of pride that it was their regiment that had been selected. Some said it was punishment for the "hunger strike" others knew better; they knew in their hearts that they were going because they were the best damn regiment the division had.

The rumors turned out to be true as is often the case and the 8th Marines soon found themselves aboard ship steaming back across the Philippine Sea to Okinawa.

Fox Company was again aboard an LST, this time it was the 923. They returned to the Ryuku Rhetto, assaulted and secured Iheya Shima (20 miles northeast of Okinawa's northern point) on 3 June and Aguni Shima (forty miles due west of Okinawa). Then, on 12 June 1945 they departed the picturesque Iheya Shima for Okinawa.

The 8th Marines went ashore on 15 June. It was exactly one year to the day since they had first assaulted the bloody beaches of Saipan, yet it seemed like a very long time ago. The III Amphibious Corps placed the 8th Marines under the operational control of the 1st Marine Division where they would remain until the end of the campaign.

The troops of the 1st and 6th Marine Divisions had been ashore on Okinawa since 1 April and had performed superbly. They were near exhaustion from weeks of savage fighting. Their dual enemies were the weather and the Japanese 32nd Army. Someone was needed to furnish the knockout blow and the Tenth Army had called in the 8th Marines.

The regiment was comprised of seasoned combat veterans, they were highly trained and experienced and in comparison to the casualty riddled 1st and 6th Marine Divisions, the troops were fresh. The 8th Marines, as a part of the 1st Marine Division would participate in the last great infantry drive of the Pacific War.

The regiment landed on Oroku Peninsula across the channel from the rubble that had been the city of Naha. Marching past the large airfield on Oroku they moved to an assembly area. They were to wait until it was nearly dark before moving out in a column of battalions. The plan was to have the 8th Marines relieve the 7th Marines by first light on 18 June.

Before moving out, the gunnery sergeant had the platoon sergeants check each of the men. They were instructed to do everything possible to silence packs, canteens and helmet liners. When this had been accomplished C-rations were issued and consumed and the troops sat around the assembly area waiting for the darkness that they hoped would cover their movement. The old gunnery sergeant moved from one platoon to the next answering questions and giving encouragement to the men as he listened to their griping.

A cloak of darkness fell over the island and the two files, one on each side of the road, commenced moving toward the southeast. Movement became difficult. The men had been instructed to each hold on to the cartridge belt of the man in front of him. To turn loose may be to break contact and separate the regiment.

The rain was merely a nuisance to seasoned troops but the darkness and the Okinawan mud presented a more serious challenge. The starting and stopping, slowing down and speeding up created an accordion-like effect that would normally have evoked oaths and threats but they were Marines and they had been told to maintain tactical silence. They did their utmost to comply and though no audible oaths crossed their lips, there were undoubtedly many curses and profane threats silently sworn on that night of misery.

As Carl Johannsen trudged along on that very dark night with no stars in the sky and the moon overly shy about peeking out from behind the rain clouds. He was in deep thought. He was re-living something that he'd survived many years before. It was the same scenario; the same kind of a miserable night with intermittent rain, practically no visibility and orders to stay closed up and keep moving. The column was long, a whole regiment long, and it was moving in two files one on each side of the nearly invisible road.

Memories, damn! He had so many memories - some of them were better than others - his memories of a night like this many years ago were memories he had long ago hoped to forget. It was unbelievably dark just like that night in France so long ago. They had been on their way up to Soissons. He was a young private back then and a green one at that. It was 17 July 1918 and here it was, 17 June 1945. Good grief, in another month it would be 27 years! Where had the time gone?

Johannsen had given considerable thought to that dark night in France. He had marched through the rain-swept forest with the 5th and 6th Regiments of Marines but he was thinking now about this march with the 8th Regiment and what they might encounter if and when they reached their intended destination. He hoped it wouldn't be a repeat performance of the bloody fighting at Soissons.

Johannsen knew that the men had doubts about this mission. They had never done this sort of thing before and many were concerned about their chances for success. He had briefed them earlier, right after the company commander had told them what they were going to do. The men listened to him because he was an old corps professional. He had told them that it had been done before by the 5th and 6th Marines and that he had been there himself and survived. He explained to the men that Colonel Wallace would never hazard his regiment unless he was certain of success. The gunny silently prayed he was right.

As the old salt watched and listened to the troops, he marveled at how much the Marine Corps had remained the same over the past 27 years. The Corps was bigger now, but so was the country and it was a bigger war. He looked at their faces, listened to their stories and jokes and to the songs they sang and found them remarkably similar. This night could easily have been France in 1918. They had a newer style helmet now and herringbone dungarees instead of AEF khakis with wrapped leggings, the bayonets were shorter and the new M-1 rifles were semi-automatic. The Marines were younger by a year or two but they were motivated, tough and they still had that Spirit of Semper Fidelis. They would make it; the night penetration would be a success. He kept right on listening to the young Marines and encouraging them.

*   *   *   *   *   *   *   *   *   *

The Point Man

17/18 June 1945

They were moving now, not rapidly and not entirely in complete silence but considering the prevailing conditions of intermittent rain and almost total darkness, they were doing reasonably well. At the speed they were moving, it was going to be a long, long night.

All hands earnestly prayed that someone up at the head of the column knew where he was going. The troops surely didn't, they were simply hanging on to one another and moving forward. It had been more than two hours since the march had commenced. All wondered how much longer it would be, but few would have guessed that they were just getting started.

Much firing could be heard off in the distance and the clouds occasionally reflected a bit of light from the detonations of artillery or star shells, none were close by and the troops were thankful. It was as quiet as one could hope for along the route of march in the 8th Marines sector. Other Marines were not so fortunate. The fighting on that Sunday, 17 June, was severe enough for someone in the 1st Marine Division to dub it the "Fathers' Day Massacre" and the name stuck.

The blood-curdling screams that suddenly pierced the quiet night took everyone by surprise. In addition to the screaming, there was a disturbance and considerable movement in the left file. The voice of Corporal Riverboat Brown was so filled with pain and panic that it was barely recognizable as human.

Eyes strained to penetrate the darkness and see what could

be done for Riverboat and to be certain there were no more Japs nearby. Visibility was restricted to little more than a dozen feet. Brown was in excruciating pain and was screaming horribly. Among those who were close enough to know what had happened, there was much vicarious sympathy pain. The screams were like a beacon in the dark, alerting the enemy to our location. Men prayed that wherever the Japs were, they were far enough away as not to hear the horrible wailing. Amidst the darkness and confusion, the screams were suddenly reduced to sobs and choking and were considerably muffled. Someone had taken a rolled-up pair of socks from his haversack and stuffed it into Riverboat's mouth.

Chic wondered who could be so cruel. Everyone liked Riverboat and no one wanted to see him suffer any more than he already had. It had been Gunnery Sergeant Paul from the Machine-gun Platoon. Paul had a tough decision to make and precious little time in which to make it; three thousand men's lives could be at risk. He either had to kill Riverboat or find a way to quiet him. He chose the rolled up socks and hoped they would work. It seemed cruel at the time but it had to be done. The decision to gag Riverboat may have saved the lives of many men.

The Jap who had risen up out of the ditch beside the road and driven his bayonet up through Riverboat's groin and into his stomach had been quickly beaten to death with rifle butts. His broken body lay in the dark just a few feet from where Riverboat was stretched out awaiting a corpsman.

Two corpsmen materialized from somewhere. There really wasn't much illumination from the moonlight when the corpsmen got to where Riverboat was stretched out on the road, but they really didn't need light to tell them that their patient was dead. The poor little guy. At least now he was free of that terrible agonizing pain. Another one of the raggedy assed Marines was wrapped in his poncho to await burial.

The column moved silently forward. Tired but ever-alert eyes pierced the inky darkness attempting to discern whether there were other Japs lying in wait beside the road. The little ditch that paralleled the road was now a place to be carefully scrutinized and greatly feared. Each of the Marines moving cautiously in the darkness with his hand on the man ahead of him could vicariously feel the pain that Riverboat must have felt as that Jap's bayonet penetrated his groin and was shoved up and into his stomach.

Riverboat was going to be missed. He wasn't an old timer. He wasn't even a regular. He was just one of the many wartime reservists that joined as a replacement prior to Saipan. Everyone had to agree, there was something very special about Riverboat. He cursed like a sailor and misquoted scripture like a drunken orator. He had opinions about everything and strangely, he had often been correct. When we lost men, he prayed for them. Chic remembered how Riverboat had controlled Hashmark while conducting a prayer service for Choirboy. He remembered too, on Tinian how Riverboat had admonished everyone to pray for Poncho when he had died. We had lost many men and he prayed for them all but he had especially singled out Poncho who most of the men considered a heathen.

Chic felt an emptiness as though he had lost a close family member as he wondered who would pray for Riverboat. Plodding along in the darkness and mud while holding on to Lucky Lane's blanket roll strap attached to the back of his pack, Chic prayed for Riverboat – and then he prayed for them all. His eyes filled with tears and he was thankful for the privacy of darkness.

Later, the silence was again shattered some distance up ahead when someone stepped on and detonated a landmine that had been planted at an intersection in the road. The regiment's strength was again reduced, this time by four. Every man must have had the same terrifying thoughts. How could the Japs keep from hearing an explosion like that and not open fire on us? The long column of apprehensive Marines kept moving. No movement could be heard from out on the flanks. Perhaps General Ushijima was purposely letting us continue the march; maybe it was another trap like on 1 April when he let the U.S. forces land unopposed and move forward until he was ready to spring his deadly trap. As a result of it, thousands died.

The march lasted from dusk on the 17th until the crack of dawn on the morning of the 18th. The Marines had fought the mud and darkness throughout one of the longest nights of their lives in order to be in position by dawn on the 18th. The effort had been necessary in order to relieve their decimated and battle-weary brothers of the 7th Marines. The 8th Marines were to take up their position on the 1st Division's right. Those who were there would long remember the night penetration, the night of the "Fathers' Day Massacre."

There's an old saying that it's darkest just before the dawn. If that were true, it would have been daylight three hours earlier because it simply couldn't get much darker than it had been then. Now, the shroud of darkness was slowly beginning to soften and the ghostly terrain had taken on a kind of murky grayness as the rain subsided and heavy fog rolled in to blanket the rice paddies in the lowlands. The men cautiously released their grips on the cartridge belts of the men ahead of them as their eyes adjusted to the dark gray of the early morning.

They continued moving forward and upward out of the paddies and low lying fog onto the ridge. The 2nd Battalion inclined to the left as they ascended Mezado Ridge. The 3rd Battalion moved over onto Kunishi Ridge. Deadly Dave put his hand on Chic's shoulder and quietly asked: "Hey buddy, do you believe in miracles?"

Chic responded with: "Yeah but I don't just believe in miracles, I depend on them."

Deadly Dave answered: "Yeah, I guess we all do. Have you looked back down to see where we've been?"

"No," Chic said, "I've been too busy trying to hang on to Lucky and keep from falling on my face in the mud, why?"

Dave glanced back pointing down and said, "Look."

Chic looked then asked, "How did we ever get through that? I can't believe it even though I'm looking right at it. This really is a miracle."

"Yeah," Deadly Dave muttered, "I thought you'd find the view of some interest."

By now, all the men were looking back in amazement. It was just barely light enough to make out the forms of several Japanese tanks enshrouded in the fog of the misty lowlands they had just traversed. There was Japanese infantry as well; enough to have badly mauled the regiment had they known the Americans were passing through them in a long narrow column in the dark. They had obviously still not seen us and would not expect us to be in the position we were now in. Lucky Lane, utterly amazed, asked: "How in the world do you think we got through all that without being detected? Who the hell was leading our column anyhow?"

Chic answered, "There's only one way we could've pulled it off and we needed a lot of help doing it. We must've had a helluva good point man up front."

Fearless quipped, "Maybe old Riverboat's ghost was up there navigating for us."

Chic admonished, "Knock it off Fearless, I'm serious! Do any of you guys really know who was leading us?"

Someone answered, "Yeah, Riverboat must have put in a good word for us when he got to heaven, 'cause this time, only God could have been the point man."

*　*　*　*　*　*　*　*　*　*

The Observation Post

Ibaru Ridge – 18 June 1945

The battalion pushed south through the early morning's mist onto Ibaru Ridge across an open slope that slanted down from Mezado. The darkness was giving way to daylight and with the light came enemy rifle and machine-gun fire from the flanks. As the attack progressed, the enemy fire increased and mortar fire soon began exacting a toll.

Their left flank was tied in with the 5th Marines, a regiment tired and worn from excessive fighting but with a combat record that could stand up to any regiment in the Corps. The 5th and 8th moved south together, the men occasionally waving at one another or giving the thumbs up sign. There was an instant rapport between the Marines of these two proud units as they advanced together.

One man from the 5th Marines was moving forward more concerned with the shots whining past him than the terrain he was walking over. His foot hit a trip-wire activating a booby-trapped white phosphorous grenade. A piece of the white phosphorous struck his chest and burned completely through him in a matter of seconds. There were no first aid measures to be taken in an incident such as this. "Willie Peter" was fast and it was deadly. Chic considered whether it might have been a forgotten American trip-wire or if the Japanese had set it. The dying man's screams of pain and fear echoed in Chic's memory as the advance continued.

They were pushing to the south. To the left front was the town of Makabe where the Japs had concentrated artillery and many troops.

It was full daylight now and a regimental observation post was established on a rugged hill on the east shoulder of Mezado Ridge. The hilltop was crowned with large coral boulders. From this OP an observer could look south to the sea over most of the remaining Okinawan terrain that was still in Japanese hands.

Major Bill Chamberlain, now the regimental operations officer, was deeply concerned as he asked, "Colonel, why in the world do you suppose the Tenth Army commander wants to come up here now? We're making remarkably good time and the order was to displace forward just as soon as possible. It could be very unhealthy to be waiting around on this hilltop much longer. We don't know what capabilities the enemy may have left."

"Bill," Wallace replied, "We're sitting ducks up here. I wanted to move the OP down the forward slope a ways where we could still observe the men without being right up here on the skyline. Tenth Army has directed us to stay exactly where we are until the general arrives."

"I know that Colonel, but why?"

"Bill I can't say why the Army does anything, but I'm sure they have their own reasons for such things. If it was a Marine general coming up here, I'd move us forward now and explain it to him after he arrived. An Army general may not appreciate a mere Marine colonel making a decision in contravention of orders, even if it is dictated by common sense."

*　*　*　*　*　*　*　*　*　*

Captain *Soichiro Ishihara* was hungry and weary. The Gods of War had not favored the 32nd Army and he knew that little time remained until the end. His regiment had been one of Japan's finest. Now, most of the guns were gone – destroyed; and his valiant men, individually and in groups, were drifting toward the Shrine at *Yasakuni* where soon, their spirits would all be reunited.

He stood in a well-camouflaged position with a handful of men, his hand upon the hilt of the treasured *Katana* that had belonged to *O-JI-san*, his venerable grandfather. They were standing beside the one remaining gun. A Type 96, fifteen centimeter field artillery piece and 8 rounds of ammunition, all that was left. His battery had included some of the best trained artillerists in the Imperial Army. Now, the men he had were a composite from what was left of the once proud unit and a few stragglers. Not all were cannoneers. Among the men with his battery were a few Okinawan conscripts, poorly trained and certainly not the caliber of soldier he was accustomed to but they too wished to make the ultimate sacrifice to honor the Emperor. *Ishihara* longed for the men who had fought with him in China but nearly all of them were gone.

His thoughts wandered back in time and he smiled softly to himself as he thought of his home and family and of his youth. All of Japan was beautiful but to him, his little island of *Minami* was the most beautiful of all. When he closed his eyes he could see the lush green paddies neatly terraced on the hillsides and he imagined the fishing boats returning with the day's catch, their sails conveying them gracefully over the water. He remembered the old men sitting on their haunches as they worked together mending the nets as their fathers and their father's fathers had done for generations.

Minami was quiet and peaceful and its people, though poor, were rich in the ways of their forefathers. Tradition, courtesy and a mutual respect for one another were among their cherished customs. He remembered those wonderful days when he was a small boy and sat for hours listening as his grandfather, *O-JI-san*, told him of the great wars. In 1900 *O-JI-san* had fought the Manchu's and their rabble from the Society of Harmonious Fists, the "Boxers," at Tientsin and he had made the march to Peking with the armies of the great western powers. The Japanese soldiers had fought well in China and had earned the respect of the foreigners. Later, *O-JI-san* had fought the big-nosed barbarians from the north in the Russo-Japanese War. It was a magnificent victory for Japan and the rest of the world knew that henceforth, the Empire of the Sun should be respected.

Shoichiro thought about school and the tremendous effort he had made to excel. He had studied for long hours and developed the self-discipline *O-JI-san* had told him would be necessary for him to gain entrance into the Imperial Military Academy. He remembered how leaving home was a bittersweet experience. He was filled with pride as he bowed to each member of his family, their friends and neighbors in turn receiving their best wishes. He pretended not to notice the lovely *Aiko Nakamura* who bowed deeply to him but when she rose up, their eyes met briefly and he felt a lump in his throat and a heaviness in his heart. He hoped no one had noticed. Secretly he wished he could have told her of the great affection he felt for her.

*   *   *   *   *   *   *   *   *   *

Dammit Colonel, look down there to our left, around that boulder." Chamberlain exclaimed. "Do you see what I see? It's a damned convoy. The Army has arrived. I can't believe they'd bring that number of vehicles right up here to the line. Look! They've got six vehicles in addition to the general's Jeep"

The startled colonel directed, "My God Chamberlain! Get someone down there to guide them up here on foot and be quick about it. I don't want to be on this damned hilltop a minute longer than we have to. The antennas on those jeeps will be a magnet for enemy fire."

"I've already got a runner standing by down there to guide them Colonel." Chamberlain answered. "I just hope they don't waste any time climbing up to us."

Arriving at the OP, the general, slightly winded, addressed the colonel in his gentlemanly southern drawl, "Hello Clarence, I've heard some remarkable reports about your progress and thought I'd come up to see things for myself."

Colonel Wallace answered, "Its nice to see the general again sir, but if you don't mind may I suggest putting your helmet back on. Its dangerous up here and I wouldn't want my men to see you uncovered. We have to set an example or some of them might decide it's alright for them to uncover."

"Clarence, you Marines never cease to amuse me with your unusual language. General Vandegrift paid me a visit a few days ago and he too commented on my being "uncovered." If it makes you feel any better, I'll put my helmet, or should I say, my cover? back on. But I do want to see these Marines of yours that are supposed to be moving out like jackrabbits."

"General," Wallace responded, "I've got two battalions down there moving forward. They're taking some hits as you'll see, but they're also taking enemy terrain, lots of it. We're hoping to advance fourteen or fifteen hundred more yards before the day is over. Here, take a look through this Japanese telescope Chamberlain has set up and you'll see the men moving forward."

Lieutenant General Simon Bolivar Buckner looked through the captured Japanese telescope for a few moments then took a step back and moved forward past the operations officer and regimental commander. The commanding general of the Tenth U.S. Army wanted to get as far forward as he could to survey the area to his front and observe the men surging forward in a skirmish line. It was a beautiful sight; two battalions of infantry, their small units, fireteams and squads, leapfrogging forward in a line that stretched across the plain.

The colonel spoke, "General, I wouldn't want you to get too far out there, this is an exposed position and its dangerous."

"Colonel Wallace, you told me to put my helmet on so I wouldn't set a bad example for your Marines. Well, let me tell you something about setting examples. In the Army, when our men are going in harm's way our officers like to be highly visible so the men can see us and know we are supporting them. We think that's part of effective leadership."

The general looked back down at the magnificent men moving forward with such precision. When wounded men fell to the ground hospital corpsmen rushed to their aid, as their buddies closed the gap and continued advancing. Where did we get such men? Had they no fear? As the line surged forward, little clusters of three or four men would dash out several yards drop to the ground and take up firing positions while other similar groups rushed forward. They were under fire but the line continued moving, in short spurts, toward their objective.

The fire discipline was remarkable, the men only appeared to fire when they spotted an enemy or identified a target. These troops moved like true professionals, they were really good. Perhaps he should have listened to Vandegrift and Geiger when they had advocated landing on the southeast coast to cut off and split the 32nd Army. A landing by the 2nd Marine Division may not have been such a bad idea after all, especially with fighting Marines such as these.

"Clarence, I haven't seen anything like this in years and I've never seen it before in actual combat. You've got one hell of an outfit down there. The fine training those men have had and their dedication to their mission is very obvious. Things are going so well here I'm going to leave you and move on to another unit."

* * * * * * * * * *

Ishihara's battery was located on a small hill about 5 kilometers east of *Mezado* Ridge. What remained of the headquarters of the 32nd Army was now at *Mabuni*. They had cautioned *Ishihara* to conserve his remaining 8 shells until the last minute or until he could identify a suitable target. His soldiers were carefully searching the area using the telescope attached to their gun.

Jo-to-hei (superior private) *Takahashi* sucked in his breath audibly, he had found something of interest. Turning from the telescope, he bowed respectfully to his captain and declared that he had seen a column of American vehicles stop at the base of a hill. Men had gotten out of them and were walking up the hill. *Takahashi* had noticed that most of the jeeps were equipped with long antennas. The men walking up the hill were not carrying rifles, they must be officers.

Jo-to-hei Takahashi respectfully asked his honorable commander to look through the glass to confirm this important target. Ishihara looked and then directed his men to sight the gun in, not on the vehicles, but on the top of the knoll where the men from the Jeeps were congregating. He carefully checked everything then layed the gun himself, ammunition must not be wasted. He sensed that it was an important target and decided to personally give the commands. He watched through his binoculars as he waited patiently, timing was very important. Finally, he could issue the command, "Fire!!"

Hazukashi! He had brought embarrassment upon himself before his men. Ishihara's heart sank as he watched his first round strike the forward slope just below the crest of the hill. It exploded in a violent cloud of dust, fire and smoke. He could see some of the Americans running around on the crest but most of them had flattened themselves on the ground for protection. With a sick feeling in the pit of his stomach he sensed that his first round was wasted, it had been too low, detonating on the forward slope. To *Ishihara*, wasting the first precious round was a decided loss of face. He cursed his bad *karma*.

The die had been cast; *Ishihara* had his target and must continue firing. Not trusting himself to sight again, he permitted his men to do it. When they were ready, he commanded them to raise the elevation slightly then to fire again and again, the remaining rounds were soon expended.

Ishihara could not know that his first round was not a result of his bad *karma*. His *karma* was much better than he could have imagined. It was Lieutenant General Buckner whose *karma* was bad this day. *Ishihara's* exploding first round had dislodged a jagged shard of coral rock that plunged deeply into Buckner's chest. Ishihara had killed the senior American officer to die in battle during World War II in the Pacific.

Ishihara could not asses the damage from such a distance, he only knew that most of the rounds fired after the first low round had been too high. Without ammunition and with only a handful of men left, he no longer commanded an artillery battery. His men would now fight as infantry. They would move stealthily out toward the enemy lines to a position from where they could launch an attack when the Americans became most vulnerable.

* * * * * * * * * *

The Naked Warrior

18 June 1945 – Near Macabe Village

It was still daylight but the Marines had been under fire all day and had advanced over 1400 yards. They were exhausted. Someone up the chain-of-command had decided the men needed a break. They were told to halt and dig-in where they were. The men were strangely silent. Their advance had been highly successful and they'd taken casualties but not as many as expected. The commanding general of the Tenth U.S. Army had been killed while with them. Deadly Dave and Fearless knew the Army would blame the Marines for not protecting their general. They wondered what the Army would do to get even.

A runner had escorted the platoon ration detail back to the CP for ammunition, water and rations. Foxholes had been dug and improved.

A gentle rain started falling and ponchos were hastily broken out, unfolded and donned. Corporal "Barnsmell" Nesbitt quickly unlaced and removed his leggings and boondockers, then he took off all of his clothing and covered everything with his poncho. He, like everyone else in the platoon, was well overdue for a shower and since it was still daylight and starting to rain, this seemed to him to be the right time and place.

As the raindrops fell dampening his body, he joyfully removed from his haversack and carefully unwrapped, the remains of a small bar of soap he had been hoarding. Standing in the rain Barnsmell soaped himself from the top of his head to his tired, aching feet. Once completely lathered, he glanced up at the rain clouds in anticipation of the inevitable downpour that always followed the first few sprinkles. This time he was finally going to put that rain to good use. Let it come! But for once, it did not come. Okinawa's monsoon season was ending.

The drops stopped falling and the clouds above drifted slowly apart. Still looking skyward, the frustrated, soapy Marine shouted at the top of his lungs, "Mother Nature is a whore!"

None of the others had thought much about it before but they could not disagree with him. She had screwed them all on numerous occasions and they had paid dearly often with discomfort and misery.

Barnsmell was doing his best to wipe the soap off with his dirty scivvy shirt when all hell broke loose to the platoon's front. A squad of Japanese soldiers had decided it was time for them to die gloriously for the Emperor and had risen up out of their positions to the front and in a ragged skirmish line moved forward firing as they advanced. They couldn't have been more than 80 yards away. They moved fast and fired their bolt action rifles indiscriminately but not very accurately.

The most humorous thing that occurred during the Okinawan operation didn't seem a bit humorous at the time, especially to Barnsmell. He was standing bare-assed naked except for the soap lather and his steel helmet without liner that he had grabbed up and quickly put on while reaching down for his rifle. There he stood, returning the advancing Japs fire wearing only a helmet that, without its liner, fit him like a large bucket. What caused Nesbitt to remain on his feet; even he could not explain when it was over. The rest of the men were firing prone and with little effort stopped the eight advancing soldiers who made no attempt to take advantage of cover. They seemed only intent on moving forward until fatally stopped by the Marines' rifle fire. From that day on the men jokingly spoke of Nesbitt as the Naked Warrior of Makabe.

* * * * * * * * * *

The Grenade

South of Ibaru - 19 June 1945

Yoshiko Sugimoto could stand it no longer. The cave she was in was not a place of security. It was a place of horror and it had become a prison. She moved out to the entrance where she felt the warm rays of the sun and could breathe clean air.

During her few minutes in the sun she could almost forget the hunger pangs that had been gnawing at her stomach. She thought of her home on Kyushu and vicariously felt the soft breezes blowing in from the Gulf of S*himabara*. With her eyes closed, she inhaled and dreamed that she could smell the aroma of steaming rice, the reek of salt fish, seaweed, the sharp smell of *daikon* and the faint scent of *shoyu*. Wonderful, delicious smells that brought her memories of the past and of a happy childhood. The sun's rays had a healing effect for which she was grateful.

She remembered how it had been before the American devils had come to Okinawa. The Japanese officers strode haughtily about telling the people of the invincibility of the Imperial Army and how the Americans would be exterminated if they ever tried to land on Japanese soil. The Americans did land and where were those arrogant officers now? There were no officers with the soldiers in the cave and the soldiers were not invincible. They were either dead or dying and the stench was horrible.

The warmth of the Okinawan sun restored within her a desire to continue living. She was grateful for these precious moments and for the healing rays of the sun. She determined that this day would be the last for her to remain in this place of horrors.

On the land below, just a few hundred meters away, she saw a line of Americans moving south. They were coming right for the heights. She doubted if they had seen her but they would see her very soon if they continued moving in this direction. It was with great reluctance that she moved back out of the healing sunlight and into the hell of the cave. She told the soldiers the enemy was approaching and the two that could still walk picked up their rifles and moved to the cave's opening.

She knew it was the duty of the soldiers to kill the enemy but why, oh why, did they have to do it now? She had planned on leaving after dark, but now the cave she hated so passionately was destined to become her tomb.

Jotohei Mori shouted for her to move quickly all the way to the rear of the cave. Blindly, she waded through the ugly black water to get to the far end. The stench of human feces and urine were overpowered by the terrible sickening smell of decomposing flesh. A few days before, this would have been more than she could stand but now, it was just another of the many horrors she routinely experienced.

The soldier *Tajiri, Iwao* tried to raise himself up on one arm but failed. His wounds were too painful and he was weak from loss of blood and from hunger. Where were the men from his unit? There had been eight stragglers with him when he entered the cave. Surely some must still be here. They were too badly wounded to go on. He knew the men on either side of him were dead but he wasn't sure about the others. The only person moving about that he could see and identify besides *Jotohei Mori* was the young woman, *Yoshiko*. He had heard *Mori* shout at her to move far back in the cave.

Even in the dim light of the cave, he could see that she was a classic beauty. Her facial features were perfectly proportioned and her skin was like porcelain. There was a natural beauty mark on her left cheek and her right arm was bandaged where she had received a gash from a mortar fragment days before. She was wearing a pair of old ragged *mompei* and a torn, dirty shirt but her natural beauty shone through. The soldier wished he had known a person such as she before the American demons had invaded Okinawa.

She squeezed through the tiny opening at the back of the cave into an out-of-the-way pocket, where there was barely space for her to curl up. Overhead loomed a petrified shower of stalactites reflected by the carpet of jagged stalagmites reaching up from the floor. These inhibited her every move. She was unable to sit up, lie down, or even stretch out her arms and legs. She simply curled up on the hostile floor of the cave as the blackness consumed her. In spite of the extreme discomfort, she was thankful to be in the protection of this tiny cocoon within the rugged coral fortress.

The two soldiers in the cave's opening started firing their rifles at the Americans and the Americans returned their fire. Bullets were whizzing around the cave and ricocheting in all directions. Suddenly there was a detonation within the cave. It had to be Private *Tajiri*. He had somehow found the strength to detonate his grenade and die honorably by his own hand.

A thundering roar and a brilliant flash of light were accompanied by the angry whirr of hot metal as fragments from an American rocket or grenade flew in all directions. She clasped her hands over her ears to prevent the concussion from shattering her eardrums. Razor-sharp pieces of steel sliced into the cave, ricocheting until they found unprotected flesh or buried themselves randomly in the cave's wall. *Yoshiko Sugimoto's* eyes burned from the cordite smoke that grew denser with each detonation.

She was fully to the rear and was behind a protrusion of rock which offered protection but she could see nothing. It seemed to her that hundreds of bullets had entered the cave but now, she no longer heard the soldiers firing outward. They were both dead.

She reached her right hand down into the pocket of her ragged *mompei* where she had a hand grenade. As her hand caressed the grenade, she felt a sense of security. She would not use it now but it was comforting to know that she had it and could use it to take her life at any time should the Americans come too close.

Outside, the sun had moved westward and was slowly dropping toward the horizon. Darkness would soon envelop Okinawa. The hated Americans had stopped shooting at the opening of the cave. They must have sensed there was no longer any danger from within as they could plainly see the two dead soldiers just outside the entrance.

As *Yoshiko* looked out of the mouth of the cave, she could see the enemy's positions. They had dug a line of shallow holes across the plain and two men occupied each of them. Tomorrow, when the Americans moved out, they would overrun the heights and the cave. The soldiers had told her how the Americans would torture and rape captured women before killing them. She reached down and clutched the hand grenade through the cloth of her *mompei* and was thankful that she had this to protect her from such a fate.

It was night now. Clouds covered the moon and darkness prevailed throughout the valley. *Yoshiko Sugimoto* slowly crawled from the filth and stench of the cave. She moved past the bodies of the two dead soldiers and started slowly downward. She was traveling light with all of her worldly possessions now gone except for the one hoarded hand grenade, which was to be used to end her life - if it became necessary.

When she got to the bottom of the steep incline, hunger and fatigue were taking their toll. She was disoriented and uncertain of which way to move to evade the Americans. The moon slowly drifted out from behind the clouds and bathed the ground ahead of her in an eerie light. She knew there were Americans in the valley somewhere but saw no one and she heard no one. She knew the remnants of the Japanese 32nd Army were to the south. Her life may yet be spared but which way was south? A loud bang and a brief muzzle blast flashed to the front and told her where the enemy was, but it was too late.

The early morning light gradually replaced the darkness of the Okinawan night and the Marines did a visual reconnaissance of the area to their front. "I know I got one of the bastards last night!" Dutch Shute said. "He was comin' right towards us. I saw him drop when I shot him. The sonofabitch was only a few yards out and he was comin' right this way. He fell right over there by that rubble. C'mon Cobber, let's go out and see what that Nip has on him. Maybe we'll get lucky and find a Samurai sword or a pistol to trade with the doggies." Shute and Jock Ross moved out stealthily, their rifles held cautiously at the ready with bayonets fixed.

As they moved forward it became obvious that there had been a garden of some sort here. That was one of the strange things about this war, every now and then you could look through the rubble and devastation and you just may notice something that had once been beautiful. Most of it was gone now, but it seemed as though one could see through the shattered trees and torn up landscape and realize that once upon a time, before the Devil had turned it into his very own little corner of hell, it must have been attractive. There was enough left to see that it had been artistically laid out and probably had been a beautiful, serene spot before the devastation of combat had all but obliterated it.

They noticed a little shrine containing a small idol and surprisingly the idol was still intact. "Heathen bastards." Beside the shrine they saw the body of a young woman. She was lying on her back, face turned up with her large eyes gently closed. There was a natural beauty mark on her left cheek and a dirty bandage on her right arm. The Marines looked down upon her and Dutch exclaimed. "Jesus, I didn't know it was a woman! My God, is this the Jap I shot? I had no way of knowing it was a woman."

Private Shute felt ill and a great deal of remorse came over him as he stood there looking down on the still form. He hadn't wanted to kill a woman but war is hell and in the dark of night, how could anyone tell the difference? She was coming from the direction of the enemy cave. They had received considerable hostile rifle fire from that cave before darkness the previous evening. She had been moving directly toward their position. Ross noticed something clutched in her right hand and as he stared at it, he pointed. Their remorse turned back to hatred as the two Marines saw the grenade! She was no different than any of the rest of them! She had probably been trying to see just how close she could get to their holes before detonating that grenade and killing a few Marines.

Ross spoke. "It's a good thing you shot her pongyo. Just think of how many of us she might have gotten if she had been a little closer and had detonated that grenade".

Shute had a heavy heart as he glanced down at the still form of the girl he had killed. She looked peaceful with her eyes gently closed and her face was not contorted as they were on most of the cadavers he'd seen. Even in death and in spite of her soiled ragged clothing there was a certain dignity about her and an almost angelic look on her pale face. Most of the battlefield dead had died with their eyes and mouths wide open. They died in horror.

As the Marines turned and started back to their position Ross' attention was drawn to the little shrine. He glanced casually at the face on the small idol and suddenly felt very strange. He couldn't help noticing the large eyes, gently closed and the statue's uncanny resemblance to the dead girl lying there in the dirt. He grasped Shute's arm and pointed to the little idol. Shute scoffed and said something about all the damned gooks looking alike. Then he looked more closely at the face on the idol and fell silent.

* * * * * * * * *

The Runner

It was the new platoon sergeant's voice. "Runner up! Who's the duty runner? Is it you Muldoon? Better get back to the CP. They're calling for a runner."

A determined Muldoon responded, "Hell no! It ain't my turn yet. C'mon you guys. Who's up to be runner next?"

Deadly Dave Donahoe got up and stretched. Reaching for his pack and BAR he said, "Guess I'm your man sergeant, I haven't been the runner in a coon's age."

"Hold it!" The platoon sergeant barked. "Give that cannon of yours to someone else and borrow a rifle. We need all our automatic weapons and if you take that thing with you it'll only slow you down. You won't be needing it anyway."

Deadly Dave exchanged rifles with Fearless saying, "Take care of my baby will you little buddy?"

Fearless grinned up at Donahoe and said, "Sure Dave, you know I'll take good care of her."

Being a runner was a unique assignment. It was frequently sought after but sometimes shunned. It was thought by some to be a great way to goof off and just relax back at battalion headquarters or sometimes even at regiment. There was always enough drinking water at battalion (they generally had a "water buffalo" attached to a Jeep) and occasionally an extra can of C-rations may be had and there was often semi-reliable scuttlebutt to listen to. On the other hand, being a runner could be a trying experience if one was dispatched over a long distance in unfamiliar terrain. It was an important job and at times it could be terrifying. More than a few runners had been lost. No one liked to be alone in a combat zone. In the platoon, the raggedy assed Marines, or what was left of them, usually rotated on runner duty. They were the old salts now.

Donahoe was a good man. He was frequently acclaimed as one of the best BARmen in the company. His tattoos, a ring of hearts around each of his wrists, were somewhat unique and he was often teased about them. They were often the subject of conversation but he never really gave an explanation for them. The less he said, the more his buddies wondered. He was a quiet man but damn he was good at soldiering! He rarely showed fear and was always welcome as a foxhole buddy. He'd seen more than his share of combat and had plenty of good sea-stories to tell. He was one of the raggedy assed Marines."

When it was his turn to be a runner, Deadly Dave had reluctantly given up his BAR to Fearless in exchange for Fearless' M-1 rifle. It was only to be for a couple of days and then the next man would rotate up and Deadly Dave would go back to being a BAR man with the platoon. Each of the Marines had taken his turn as runner and now it was Donahoe's turn again. It may be pretty nice going back from company headquarters to battalion and even sometimes to regiment. He'd get to see how the anointed ones in the rear echelon lived.

A staff sergeant at the battalion message center explained to Donahoe just where he should go in order to find the regimental CP. He was not to waste any time, as they would soon be displacing to a new location. When he returned, the battalion would be in a different area as well. The sergeant gave Donahoe a well-worn topographical map and marked the co-ordinates where the new battalion CP would be when he returned. It would soon be dark and runners did not want to be out on their own after dark. The staff sergeant had told Deadly Dave to remain at the regimental message center until the next morning when they would give him something to bring back to the battalion.

Donahoe was traveling light and he moved out quickly. The M-1 was a featherweight in comparison to the BAR and heavy belt of ammunition he had been carrying for the past couple of years and he wasn't encumbered by a pack. He was moving almost at a trot as he had to beat the impending darkness. He wished he had gotten an earlier start. The staff sergeant had warned him about Makabe Village. There were still bypassed Japs in that area. Deadly Dave had been an outdoorsman all his life. An assignment like this was a natural for him. He wondered what he might be able to scrounge that he could take back to the squad after he got to regimental headquarters.

* * * * * * * * * *

It came as a tremendous surprise being caught in a snare and then pounced upon simultaneously by two Japs whose hands moved like lightening. He wasn't expecting it and found it hard to believe that they had him down and hog-tied him in mere seconds. Shouting wouldn't help and he couldn't fight back with his hands lashed behind him. He knew he was in enemy territory and anyone who might hear him would be Japanese.

The knife slash in his side was painful and it was bleeding. He knew it was a serious wound but still, they made him stand and walk with his hands tied painfully behind him. The communications wire they had used to tie his hands was much too tight and he knew it was intended to cut the circulation and cause pain. After all his combat, Dave Donahoe was a prisoner of the Japanese! How could such a thing have happened and what were they going to do with him?

*　*　*　*　*　*　*　*　*　*

The body was obviously that of a U.S. Marine. It was clad in faded herringbone dungarees that were spotted with dried blood and body fluids. The Marine field shoes and leggings were still easily recognizable. The entire stomach and center of the torso and groin were just raw meat coated with blackened dried blood that had run out of wounds probably inflicted by repeated stabbing or multiple hits from an automatic weapon. The victim had been tied to a stake that was actually the trunk of a young tree, the top of the tree had been shot or broken off. There was communications wire wrapped around the chest and waist and his hands had been pulled behind the stump and tied tightly with the comm wire. His head was leaning forward with protruding eyes looking down at the ground. The body was already beginning to blacken and was so disfigured from swelling as to be unrecognizable.

The swarming flies were like a dark cloud and the stench was awful. Behind the post where the swollen hands were tied, if one looked carefully at the blackening wrists he could see that each had a ring of red hearts tattooed around it. The Japs had done many terrible things but Chic had never seen anything quite as bad as what they had done to his friend, Dave. He thought about who he needed to tell but then he realized that most of the buddies who would really care about Deadly Dave were already gone, except for himself, Lucky and Dutch Shute. Sometimes it was difficult keeping score.

He could hear muffled voices all around him speaking softly. Someone uttered, "Damned Japs! They ain't human those little bastards. They just ain't human!"

They were cursing the Japs and swearing oaths and he recognized the voice of the new lieutenant.

"Okay men, that's it! We're not takin' any more prisoners! Do you men hear me? No more Jap prisoners!"

Chic wondered just what kind of vermin would do such a horrible thing. Why couldn't they just have killed him and had done with it? Why go to so much trouble to defile his corpse? The lieutenant's words seemed to echo in Chic's mind. "No more Jap prisoners"!

He knew how they felt. Hell! He probably felt it more than any of them. Donahoe had been his buddy for a long time. They had been on liberty together and they had often fought side by side on these lousy islands. There was no way he would ever forget or forgive this grotesque deed. Yet, there was something deep down inside him that wouldn't let him forget Suzuki and the canteen and the crucifix and what had happened on Saipan.

Had Suzuki and his men been capable of such an atrocity? Maybe this is what they had planned for him. Suzuki could have killed him at any time yet he had given him a canteen of water and had let him live. Chic would never know why Suzuki had done it, he often wondered what Suzuki's motive had been. He would be forever grateful. The Japanese were like anyone else, some were bad beyond description. Others were merely victims of a fanaticism that had engulfed their whole race and destroyed their power to reason intelligently. Chic looked quickly away, he'd seen enough. "Semper Fi, Dave old friend. God how we'll miss you!"

The new lieutenant and the platoon sergeant had recovered Donahoe's pack from the CP and were going through his personal effects in preparation to having them shipped home to his dad. When they opened his wallet the sergeant ex-

claimed, "Hey Lieutenant, look at this. He had a life membership in the VFW. Here's his card."

Chic remembered Deadly Dave's remarks when he'd received that card in the mail back on Saipan. Donahoe's pre-
diction of death before going to his first VFW meeting had
come true. It just did not happen the way he had predicted.
Chic felt really sorry for the new lieutenant. He had some very
difficult letters to write. He felt sorry for Dave's father too, a
widowed, disabled veteran who'd lost an arm fighting in France
during World War I, and now he had lost his only son.

* * * * * * * * * *

Fearless' Farewell

Fearless Frank Quinlan had not been himself since
Donahoe's mutilated body had been found. He was used to
death, they all were, but what had happened to Deadly Dave
was something none of them had seen before. They could not
accept the fact that he had been killed in such a brutal manner. Fearless had tried to make a few notes, which he was
going to put in a letter to Donahoe's dad after the island was
secured, but whenever he started writing, his hands would
shake and his stomach became upset. Francis Xavier Quinlan
had finally seen too much combat.

One campaign after the next, how much longer could they
take it? The platoon was now hardly recognizable. Most of the
faces in the company belonged to replacements. The remnants
of the raggedy assed Marines, Chic, Lucky, Fearless and Dutch
and sometimes the music, tried to maintain their distance
from the new men. They had lost too many friends and did
not want to make new ones only to have them slaughtered as
well.

When the company moved out Fearless didn't look like
himself. He had given up and just walked upright and took
no notice of the available cover. Somehow, he looked out of
place carrying that Browning automatic rifle. It was too heavy
and too big for him. He shouldn't have kept carrying it, but he

said he didn't want to give it up. The troops all knew it had been Deadly Dave's BAR. Fearless and Deadly Dave had always been good friends. He had obviously been thinking of Deadly Dave who was always proud of being a BARman.

Fearless had developed the "thousand yard stare." He was close to cracking up. He'd seen too much combat and too many deaths. There was nothing for him to look forward to but more combat. It was late June of 1945 and the saying was still, "Golden Gate in forty-eight, bread line in forty-nine." Who the hell could last until 1948?

As they moved forward, the stillness of the Okinawa morning was shattered by the chattering of a machine-gun. Fearless Frank Quinlan's BAR barked a few short bursts and then fell silent. The heavy rifle dropped from his hands as he slumped forward, his knees touched the ground at the same time. Both of his hands were clutching his stomach as he slumped forward his face fell into the dirt and then he rolled over on his back, slowly, painfully.

Chic had only been a few steps behind Fearless. He dropped into the prone position and started crawling forward as the others did their best to lay down covering fire. He wished they could spot that damned Nambu. It was really close, but was well concealed.

Fearless Frank Quinlan was down for the count. He suspected it and Chic knew it. The blood was flowing freely. How the hell do you stop the bleeding when its coming out everywhere? "Corpsman! corpsman!! Its Fearless, he's hit bad!"

Butcher came lumbering across the ground like a rampaging elephant. He was carrying a lot of weight and just wasn't able to move fast enough. The Butcher was an easy target. He went down less than a dozen yards from Chic and Quinlan. The Butcher was dead. Fearless Frank Quinlan would not be treated by a Navy corpsman.

"Chic, its real bad isn't it? I think I need a corpsman. When you get the corpsman, tell him to bring a priest. I think I need a priest too."

"Okay Fearless," Chic lied, "Butcher's on his way, he just has to move carefully, the Nambu that got you is still out there somewhere."

Chic hated to lie to his buddy. Butcher was dead and Chic

knew it. He could see his body lying right where he had fallen. He just didn't know what else to say. He believed that telling Quinlan help was on the way would comfort him some.

"Yeah Fearless, it looks pretty bad, and right now we've got a big problem. We've got to stop the bleeding."

Quinlan dug his clenched fists hard into his abdomen and held them there. Blood kept oozing out around his hands. He must have been hit with two or three rounds.

"Chic, Chic, I've got to talk to you. We're buddies ain't we? We've been together a long time. Tell me I can trust you?" Chic could still understand but Quinlan's voice was changing and sounded strange.

"Of course you can trust me. But don't try to talk now, we've got to keep you calm and we've got to get the damned bleeding stopped. I don't want you going into shock on me."

"Chic there's some things I've got to tell you. I don't really hate all those corpsmen, it was just sort of a gag, that's all. I know they're good guys. I just fought with them 'cause they didn't like to fight as much as other sailors, that's all. I knew my chances of winning were better with corpsmen. They always wanted to subdue me and get me in an ambulance. I never really hurt any of them, it was just an act. Oh God, my back and belly hurt! Chic, I've lost the feeling in my legs!"

"Was I shot there too? Did they get me in the legs?"

"No Frank, I don't think they got your legs. It's just your stomach. But please try not to move. The more you move, the more blood you'll lose. Corpsman! Please, somebody get a corpsman over here!"

With Butcher dead, there were no corpsmen. Chic needed help with Fearless. His hands trembled uncontrollably as he took his first aid packet out and removed the gauze bandage and shoved the compress into Fearless' stomach in a futile attempt to arrest some of the bleeding.

No one dared approach them until the Jap machine gun could be silenced. Chic cradled his friend in his arms and watched the color rapidly draining out of his face. The Nambu fired another burst, it was too close. Chic leaned Fearless down on his back and lay down beside him with his arm supporting the dying Marine's head and his hand squeezing Fearless' blood soaked right arm.

Fearless mumbled, "Chic, the girls. I've got to tell you about the girls. You're not gonna believe this but I want to tell you. Chic, I never got to first base with any of those girls. I really tried, but I just couldn't score. I'm still a virgin Chic. What do you think of that? The great lover, Francis X. Quinlan never even got laid."

"Please Fearless, knock it off! Don't try to talk, you're just making it worse. Hell, I never got laid either. I didn't have any better luck with women than you did. Half the guys in the outfit who bragged about all their conquests are probably still virgins too. Just like you and me. You just tried a little harder than the rest of us that's all. Now stop moving until we can get some help over here for you."

When Chic removed Quinlan's BAR belt, he had taken a hand grenade from it. Now may be a good time to use the grenade. No one had been able to get near them and Chic had guessed at the location of the Nambu in the treeline and thought maybe with a little luck, he could lob the grenade far enough to at least get a little shrapnel close to the machine gun and maybe do some good. He took his arm from under Fearless Frank's neck and carefully, gently laid his head down.

Getting up on one knee, he armed the grenade and carefully measured the distance to where he believed the Japanese were. It was a long way to throw. He cursed himself for not having played more baseball as a kid and at the same time he prayed that the grenade would go where he aimed it and silence the Nambu. Chic fervently wished old Hand Grenade Harrington hadn't been killed. This throw would have been "duck soup" for him.

Chic was torn between a sickening fear and the overconfidence born of absolute necessity. He knew he was going to make it. He had to. Everything depended on making that grenade reach. He threw his only hand grenade with all of his strength and immediately knew it wasn't good enough. The grenade hit the ground and bounced once toward his intended target, but far short of it. He flattened out and burrowed his face into the dirt beside Quinlan as the detonation propelled grenade fragments and coral pieces in all directions.

"Did you get him Chic? Did you get him?" "No Frank, I couldn't have, they're still shooting hell out of everything around here!"

Quinlan took one of his bloody hands out of his stomach and reached up with it faintly attempting to make the sign of the cross. Chic knew he was praying and could understand some of the words he was saying,

"....Holy Mary Mother of God, pray for us sinners, now and at the hour of our death...." It doesn't hurt as much now Chic, I don't feel that awful pain anymore - but I can't move!"

Yancey grabbed Quinlan's bloody, elevated hand and squeezed it.

"That means you are going to be alright Fearless, you're gonna make it. I knew you would." Chic lied.

The grenade may have fallen short, but it made someone mad as hell. The Japanese opened up with several more bursts from the machine-gun. The response was a reaction. It was not carefully aimed fire and proved ineffective. It was however, a dead give away as to the Japs' location. Marine rifle fire took up the fight and soon was supplemented with 60mm mortar fire. The mortars had the desired effect.

When the smoke cleared, the Nambu had stopped chattering and all was quiet, including Francis Xavier Quinlan. They had been together a long time, Chic and Fearless Frank, and it was not easy saying goodbye.

Francis Xavier Quinlan, veteran of too many campaigns, the greatest lover in the company and one helluva combat Marine was dead. The enemy fire had ceased and the troops were cautiously moving forward. Sergeant Childs and Gunny Johannsen appeared out of nowhere and helped Chic cover Quinlan's body with his poncho.

Chic felt Gunny Johannsen's gentle hand on his shoulder and knew it was time to move forward with the rest of the men.

"Nice throwing kid, real nice."

"Thanks Gunny."

Chic felt very old and lonely as he realized that the raggedy assed Marines no longer existed. For the time being and until this war was over, the Marine Corps wasn't going to be much fun anymore.

He thought about the article by Ernie Pyle that Donahoe had gotten from his dad just a few days before the Japs had tortured him to death. "I lay there in the darkness thinking.... and thinking of the millions far away at home who must remain forever unaware of the powerful fraternalism in the ghastly brotherhood of war."

* * * * * * * * *

Night Patrol

Okinawa - Late June 1945

Over on the right flank, an automatic rifle barked a series of put-put-puts into the stillness of the night. The men instantly dropped and froze as their hearts beat wildly. The automatic rifle repeated put-put-put, put-put-put.

Corporal Nesbitt swore, "Dammit! That's a BAR, its one of our own people firing at us. That trigger-happy S.O.B.! The word was passed to those jerks that we'd be reentering the lines right here and at 2300 and that's what it is right now. If I ever find out who that BAR man is I'm gonna turn him every way but loose."

Lucky admonished, "Knock it off Barnsmell! You're talking too loud. If the Nips hear you, we'll have both sides firing at us."

Remaining in the prone position the patrol started inching slowly forward taking advantage of the slightest folds and depressions in the ground. They moved in this manner until they found suitable cover in a shallow ditch. It seemed to take them an eternity.

Beads of perspiration saturated Chic's forehead. He could feel a rivulet of sweat running down his back. His heartbeats were strong enough to be annoying. He could hear them pounding in his ears yet he felt a fearful weakness come over him. Silently he said a prayer and then wondered if many of the other Marines felt this terrible fear in the same way he did. The patrol would never make it in before daylight without getting shot up. These new replacements were too damned trigger-happy. Chic listened as Barnsmell briefed the men as quietly as he could:

"Okay you guys, 50 percent alert and I mean alert! We can't get back in now with that fool's finger on the trigger of his BAR and we sure as hell don't want to go back where we've been and cuddle up with the Nips. We'll stay right where we are in this ditch until daylight and then we'll go in. I'm gonna find out why they weren't expecting us and you can bet somebody's head is gonna roll for this!"

Chic was awake and alert. The Marine beside him was just a kid, one of the new replacements. It was time for him to rest and let the kid watch for awhile but Chic wasn't sleepy. He decided, what the hell, he'd let him sleep a bit longer. He looks peaceful curled up there in the ditch. Poor bastard, he'll be dead soon enough, just like all the others.

He laid his forehead in the crook of his arm and silently sobbed. He was thinking of Jerry Bronson and Shanghai. He thought about Fearless and the Weasel and of poor little Kevin Mulcahy and of Big Ski and Little Ski. He thought about Donahoe's torture and Whitey Schultz and Mac and Riverboat Brown. Oh God, just think of what happened to old Riverboat. What a hell of a way to die! The poor little guy never hurt anyone in his life and he had to suffer so much when he was dying. Damn! There's no justice in this life. Chic thought about Corporal Thompson's death and he thought about Poncho and wished he could have known what a good Marine Poncho would turn out to be before he was killed. He would never forget Marine Gunner Robinson and he remembered Blackjack's brother Milt and how he had died on Tinian trying to get help up to us during that last banzai attack. Chic wondered how much time he had left before it would be his turn to join the others. It was a very long night and he was relieved to see the first crack of dawn. As the Okinawan sky lightened, maybe they could find a way to convince those trigger- happy boots to let them back into friendly lines.

* * * * * * * * * *

The change had been subtle and had taken place over a

long period of time. A few new replacements here and there to replace men who had been lost. The squad, the platoon and the company were different now. They were made up mostly of newer men. The replacements all looked pretty much the same. They were Marines, but anyone who had been a member of the company for awhile could see that it was now a company of strangers.

When a Marine encountered an old hand from another platoon who had been with the company for awhile even though they may not have known each other well in the past, a nod, a faint smile or a profane term of endearment would pass between them. They now felt deeply for one another, these "old timers." They had become members of a shrinking but elite fraternity within the company. Each wondered how much longer the other would survive. It is terribly depressing to be a proud young Marine and have more friends who are dead than alive. Chic thought to himself, "Golden Gate in Forty-eight..." My God, how will I ever survive that long?

Okinawa was secured now, so why were we on night patrol and still living in holes in the ground eating crummy C-rations and going out after prisoners and killing Jap holdouts every day? It was the same old routine as on Saipan and Tinian. No one likes war, but combat Marines, the men who have to fight the damn wars, hate it the most of all.

* * * * * * * * * *

The regiment was headed back to Saipan to be reunited with the rest of the 2nd Marine Division. The men wondered what new adventures were in store for them. Scuttlebutt aboard ship was that they were not going to go to China. Some damned fool back in Washington who was not being shot at had decided to have us invade Japan itself, and soon. Chic hoped the scuttlebutt was just a figment of someone's imagination. He remembered something the music had said before they left Saipan the last time and he found it disturbing. Netherland had told them the next big operation was planned for November and would be the invasion of Japan itself.

He could not forget the *banzai* attacks he had survived

and he realized that an invasion of Japan would result in fanatical defenses and wave after wave of the invaders were certain to be decimated. The Marines were sure to be among the first waves of an attacking amphibious force.

He remembered the Okinawans walking single file along the dykes attempting to surrender. Many women and children had babies strapped onto their backs, others carried bundles on their heads. Long lines of them were shot down en mass by the Japanese soldiers. An invasion of Japan could result in the near annihilation of the Japanese race! Their own soldiers will shoot down the ones we don't kill. Chic knew the people back home in the United States would never be able to fully understand the total brutality of the Japanese fighting men. He did not look forward to invading Japan.

The company gunnery sergeant told the platoon sergeants to have the men strike their shelter tents, roll their gear, bury their trash, fill in their holes and stand–by for orders. The orders came soon enough when the first sergeant bellowed at the men to fall-in. They had a tough day ahead of them. The regiment was marching to the floating docks down by Naha to go aboard ship.

The USS *Admiral Capps* PA121 had been a luxury liner before the war. She had been converted into an army transport and was manned by a crew from the US Coast Guard. She was a large transport ship and was cleaner and more spacious than most. She was also a good feeder. The men considered themselves lucky to be aboard, even if she was taking them back to Saipan.

* * * * * * * * * *

The Bombs

Field Music First Class W. Max Netherland was back from the Army hospital with plenty of new material for his infamous rumors and scuttlebutt. The music was taking more than a small amount of ribbing over the location of the wound that got him out of the field and into the hospital in the first place. From now on, whenever he said something was a pain in the ass, he would have a reference point and some real credibility.

"Dammit men, you'd better listen to what I'm telling you. Our next operation is gonna be a really big one. I told you guys before we left for Okinawa the last time that our next campaign would be in November and we are going to invade Japan. In fact, I can even give you the code name for the operation and tell you where we're gonna land."

Lucky spoke up with, "Look Music, we just got back from Okinawa. They're not going to send us back into combat again after all we've been through, they've got to give us a break and enough time to get more replacements and get them broken in and trained."

"Okay, have it your way," the music retorted, "I don't know anything. Forget about all the times I told you guys what was going on and I turned out to be right. Just remember, when you start hearing talk about Operation Olympic or see them breaking out maps of the island of Kyushu that you heard it first from your friendly field music and don't ask me anything else about it because I'm not going to share anymore damned information with you guys. When this outfit is going up the gangplank of some rusty old bucket in October, I'm going to be standing right there on the dock sayin' I told you so!"

The balance of July was spent doing some pretty intensive training. Something was up; all the men could feel a tenseness in the air and they felt a renewed sense of urgency about everything. None wanted to admit that the music had been right again until one day when the new company commander was speaking to them and mentioned Operation Olympic.

News of the dropping of huge, devastating bombs on Hiroshima and Nagasaki came with a startling suddenness in the midst of our all-out training and preparations for the amphibious assaults on Japan.

Private Nelson, a buddy of Epstein's had been walking his post which included the company street in front of the 2nd platoon's tents. Shortly before reveille, Nelson stuck his head into the tent and awakened Epstein to relate to him that the corporal of the guard had told him that some nut had started a rumor that the United States had a bomb that was so big that just one of them could wipe out a large city.

They were calling it an Atomic Bomb and we had allegedly dropped one of them on a place called Hero-sheema in Japan. Epstein, along with everyone else in the tent, was skeptical and had questions but Nelson was fearful of being put on report for violating his 5th and/or 7th general orders and resumed walking his post without another word. Of course, no one really believed the rumor but it was almost time for reveille and the men, now that they were awake, lay in their bunks speculating and discussing the Atomic Bomb while waiting for reveille to be sounded.

Corporal Jerden wasn't buying it as he stated, "You know, it's a pretty weird story. In fact, its even a taller tale than something the music might come up with. Where do you find your nutty friends Epstein? There's just no way this could be true."

"Of course not," Chic scoffed, "What do they take us for? There hasn't been a plane built that's big enough to carry a bomb that could wipe out a whole big city. If they did try to build a plane that big, it probably couldn't fly."

The music had left the tent earlier to sound first call and reveille and then, as usual, to be the first in line for early chow. The men were up and dressed and were squaring the tent away when he re-entered the tent with the latest rumor. "Hey you guys, wait 'till you hear what I just heard up at the battalion mess. Remember Golden Gate in Forty-eight and Bread Line in Forty-nine?" Someone mumbled, "Yeah we've all heard it enough times, why?"

"Well now they're sayin' Home Alive in Forty-five!"

Lucky felt that this rumor, or sick joke or whatever it was, had gone far enough and said so.

"You gotta be kiddin'! Don't be sayin' things like that and get everybody's hopes up Music. You know the war is still gonna last a long time. Now, unless you really know what you're talkin' about, knock it off!"

At morning chow the rumors were rampant. No one seemed to know very much about this Atomic Bomb except that it was dropped on a city with the unlikely name of Hero-sheema which of course no one had ever heard of. The company continued going out on routine patrols to look for the die-hard

Japanese holdouts every morning or afternoon. They spent the other half day training. It was obvious to the men that no one had cancelled the plans for Operation Olympic, their upcoming invasion of Japan. And yet, the rumors persisted.

By the 9th of August, the rumors about the big bomb had just started to die down a little when a new story started to circulate about another Atomic Bomb. This one was supposedly dropped on the city of Nagasaki.

Chic found this hard to believe and so after hearing the rumor about our bombing Nagasaki, he went to see Chaplain Wickersham. "Father, I need to know something and I'm sure you will tell me the truth. Is there really such a thing as an atomic bomb or are the rumors just a bunch of scuttlebutt? If there are such bombs, did we really drop one of them on Nagasaki?"

The chaplain confirmed what Chic already knew had to be true. He even stated that he had heard that one lone bomb could completely obliterate five square miles of a city. Chic asked the chaplain how much he knew about the city of Nagasaki and was surprised to learn that he knew quite a bit about it. Father Wickersham confirmed what Chic had learned from the chaplain in the Army hospital the previous year. Nagasaki was the Christian capital of the Orient. It was a sullen Chic Yancey that returned to the company area. He was in the company street speaking with Dutch Shute, Epstein and Lucky Lane: "Do you guys know what the chaplain just told me? There really are Atomic Bombs and we did drop two of them just like everyone's been saying."

Lieutenant Grosscup just happened to be walking down the company street at this moment and Chic saluted him and confronted him with:

"Hey Lieutenant, we heard the Atomic Bombs are real. Chaplain Wickersham told me so. Do you know anything about it?"

"Yes, of course I know about it. The officers got the official word about the first one a couple of days ago. We bombed both Hiroshima and Nagasaki and wiped them right off the map. For all practical intents and purposes, neither city exists anymore. The Japs got just what they deserved."

"Oh no! Why did we have to bomb Nagasaki?" a crestfallen

Chic asked, "That was really stupid and it was cruel as hell. I can't see how our country would ever stoop to such a miserable thing."

"Yancey!" the lieutenant snarled, "What the hell are you, some sort of subversive? You don't like the United States anymore? You sure sound like a goddam Jap-lover to me! Didn't you see what those bastards did to your buddy Donahoe when we were on Okinawa?"

"Yes Sir, I saw what they did to him and I still say we were way outa' line to drop that bomb on Nagasaki."

The lieutenant was becoming emotional as he directed, "Yancey, get your Jap-lovin' ass up to the company headquarters tent and wait there for me. I want to talk to you and I want the company commander to hear what you have to say. I think we may have grounds for a court martial here."

Fortunately for Pfc Yancey, the new company commander was a bit more understanding than Lieutenant Grosscup. Chic attempted to explain about Suzuki sparing his life. He had been from Nagasaki. He also related what the Army chaplain had told him a year before and what he had just learned from Chaplain Wickersham. There were far more Christians in Nagasaki than in all the rest of Japan combined. If we had to fight in Japan, why would we start by wiping out the Christians? Weren't they more likely to help us than anyone else in Japan? Why did we have to bomb Nagasaki when there were plenty of more suitable targets at powerful bases like Yokohama, Kobe, Yokosuka and Sasebo? Chic was dismissed with no action taken but the company officers would remember Pfc Yancey and would reward him with another month on mess duty.

A little after 2100 on 10 August, scuttlebutt started and swept through the battalion area like wildfire. Someone was spreading the exciting rumor that Japan desired to surrender unconditionally. People back in the United States were celebrating wildly. In places like New York City and San Francisco they had celebrations that are yet to be surpassed. News of the war's end was met with joy, happiness and wild celebrations throughout the world. On Saipan, men started milling about in the darkness out in the company street and they were talking about the end of the war but not a shot was fired and there certainly was no big celebration. There may have been many hopeful prayers, but the prayers were said quietly and privately. The men were all hopeful but it seemed too good to be true. We all knew that the war was not supposed to be over until 1948.

On 14 August 1945 the war was officially declared over. The 14th was being called VJ Day (victory over Japan Day). There would be no more beachheads, no more killing, and no more nasty little Nips firing at us from unlikely places. It was like someone on death row getting a reprieve. Now, we who had survived thus far finally had a right to believe we would live to see home again. What a pleasant surprise it was to men who had often wondered whether they would even survive until the end of the day.

* * * * * * * * * *

Teeth of the Dragon

September 1945

What a good feeling it was to be in a convoy on the moonlit sea and not have to darken ship. The ship's lights were on as were those of the other ships in the convoy and it was exciting. We had never expected to go to Japan in this manner. Most of the battalion was aboard the troop transport USS *Menard*, an APA, but it no longer seemed like an APA. The war was over and most of the shipboard regulations had been relaxed.

The doors, hatches and ports were open all night; the decks were lighted; the air was free and the sea was no longer a haven for hostile submarines. We kept marveling to ourselves, those of us who had known the fury of combat, and we found it all very difficult to believe. The war was really over and we, at least some of us, had survived.

Cruising into the bay at Nagasaki was a memorable experience indeed. As the dark, early morning sky gradually lightened nothing could be seen through the thick blanket of fog that hung low over the water. It was as though God had decided to keep us in suspense until the last possible moment when he was ready to raise the curtain and reveal the next act in this drama.

As Chic and his friends stood at the ship's rail, straining to get their first glimpse of land, they became aware that they were gliding past dark shadowy forms to both the port and starboard. The persistent cloak of fog hung over the water like a pall. Then, as the fog gradually started lifting, the forms came into focus more and more clearly until suddenly, there they were! Jagged spires of rock rising vertically up out of the sea to stab through the dull gray of the morning fog. They were as the teeth of a giant dragon that had been positioned to guard the entrance to hell - or to the Empire of the Sun - or whatever the beholder's imagination dictated at the time.

The natural grandeur of this unique country was breath-taking. It was exotic and in its own peculiar way, it was beautiful. Chic could not compare it to anything he had ever seen before, these great pinnacles from the sea that they were gliding through - the dragon's teeth. As the fog slowly diminished and the dawn continued to brighten the sea and the sky; some of the exotic beauties of the Orient were slowly being revealed on that early Sunday morning in September of 1945.

There was land now, it was all around us. Small islands rising sharply up from the water. Oriental trees, lush green terraces and delicately manicured gardens. They could see a few buildings. The houses were small, some had classic tile roofs that turned up at the corners; other roofs seemed to be made from multiple layers of thatch. The houses appeared to be ancient and the whole scene was very picturesque. It was like an oriental painting on an old picture postcard.

Chic thought of the children's story of Alice in Wonderland and remembered Alice stepping through a looking glass into the Wonderland of her story. He felt as though he had just sailed through the teeth of a dragon into his wonderland. He had entered the Empire of the Sun and wondered if it was real or if he was just dreaming?

*   *   *   *   *   *   *   *   *   *

The landing party climbed out of their "Mike Boats" and

scampered onto the Nagasaki pier. A handful of haggard young men from the 8th Regiment of Marines, cynical, weary of combat and aged well beyond their years stood on the outskirts of Nagasaki, Japan. They were the survivors of the raggedy assed Marines. They silently viewed the awesome devastation of that once great Christian city. Glancing around at the other Marines landing beside them they looked into their faces. Most had an aura of innocence about them that the raggedy assed Marines had long since lost. They were the new men, the replacements. They had been trained to fight but had yet to be tried. There were lots of replacements in the ranks now. So many of the men who had earned the right to be here were gone. They had been buried, some at sea and others on Guadalcanal, Tarawa, Saipan, Tinian and Okinawa. They were the true heroes of the 8th Marines, and would be the subjects of the regiment's legends that would be handed down from generation to generation of future Marines. We are a Corps steeped in tradition and we glory in our history and take pride in the accomplishments and the sacrifices of those Marines who have gone before us.

Chic quietly prayed his thanks to God for his own life that, for some unknown reason, had been spared again and again while so many others had not. He tried to pray for the others, the ones who gave their lives so he could be here now, the first dozen or so were easy but there were so many faces and names to remember. It was difficult to concentrate on our dead while viewing the ruins of this once great city of Nagasaki. The voice of the new platoon sergeant shattered Chic's thoughts.

"Alright you guys, saddle up! We're shovin' off for an assembly area. Move out in a column of twos, one file on each side of the street an' square your shoulders and stay in step. Let's show these damned gooks what real fightin' men look like!"

Lucky Lane spoke in a stage whisper but all the men around him heard clearly, "Who the hell's he kidding? The real fighting men are dead, we left them behind on those stinking lousy islands in an ocean that some fool named the Pacific. And whoever it was that named it the Pacific Ocean was either crazy or he didn't have a dictionary to tell him what pacific actually means."

Curious, Chic asked: "What do you mean dictionary Lucky? Have you actually looked it up?" "Yeah and guess what it means? '...of a peaceful nature; calm; tranquil. Also, Making or tending to make peace."

Netherland couldn't help but smile as he said: "Ain't that somethin'? Why the hell was I so seasick if its calm and tranquil, and what about the damned typhoons? And 'making or tending to make peace' sure as hell doesn't seem to equate with the war we just fought. I guess we must be part of the ten percent that never gets the word."

The regiment was moving now; a column of files on each side of the street. The men were at sling arms with bayonets fixed. A clip of M-1 ammunition, just eight rounds, was in the first pocket of every man's cartridge belt. Most of the buildings had been badly damaged but a few were still reasonably intact. It was very noticeable that there were no unbroken windows or undamaged shoji panels even five miles out from the center of the city. The atomic bomb was all they had said it was.

Japanese civilians and a few soldiers lined the route of march. They stared but showed no animosity or emotion. Their faces were ashen and their expressions blank. They looked worn out. They were as tired of the war as we were. Most of the men were in old army uniforms and nearly all of the women were wearing wartime *mompei*, it was obvious that this was all they had left. They surprised us by courteously bowing low as we passed. They were quiet and docile. Was this the vicious, brutal, fanatical enemy that we had fought for so long? How could it be possible?

These people were truly a paradox. They were changed completely from the Japanese we knew and had fought. As Chic looked into their expressionless faces he thought of the hundreds he had seen lying dead on the field of battle. Yes, these were the same people. Their Emperor had told them not to offer resistance to us and they did not. They were being totally obedient to their beloved Mikado. If he had told them to fight to the bitter end, every one of them would have done so. Chic would always remember the *banzai* attacks and the *Kamikaze*. Every man, woman and child in the Empire of the

Sun would have fought to the death if they had been ordered to do so. Thank God for the Atomic Bombs! It is the only way this brutal war could have ended without virtually wiping out the Japanese race. Not to mention perhaps as many as a million or so Americans.

The bayonets on our rifles seemed out of place as did the eight-round clips for each rifle. The single clip of ammunition that had seemed so inadequate when we were coming ashore was now almost an embarrassment. The war really was over. Now finally, we believed. The Japanese we had fought had been totally transformed. The devastation of the Atomic Bomb was beyond understanding or adequate description. The people here were so pathetic. The enemy existed now only in our memories. Our hearts went out to these poor souls. As they bowed deeply in submission, their expressionless faces and threadbare clothing told a story of bitter deprivation and defeat.

The Marines had marched past part of the destruction and were now behind a hill that looked out over the port of Nagasaki. From the hilltop they could view the utter destruction of this once great bustling city. The reverse slope of the hill had offered some protection from the devastation of the atomic bomb and the damage was considerably less than that which they had just marched past and viewed from the hilltop. A waiting train sat on railroad tracks just a few yards from where the column of Marines was assembled. It was twenty-two cars long and at the door of each car was a black-uniformed railroad employee waiting to serve the expected passengers.

On one side of the assembly area was a road and beside it, a row of Japanese houses that had hardly been damaged by the atomic bomb.

While the men were waiting for the word to board the train, they were standing in the road talking and killing time. Chic noticed something strange about Dutch Shute. He was looking toward one of the houses and was staring as though there was some special attraction or mystique about it. Chic asked,

"Hey Dutch, what is it? What's so fascinating about the house?"

"Look Chic, its not the house. Look at the little garden in

front of it. Do you see that shrine with the little idol?"

The little shrine Dutch had noticed in the garden in front of the small house was much like one he had seen on Okinawa. The shrine beside the body of the Japanese girl that he had killed. The Marines had no way of knowing then the significance of the shrine or the idol. Dutch Shute only knew that, in his mind, the girl he killed and the little idol had exactly the same lovely facial features.

"Yes, of course I see it but all of these little Shinto shrines look the same to me. What is there about it that interests you?"

"Don't you see it Chic? Its her, its the girl from Okinawa. The girl I murdered."

"Dammit Dutch, you didn't murder anyone! You shot that girl because it was dark and you thought she was a soldier and you know damn well she had a grenade in her hand. She might have killed all of us with that grenade if you hadn't stopped her."

"Chic please, look at the face on the little idol in that shrine. Its her again, its really her."

The Battalion Sergeant Major was carrying a clipboard and had an interpreter with him as they were walking down the line of cars. The interpreter was stepping up into each car's doorway and asking something in Japanese then relaying the conductors' answers to the sergeant major. Apparently they were trying to determine if the cars had been made ready and had been inspected. When they were abreast of the platoon Chic looked at the sergeant major and excused himself then he spoke directly to the interpreter.

"Will you please do us a favor and take a look at the little statue in that Shinto shrine over there in the garden? What can you tell us about it anyhow?"

"Oh yes, I know about it. Yes, that is not Shinto shrine. That is the goddess *Quan Yin*. She is Buddhist. The Japanese say '*Kannon*' but I am Chinese and she is *Quan Yin*."

Dutch Shute took Chic completely by surprise and surprised the Chinaman as well by stating: "She's beautiful, she's really beautiful."

As Chic was recovering from Dutch's unexpected outburst, he tried to ask the Chinaman to tell them something about

Quan Yin but the sergeant major had better things to do than to let his interpreter get sidetracked by a couple of curious Pfc's.

"Come on Mr. Wu, let's check the rest of these cars. We're going to be moving out soon. You men stand by to mount up!" Mr. Wu continued walking down the tracks beside the waiting train with the sergeant major but not before blurting out to Dutch: "She is *Quan Yin*, the Goddess of Mercy."

"The Goddess of Mercy?" How strange that Dutch Shute's little idol would turn out to be the Goddess of Mercy. *Quanyin* and all of the other Gods surely had been working overtime on this day to allow the occupation forces to land unopposed. It had to be the most merciful landing in the brutal history of World War II. And so the men of the 8th Marines boarded a passenger train for transportation to Isahaya, Kyushu.

As the men came aboard, they stowed their packs on the luggage racks, adjusted the seats and prepared themselves to be comfortable while on the trip to a place none of them had ever heard of, Isahaya. The Japanese trains were smaller than trains back in the States but they were otherwise very similar. The train lurched then started moving smoothly forward with a minimum of jerking. A locomotive whistle sounded and Chic felt a wave of nostalgia come over him as it sounded remarkably like the train whistles back home. He began to realize once again just how much he had missed being at home during the war years.

The train rolled beyond the desolation of what had been Nagasaki. As they started moving upward, the hills were bare and colorless except for the depressing dull gray that had settled over everything. The gaunt trees had been blown outward and lay on the gray hillsides stripped of every leaf. The train was approaching the first of many tunnels and the whistle shrieked as the train rumbled into the darkness. It wasn't long before windows started slamming shut and oaths were heard coming from the coughing Marines in the smoke-filled cars.

As the train finally emerged into the brightness of daylight the Marines cursed themselves for not having closed the windows sooner. They had become human magnets to the soot and cinders in the tunnel. This minor discomfort was immediately forgotten as the men realized that they had emerged into a completely different world than that which they had left at the other end of the tunnel. The change of scenery was breathtaking. It was fresh and green and beautiful in comparison to the grim desolation of the atomic bomb. Slowly, one by one, the windows were lifted by Marines eager to clear the smoky air in the passenger cars and breathe the freshness of the wonderful countryside that now surrounded them.

The train passed through another half-dozen or so tunnels but the Marines were alert and closed the windows in plenty of time. As the train skirted the Gulf of *Shimabara*, they gazed at a beautiful inland sea called the *Omura Wan*. Across the *Omura*, green hills rose sharply up from the water and off in the distance behind the hills were Kyushu's majestic mountains. The railroad followed a curving seawall and cut through colorful country villages. The beautiful blue of the *Omura Wan* complimented the lush green of the trees, bamboo forests and terraced rice paddies of this enchanting land of our erstwhile enemies.

Arrival at Isahaya brought the Marines back to reality. They disembarked from the comfort of the train and fell-in beside the tracks. The 8th Marines was, and always had been, an infantry regiment. They were about to be reminded that the infantry walks. There were no trucks, trailers, Jeeps or any type of transportation to move the regiment to the base they were to occupy. The command was soon given, "Forward March!"

As the regiment of Marines surged forward, carrying all of their worldly possessions including the field transport packs on their backs, rifles, helmets and any incidental items that would be needed to make camp. The command "Route Step March!" was quickly given as the men staggered forward under their heavy loads. The leisurely days at sea had not prepared them for this. They arrived hot and sweaty just before sundown and the men had to move fast to take advantage of the remaining daylight.

The former Japanese air base at Isahaya was not luxurious but it was an improvement over what they had been accustomed to. The men soon learned that Kyushu mosquitoes are nearly as bad as those of the tropical islands they had just left. Fox company was billeted in a large aircraft hangar. The sweaty Marines couldn't wait to get their packs off, spread their shelter halves and blankets on the concrete and relax. It had been a long and very warm day. When the sun went down, the warmth vanished and a regiment of very cold Marines lay wrapped in their blankets shivering on the concrete decks of the hangars. Lucky Lane observed that what he had thought to be a hanger was obviously not. It was a wind tunnel and there seemed to be only one kind of wind at Isahaya, cold.

Reveille was not always welcomed with much enthusiasm by Marines but this, the first morning at Isahaya it couldn't come soon enough for the freezing troops. They were up and doing physical exercises before daylight. A cadence of multiple thuds resounded throughout the hangar as heavy Marine boondockers struck the concrete alternating with the sound of hands clapping overhead. "Side-straddle hops" was the preferred exercise on the first morning.

With the rising sun came a dramatic rise in temperature. It was warm again. At precisely 0755, the brassy sound of the field music's rendition of "First Call" resounded throughout the former enemy base and at 0800 the music played "Morning Colors" as the flag of the United States of America was smartly raised to the peak of the Japanese flagpole. What a momentous occasion this was in the history of the 8th Marines; the first American regiment to deploy overseas at the beginning of World War II, and the last regiment in combat at war's end. Now, they had the honor and privilege of raising the American flag on the Japanese homeland.

Supplies were received including folding canvas cots and suitable rations. Life was rapidly improving. A battalion messhall was established and a tent was erected to serve as the battalion Officers' Mess. Chic had mixed feelings about being back on mess duty. He had enthusiastically embraced it on Tinian when he thought he was near starvation and weighed but 93 pounds and he would have welcomed it aboard ship where messmen were always able to help their buddies by smuggling a little extra food to them. He would have to wait awhile to see if mess duty was going to be good duty or a problem in Isahaya.

What a break! The very officers who had put him on mess duty turned out to be his salvation. The cooks all knew Chic from his last tour of mess duty and they were friendly to him. He would get the softest job he'd ever had. When the word was passed that they needed two sharp messmen to work in the officers' mess, Chic was one of the two. The hours were short, the work was easy and the chow was the same as that eaten by the battalion officers. He couldn't ask for anything better.

The hangar offered protection against the frequent rains and the ever-present mud and was a vast improvement over the "accommodations" of the past two years. When Chic wasn't in the officers' mess he was back in the hangar with the platoon. There were very few duties other than the routine security guard and working parties. Training had been all but suspended for the time being. The men knew it was all too good to be true and it was. In less than a week the word was passed that the regiment was moving. We were going to a place called Kumamoto, a Japanese industrial city. None of the Marines had ever heard of Kumamoto.

* * * * * * * * * *

Yonen Gakko

The 8th Marines was headquartered at Yonen Gakko. It was three miles from Kumamoto City and had been the military academy of Kyushu and home of the Japanese 6th Cavalry Division. The large wooden barracks were two stories high. The Japanese barracks were not much different from old barracks anywhere except that these were bigger and were of untreated raw wood that had aged and was very dry.

When the Marines inquired about the long bamboo poles that were angled up and propped against the buildings in close proximity to the second story windows they were more than a little surprised at the answer. The long bamboo poles were their fire escapes. In the event of fire the men were expected to climb out the windows and shinny down the poles to the ground, two stories below. They had often heard of the proverbial "Chinese Fire Drill." They were in Japan now but perhaps Japanese fire drills were not much different than Chinese fire drills. The men all hoped there would be no fires.

The Supreme Allied Commander, General of the Army Douglas Mac Arthur, had issued an order that there would be no liberty, at least not for the time being. The men were required to remain in the barracks area. Field Music First Class W. Max Netherland had heard an unfounded rumor that Army troops in the Tokyo area were being granted liberty. If the music looked hard enough, he could always find bad news.

Pfc Epstein was looking out the 2nd story window when he noticed a pair of two wheeled carts rolling into the yard below, each was pulled by a Japanese man wearing the traditional straw coolie hat. Epstein watched the carts being off-loaded and out of idle curiosity he wondered what the objects could be that were in the boxes that were being taken off the carts. Whatever they were they were individually wrapped in straw. What a pleasure it was when the word was passed to get a working party outside to carry the beer ration in.

The Marines were introduced to Kirin Beer in large full-liter bottles that had been individually wrapped in rice straw to protect them from breakage. Beer was rationed to the men at the rate of two of the large bottles per man. Epstein declined his beer ration. He didn't think the Japanese would have very good beer and there was no telling what they might have put into it. Surprisingly, a few other Marines felt the same way. In an unprecedented but welcome move on the part of the company officers, permission was granted for the men to drink their beer in the barracks. Kirin Beer, like all Japanese beers, turned out to be excellent.

The men sat around the squadbay drinking beer and contemplating duty in Japan when Chic suddenly asked, "Hey Smith, I remember you once telling old Riverboat that you are a Baptist. What do you know about Jonathan Goble, he was a Baptist?"

The surprised Corporal Smith responded with, "So what if he was? There's lots of Baptists. I can't tell you anything about him. I've never even heard of him before. Who is Jonathan Goble and why are you suddenly interested in Baptists?"

Chic proudly proclaimed, "Because of the *rickshaw*, he invented the *rickshaw*."

Lucky Lane entered the conversation as he asked, "Who the hell do you think you're kiddin'? The Orientals have always had *rickshaws*, dammit, that's a part of their culture like *kimonos* and *obis* and *toriis* and pagodas. I've seen pictures of *rickshaws* all my life and I know they had them long before any white man ever came here."

A confident Chic Yancey replied, "Well, that's where you're wrong buddy. A U.S. Marine private, who became a missionary, invented the rickshaw and Jonathan Goble was that Marine."

"You know, you are beginning to sound a lot like the field music. That's the sort of thing I'd expect Netherland to come up with. Where the hell did you ever get that information anyway?"

"Well, Netherland and Father Wickersham were talking about Goble the other day. The father said that what Goble did made a lasting improvement on life throughout Japan. He was just trying to illustrate that one Marine, if he is innovative and uses his imagination, can really make a difference. I always thought the rickshaw was Japanese too. I would have never guessed that a thing we thought was so typically Japanese could have been invented by a Marine. But the chaplain knows a lot about these things and he wouldn't say it if it wasn't true - you know chaplains don't lie."

Lucky snapped, "The hell they don't! You've got a short memory little buddy. Remember when that chaplain told Jerden we weren't going to have any more air raids on Saipan? Later that same night the Japs bombed the hell out of everything? But, if Chaplain Wickersham said it, its probably true, he's a pretty reliable guy. We'll all have to be innovative and start using our imaginations more. Who knows what some crazy Marine may come up with."

In seeing that the terms of the surrender were being carried out, the 2nd Marine Division was responsible for: Demobilizing Japanese military personnel; taking over their military installations; locating and disposing of weapons and explosives; apprehending war criminals and processing the military and civilian personnel returning from various parts of the former Japanese Empire. The U.S. Army of Occupation had two Marine divisions and one Army division, approximately sixty-thousand men, to occupy the Island of Kyushu and be responsible for over twelve million Japanese.

Company and platoon-sized patrols left Yonen Gakko daily to scour the countryside for caches of Japanese weapons. Surprisingly, the people themselves often helped by showing the way and assisting in locating weapons and military equipment. The Emperor had told them to cooperate with the occupation forces and they were doing just that. It seemed very strange that the Japanese people who had been totally hostile during the war were so cooperative now.

There were some surprises revealed during the occupation, especially regarding the war-making capabilities that the Japanese still had. We initially thought that they were completely defeated but a tremendous amount of weapons of all descriptions and considerable stores of ammunition remained. The Japanese still had in excess of seven thousand airplanes dispersed throughout the country, many of which were hidden in large caves and underground hangars.

"Hey Lucky," Chic asked, "What did you think when you found out that the Japanese still have seven thousand planes?"

"I thought, thank God for the atomic bombs! It's the only way we could have ended the war without the Japanese being wiped out. Every man, woman and child of them. You know how they fought us on the islands. When we invaded their homeland, they would have been even more fanatical. They would have all fought to the death, all 88 million of them and you can bet your ass we would have lost at least a million men ourselves. Just think about the US 5th Fleet with nearly 600 ships lying off the coast of Japan in preparation for an amphibious landing and then being attacked by seven thousand Japanese planes flown by those crazy *Kamikaze* bastards. It would have been the greatest naval slaughter in world history. We're really lucky the war ended like it did 'cause if it hadn't, none of us would be alive now."

Dutch Shute was unusually quiet. He drank beer with the others in the squad but just didn't say much to anyone except those who had been closest to him for a long time. The changes that had started coming over Dutch back on Saipan were more pronounced now. He was moody and quiet and he always seemed to have something serious on his mind. When it was called to the lieutenant's attention that Pfc Shute may need help of some kind, he surmised that Dutch was just eager to get back home like so many of the other men. Lucky and Chic knew better, they had been with Dutch for a long time and had seen him operate under pressure. He had always been a good Marine. They thought Dutch's problem was something more serious and tried to cheer him up whenever they could. Chic was glad when his mess duty was over so he could spend more time with his buddies, there were only a few of them now.

There were some hard feelings and considerable grousing among Marines who felt that they should be granted liberty to go into the city of Kumamoto. Rumors persisted about the Army being permitted liberty up in the Tokyo area. Whether it was true or not was never substantiated but it did little to build good relations between soldiers and Marines. The survivors of the raggedy assed Marines considered it an affront to their dignity and a challenge to their initiative to be kept aboard now that they'd won the war. Why, they had even managed to go on liberty back on Saipan where there was no liberty. They were possibly the only Marines in the outfit who had ventured forth undetected on liberty nearly every Sunday.

Late one evening, following a fairly serious Kirin beer drinking session, a top level, top secret, conference on strategy was called. An operation plan had to be devised.

"Forget Kumamoto," Chic said, "It's a big city and there'll be M.P.'s everywhere. Let's go the other way. Outside of the fence are plowed fields. If you look across to the other side, there is a hamlet with several Japanese houses in what appears to be a big grove of trees. The houses look pretty nice. Most have those oriental style fancy tile roofs that turn up at the corners."

"Yeah," Dutch responded. "That's all we can see from here, just the treetops and the roofs. It looks like a pretty long walk through those fields."

"Well if you think its too far to walk Dutch, may I ask you a simple question?"

"Sure Chic, what is it?"

"What the hell are you doin' in the infantry?"

It was determined that Lucky, Chic and Dutch would have to maintain the reputation of the raggedy assed Marines and that, for the time being, they would consider the music a security risk as he was not always good at keeping secrets. They would not include him. The music was usually tied up with special projects he was doing with his newfound buddy, the chaplain. Their first challenge was to find a friendly sentry that could be bribed not to shoot them on their return and then they had to find a means of getting through the fence; which was negotiated with little trouble.

It was awkward walking across the plowed fields in the dark but they soon adjusted to it. The fog was thick enough so they probably could have made it without the cooperation of the sentry but coming back may be another matter. The sounds of railroad trains clicketty-clacking along on distant rails brought Chic a touch of nostalgia; he had always liked the sound of trains in the distance. The moaning of the train's whistle and the humming of the wheels were amplified in the darkness and the damp quietness of the night. It was a sound he had missed while overseas, until coming to Japan, and it made him think of home

On the far side of the field the trio entered a small picturesque hamlet of several houses. Old fashioned oriental lanterns flickered and cut into the foggy darkness without providing much useful illumination. The Marines walked down the lane looking at the houses, many of them had high privacy fences around them. The gates were all open or ajar and the men tried to peek in without seeming too obvious. The village was clean and orderly and even in the darkness it looked like something out of a storybook. It was very picturesque.

At the first intersection they glanced through an open gate and saw a man sitting in his house. The sliding panels were open and as he sat cross-legged at a little table he smiled and waved to them.

"Herooo!!" He pointed to his chest and stated: "I are *Chin Kyo Go*." Bowing and waving to them intermittently, he indicated that they should enter. All entered, removed their boondockers and leggings and mounted the platform where the man sat. They attempted to sit cross-legged around the little rectangular table, emulating their host. The little table was only about a foot high.

Having entered their first house and having just met their first local citizen, they immediately realized that the world is full of characters and Japan was certainly no exception. He repeated, "I are *Chin Kyo Go*!" as though he was some kind of a notable personage and his name should mean something to his foreign guests. Obviously, it did not. His next gesture did have some meaning to the Marines. He clapped his hands together and an elderly lady slid back a wooden frame with paper panes that comprised a part of the wall. They soon learned it was called *shoji*. She bowed to the guests repeatedly and in response to something the host commanded her, she promptly produced four large bottles of Japanese beer. The old lady turned out to be *O-KA-sahn*, their host's mother.

Dutch Shute had just started to unfasten his belt to use his Marine Corps issue buckle to open his bottle of beer when they were all startled by their host. *Chin Kyo Go* proceeded to pick up a bottle of beer and opened it with his teeth. Placing the bottle on the table, he reached for the next bottle and the next. When all four bottles of beer had been opened, all raised them in an American/Japanese toast. The Marines had never known anyone before who opened bottles of beer with his teeth. None of them were quite ready to try it themselves.

The next remarkable thing their host did was to proclaim "Me dentisto!" As far as the Marines could make out, *Chin Kyo Go* not only had very strong teeth, he was actually a dentist. He was the one person who certainly should know better than to open beer bottles with his teeth.

Chin pointed to himself again and proudly stated "I are *Chosen-jin*," which meant exactly nothing to the Marines at first but as the evening wore on, they realized that he was telling them proudly that he was not Japanese, he was Korean. He was also a man of means, or so it seemed, as he apparently had an endless supply of *Biru* Kirin which he gladly shared with his newfound friends. *O-ka-sahn* served them some fairly exotic food. Except for the rice; they had never seen anything quite like it but after several bottles of beer they were hungry and the food was spicy and tasty. Chin produced a small pocket-sized Japanese/English dictionary which kept them all busy for the rest of their visit.

They enjoyed their clandestine sojourn to the village but now had to get back across the plowed fields and through the fence before daylight and they had to do so without being shot by one of their own sentries. Dutch Shute had acted strangely throughout the evening and seemed more reserved than ever. He obviously had something on his mind that he was not ready to share with his buddies.

The next morning the three warriors wished their host of the previous night had not been quite so generous with his beer. They were all nursing headaches. Making their way to the messhall, the three found that they were less than popular with their shipmates. In fact, for some reason still unknown to them, they were ostracized. None of the other men wanted to talk to any of them or have any close contact with them.

Corporal Heckendorn was an assistant cook who Chic had gotten to know while he was on mess duty back on Tinian. Heckendorn approached the three hung-over Marines to say hello when he suddenly stopped and reeled back from them exclaiming "Keerist what have you guys been eating?!!"

None knew and so obviously could not give him a straight answer.

"I've never smelled anything as bad as you guys before in my life! What the hell is it?"

Chic feebly mumbled;

"We were dinner guests of a dentist friend last night and when he offered to share his food with us, we didn't want to offend him."

"Offend him! Well let me tell you something *Cobber*, you may not have offended him but you sure as hell are going to offend everyone else you speak to until that stuff wears off. Its awful, you guys must have been poisoned!"

"Omigod, poisoned! We really do feel bad but I thought we just had hangovers from all the beer we drank. We'd better get to sickbay and find out if we're alright."

"Sickbay! You think the docs are going to let you characters into sickbay? Not smellin' like that they aren't. Don't kid yourselves, the closest you are gonna get to sickbay is maybe the shitter and they'll probably lock you in and make you stay there until it wears off, whatever it is."

The raggedy assed Marines had unwittingly been introduced to the famous Korean delicacy *kimchee*. Many other Americans would become familiar with *kimchee* while serving on the Korean Peninsula in a subsequent war five years into the future.

*   *   *   *   *   *   *   *   *

The Fire Chief

On a subsequent clandestine visit to the little hamlet the three Marines were welcomed into the home of *Shigenaga Na Unae* and his grandson, *Takatsugu Tajiri*. Shigenaga Sahn was a venerable old man who claimed to be 93 years of age. He had been born in 1852, the year that Commodore Perry's fleet first visited Japan. So many remarkable changes had occurred in his homeland during *Shigenaga Sahn's* lifetime that it was hard for the young Marines to fully comprehend it.

Much mention was made by *Shigenaga Sahn* of the *Satsuma* Rebellion. He was in his mid-twenties when it had taken place in 1877 and it was apparently his first and only combat. From his descriptions, the Kumamoto Castle and all of the people of Kumamoto played a major role in the *Satsuma* Rebellion. Chic sipped his beer and looked into the future with sadness. He saw himself someday as the old man was now. *Shigenaga Sahn* knew his life was growing short and he was desperately trying to tell the story of his experiences in the great rebellion in which he had fought. He just had to get it out, to make someone hear it before it was too late. These *gaijeen* from far across the sea were warriors, they had fought in a war and so they would understand him. The old man's frustration grew by the minute as he tried to relate his tale and was constantly interrupted by his grandson using that damned dictionary to translate.

Shigenaga Sahn had seen his country's victorious army invade and occupy China, Manchukuo and Chosen. He learned of the successful attack on Pearl Harbor as his nation launched into a full scale war against the great western powers. Many victories followed in quick succession as Guam, Wake the Dutch East Indies and Singapore fell to Japanese forces. A succession of American, British and Dutch ships were sunk and French Indo China was occupied; then the Philippines were taken. The Japanese victories were amazing and he could see that the Greater East Asia Co-Prosperity Sphere was beginning to encompass much more than just greater East Asia. Japan would soon control all of the Pacific.

Then came a real shock for the people of Japan; expecting an early victory, they were forced to accept the continuous bombing and strafing by the allied air strikes and the fire bombings of Tokyo and many other cities when they had been told repeatedly that victory was nearly at hand. The Japanese had trusted and believed in their government. When asked about the atomic bomb, the old man simply said that he had heard about it and when he had seen its blinding light he knew that the Gods had a new plan for Japan and for its people. He knew the war would soon end and the Empire of the Sun would be facing new challenges.

The grandson, *Takatsugu Tajiri*, was a long-time soldier and had been a sergeant in the Imperial Japanese Army Tank Corps. He had served in China with the Army but his unit had been recalled to Japan apparently to assist in its defense. He was very proud of his army service yet seemed to have no animosity toward his country's conquerors. He was respectful and friendly. His two young cousins *Yoshiko* and *Aiko*, waited on them, frequently bowing and though responsive to requests always remained a respectful distance away from the men.

Shigenaga Na Unae was pleased to have an audience willing to listen to him. He spoke of the history of Kumamoto and of the castle and told of the great warriors that had come from this area and of a great battle in the distant past. He spoke of various horses he had owned as a young boy and was saddened now that there was only one old work horse in his stable. He told them of the big festival they had in 1922 when the whole city of Kumamoto had been electrified. One could sense that he was still in awe of the great miracle of electric lighting. The Marines were fascinated by the old man's stories but they grew weary of the poor quality of translations rendered by *Tajiri* who found it necessary to look up nearly every word in the dictionary. A statement by the old man that took less than two minutes in the telling would often take more than ten minutes to translate.

The years were telling on *Shigenaga-sahn* and he soon tired of story-telling, it was time for him to sleep. He excused himself in a courtly manner and the girls assisted him from the room.

Dutch Shute studied *Tajiri's* face for awhile and then asked:

"Do you guys remember when Blackjack and Shanghai had me murder that poor little Jap with the machine gun? I think he looked a lot like *Tajiri-san.*"

Astounded at Dutch's use of words, Chic answered, "They didn't have you murder anyone dammit. They had you guys shoot those machine-gunners before they spotted us and started killing Marines. You probably saved our lives. Besides Dutch, you are nuts! There's no way you could have gotten a look at that Nip's face, he was at least two hundred yards away from you and he was in the shade of that stone overhang. There is no way you could have seen what he looked like."

"Well I did see him and he looked just like our friend here. Hell, he might have been his brother or his cousin or somethin' and I killed him."

Dutch had a strange fascination for *Aiko* and kept glancing at her. The sisters were both very quiet and reserved but Aiko didn't seem to mind the interest Dutch showed in her. His looks caused her to blush from time to time but except for blushing, she didn't seem to mind his stares. Shortly after arriving for one of their evening visits with *Tajiri-san, Aiko* presented an apple to Dutch saying *omiyagae* and bowing. He thanked her and attempted to teach her to say apple in English but quickly learned that there were some sounds that she simply could not pronounce. "Aperoo" just didn't sound to him anything like apple. Dutch decided that it would be much simpler for him to learn to say apple in Japanese so he tried repeating *omiyagae.*

Communicating with *Takatsugu Tajiri* was challenging but

it was fun. His dictionary received a great deal of attention. The Marines marveled at his ability to remember words and their meaning from one visit to the next. The evening visits had become, more than anything else, English lessons for *Tajiri-san*. Dutch wanted to remember how to say apple in Japanese but found that he had forgotten the word after his second beer.

Leafing through the English-Japanese dictionary he found that *omiyagae* did not mean apple at all, it was Japanese for present or gift. With much laughter and bowing, he now knew that *Aiko* had said she was giving him a gift. She quickly learned that gift in English was present, which she pronounced presento and Dutch learned that he could easily pronounce apple in Japanese which was *ringo*.

As they tramped clumsily across the plowed field on their return to the base Dutch, who had been very quiet, asked no one in particular;

"Did you see what she did tonight? She was so damned nice the way she gave me that apple and smiled. I really feel like a rat after all I've done. You know, I think she knows about me and still she seems so forgiving. She really does seem like a little Goddess of Mercy."

Lucky responded with, "How much beer did you drink tonight? You sound like you've completely lost it Dutch. What's wrong with you anyway? There's nothing to forgive, you're just a Marine who did his job that's all. You should be proud of all you've done, there ain't many guys in this outfit that are as good a Marine as you are and you know it. For Crissake man, stop thinkin' about the Goddess of Mercy, you ain't a Buddhist, you're a Marine."

"You guys don't understand. You don't have to live with it. I damned near killed that little baby and her mother and the other people in that cave on Saipan. Then I killed that poor guy with the machine-gun who wasn't even shootin' at us. Then I killed that beautiful little girl on Okinawa, *Quan Yin*, the Goddess of Mercy, you know it was her, you were there."

"Dutch! You saved that baby and her mother on Saipan and all the others that were in that cave. You know we'd have blown it if it wasn't for you. Hell, if you had been in the Army they'd probably have given you a medal. Now stop talking like an ass and eat your apple."

Dutch Shute did not eat his apple. He treasured it as if it were made of gold. After all, it had been given to him by *Aiko* or *Quan-yin* or Kannon or whatever the Goddess of Mercy wanted to be called.

On subsequent visits, the Marines managed to bring small items that were needed and appreciated in the household. Food items were always gratefully received. The war had punished the people of Japan severely and many of the necessities of life were in short supply, especially food. Chic had given up cigarettes on Saipan during the campaign and found that his cigarette ration was a valuable commodity to Tajiri-san. American cigarettes were practically legal tender in the postwar Japan of 1945.

The evening visits to the hamlet had become nearly a ritual and consisted of the men paying their respects to *Shigenaga-sahn*, being good listeners until the old man tired and then a two hour session with the dictionary and repeated pronunciation lessons for Tajiri-san during which two to three bottles of beer were consumed by each of the men. One evening, *Takatsugu Tajiri* proudly announced that he had made application to work on the Marine base. An interpreter employed by the Americans had told him that his application would receive favorable consideration since he was studying English and had valuable experience. When asked what the job was, he announced that he had applied to be the base fire chief. This came as no little surprise to the men even though they knew he had experience fighting fires in Tokyo during the fire-bombing by American B-29's but they knew he also had experience in a somewhat related field. *Tajiri-san* had been a sergeant in the Imperial Japanese Army Tank Corps. If he could drive a tank it stood to reason he could drive a fire truck. It turned out that the fire chief's job on the one-truck fire department was to supervise the firefighters and be the driver of the truck. The ex-sergeant, *Tajiri-gunso*, was a natural for the job.

* * * * * * * * *

As the men were walking from their barracks to the

messhall for noon chow one brisk autumn day they beheld a strange sight. The camp fire department had completed renovation of an old Japanese truck and had painted and equipped it as best they could to be a fire engine. The truck was proceeding very slowly, almost ceremoniously, down the street past the wooden barracks on its maiden run, its Japanese fire crew were hanging on at their appropriate positions. The Marines came to a dead stop, staring open mouthed as the truck moved slowly past them. The driver climbed up onto the seat in the open cab behind the wheel, as he stood upright on the driver's seat he bowed respectfully to the raggedy assed Marines. The other occupant of the cab trying furtively to keep the truck moving smoothly forward and control the steering wheel which Tajiri had totally abandoned in his eagerness to mount his moving pedestal. It was obviously *Takatsugu Tajiri's* way of greeting and honoring his special Marine friends and would-be English teachers. The three raggedy assed Marines standing in a row dutifully bowed to the esteemed fire chief.

"What the hell is going on around here?" gasped Gunnery Sergeant Carl Johannsen.

"Oh nothing, Gunny," Chic answered, "We just thought we would return his bow so as not to make him lose face."

"What do you mean lose face? Who the hell is that clown anyhow? Dammit, you men don't bow to the Japs. Let them bow to you and keep it in mind that we won the war. They lost it - and we'd better not ever let them forget it, not ever!"

The gunny was an Old Corps Marine and had very strong feelings about the Japanese. The men were glad to move beyond their gunny and enter the relative safety of the messhall.

* * * * * * * * *

Kumamoto Liberty

Limited daylight liberty was finally granted.

There was little to see or do in Kumamoto in the Fall of 1945. Only a small number of restaurants could be patronized and they were identified by placards that had been posted on the front doors proclaiming in english that the food served therein had been inspected and was authorized for consumption by U.S. Occupation Forces. The Japanese merchants were feverishly working to repair and reopen their shops and stores. In 1945, Kumamoto, Japan had no nightclubs or bars and not a single neon sign was to be found in the city.

Chaplain George Wickersham was always on the job looking out for his Marines and through an interpreter and members of Kumamoto's small Christian community, he made several contacts in the city. One of his proudest accomplishments was arranging a visit to some French nuns at a convent. The nuns had an old Victrola and some 78 rpm records and they decided to welcome the Marines by having a dance. Stash, a Catholic, was flabbergasted as he asked:

"Who ever heard of going to a dance in a convent? I just can't believe it. Its probably some kind of a trick to get us out and then tell us we're on a working party or something. You know we can't trust chaplains. Remember Father Grace on Saipan who told Jerden to let the troops know that we weren't going to get bombed anymore. That very night we had an air raid and the Japs dropped bombs all over the damned island?"

Giving Stash a knowing look, Lucky answered, "Yeah, I remember but this time it may be different. Father Wickersham is an Episcopalian. I'm gonna give it a try, what have we got to lose Stash? Besides, maybe we'll meet some nice girls."

"That's not the kind of girls I had in mind, but I guess I'd better sign up and go just to keep you guys out of trouble."

The "convent" was not exactly what the men had expected. It was more of an orphanage for young girls. The French nuns were nice but most reminded the men of drill instructors they had known back in boot camp. O'Keefe said one of them had to be related to a brig warden he'd once met at Camp Elliott's red-line brig. She had his looks and all of his same characteristics - and he hadn't even known the warden was French.

Marines were wearing their heavy Marine Corps issue boondockers. The young ladies were formally attired in their *kimonos* and *obis* and were wearing wooden *geta* which made them seem much taller but were not conducive to dancing. This was the first time since their arrival in Japan that the Marines had seen anyone wearing the traditional, colorful Japanese silk *kimonos*. The ever-watchful Mother Superior saw to it that partners were changed with great frequency, (a simple security measure). The men recognized instantly that young ladies wearing heavy *kimonos* with large *obis* tied ceremoniously at their backs were not equipped for western style dancing, even without their high wooden *getas*. The geta were soon exchanged for straw *zories* which tended to make the girls two to three inches shorter but were slightly less clumsy to dance in.

Netherland, the music, told the others that he had found out that the Mother Superior, who he referred to as, "the Nuns' Senior DI," had prescribed the uniform of the day for the girls. No one could find a reason to doubt the veracity of this pearl of wisdom. The lack of a common language was a problem and a serious deterrent to budding friendships. The girls were wearing such heavy and awkward costumes that they tired quickly (exactly as the Mother Superior had planned) and as nice as the men tried to be to them, it was obvious that they were not quite ready for any fast friendships with Marines with whom they could not communicate and who had been killing their countrymen just a couple of months before. Heavy Marine boondockers were a deterrent to smooth dancing and could almost be classified as dangerous weapons by the small Japanese girls who were often in the line of fire of the clumsy Marines' big feet. None of the men claimed to be good dancers but they were at least willing participants.

The nuns brought out the smaller children who were also attired in their finery and they stole the men's hearts. They were easier to communicate with than the older girls using a combination of sign language, broken English and badly fractured Japanese. A few minutes with these colorfully attired three, four and five-year-olds made the day. The men left broke but feeling good about themselves. Even the Mother Superior seemed pleased at how things had gone. Score one for Chaplain Wickersham.

Walking down the streets and looking at little Japanese shops that had started to reopen told Chic, Lucky and Dutch that these were a very industrious people who would not wallow in their defeat. They would soon recover from the devastation of the war and would continue to rebuild their nation. There was activity everywhere. Buildings were being repaired, broken glass windows in the shops were being replaced and Americans were eagerly welcomed as paying customers.

One of Kumamoto's highlights was the *Suizenji* Park. The Japanese proudly mentioned the *Suizenji* gardens as the place to go, the Marines couldn't understand why. One park seemed the same as any other to them even though this one was distinctly Japanese with a man-made mount *Fujiyama* as it's centerpiece. Overall the park was beautifully laid out and like so many Japanese gardens it was so green and beautiful as to almost seem artificial. Lucky and Chic encountered a little boy in the park who tried to converse in English. His mother, dressed in western-style clothing, was obviously a well-educated lady. She said she had worked for an American company before the war and had read and studied much about the United States. She believed that Japan would ultimately lose the war. She claimed to have taught English to her son from the time he began talking. He was a bright child who asked a multitude of sensible questions. The mother was the first western-style Japanese they had encountered. She gave them a brief tour of *Suizenji* Park and proudly mentioned that *Suizenji* had been founded in 1632, which caused a surprised Chic Yancey to reflect,

"Damn, this garden is 140 years older than the Marine Corps!"

They considered mother and son to be very unusual and knew these two would make many friends among the Marines. The woman was eager to talk about Kumamoto and its history and as the group strolled through the park she kept up a running commentary in her excellent English. They never saw the mother and son again.

Strolling down the streets of Kumamoto and just looking at the sights was an interesting experience. They were learning that cities throughout the world have many similarities and yet in the Far East there are some stark differences. Glancing up, Chic's eyes followed along a very large, smooth stone wall that seemed to curve outward near the top. As he looked up beyond the top of the wall he could see the decidedly Japanese architecture of a large medieval castle. It was right out of a storybook. Chic had not known that such places really existed until old *Shigenaga-sahn* had tried to tell them of it. This was the famous Kumamoto Castle that the woman in the park had also mentioned to them. It was another of Kumamoto's special places of interest.

While Lucky, Dutch and Chic were inspecting the castle, Chic realized what old Shigenaga-sahn had been trying to explain to them. The old man's stories would really have been interesting if only they'd had an interpreter besides Tajiri-sahn and his dictionary. As Chic looked at the high, delicately curved stone walls which had obviously been designed for defense, he knew it would be impossible for anyone, even a monkey, to climb them. The tower and the turrets and the fenced well inside the walls seemed like they were all part of a movie set, but they were real. He had certainly never expected to find a huge, medieval castle perfectly preserved right here in the middle of the island of Kyushu. Japan had been full of surprises for him, the castle being only one of many.

Chic thought that back in the days of feudal Japan when the *Shoguns* ruled, the castle would have been an easy place to defend. For anyone attempting to assault, it would almost surely have resulted in disaster. It was one of the three premier castles of Japan. The men enjoyed inspecting its defenses and roaming through its six stories of rooms, passageways, tunnels and dungeons. They later learned that after the *Meiji* Restoration, the Samurai warriors who resisted the new order had fought their last great battle at this very place. Imperial forces had barricaded themselves in the Kumamoto Castle and survived 55 days of fierce attacks by the rebel Samurai. Some of the major buildings were burned down in the battles but later had been restored.

For transportation back to camp they were to assemble at

the Kumamoto Railroad Station by 1700. They soon learned that the railroad station was called the *Teishaba*. At the *Teishaba* a female voice was heard over the public address system announcing arrivals and departures in Japanese. The voice changed easily from Japanese to exellent English and was clearly heard but its Nisei owner was never seen by the Marines. They were busy boarding trucks outside the station for transportation back to their barracks.

"Hello you lucky people! You'll soon be going back home to the States. Oh, how I envy you. Good luck and God bless you all."

The tone of her voice was sad and moving and told the listener that she meant it with all of her broken heart. Chic knew that if he could see the face that voice belonged to there would be tears in her eyes. He had often thought about the awful plight of American prisoners of war in Japan but until this moment he had never considered the Americans, like this Nisei girl, who had been trapped in Japan by circumstances beyond their control when the war started. Life for them must have been extremely trying.

Once back at the barracks, the men didn't have a lot to say about their liberty in Kumamoto, there just wasn't that much to it. They drew their ration of two beers and looked forward to going out on patrol the following day to round up more Japanese weapons and munitions.

* * * * * * * * *

Hiking through the countryside it was refreshing to see so many larks in the grassland and around the cultivated fields. During the war the Marines hadn't seen many birds on the Pacific islands. Most had been blown out of the air and killed by the concussion from the naval gunfire, bombing or artillery. The birds helped them to remember a little of what life had been like at home before the war.

As the patrols passed people working in the fields or even walking along the roads, they would stop what they were doing and formally bow to the Marines. At first it gave the men an awkward feeling but they soon came to accept it as the Japanese way of greeting and answered the bows with a friendly word and a wave. In October, they had started seeing pretty purple flowers with five petals. When they mentioned the "*murasaki*" flowers at *Shigenaga-sahn's* house, the *Tajiri* girls took five minutes with the Japanese-English Dictionary to explain that the gentians were the special flower of Kumamoto.

While they were out they saw quite a few big camphor trees like the ones in and around the Kumamoto Castle grounds. They didn't dare to mention the camphor trees to the girls. If it took five minutes to translate the importance of a little flower, there's no telling how long it would take to explain about the big trees. The men had little enthusiasm for their prolonged sessions with the dictionary. Once the patrol had returned to the barracks, there was barely time to clean weapons and prepare for evening chow.

The raggedy assed Marines waited until after dark and then quietly crossed the fields to "their" hamlet and another session with the venerable old *Shigenaga-sahn*. It wasn't very exciting but the people were nice to them and greeted them as friends and sometimes trying new Japanese foods that were offered to them could be an adventure.

They had learned after their first visit to *Chin Kyo Go* and their bout with *kimchee* to decline his offers of food but his beer was entirely acceptable. There were no shops in which to buy things in the little village but bartering was easy and American cigarettes were highly prized. An added advantage was - no competition. The other Marines, attracted to the big city, had not yet discovered the little village.

* * * * * * * * *

Sayonara

Many of the wartime Marines were going back to the States for discharge and several of the company's high point NCO's were in the first draft. With the loss of NCO's the company was authorized to promote three men to corporal. A promotion board was convened and an examination was given to all the eligible Pfc's. Chic felt good about the corporal's test. He finished the exam quickly, looked over his answers and knew he'd gotten them right. The promotion board consisted of all the company officers and the first sergeant and gunnery sergeant. They were going to examine the men who had successfully passed the test and decide which three would receive the promotions to corporal.

Chic reflected aloud, "You know, I really don't mind this duty so much; it's an improvement over what we had for the last couple of years and the chow is getting better all the time. Maybe I'll ship over and ask them to send me to the 1st or the 6th Division over in China. I've always wanted to go to China."

Gunnery Sergeant Johannsen walked into the squadbay where Yancey was sitting on his folding cot writing a letter home.

"Hi kid, how ya doin'?"

"Fine Gunny, what's up?"

"Not much, just the same old seven-come-eleven, things don't change much in this outfit. Mind if I sit down on your bunk for a spell?"

The surprised Chic responded, "No, of course not Gunny, make yourself comfortable."

"Kid, the Top and I wanted you to know something and that's what I'm doin' here. We were both on the company promotion board and we both rated you number one, but you still ain't gonna make corporal, not in this outfit. The Top and I rated you first and the officers all rated you last. I know you've got more than enough points to go home and that's exactly what you'd better do. Forget about reenlisting until you get away from the lieutenants. Mr. Grosscup has the others convinced that you're a wise guy; he's never liked you and you know you can't fight city hall."

"But Gunny, I was thinking of reenlisting and staying right here or asking them to send me over to China."

"If you want to reenlist go back to the States and do it. That way you'll be away from these lieutenants. Once you leave here you won't see them again. They are all reserves and they'll be going home and getting out just as soon as they acquire enough points."

Stash and Lucky had overheard what the gunny said. Chic smiled and pretended that it didn't mean anything to him.

"Gee Chic," Stash exclaimed, "That's really a bad break."

"Aw heck, as far as I'm concerned it doesn't mean a thing. I sure don't want all the added responsibility that goes with being a corporal. I've been a Pfc so long now that I just wouldn't feel comfortable being anything else. I guess I was lucky to keep my Pfc stripes this long the way those lieutenants feel about me."

Chic Yancey was crushed. He really did want to be a corporal. He wanted to be a corporal more than anything else he could think of. He had really tried to be a good Marine but he had obviously not been good enough. It was going to be tough going home to face his family and friends still just a Pfc, they'd think he had been a failure as a Marine.

Chic confided, " I've made up my mind, I'm goin' home!"

"Yeah," Smith said, "I hear old Lucky and Stash have enough points to go stateside too. Gee, things are sure gonna seem different without you old salts around to keep reminding us of what this outfit was like back in the Old Corps. I guess we won't be hearing any more stories about the world's greatest squad leader, Shanghai Pooley; or Fearless Frank or Deadly Dave or Hand Grenade Harrington or the Knife Fighter or .... Hey, where'd those guys get all the crazy nicknames from anyhow?"

* * * * * * * * * *

A draft of high point men from the 2nd Marine Division was assembled and transferred to Sasebo to join the 5th Marine Division. The 5th was taking it's colors back to the United States and would be decommissioned at Camp Pendleton. Sasebo had been a major Japanese naval base prior to the surrender and had served as headquarters for the 5th Marine Division during the occupation.

A Marine sitting across the mess table from Chic and Lucky asked, "Hey, you guys came from the 8th Marines in Kumamoto. What did you think about that jerk in the 8th who blew himself away? I guess he couldn't stand being left in Japan when his buddies were all going back to the States? How stupid can you get?"

Chic felt a chill creep down his spine leaving him with an

ominous feeling of depression and apprehension. He had just left Kumamoto and the 8th Marines. He hoped it was not any-one he knew but he had a strange premonition that it was someone he knew very well. He mumbled silently to himself "*Quan-yin*, be merciful" as he thought of Dutch and prayed that he was wrong.

* * * * * * * * * *

To Herman "Dutch" Shute, the Goddess of Mercy was a lovely oriental maiden whose full lips appeared ready to break into a smile at any moment; her large eyes were gently closed in peaceful contemplation. To him, she represented all that was good and pure. He believed he had brutally violated her on a dark Okinawa night by shooting her down like an evil beast.

Dutch's conscience and imagination had tormented him to a point beyond reason. He repeatedly saw the angelic young face and the gently closed eyes of the girl he had killed on Okinawa and he saw that same face on the little statue in the shrine beside her still body. Three months later on the out-skirts of Nagasaki he saw another idol in a shrine and knew that it was she; here she was welcoming him to Japan and letting him know that wherever he went, she would always be there waiting. He was astonished in Kumamoto when *Aiko Tajiri* looked down, smiled and gently closed her eyes. He knew then that she was the Goddess! She had been reincarnated and had come back to torment him with kindness and gentle-ness for the terrible thing he had done to her.

It was his rifle, the same M-1 rifle he had fired when he killed the machine-gunner on Saipan and the same rifle he had fired on that awful night on Okinawa when he murdered the goddess of mercy. She was thought to be an enemy sol-dier moving toward their position in the darkness. Trembling and with a heavy heart he deliberately placed his mouth over the muzzle of the rifle and put his thumb in the trigger guard.

* * * * * * * * * *

The Marines of E Company, 2nd Battalion, 28th Marines

were standing in formation on the dock at Sasebo. They moved out on command in a column of files from the right and as they approached the accommodation ladder, each sounded off with his name to Lieutenant Daskalakas and the first sergeant who checked them off the list affixed to his clipboard. Each Marine saluted aft then inboard as they stepped onto the deck of USS *Sarasota*. For most of them it would be the last time they rendered the double salute on boarding a U.S. Navy vessel in the line of duty. They were headed home to be mustered out and discharged from the United States Marine Corps.

Lucky Lane was deep in thought. There was no question in his mind as to what he was going to do when he got home. He would reenroll at Ohio State as soon as possible and would finish his senior year. He was determined to get the degree he should have had three years earlier. He had another thought that kept bothering him. The Marine Corps, he liked the Corps and he had liked most things about being a Marine but he had gotten some very bad breaks. It was disappointing and embarrassing going home a private when nearly all of his former classmates had been commissioned in the various services.

Lucky knew he had been a good Marine. It was almost as though the company officers were playing a game to keep him from being promoted. He never made Pfc. Standing on the deck of that homeward bound ship and looking out across the vast Pacific, Lucky made a decision. He would stay in the Marine Corps Reserve, and do his utmost to get promoted and after graduation he would apply for commissioning in the Marine reserves. If he ever went to war again, he wanted to be an officer. He wanted to be the kind of officer Lieutenant David Stacey had been or Captain Marty Barrett, their old company commander.

If he ever went to war again, Lucky wanted the troops to have the kind of lieutenants they deserved. He knew his personal experiences and his love of the Corps would help him to be that kind of an officer.

Crossing the Pacific was different this time. There was no need for the ship to zigzag and there were not as many drills. Shipboard life was much more relaxed. The war was over.

The war was really over! Everyone, Marines and Sailors alike were concerned about getting back to the States and picking their lives up where they had left off. They talked constantly about their future plans.

Chic Yancey was lost, he didn't have any future plans. He had grown up in the Marine Corps. When he entered boot camp he was a boy and he had grown to manhood in the Corps. He had wanted to be a Marine for so long that now that it was time to get out, he didn't know how to be a civilian.

There was much talk about a new G.I. Bill of Rights for veterans. It was rumored that the government would subsidize a college education for veterans and even pay them while they were going to school. Chic thought this was wonderful and wished he could take advantage of such a program but he knew that he would not be acceptable to a college without first getting a high school education. He also knew he could not return to high school after his life as a raggedy assed Marine.

The ship's captain and crew did their best to expedite the trip back to the United States. They too wanted to be home for Christmas and the scuttlebutt was that they were going to make it. Chic thought about Dutch. Dutch was not the only one of Chic's buddies that was not returning to the United States, he was just the only one who had made the decision for himself. Chic often thought about Deadly Dave and Fearless and when he did, all the other faces and names would come rushing back to him. All were great guys and some could even be considered exceptional. A few were real characters and vastly different from one another like Poncho and Riverboat, and Hand Grenade Harrington and Shanghai but they all had one special thing in common, they were his brothers, they were Marines and he missed them all. God, how he missed them!

Chic thought about the people he would soon be seeing, family members and friends. He was glad they did not have to experience what he had seen and lived through and yet, in a way, he felt sorry for them, there was so much they had missed and would never be able to understand. If he made it back to the United States, he knew that he would not be the same as before the war. He would not be comfortable trying to fit into civilian society. He would want to talk about his buddies and his experiences and adventures but he wouldn't dare do so. He didn't think anyone would be interested or could fully understand. They probably wouldn't even believe him. Chic had lived through it and already, he was beginning to wonder whether it had all really happened or if it was just a bad dream.

The ship continued on its course toward the West Coast of the United States as Chic thought to himself: "Golden Gate in '48.... My God, there's only two more days left until Christmas - and its still 1945!"

Chic Yancey reluctantly left his beloved Marine Corps following his return to the United States. He tried civilian life but was disappointed. He was a man now and had grown wary of the ways of the world. He missed the soldiering, the discipline, the close-knit brotherhood, the travel and adventure and the simple honesty he'd found among Marines. He missed the Spirit of Semper Fidelis.

Deciding to reenlist in the Corps, he was embarrassed at being a hashmark Pfc. Soon after returning to the Corps he was promoted to corporal and subsequent promotions came rapidly until he was a gunnery sergeant. In his twelfth year of service he received an unrestricted commission as a second lieutenant in the regular Marine Corps.

He was privileged to serve on land, at sea and in the air. In addition to World War II, he participated in the Korean and Vietnam Wars. The proudest moment of his life came when he had the privilege of commissioning his only son a lieutenant of Marines. Both father and son are now retired from the Marine Corps and reside in Northern Virginia.

The remaining raggedy assed Marine, Private Daniel R. "Lucky" Lane, joined the Marine Corps Reserve and returned to Ohio State where he completed his senior year and graduated. He became a high school mathematics teacher and football coach. Second Lieutenant Lane, USMCR returned to active duty during the Korean War and stayed on to complete 30 years of active service.

Chic Yancey and Lucky Lane served together at Camp Pendleton, California for two years during the Korean War. They played vastly different roles than they had during World War II when they were raggedy assed Marines in the 2nd squad.

Yancey and Lane remained lifelong friends.

The 28th of November 1994 was a bright sunny day at the Quantico National Cemetery. An elderly Jim Yancey stood quietly at attention beside Lieutenant Colonel Daniel R. Lane, Jr., smartly attired in his dress blue uniform with polished medals and the traditional Mameluke Sword of a Marine Officer suspended from his Sam Browne belt. Yancey's own son was not present. He was with his battalion deployed somewhere in the Far East.

The Marines were paying final respects to one of their own. Pallbearers flanking the coffin faced inboard and smartly folded the flag into the traditional triangle. It was handed to a colonel who presented it, "In the name of the President of the United States," to the next of kin, Lieutenant Colonel Daniel R. Lane, Jr.

A squad of seven Marines fired the customary three volleys and a lone bugler sounded taps. Major Jim Yancey, USMC, Retired, eulogized Colonel Daniel R. "Lucky" Lane, Sr. his old foxhole buddy and friend of more than 50 years. He ended with the traditional; "I bid you fair winds and following seas old friend. Semper Fidelis."

Turning to the lieutenant colonel the old man quietly said: "Come on over to the Globe & Laurel, Dan. We'll break out the family silver (old canteen cups) and have a drink in memory of your Dad. Then I'll tell you about the raggedy assed Marines."

Semper Fidelis

Saipan, 1944 (USMC Photo)

Saipan, 1944 - A Marine tank blasts a thicket in Saipan. (USMC Photo)

Lt. General Holland Smith at 2nd Division cemetery, Saipan. (USMC Photo)

2nd Marine Division cemetery, Tinian Island. (USMC Photo)

Marines prepare to assault on Saipan beach. (USMC Photo)

A Marine eliminates cave defenders on Okinawa. (USMC Photo)

Jungle and cliffs of Saipan.

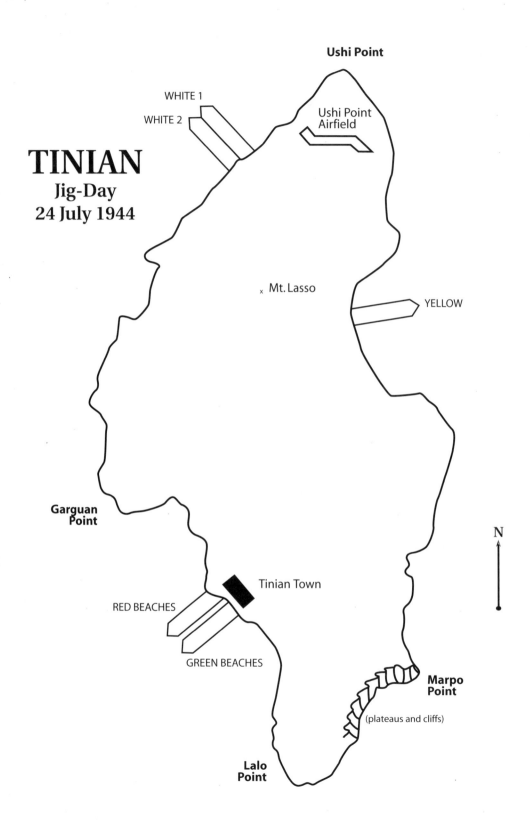